Gil

Gilded Dreams

Kristy Daniels

WARNER BOOKS

A *Warner* Book

First published in Great Britain by
Judy Piatkus in 1993
This edition published by Warner in 1994

A CIP catalogue record for this book
is available from the British Library.

ISBN 0 7515 0900 0

Photoset in North Wales by
Derek Doyle & Associates, Mold, Clwyd.
Printed and bound in Great Britain by
Clays Ltd, St Ives plc

Warner Books
A Division of
Little, Brown and Company (UK) Limited
Brettenham House
Lancaster Place
London WC2 7EN

Chapter One

Diamonds. Everywhere he looked, there were diamonds: as far as he could see, a blanket of diamonds covering the hills, glittering in the morning sun.

The young man brought his hand up to shade his eyes as he stared out over the rolling countryside. It had snowed last night, the first snow of the year. All week, it had been overcast, and the dun-coloured hills and barren trees had a beaten-down look from trying to hold up the November sky. But finally, the snow had come and, with it, the transformation he loved. Everything was pure and clean, white with glittering promise.

Jonathan Caras turned and started down the hill. He reached the opening of the small gorge that surrounded the pond and paused. The snow had turned the hidden glen into a little crystal palace. Fir trees and rocks rose up around him, cloaked in snow. The pond was iced over; the small stream that fed it from above was a frozen cascade of icicles. It was eerily quiet, so quiet he could hear the slow dripping of water. So quiet he could hear his blood surging through his heart.

His eyes found the large flat rock, covered with a blanket of snow, and he shivered. Thinking of a white-hot day in August. Thinking of the rock hot against his back. And the feel of Marion's body next to

1

his, and her lips soft on his breast . . .

He stood staring at the rock for a moment longer, then picked his way through the drifts out of the gorge. He started back, walking slowly at first, then breaking into a slow trot. By the time he reached the road he was running, his lungs pulling in the stinging cold air, his face burning. He ran, his eyes watering from the glint of the sun off the snow.

'*Look Ma, diamonds! The snow looks like a million diamonds!*'

'*Oh, Jonathan, you say the strangest things sometimes. You keep that scarf on, hear? Where you running to now?*'

'*Don't know, Ma. Don't know . . .*'

As he approached the farmhouse, he slowed. His eyes travelled over the house's flaking paintwork, once a cornflower blue but now faded to grey. His gaze came to rest on the flower box under the kitchen window, its hard earth and neglected twigs half covered by the snow.

'*What are you planting, Ma?*'

'*Geraniums, Jonathan. The reddest ones I could find to brighten up this tired old house.*'

'*They're pretty.*'

'*Yes, but they don't last long. Come November, they'll be gone.*'

'*But they'll come back after winter, right?*'

'*No, not these. Flowers this special never come back.*'

Jonathan stood, his breath coming slower now, making clouds in the air. His gaze went to the barn, a valiant stand of weathered grey planks listing under its cap of snow, and then out again at the hills beyond. He turned and went into the house.

He paused in the pantry to stamp the snow off his shoes and hang his scarf and coat on a peg. The kitchen was filled with the warmth and fragrance of food: pumpkin pie, a piercing sensory stab that brought back to him another image of his mother bending over the oven, her heat-flushed face turned up to him, the sun from the window haloing around her dishevelled hair. He could hear her laugh fading like an echo in the empty kitchen, and he knew suddenly that she was the source of the slight melancholy that had been with him all day. Why, he thought, is the house so full of her today? Why is she with me today?

'Oh, Jonathan, you're back.'

Hannah, the housekeeper, came in, rubbing her hands on her apron. 'Dinner'll be ready soon,' she said.

Jonathan ventured further into the kitchen and surveyed the array of food crowding the counters and tabletop: bowls of yams and vegetables, cranberries and a turkey waiting to be placed on its blue and white china platter. All the makings of a Thanksgiving feast.

'I hope you brought an appetite with you,' Hannah said, smiling. 'Your father wanted this dinner to be special, in honour of your homecoming.'

He looked into her keen eyes, little blue buttons sunk into the pleated pink cushion of her face. 'Everything looks fine, Hannah, just fine. Where is my father?'

She gave a derisive but possessive little shrug. 'In the parlour, with his nose stuffed in one of those dusty old books, as usual. Maybe with you being home now he'll take the time to eat a decent meal.'

Jonathan smiled and started towards the parlour. At the door he paused. As a boy, he had always thought the room was beautiful. In an attempt to give the little room the grandeur of a real parlour, his mother had draped the two windows with heavy fabric, papered the walls in deep-red brocade and crowded in a few hulking pieces of dark Victorian furniture. But the brocade had faded and the upholstery had turned threadbare. Several years ago, his father had finally claimed the room as his study, filling it with towers of books, and now even Hannah's

3

ministrations could not stave off the invading shabbiness.

In one corner was an oak desk, where his father sat, head bent low over a book. Sensing Jonathan's presence he looked up, the round lenses of his glasses catching the light of the oil lamp at his elbow.

'There you are. Where'd you go?' his father said.

Jonathan moved a pile of books from a chair and sat down. 'I walked down to the pond and back.'

'Ran, you mean. Your face is still red.'

Jonathan smiled. There was a pause. 'You should have the porch fixed,' he said finally. 'It's falling apart.'

'Yes, I've been meaning to get to it.'

'Why don't you just get Uncle Jake to do it?'

'He's got his own work to do. I'll get around to it, in the spring. Right now, I'm too busy.' His lips, in the bush of his peppery beard, turned up and his hazel eyes caught the light.

'Don't want to waste any of your white time, right, Pa?' Jonathan said.

White time. Charles had not thought of that phrase for years. It referred to winter, of course, but also to something more significant. Charles Caras was a farmer, just as his father had been before him, working the same land near the small town of Dryden, east of Ithaca, New York. Like most boys his age, Charles had left school after the sixth year and begun his life's work. Every day, he had worked in the maize and alfalfa fields 'from can-see to can't-see' – dawn to dusk. Charles missed school, but he was content to slake his dreams with books read by candlelight in bed. He developed a love of Shakespeare, finding within the plays every foreign world, every human passion he needed. And always he waited for winter to come. Winter was 'white time'. With the fields fallow, there was more time, precious time to read. Time to lose himself in the pure, white expanse of his dreams.

'White time . . .' Charles repeated. 'I remember when you first called it that. You were just thirteen and I'd caught you lying in a field reading instead of doing your chores. You looked up at me, real serious, and said, "I'm taking some white time, Pa. A man's just got to have his white time." ' He chuckled.

'You made me clean out the barn for cheeking you,' Jonathan said, laughing.

'But I never forgot that phrase.'

Charles's smile lingered as he stared at Jonathan's face. Right from the beginning, the startling originality of his son's mind had amazed him and it was with some pride that he had always looked at Jonathan and seen something of himself there. But as Jonathan became older, it was not himself he saw so much as his wife, Vivian.

Vivian . . . Jonathan had her restlessness. Unsettled, moving, always moving . . . they were so much alike, each surrounded by an aura of energy so powerful it seemed to electrify the air. It was, he remembered, what had first drawn him irresistibly to Vivian Linquist so many years ago. He had seen her standing in the sun, as he came out of the store in Dryden. She was only fifteen, a pretty blonde girl from a nearby town. People around Harford said she had too much spirit. And when Charles began to court her, they wondered what a wild girl like that saw in the quiet young farmer, not knowing that what Vivian Linquist saw was a haven from a father who beat her. She and Charles were married and, after a year, Jonathan was born. A year later, another baby boy came, but he died of pneumonia in the long, brutal winter. After that, life settled into a monotonous rhythm, punctuated by the changing seasons.

Charles stared at Jonathan, searching now for physical signs of himself, but still seeing Vivian. Jonathan had inherited his wavy black hair and the strong features of

5

his Greek ancestors, but Vivian's Swedish blood had sculpted his face, giving it finer angles. And he had her eyes . . . memorable eyes, pale blue and fathomless, like the fractured interior of a glacier hit by sun. Jonathan was tall and muscled like Charles, but without his father's burliness. He was slender, with long legs. Runner's legs.

An image flashed into Charles's mind: Jonathan at fifteen, running across a field, framed by the sunlight, brown and bare-chested, with his body and head held high, his cadence as natural and sensual as an animal's. Running, always running . . .

At first, it had not been hard to keep Jonathan's restlessness at bay. When he was a boy, the world within the farm's fenced acres was fertile enough to feed his imagination. He prowled through the towering maize hunting leopards in a jungle forest. He lay on the slippery creek bank launching flotillas of leaf-boats on journeys to the ocean. He sat high in the branches of a tree, seeing the faces of strangers in clouds and wondering, always wondering, where they were going. Charles had seen it all very early, there in his boy's face.

As Jonathan grew older, the fire to see what lay beyond became stronger, and Charles was pleased when it struck an intellectual spark. Jonathan grew to love school and books. Sometimes, Jonathan would come home from school late for his chores, and Charles would know that the boy had been in Southworth Library on Main Street. He brought home books of adventurers: Robinson Crusoe, Huck Finn and Ulysses. But what he loved most were the newspapers. Not the weekly edition of the *Ithaca Journal*, filled with farm reports, but its daily edition, which contained foreign news and spicy stories of crimes and suicides that were deemed too sensational for the rural edition.

As Jonathan's sixth school year drew to a close,

Charles insisted that he continue and at eighteen, Jonathan received his high-school diploma. There was a small ceremony at the school and, afterwards, Charles pressed something into Jonathan's hand. It was his pocket watch, a plain piece but gold nonetheless. 'I'm proud of you, son,' he had said. 'It's time you had this.'

Now, Charles's eyes drifted from Jonathan's face down to the watch chain looped on his vest. The watch was still there, but with a new elegant fob added. His gaze travelled over Jonathan's suit as he considered his adult son with a small feeling of sadness. The boy was gone, replaced by a man. A college man. Four years of college, and what had been unbridled energy in the boy was now refined into an air of raw power pushing to be released.

His thoughts tripped back once more, back to the day Jonathan had first brought up the idea of going to Cornell. It was a spring evening and they had been coming in from the barn. He had known something was on Jonathan's mind for days and finally Jonathan just blurted out that he wanted to go to college. His father stopped in mid-step and stared at him.

'How would you pay for it, Jonathan?' he asked finally.

'I've qualified for a small scholarship at Cornell, Pa. And I can get a loan, if need be,' he answered firmly.

Charles's gaze was steadfast. 'Ithaca's a ways from here.'

'Only twenty miles. I can get up earlier, do the chores and take the buggy. I'd be home by eleven each night.'

'What would you study?'

Jonathan hesitated. 'I was thinking of agriculture. Or maybe literature.'

Charles looked at him intently as Jonathan held his breath. Then Charles ran his hand, dirty and callused, over his face. 'Literature?' he repeated softly. He started

7

towards the house, stopped and turned back to face Jonathan. 'We'll find you boarding in Ithaca,' he said. 'Won't do for you to be wasting time travelling from here to there.' He paused, seeing doubt fight with the joy in his son's eyes. 'Don't worry, Jonathan,' he said, smiling slightly. 'We'll find a way to pay for it. You'll go to college. And you'll study literature.'

That autumn, Jonathan Caras had become a member of Cornell's class of 1894. Ezra Cornell, a farmer who had made a fortune in the telegraph business, had founded the school on the belief that the lower classes had just as much right to higher education as the rich, and scattered among Cornell's wealthy students were many others like Jonathan. But Jonathan did not want to be like the other farmers. Eager to compensate for his social disadvantage, he studied hard. After his first year, he emerged first academically among his classmates in the Arts and Sciences College. Though he couldn't afford the time or money needed for social clubs, he couldn't resist joining the running team. And he finally succumbed to one other diversion: the student newspaper, the *Cornell Daily Sun*. For the next three years, he worked on the newspaper, rising to editor-in-chief in his senior year. It was his love of the *Sun* that finally gave him the direction he had been seeking.

Since his freshman year, he had pondered his future with increasing anxiety. Finally, he realized the answer had been there in front of him – newspaper journalism. He sent off letters to big city newspapers and finally received an offer from the *New York Herald*. The city editor was pleased to be getting an Ivy League man, but told Jonathan he wouldn't have an opening until December. That was fine with Jonathan; he wanted time to break the news to his father. But no matter how many times he tried, he hadn't been able to find a way to tell his father of his plans.

Now, as he sat in the parlour, looking into his father's face, he knew the time had come. His eyes travelled round the room. Yet another image of his mother sprang to his mind, of her dusting the mahogany tabletop.

'I can see my face in the table, Ma, it's so shiny.'

'So you can! This table's a fine piece of furniture, Jonathan. Fit for a queen. This whole room is fit for a queen . . .'

'Like you, Ma.'

'Yes, like me.'

Jonathan stared at the faded red brocade walls, seeing the room as if for the first time. It was, he knew now, tasteless, as obvious as a bright-red geranium. The thought, coupled with all the other ones of his mother that had crowded him so all day, left him saddened; the question that was always there with him, haunting his mind, pushed its way forward.

Why did she leave?

It had happened just before his return to Cornell for his senior year. She had simply packed a bag and left before dawn. He had come into the kitchen in the morning to find his father sitting at the table, holding his head in his hands. Without a word, he handed Jonathan an envelope and left the house. Jonathan tore open the letter addressed to him and read the note.

My dearest son, I have to go.
Remember that I love you.
Forgive me. Your Mother.

There was nothing else, not even a note to her husband. Jonathan read the note over and over in dumb disbelief, looking for clues, but there was nothing. Except, he realized later, the memory of one night. At the time, it had seemed insignificant, but now it burned bright in his head.

It had been a week before she left. It was late, and the September night was sultry, with the fading Indian summer breeze stirring the curtains at his bedroom window. He was awakened by a soft sound and recognized his mother's voice outside. She was singing softly, a slow melody like a lullaby. He got up and went out to the porch. She was sitting in a rocker, her face profiled by the moonlight, staring out over the fields. She was singing, and crying.

'Ma?'

She turned to look at him, smiling slightly.

'You all right, Ma?'

She nodded. 'Come sit with me, Jonathan,' she whispered.

He sat down on the stool next to her, running a hand over his eyes. It was about three in the morning, and the air was strangely heavy, still and silent. He stared at her face as she looked out at the fields, then up at the stars. Her eyes were bright with a strange light.

'Look at them,' she murmured.

He did, and when he looked back, she was staring at him. 'I'm so proud of you,' she said, her eyes brimming. 'A grown man, a college man . . . with that big, beautiful world just sitting out there waiting for you.'

His heart was beating fast and he didn't know why.

'Don't settle,' she said suddenly.

'What?'

'Don't settle, Jonathan.' She looked away, back out over the fields. 'If you can dream something, then you can get it. Just don't settle.'

The words came out soft but with a startling fierceness. He had never heard her talk this way.

'Promise me,' she said, 'that when you go away from this place you'll never come back.'

He stared at her, not knowing what to say, 'Ma—'

She took his hand, squeezing it hard. 'Promise me.'

10

Her strength surprised him. Finally, he whispered, 'I promise.'

She released his hand. She searched his face with burning eyes, then took it gently in her hands, pressing her warm cheek against his and brushing her lips against his eyelids. He felt her hand run through his hair, pushing it back, as if he were a boy again, and the warm rush of her breath against his ear. 'Go back to bed, Jonathan,' she whispered.

That was the last time he saw her. She never returned to Dryden. She never wrote. She had simply disappeared.

He was filled with questions, but his father refused to talk about it. Though Jonathan felt guilty about leaving his father alone, his father finally insisted that Jonathan go back to school. '*Let's get on with our lives*,' he had said, and then added, '*Don't worry about me. I have my work to keep me busy*.'

Jonathan's eyes travelled over the books stacked in the shadows of the parlour. In some ways, Jonathan greatly admired his father's zeal. After all, how many of Dryden's farmers bothered to read any book, let alone scholarly Shakespearean treatises? But he also believed his father's project was an escape, a way of coming to grips with his wife's desertion, a way to fill the loneliness.

Jonathan ran his hand over his eyes. How am I going to tell him? he thought. How am I going to tell him that now I have to go, too?

He sat forward in the chair, elbows on his knees. 'How's the studying going, Pa?' he asked softly.

'It's going well, really well. I've made great progress this year. I'll make even more now that winter's here.'

Jonathan stared at his hands. There was a silence, broken by the sound of Hannah setting out dishes in the dining room.

'Something's bothering you, Jonathan,' Charles said finally. 'What is it?'

Jonathan looked straight into his father's eyes. 'I'm going away, Pa, to New York,' he said. 'I've got a job lined up there. I'm going to work on a newspaper.'

Charles stared at him for a long time, then slowly took off his glasses. 'When did you decide this?' he asked.

'I've known for some time now.'

Charles drew in a breath and let it out.

Jonathan held his father's eyes, but didn't know what to say. He heard the kitchen door open – Uncle Jake coming in from the barn, stamping his boots in the pantry. And a strange voice in the kitchen with Hannah.

After a while, Hannah came to the door. 'Marion's here, Mr Caras, so we can start dinner whenever you and Jonathan are ready.'

'We'll be right in, Hannah,' Charles said.

Jonathan waited for her to leave, then turned to his father. 'Marion's here?'

Charles smiled. 'She's been coming by pretty regularly since you've been at school. I enjoy her company. She tolerates my foolish talk about my work.' He paused, seeing the look on Jonathan's face. 'You don't mind that I invited her, do you?'

'No, no . . . not at all. It's a nice surprise,' Jonathan said. He fell quiet, looking up at his father, who was still wearing the same small, thoughtful smile of a moment ago.

'You're worried about leaving me alone,' his father said.

'Yes.'

'Don't be, Jonathan. You must go. I've known that for some time, and now I see it in your eyes. All young men feel what you're feeling now.'

Did you? Jonathan thought. Did you feel it once?

'But not all young men act on it,' his father went on. He glanced at a book lying on the desk, and ran his fingers over its frayed leather cover. 'I was too much like

12

young Hamlet here, I guess. My mind is tipped more towards contemplation than action.' He looked back at Jonathan. 'But you're different.'

Jonathan was quiet, his throat constricting. He wanted suddenly to embrace his father, but such overt displays of affection had long ago been tucked away, like toys, in the storage chest of childhood behaviour. He was an adult now. The emotion welled up in him and he grasped his father's hand. 'Thank you, Pa.'

Charles squeezed his son's hand, then stood up briskly. 'Well, we'd best get in to dinner or Hannah will have both our hides on a platter.'

Sitting at the table, Jonathan felt overwhelmed with conflicting emotions. The sight of his father sitting at his usual place and of his mother's empty chair pulled at his guilt. He glanced across the table at Marion. He was happy to see her. They lived on neighbouring farms and he had known her all his life, finding in her friendship a replacement for the brothers and sisters he had always wanted. But tonight her unexpected presence filled him with a strange sense of nostalgia, as if he were already yearning for everything he was about to leave behind. Still the single strongest pull he felt was an exhilarating impatience. It was time to go.

After dinner, he and Marion helped Hannah clear the table and then they decided to go for a walk. Outside, in the cold, still air, Jonathan began to relax. He had not seen Marion for months, but such absences never seemed to affect their relationship; they had grown up together with an ease that precluded shadows and secrets. But there was a secret now. And as they walked, she seemed to sense it, and was quieter than usual.

Black clouds, haloed by the moon, scuttled across the night sky; the only sound was of their shoes crunching through the hard snow as they walked towards the barn. Jonathan touched her arm. 'I have something

13

to tell you, Marion,' he said.

Her clear grey eyes held his. 'It's cold. Let's go inside,' she said.

He followed her into the barn – warm and fragrant with the smell of hay and animals – and lit a paraffin lamp. He turned to face Marion. The lamp's light gave her even-featured face the soft glow of a cameo, and Jonathan was struck by how pretty she looked. A sudden memory overwhelmed him . . . sitting between his mother and Marion on the pew in the beautiful white frame church in Dryden. Listening to the lulling hymns, watching the sun filter through the green glass windows, bathing his mother's and Marion's faces in a cool, ethereal glow.

Marion dropped her shawl to her shoulders and patted her shining brown hair back from her temple, a nervous little gesture. Her large eyes focused on Jonathan. 'What did you want to talk to me about?' she asked.

'I'm going away, Marion. I've taken a job as a newspaperman, in New York City.'

She stared at him, 'New York City . . .' she said softly.

Suddenly, his excitement could no longer be restrained. He wanted to share it with Marion. 'Think of it, Mari,' he said, a smile spreading across his face. 'Me in New York! Next week, I'll be there. I'll be starting a whole new life.'

'But why New York, Jonathan?'

He took a step towards her, his excitement now unbounded. He grasped her shoulders, his eyes bright. 'Why, it's the greatest city in the world, Mari! In a place like New York, a man can make his mark, and no one cares where he comes from or how much money he has. In New York, a man can raise himself up by his talent, his mind and his drive. In New York, a man can be whatever he wants to be!' She was staring at him.

14

'What's the matter, Mari? You're looking at me as if I was a madman.'

He laughed and pulled her to his chest in a happy embrace. Suddenly, all the memories that had crowded around him all day were fading. He was going. Finally, he was going.

'Oh, Mari, be happy for me!' He laughed. 'This is what I've always wanted. I feel like my life is just beginning!'

She pulled back, and her eyes looked up at him round and solemn. She stared at the face she knew so well with new eyes, as if to memorize every detail. She was losing him, she knew that now. For years, she had kept him to herself, deflecting the flirtations of all the other Dryden girls who had wanted him, kept him even after he went away to college. College had changed him, making his fire burn even brighter. But after winter, every spring, he had always returned to her. And even as her mind told her that one day he was destined to leave, her heart denied it and kept alive the hope that they might be married. But now she knew: this time, he was leaving for good. She was losing him.

She stared at him, wanting him to kiss her, aching for him to kiss her as he had that one day four summers ago. A breathless, hot day, with a white-heat sun. The day was seared in her memory. It was August, the week before he was due to leave for his freshman year at Cornell. Seeking relief from the heat, they had gone to the pond to swim. It was a secret place, shut off from the world by walls of high mossy boulders and dark trees. As children, they had used the place as their playhouse, but had not been back in years. They were both quiet, strangely expectant. She had lain on the flat rock, feeling its heat radiate up into her skin. He called to her and she looked up, squinting in the sun, to see him standing on a ledge above, poised to dive into the water. She stared at him, mesmerized. Then came three quick images: his perfect body motionless . . . suspended in the white-hazed sky . . . then cleaving the green water. He joined her on the rock and they lay side by side, silent, eyes closed to the sun, their bodies pressed against the hot stone. She raised herself up to look at him, at the beads of water glittering on his brown chest, and without thinking, she leaned down to kiss him, taking his nipple gently between her lips. Then, he was kissing her, deeply, slowly, as he had never done before: sounds she had never heard from him before, feelings she had never felt in herself before and the press of his body hard and warm and wet against hers. Then, suddenly, he had stopped, pushing himself gently away, breathing heavily, at first unable to meet her eyes. 'Not here, Marion,' he had said, 'not this way . . .' Later she was glad he had stopped, because she would not have been able to.

She stared at him now, wanting to kiss him, but, after all their years of closeness, suddenly not knowing how. He had changed so much. And she was losing him.

'I'm going to miss you, Jonathan,' she said softly.

His face became sober. 'New York's not far,' he said, the words coming out with a quiet hollowness. 'We'll see each other, Mari. Maybe in a couple of months, after winter, I'll come back—'

'No,' she murmured, 'you won't come back.'

'Mari . . .'

She tried to smile but couldn't. 'You're special, Jonathan. You were meant for the wide world, not this place. I've always known it. Everybody's known it. *You've* known it.' She paused. 'I was born for this, but you weren't.'

They stood there silently, Jonathan's arms still wrapped around her waist. She reached up to touch his cheek and parted her lips. She pressed closer against him, and she could feel him begin to stir against her. He

16

kissed her softly, lingeringly, on the lips, then pulled back slightly.

'Let's go back in,' he said.

She quickly dropped her eyes and took a step back, away from him.

After a moment, he held out his hand. 'Mari . . .'

She hesitated, then put her hand in his. They walked out of the barn and towards the house. The moon emerged suddenly from behind a cloud, bathing the barnyard in a coldly beautiful, unworldly light. Jonathan stared at the snowy hills, at the diamonds, as far as he could see.

Chapter Two

The room was cold, but the young girl didn't feel it. The wind rattled the closed shutters, but she didn't hear it. She heard only the music and its soft vocal accompaniment – '*Un, deux, trois, et quatre . . .*'

She was tired and her feet ached unbearably, but she ignored the pain, her hands gripping the chair, her mind attuned to the music and the voice. '*Un, deux, trois . . .*'

The music stopped suddenly. '*Non, non, non!*'

The girl looked quickly towards the old woman sitting behind the piano.

'You must push your foot over the toes,' the old woman said.

'But it hurts, Mémé.'

'I know. Soon it won't.'

The music began again. The girl gripped the chair tighter and rose up on her toes. The pointe shoes gripped her feet like vices, sending pains shooting up her legs, but she pushed, bending her arches until her feet curved like commas. Oh, how could something as pretty as these pink satin ballet shoes hurt so much? She had been so happy and proud when Madame had given them to her. But now, after a month, she had grown to dread putting them on. How did others dance in these things? Madame promised it would get easier, but it hadn't.

'Better . . . that's better . . .'

A trickle of sweat made its way down the girl's back and she bit her bottom lip. The music stopped. 'That's enough,' the old woman said.

The girl closed her eyes, leaning against the chair.

'Come here, Cendrine.'

The girl went obediently across the room with a slightly hobbled walk. The old woman guided the girl down into a chair and, with some effort, knelt on the floor and began to untie the ribbons of the ballet shoes. When she pulled off the first shoe, the girl winced but remained silent. Her toes, wrapped in lambswool, were bloody.

'You worked hard today, *ma puce*,' the old woman said softly, gently swabbing the girl's feet with the hem of her skirt.

'I'm not getting any better, Mémé,' the girl said.

The woman smiled and began to massage the girl's calves, her fingers expertly assessing the progress; Cendrine's legs were thin but getting to be as hard as iron. 'First comes strength, then beauty,' the old woman said.

'But all I ever do is exercises,' the girl said. 'I want to dance.'

'Slower is faster.'

The girl sank back in the chair. 'Slower is faster, slower is faster – I don't understand.'

The old woman got to her feet. 'You're fourteen, Cendrine,' she said, 'and you've had a late start. If I push you too fast, you will develop bad habits and never be a dancer. Slower is faster.'

Cendrine sighed, but when she looked back at the old woman, she was smiling. 'I bet you didn't go slow, Mémé.'

The woman's lips tipped up slightly as she wound the ribbons around the pink shoes. 'It's cold. Get dressed.'

Cendrine quickly pulled her dress over her petticoat.

The old woman thrust some wood into the porcelain stove and went to the kitchen to fill a kettle for tea. Cendrine watched her, her eyes moist with affection. Four times a week, Cendrine came to the cramped apartment for her ballet lesson, and for an hour, the old woman treated her as a student, barking out instructions and endless corrections. But then came tea, and the relationship between the girl and old woman turned intimate. That was why Cendrine called the woman Mémé. To her, the woman was like the grandmother she had never known, or like the mother she wished her own could be.

The sound of the kettle whistling made Cendrine smile. She didn't really like tea, but she loved the dignity of the ceremony that the old woman wrapped around it. Sitting in Madame Kchessinskaya's apartment made Cendrine feel as if she were a grand lady living in some wonderful big city – Paris, perhaps – not a girl stuck in a little village clinging to the hills above the Mediterranean in Provence. Cendrine's eyes travelled over the apartment. What a glamorous place it was! The walls were covered with red flock wallpaper from Paris, and the furnishings were delicate gilt antiques. The large black piano was draped with a purple silk shawl from the Orient; every inch of table and shelf space was covered with pretty bibelots. On one shelf, there were strange little Russian figures with forlorn faces that Madame called icons. Cendrine especially liked the apartment in winter, as it was now. When it was cold, Madame kept the shutters closed and burned patchouli candles even during the day. The candles covered the smell of mildew and gave everything a soft glow, hiding the chips on the gilt furniture and the big water stain on the wallpaper above the window.

Cendrine pulled a shawl over her shoulders and went to the piano, trailing a finger over the yellowed keys, her eyes focusing on the sheet of music. She wished, not for the first time, that she could read it.

'Have you been practising your English?' the old woman called out.

'Yes, Mémé. And the Russian, too.'

Cendrine continued her circuit of the small apartment, her eyes lingering on the pictures of dancers. Russian – what good was it? No one in La Turbie could speak it. Maybe no one else in France spoke it. Now, English, that was different. She had heard it once in the café, two lost strangers passing through asking for directions. English – that would be useful some day.

Cendrine picked up a picture frame from the piano. It was a portrait of Madame taken thirty-five years ago, in 1859, before her debut in *Giselle*. Cendrine took in the details of the peasant costume and the garland of flowers in Madame's hair; unconsciously, she tilted her head slightly, mimicking the pose.

Madame came in bearing a tray. 'Come here by the stove, Cendrine,' she said.

Cendrine put the frame back in its place and took a chair next to Madame as the old woman poured the tea carefully from a beautiful Spode china teapot. 'I love this pot,' she said. 'I used to have an old samovar in my dressing room, but Gerald said it was a barbaric contraption and he bought me this. It was the first thing he ever gave to me.'

Cendrine took the lustrous white cup, her eyes sparkling at her stroke of luck. Madame could be cantankerous, but today she was in the mood to tell her stories. 'Did he give you other things, Mémé?' she asked.

'Of course. A pearl necklace, a diamond tiara . . . and a Beresford bulldog.'

'Do you still have it?'

'Pépé died decades ago, child.'

'No, the tiara, Mémé.'

The old woman laughed. 'I had to sell it.'

Cendrine took a sip of tea. The room was warm now, cozy from the stove and candlelight. Madame sat in her chair, her cup held delicately in her lap, her eyes half-closed. Cendrine, afraid the old woman was dozing off as she often did, rattled her cup gently and Madame's eyes fluttered open.

'Tell me about how you met Gerald, Mémé.'

'Oh, not again!'

'Please.'

The old woman sat up slightly. 'It was after my debut in *Giselle* at the Imperial Theatre in St Petersburg. I was in my dressing room, and I looked up and saw this man standing at the door.' She paused, smiling slightly. 'He had red hair – and the most beautiful beard. He was tall and distinguished-looking. He said something to me, rather shyly, but I didn't know any English then. Finally, he handed me some flowers, kissed my hand, and left. The next day, I found out he was an English lord. We were married three months later.'

'And you went to live in a castle in England,' Cendrine said eagerly.

'A manor house, child. With a terrible tax debt.'

'And you moved to France to live in a villa.'

'To Menton. A very small villa.'

The apartment was quiet for a while. Cendrine knew the rest of the story: how Gerald had died leaving Madame with the tax debt that forced her to sell the villa by the sea and retreat up into the hills to La Turbie. That part of the story she didn't want to hear again. A question had been bothering her lately, but she had been afraid to ask it. Yet she needed an answer. Cendrine set her cup aside.

'Why did you stop dancing, Mémé?' she asked softly.

The old woman's eyes had closed again, and it was a

moment before she opened them to look at Cendrine. 'Because Gerald wanted a wife.'

'But didn't you miss it?'

The old woman poured herself another cup of tea. She stirred some milk into it, taking her time, the spoon tinkling like chimes against the china. She raised the cup to her lips with a gracefully choreographed movement of arm and hand, then set the cup aside, her gaze distant. 'Yes, I missed it,' she said softly.

Cendrine waited, looking at the old woman's face, waiting for her to return from whatever place she had gone in that moment. Finally, Madame looked directly at her and smiled. 'But what times I had! What places and things I saw!'

Cendrine sat forward in her chair.

'I studied with the great Taglioni,' the old woman said. 'I saw Milan and Copenhagen. I danced in *Faust* and *La Sylphide*, at La Scala and the Comédie Française with Marius Petipa himself.' She glanced at Cendrine. 'I had many great partners. A different man every night, and I loved them all.'

'But you loved Gerald,' Cendrine blurted out.

'Yes, but a ballerina cannot help falling in love with her partner on stage. For a brief moment, it is perfection: just the two of you, alone in the light together, and you are in love. Then, of course, it ends and you return to reality.'

Cendrine smiled. 'What makes a great partner, Mémé?'

Madame laughed lustily. 'Well, he must be tall, of course. And handsome, with fine features and a proud bearing.' She paused theatrically. 'He should also have a mark of tragedy about him . . . but with a certain gravity so he is not pathetic.'

Cendrine giggled.

'It's true! You cannot be a great ballerina without a

23

great partner! You must have a man who is strong and courteous. And when he moves, he should soar like an eagle, not dart like a swallow.' She paused. 'And he must, above all, be passionate.'

'Passionate . . .' Cendrine repeated, nodding.

The clock on the table chimed softly five times. Cendrine looked at it in alarm. 'Oh, no! It's late, I have to go!' she said quickly, jumping to her feet. She was halfway out of the door when she heard Madame calling her back.

'Your shoes, Cendrine!'

The girl ran to the piano, grabbed the heavy black boots and thrust them on her feet. The old woman came over to her and held out something. 'Here, this came today. Take it with you.'

Cendrine's eyes widened when she saw the magazine. It was the latest copy of *L'Art et la mode*, the Parisian fashion and society magazine. 'But you haven't even opened it yet, Mémé,' she said.

'What do I need fashion for at my age? Take it.'

Cendrine smiled and took the magazine. She kissed the old woman quickly and ran down the wooden stairs into the dusk.

It was raining and she paused in the courtyard to pull the shawl up over her head and tuck the magazine beneath it, before dashing out into the narrow street. She made her way quickly through the dark labyrinth of cobbled streets, past crumbling old buildings with shuttered windows leaking candlelight and oily smells of cooking. She hurried, wishing she did not have to go home, but knowing that she would be punished if she were late.

As she approached the village square, she felt her heart drop in her chest. What an ugly village La Turbie was! That day it was made even more depressing by the winter rain. The square was just an empty circle, usually

24

dusty but now muddy and rutted, ringed by faded shops, a squat stone church and stunted plane trees, their leafless branches reaching up to the grey sky like claws.

It began to rain harder and she ran the rest of the way to the café. Inside, she paused to hang up her wet shawl and shake the folds of her dress. There were only a few men hunched over glasses of Pernod at the bar and no one looked at her. Her father was nowhere to be seen. Gripping the magazine to her chest, she went quickly up the stairs.

She reached her room in the attic and shut the door, letting out a breath of relief. She stood for a moment, listening to the sounds below, the water from her dripping skirt pooling around her feet. The attic was cold and she shivered. Carefully smoothing the cover of *L'Art et la mode*, she slipped it under the mattress and began to pull her wet dress over her head.

A knock made her jump.

'Cendrine? It's me, Roland.'

The door opened a crack to admit a mop of blonde hair and a pair of blue eyes. Cendrine motioned her brother into the room. She was wearing only a camisole and a petticoat, but felt no need to cover herself; Roland had seen her undressed before. All their lives, they had slept in the same bed together, until three months ago, when Cendrine, in a small act of independence, had finally claimed the space between the eaves as her own.

'He's been looking for you,' Roland said quietly. 'Where have you been all day?'

'At Madame's.'

Roland's mouth drew into a line. She had confided in him her secret about the ballet lessons, but he was always afraid that she would be discovered. 'You said you would go there only twice a week, Cendrine,' he said. 'Now you go four.'

'I have to. Madame says I must work hard to catch up.'

He stared at her, his brows furrowed. She reached out to brush his hair off his forehead: hair so much like her own, straight and silvery blonde. A face so much like her own, pale and childish, with grey-blue eyes. He was a year younger than she was, but sometimes she felt as if they were twins, so strong was the bond between them.

'I made something for you,' Roland said, holding out a piece of butcher's paper. It was a drawing of a ballet dancer, copied carefully from one of Madame's old issues of *L'Art et la mode*.

'Oh, Roland, it's beautiful,' she said softly. 'I'll put it here.' She got up on the bed to hang it on a beam. Turning back to Roland she suddenly froze, the smile slipping from her face. A heavy sound on the stairs: Roland heard it too and stepped away from the door, into the room.

A figure appeared, filling the door frame. Gustav LeClerc stood there, his eyes going from Roland to Cendrine. He was not a tall man, but his arms and chest were thick and his face was ruddy and swollen from the wind and too much drinking. He had been in the cellar bottling wine, and the attic became filled with his smell, an acrid odour of sweat, tobacco and rotten grapes.

His eyes went up to the drawing. He stepped past Roland and pulled it off the wall. He stared at it for a moment, then, in a lightning-quick move, flung his arm backward, striking Roland across the face. The blow knocked Roland against the door and to the floor. Cendrine stood there, on the bed, too terrified to move.

'I want those bottles washed – now,' Gustav LeClerc ordered without looking at Roland.

Roland got to his feet. The right side of his face was red, blood trickling from his nose. Cendrine watched him, her heart hammering, her eyes filling with tears. She had seen Roland get hit so often and often she had seen him cry. His eyes were bright now, but she knew suddenly that this time it was not from tears. It was pure hatred she was seeing, and it scared her. She held her breath, knowing that if Roland struck back, their father would kill him.

With her eyes, she willed Roland to leave. Finally, he turned and went down the stairs. She closed her eyes in relief. When she opened them, she saw her father staring at her; she realized suddenly she was wearing only her underthings. And her father was staring at her breasts. Her mind tripped back to when she was twelve, the time when her father, full of drink, had tweaked her budding nipples beneath her blouse and roared to his wife, 'Look, Marie, how our little one's growing!' She had run from the kitchen, crying in shame, wondering why her mother had not followed to comfort her.

So many times after that, she had caught him staring at her with strange, liquid eyes. He was looking at her that way now, but there was something different this time. His mouth hung slightly slack and his breathing was heavy and slow. She folded her arms across her chest. She was suddenly terrified: terrified not that he would hit her, but that he would touch her.

'Get down,' he said.

Cendrine jumped down from the bed, trying to move away from her father in the small space. He took a step towards her and she waited, her heart hammering against her ribs. A noise rose up from the café below, men's laughter followed by her mother's soft voice. Gustav LeClerc's eyes flicked towards the door and back to Cendrine. He stared at her for a long time.

'Go help your mother,' he said, and left the room, Roland's drawing crumpled in his hand.

Cendrine shut the door, sinking down on the floor. She began to tremble, a trembling that grew quickly to a shaking so violent that it left her weak and nauseous. She drew her knees to her chest, pulling herself into a tight

27

ball, but she couldn't stop her body from shaking. She didn't know how long she stayed like that, but finally, the light from the small window was gone and the room was dark. She got up, put on her dress and went downstairs to help her mother.

A ballroom. Gentle-faced men in black dress coats and beautiful women in gowns swirled like flowers caught in the wind. Crystal chandeliers rained down rainbows. Mirrors tossed back the light, igniting the jewels on the women's necks into rings of red, blue and green fire.

The drawing in *L'Art et la mode* was done in black and white, but Cendrine could see all the colours, could hear the music and smell the women's perfumes. Her eyes hungrily took in the details of one woman's dress, the feather in her upswept hair, the jewels at her throat, the flounce of flowers and bows at her wispy, corseted waist. Did such women really live? Did worlds like this truly exist?

Cendrine yawned, shifting in the narrow bed. It was quiet, and the candle on the nightstand had burned down to a stub. She had been reading for hours and knew she should get some sleep, but she couldn't set the magazine aside.

She turned the page to a new illustration. It was of a couple in a chaste embrace. The man, handsome and dark-haired, was holding the woman's hand, and her eyes were demurely downcast. His lips were poised just above her plunging neckline, as if he were about to kiss the delicate shadow between her breasts. Cendrine ran her fingers slowly across the illustration, her heart beating more rapidly.

Making love . . . this is how it is supposed to be, she thought.

She knew little about sex. She had watched animals mate, and knew instinctively that men and women did the same. But she believed that it had to be something more, and finally asked Roland.

'It's not,' he had told her, his maleness giving him for once an edge of knowledge over her. 'It's just sex. It's what animals do. It's what he does to Mother.'

She had heard the sounds coming from her parents' room: the grunting noises and the whimpering of her mother. But it had nothing to do with love. It was brutality, no different from what he did to Roland.

Cendrine stared at the illustration in the magazine till the embracing couple became a blur. She had to get some sleep. She stuffed the magazine under the mattress and blew out the candle.

It was just before dawn when Cendrine was roused by a strange, heavy weight in her bed. She couldn't see her father's face; it was his smell that came to her, snapping her awake. Her heart began to pound, afraid that he had somehow found out about her ballet lessons and had come to beat her. He raised his hand and she flinched. Then she felt his fingers, rough and heavy, touching her throat, moving downward under her nightgown and over her breasts. Her body went rigid with shock.

'*Cendrine, ma belle Cendrine, ma petite . . .*' he murmured. His breath was hot and rancid on her face. His fingers closed on one of her nipples, squeezing, and she cried out. He struck her across the mouth just hard enough to shock her into silence.

'*Tais-toi!*' he said. 'Shut up!'

His hands began to move beneath her nightgown again, cupping the mound between her legs. Tears filled her eyes and streamed down her cheeks but she forced her mind to go blank, blotting it out. She was terrified that he would do what he did to her mother.

Eventually he stopped and got up. 'Don't tell anyone, Cendrine,' he said. 'If you do, I will beat you so hard you

29

won't be able to walk. You'll be a cripple.' And he was gone.

She lay there rigid, unable to move, listening to his tread down the stairs, followed by the usual sounds of his morning routine as he went out the café's back door towards the chicken coop. A few minutes later, she heard her mother stirring.

Suddenly, the room felt as if it were closing in around her, suffocating her. She couldn't face anyone. She had to get out, away. She swung her feet over the bed and sat there for a moment, trying to calm her breathing. Then she dressed quickly, crept silently down the stairs and out of the front door of the café.

It was still dark, the only light coming from the *boulangerie*. The air was cold and windy, fragrant with the smell of baking bread. She ran across the square and into the narrow streets, moving without thinking, her breath coming in short gasps. Disappearing into a grove of cypress trees, she emerged into a clearing that was dominated by a massive stone ruin. She didn't stop to look at it. She ran into its courtyard and only then did she stop. She stood there for a moment, wavering. Then she dropped to her knees in the wet grass and cried.

Cendrine stayed there for a long time, hunched into a ball, great sobs racking her body. Finally, she fell silent. When she raised her head, the sky was grey with the breaking morning and it was quiet except for the rushing of the wind through the cypress trees. She looked down at her hands, clenching fistfuls of grass.

Slowly, she got to her feet and straggled across the lawn, her eyes drifting vacantly over the fallen stones and the crumbling pillars. She felt safe here. The old Roman ruin was her secret place, a place where she had always come to play and dream. The ruin had been abandoned centuries ago, and was being slowly eaten away by the sea air. No one ever came to see it.

No one ever bothered her here.

At the edge of the clearing, on the lip of a sheer cliff, there was a stone bench that overlooked the Mediterranean. She sank down on it, watching the details of the coastline, so far below, emerge. The pretty village of Beaulieu-sur-Mer took shape, its red roofs glowing pink as the sun hit them. The sea changed colour from grey to soft blue and she could see a white yacht sitting at anchor.

Suddenly the feel of her father's hands came back to her and she drew in a sharp breath. What was she going to do? She couldn't tell her mother, Roland or even Mémé. She was too frightened and too ashamed. Tears burned in her eyes, but she wiped them roughly away, staring at the yacht far below, concentrating on it, trying to imagine where it came from, what great man owned it. Anything to blot out her father.

Away . . . she had to get away.

But where? How?

She closed her eyes. Get away . . . but not like the other girls. She would not marry some stupid village boy just to escape. She wouldn't be trapped here, like her mother had been.

She would dance. Dancing would bring her freedom. Dancing would take her away.

She shivered, dreading going back to the café, but she knew she had no choice at the moment. Somehow, she would find a way to survive. She had to, until she was old enough – until she was strong enough to get away for ever.

She opened her eyes and squinted at the sun. It was higher in the sky now, glinting off the sea. She looked down at her hands, cradled in her lap, still clutching the grass.

She raised her hands and opened them. The wind caught the blades of grass, scattering them in the air.

Chapter Three

It began as just another March storm, a tempest of wind and rain in the night. But by morning, New Yorkers woke to find their city paralysed by a blizzard. The elevated trains started down from Harlem as usual, picking up workers heading towards the lower end of the island, but finally all trains sputtered to a stop on the clogged tracks. By nine, everything had come to a standstill; even horsedrawn rigs lay abandoned in the streets.

Jonathan was awakened by the shivering of his own body. His flat was ice cold, filled with a gloomy light, the window nearly covered by a wall of snow. He tossed off his blankets and looked down on the amazing scene below. Nassau Street was heaped with drifts, some two storeys high, and the snow was still coming down. He dressed quickly. He knew he had to get to the newspaper office as soon as possible.

Downstairs, he helped two men who were using coal shovels to dig through the massive drift blocking the stoop. Once out on the street, he paused to catch his breath and take in the unusual spectacle. The street was a vast, white desert dotted with hapless people caught up in snowy whirlwinds. Signs were obliterated and doorways hidden. Broken trees poked out of mountainous white ridges. Buildings were festooned with ice and ornamented in fantastic white gargoyles. He looked across the street, up at the bank clock by which he set his watch each morning. Its hands had stopped at seven minutes past twelve. It was as if the whole world had come to a stop, and his street, usually filled with grime and noise, had been transformed into a dream world of surreal, desolate beauty.

He wound his muffler up over his face, and started down the street. At the *Herald* office, he went quickly up to the city room. Usually, at this time of the morning, there were a dozen reporters and editors lurking about, but now only three men sat around the table. One of them was the news editor, Roscoe Barnes, whose shadowed eyes clearly indicated the sleepless night he had endured. Roscoe saw Jonathan and came towards him eagerly.

'How the hell did you make it in?' he asked. 'Never mind – you're here, thank God!'

Jonathan began to peel off his coat and muffler. 'You look terrible, Roscoe,' he said, smiling.

Roscoe rubbed his bristly chin. 'I stayed late after the final edition last night, and stuck around to have a drink with Charlie and Tom. By three in the morning, we were trapped. All the telegraph and electric wires are down. We're completely cut off.' He eyed Jonathan anxiously. 'What's it like out there?'

Jonathan sat down, rubbing his hands together to get the blood moving. 'Incredible. You wouldn't believe it.'

'A hell of a story. We have to get moving on it. Now!'

Roscoe's eyes were avid. Jonathan did not have to be told that he was expected to go back out into the snow. He glanced at Charlie and Tom. Charlie was a rewrite man, near retirement; Tom was eighteen, a copyboy who wanted desperately to move up to reporter. Jonathan stood up and began to put on his coat.

'You'd better hope somebody else makes it in here,

Roscoe,' he said with a laugh. 'Young Tom and I can't do this alone.'

Roscoe smiled. 'You're the best newsman in town, Jonathan, and I'm the best news editor. We'll pull it off. Can't let the *Times* hand us our shirt on the biggest story of the year.'

Tom, now bundled up in his overcoat, came to their side and looked at Jonathan for instructions. Jonathan himself had been at the *Herald* only three years now, and he was twenty-four, not that much older than Tom; yet his diligence, drive and uncommon ability to paint pictures with words had earned him the respect of his colleagues. Tom idolized him.

'All right, Tom,' Jonathan said. 'You go to Wall Street and stop at police headquarters. I'll hit City Hall and then head up Broadway. And don't just get facts and figures – use your senses. All of them.'

Roscoe held out a flask. 'Here – you might need it.'

Jonathan slipped it into his coat pocket with a smile. 'I hope it's not that usual rotgut you drink.'

'You get cold enough, you won't care,' Roscoe said.

Outside, Jonathan struck off through the snow and made his way to City Hall, where he found out that all the city's transportation had come to a halt, including railways and ferries from the boroughs. Three hundred people had spent the night in Grand Central Station and hundreds were still stranded in carriages on the el throughout the city. Business was immobilized; was impossible for anyone to reach the lower end of the island. There was no electricity, and all the electric clocks in the city, which operated on one circuit, had stopped at exactly seven minutes past twelve.

The facts were sketchy, but Jonathan knew he had to do just what he had told Tom: use his senses. It was, he knew, the people and all their small stories that would go to make up the bigger story.

He made his way up Broadway, past snow-barricaded shops with signs announcing spring sales, past strangers with cold-puffed faces and frozen whiskers. At Macy's, he discovered that the sales clerks had spent the night sleeping in the store. Along Broadway, he found all the grand hotels completely booked with wealthy refugees who had been unable to get back uptown.

He saw incidents of small kindness. Near 14th Street, he saw a woman huddling in a doorway, crying bitterly, holding an infant, until passers-by steered her into a restaurant. He passed a cart caught in a drift, its exhausted horse near death, the driver slumped forward, still clutching the reins. Two workers got the unconscious driver down, rubbed his face with snow and helped him to a police station while someone led the horse to shelter. Children, taking pity on the sparrows wandering near-frozen on the ground, warmed them gently between their mittened hands.

He saw, too, examples of unscrupulous behaviour, such as the man who extended a ladder up to a stalled el train and charged passengers a dollar apiece to climb down. The rich were being equally exploited; Jonathan watched a cabman lead a furious bidding war among a group of finely dressed men who needed a ride to the Exchange. Finally, a man won the ride for $100. 'This is one day when even big money won't make the mare go,' one of the losers quipped to Jonathan.

It was true, Jonathan thought. The snow had acted as a great equalizer, erasing the hard line of demarcation between the city's rich and poor. For the moment at least, nearly everyone was infused with compassion. That was what he would write about, he knew: that feeling of humanity and how it had transformed a city.

When the grey afternoon light began to wane, Jonathan started back down Broadway. He had told Tom to meet him at Herald Square at four, but by the time he got to the square, the snow was coming down hard again, and he could barely see. Finally, he spotted Tom across the square and started across the street.

Suddenly, in the haze of the driving snow, he saw a pair of horses and a wagon bearing down on him, lurching in the snowy ruts of the street, out of control. He saw, too, in that split second, a small boy dart across the street. Without thinking, he hurled himself at the boy. He felt the small weight of the boy's body, heard the crashing rattle of the wheels, and then felt a sharp strike against his left leg. Then there was nothing but the damp cold of an enfolding snowbank.

He became aware of arms pulling at him, and then of the whimpering of the boy beneath him.

'Jonathan! Are you all right?'

He was pulled to his feet, and it was a moment before he recognized Tom's terrified face. He wiped the snow off his face, dazed. 'Yes, I'm fine,' he murmured.

He heard the whimpering again and looked down to see the boy sitting in the snow, scared but unharmed. Jonathan started to reach out to him when a woman suddenly thrust herself between them, kneeling in the snow to take the boy in her arms. She started to sob, rocking the boy back and forth. Jonathan's practised eye took in the details of the woman's dress: an old, shapeless black coat and tattered scarf. He saw a basket of clothing lying nearby where she had dropped it, and his eyes went to her bare hands cradling the boy's head: chapped, red hands that identified her as a laundress. He stooped to gather the spilled laundry back into the basket. After a while her crying lessened and she looked up. Slowly, she struggled to her feet, and took the basket from Jonathan.

'Thank you,' she whispered.

Someone stepped forward to help her and the boy, and Jonathan watched as they walked away. The woman looked back over her shoulder at Jonathan, then was swallowed up in the snow. The crowd dispersed with a murmur.

'That was a crazy thing to do,' Tom said. 'You could have been killed!' His face was filled with awe.

'I didn't think,' Jonathan said., 'It was a reaction, that's all. A reflex.' He began to shiver. 'Let's get going.'

He took a step and winced. Tom saw it and looked down to Jonathan's leg where a dark-red spot stained his trousers at the calf.

Tom blanched. 'We've got to get you back to the office.' He began frantically to look around the streets.

Jonathan smiled slightly. 'Tom, I don't think we're going to find a ride tonight. Let's get walking before we freeze to death.'

He held out his arm, and Tom fit his shoulder beneath it, bearing Jonathan's weight. Together, they made their way down the street.

Back at the office, Roscoe installed Jonathan in the editor's office on a sofa, while Tom related the details of Jonathan's deed to the small but rapt newsroom audience. Yet the excitement was soon forgotten in the amount of work that was yet to be done. Only two other reporters had made it to the office and their reports, with those by Jonathan and Tom, were now ready to be fashioned into one story. Jonathan, shrugging off Roscoe's threat to call a doctor, limped out to the newsroom, gathered up the reports and sat down at his desk behind the typewriter. No protest from Roscoe could deter him. He wanted to write the story.

After half an hour, Roscoe came over and picked up the first two pages of the story, reading them carefully. 'You writing a novel again?' he said.

'You don't like it?' Jonathan asked.

'I didn't say that. It's just not the usual style.'

Jonathan resumed typing. He and Roscoe had been

through this before; it was such a familiar argument it had almost become a game. It had started three years ago, the day Jonathan turned in his first story, a naively melodramatic piece about a fire that Roscoe made him rewrite twice. Jonathan had come to the *Herald*, braced by his experience at the *Cornell Sun*, believing he knew how to write news; but he quickly discovered that the courtly style of writing he had cultivated at Cornell had no place in a real newspaper. 'I want facts, not this romantic rubbish,' Roscoe had told the deeply embarrassed Jonathan. So Roscoe taught him how to gather facts and pare them down into the tight-knit, prosaic style that defined newspaper writing. But Jonathan's own writing instincts could not be suppressed, and into the fabric of facts he wove subtle threads of colour and drama. The result was a compromise – lean, evocative reporting that told the news while hinting at the larger human truths beneath. Over the years, the two men had developed, if not a friendship exactly, then certainly a respect for each other. Roscoe had taught Jonathan about the gritty reality of newspapers – Jonathan had taught Roscoe about the power of the imagination.

'Not the usual style,' Roscoe repeated, enjoying the game.

'Ah, but this isn't the usual story, Roscoe,' Jonathan said, smiling. 'It's not about how many feet of snow fell and how many trains stopped, although you'll find all that in there. It's about small heroics. And humanity.'

Roscoe saw the sparkle in Jonathan's eyes. With a grunt, he took the pages back to his desk.

He returned a short time later. 'All right, I'm buying it,' he said. 'New Yorkers turn heroic . . . people will eat it up. It'll make them feel good about themselves. I like it so much, we're going to run our own hero story. I told Tom to write up how you saved that kid.'

'What? It was nothing, Roscoe. I told you that.'

'It's a heart-warming tale. It'll sell papers.'

Jonathan glanced over to a nearby desk, where Tom was feverishly typing, his brow knitted in intense concentration. The sight reminded him of himself, on the day he had started at the *Herald*, fresh from Cornell. 'Tell Tom not to get too carried away,' he murmured.

After Roscoe left, Jonathan sat there, staring at the page in his typewriter. He rubbed his hand over his eyes, feeling suddenly exhausted, very aware of the throbbing pain in his leg. Pulling out his pocket watch, he registered that he had only fifteen minutes to finish his story. He ran his thumb lightly over the watch's face, thinking of his father. Then he snapped the watch shut and put it away. He rested his fingers lightly on the typewriter keys and closed his eyes, concentrating, willing his mind blank, until he saw nothing but an expanse of white, as clean and empty as the snow. White time. Time to write. After a moment, as always, the images formed in his mind and the words began to flow.

Chapter Four

On the third morning after the blizzard, Jonathan was awakened by a knock on his door. A boy stood there, holding out a letter. 'Mr Caras? This is for you. I was told to stay for an answer.'

It was an invitation to dinner that night, from his friend, Sumner Briggs. The postscript – 'I promise you a feast fit for the city's biggest hero' – brought a smile to Jonathan's face.

Sumner . . . he hadn't seen him in nearly a year, since he had gone to live in Europe with his family. Jonathan rubbed the expensive paper of the invitation between his fingers. The prospect of getting out of the flat for dinner at Sumner's apartment cheered him, even if it meant enduring his friend's taunts.

'Tell Mr Briggs I'll be there,' Jonathan said, handing the boy a nickel tip. 'Say, are the trains running yet?' he called out as the boy ran down the stairs.

'The Ninth Avenue's up,' the boy called over his shoulder. 'Thing's just like they was before.'

Late that afternoon, Jonathan bathed and laid his best suit out on the bed. He was glad now that he had bought the suit, though it had cost him a month's salary. He wanted to look his best to see Sumner.

Adjusting his tie at the mirror, his hands paused as his thoughts drifted back to his years at Cornell. He hadn't thought much about college in the last three years, but now the memories of his years there were vivid. Cornell and Sumner . . . the two were for ever tied together in his mind. He stared at his reflection, and his mouth turned up in a sheepish half-smile as he remembered his first few weeks at school. What a figure he must have presented on that first day!

The Ithaca train station, freshman year. He could see himself standing with his suitcase, waiting for the upperclassman who, by tradition, was supposed to meet each new student. A young man had come towards Jonathan and thrust out his hand, smiling broadly. He was tall and thin, with thick spectacles and straight blond hair worn slicked back on his head. He was dressed in a splendid tweed suit that made Jonathan acutely aware of his own poor clothes. But the man did not seem to notice what Jonathan wore. He began a nonstop stream of talk that had put Jonathan immediately at ease. 'Well, you must be Caras! Welcome to Ithaca. I'm Sumner Briggs. Good to have you here. Marvellous day, isn't it? Should be splendid for the game! That your bag? You travel light! Well, let's get started up the hill.'

The cab took them up a steep hill, leaving them at the summit. If Sumner Briggs had been impressive, Cornell itself was even more so. The campus was set high above the town of Ithaca and Lake Cayuga, which looked like a long silver mirror flung down in the folds of a dark-green velvet robe. All around were towering elm trees, sweeping green lawns and stately buildings, set in a sylvan glen cut through with rushing waterfalls.

And the people! The campus swarmed with handsome young men and pretty women. As he walked with Sumner across the quadrangle, a green carpet littered with red and gold leaves, Jonathan heard snatches of foreign words – Spanish, and something he guessed was

Oriental. He saw a dark man wearing a suit and a white turban. At one point, he had simply stopped, standing there staring at the buildings, the trees and the people, filled with strange emotions: apprehension at being in a new, foreign world but, most of all, a thrilling elation about the future. His future.

'Is something wrong?' Sumner had asked.

'This place,' Jonathan said. 'It's beautiful. Like Olympus, far above the real world.'

He looked quickly at Sumner, expecting laughter. But Sumner had only smiled and said, 'A romantic! That's good. We're a dying breed, you know.'

Now, standing before the flecked mirror in his apartment, staring at his reflection, Jonathan smiled as he recalled the incident. He smoothed the lapels of his suit, picked up his overcoat and hurried out of the door.

Outside, he paused. The late-afternoon sun was shining in a clear, blue sky, but what the messenger boy had said earlier was true. Deprived of its pristine white cover, New York looked just the way it had before – noisy, dirty and incredibly ugly.

At Ninth Avenue, Jonathan boarded the el. It was crowded with people going home after a long day, smelling of wet wool, sweat and fatigue. As the train lurched its way uptown, spewing cinders and steam, Jonathan clung to a leather strap, wishing that Sumner did not live so far uptown – or that he had enough money for a cab.

Money . . . It made all the difference. He had learned that at Cornell. He had learned it from sitting next to the sons of the wealthy, from watching the way they dressed and acted. He had learned it especially from Sumner.

Right from the start, Jonathan had wondered why a person of Sumner's background sought out his friendship. His father owned one of New York's biggest banks and his family was listed in the social register. But

Jonathan soon discovered that, despite his family's wealth, Sumner did not fit the mould of the other privileged students. He was unathletic and, because of his plain features, unsuccessful with women. He was also studious and shared with Jonathan a passion for great books, despite the fact he was actually studying business in order one day to take his place in his father's New York bank. It was a simple intellectual bond that sparked their friendship, but it was more complex needs that fed it. In Jonathan, Sumner saw what he could never be: a man free of convention with enough courage, talent and energy to reinvent himself. In Sumner, Jonathan saw what he wanted to be: a man of status, able to move with confidence in any social circle.

Sumner was more than willing to be Jonathan's unofficial guide. He belonged to Chi Psi, living with his fraternity brothers in a magnificent gabled mansion on campus. Sumner offered to sponsor Jonathan's initiation into the fraternity, but a fraternity man was expected to maintain the correct wardrobe and have enough cash on hand for dinners, initiation fees and athletic tickets – about $1,000 a year, a fortune to Jonathan.

So Sumner included Jonathan in as many of his fraternity's activities as he could, and Jonathan began to change in fundamental ways. His education extended beyond libraries and labs, as he learned from Sumner the rules of the social game: everything from correct cutlery to polite conversation. He fell into the easy rhythms of college life, gauging the change in seasons no longer by the colour of the earth or the birth of animals, as he had done on the farm, but by more selfish sensual pleasures. Yet despite his new confidence, a part of him remained in awe of Sumner and the other wealthy students. There was something innate in their looks and behaviour which Jonathan knew he could only ever hope to imitate, no matter how hard he tried. They came from 'good' families, from important cities like New York and Boston. They looked different, always crisp and clean in their smart cutaway suits, their pale faces rendered smooth by barbers, their short hair smartly parted in the middle. Their manners were as smooth as their carefree faces, and even their speech had the musical sound of money.

Jonathan watched them playing on the tennis courts or boating on the lake, looking like splendid young gods in their straw hats and white flannel trousers. And at their sides were their goddesses, young women so incredibly beautiful that often Jonathan could do nothing but stare crudely. Sometimes, at night, as he lay in his bed with his books across his chest, the women would come back to him, dancing along the periphery of his mind. The sweeping S-curve of their figures, the tantalizing juxtaposition of their tiny constrained waists and soft, uplifted bosoms. The passing scent of their shining, upswept hair. The glimpse of pale cheek beneath a parasol. It was the women who, in the end, caused him the deepest, most aching envy. Women like that never looked his way. Women like that moved in a different world of wealth and ease, a world to which he had no entry.

Money . . . For all their closeness, he and Sumner were still separated by it. When Sumner graduated and went to work for his father's firm, they kept in touch by writing. But Jonathan's life at Cornell was never the same again and it was not much later that he decided to become a journalist. Fortunes were being made in America every day from strange new sources – steel mills, oil. Why not newspapers? Other men had accumulated power and money owning them; there was no reason why he couldn't. Newspapers would be his entry into the blinding white world of wealth he had found at Cornell.

The train took a sudden turn, throwing Jonathan against the man next to him, pulling him back to the present. Jonathan uttered an apology but the man rudely pushed Jonathan back and turned away.

Jonathan looked out of the window, down at the tenements hidden in the track's shadow. Money . . . It seemed he was always thinking about it now. Three years of living in New York, a city cruelly divided by money, had meant he couldn't avoid the preoccupation. There were so many rich people; every day the newspapers were filled with stories about the new luxury hotels being built, about how a sleepy seaport was becoming a world capital and how wealthy families named Vanderbilt, Gould, Frick and Rockefeller were spearheading a new phenomenon called high society. New York was an exciting, romantic place – if you had money.

But if you didn't . . . He looked down again at the small windows of the tenements, opaque with soot, wondering how people survived, crammed into those airless rooms, living for ever in the gloom of the railway tracks. He wondered, too, about the countless vagrants he saw on the streets and the people living in shacks on the acreage that had been set aside in the middle of the city for a new park. And the children, legions of dirty orphans sleeping beneath bridges or huddled like rats in the hay barges on the East River.

He closed his eyes, thinking now about his news story and how foolishly romantic it had been, his vision of a city transformed. The truth was that New York was a hellish place, nothing like the dream he had conjured up in his days back on the farm. The reality was, for most New Yorkers – even for working men like himself – streets filled with dung, dead horses, cacophony and the constant struggle to survive.

His thoughts turned now to his job at the *Herald*. He

45

was making a decent wage, and the work was interesting enough – competing for stories with the city's best newsmen, covering murders and political scandals. But he had known right from the start that he wanted to be more than a reporter. He wanted to learn the business, move up to editor. And then, some day, be in a position to buy his own newspaper.

It was only after he had been with the *Herald* for a year that he discovered he had little chance of advancement. There were too many older men ahead of him, and the paper itself had stagnated. Its circulation was nearly half a million, but it was slowly losing ground to other, more vital papers. The *Herald* desperately needed ambitious men to help it, but a sad sort of inertia had settled in, born of men too worried about their futures to take chances. No one seemed to care and that included the owner. The *New York Herald* was, Jonathan had discovered, a rudderless ship. It was owned by a man named Alexander Profitt, the son of the newspaper's founder who had died five years ago. The younger Profitt had a reputation as a playboy and hard drinker, and it was generally believed he lacked the talent of his late father. To make matters worse, he didn't even live in New York. Several years ago, he had moved to Paris and had started a newspaper there, apparently as nothing more than a diversion for his wealthy friends. To fund this Paris edition, Profitt had cut back expenditures for the *New York Herald*. Resentment simmered on the New York staff, yet no one seemed to have enough power – or courage – to question Profitt's moves.

Jonathan had heard all the stories about Profitt's extravagant lifestyle; they had the power of myth in the *Herald* newsroom. The favourite explained why the man had had to leave New York several years ago. It seemed that during a dinner party, the drunken Profitt had urinated into the fireplace at his socialite fiancée's home and her enraged brother had challenged him to a duel. The engagement broken, Profitt had run off to Paris to avoid a scandal and had remained an expatriate ever since, turning his back on the New York society that had shunned him.

Jonathan did not know if the stories were true, but they bothered him. What chance for advancement did he have on a newspaper whose owner was a drunk who never set foot in New York, let alone his own newsroom? And how much longer would the mere satisfaction of his writing sustain him? He wanted to move up, to make his mark. He had ideas for improving the *Herald*. A couple of times he had written letters to Profitt, outlining his ideas, but had not mailed them. What good would it do? he had thought. The man obviously didn't care. He had vented his frustration to Roscoe, and so far, the news editor had managed to talk him out of going to another newspaper.

But now, as he stared out of the train window, Jonathan knew he had to do something. He had put off the decision too long; the invitation from Sumner – and the memories of Cornell that it had rekindled – had been a sign. It was time to move on. On Monday he would go and see the city editor at the *New York Times*.

The train came to a stop and the conductor announced 60th Street, end of the line. Jonathan emerged into the twilight and started walking. It was twelve more blocks to Sumner's apartment, but Jonathan was glad to be out of the train. It was a pleasant walk this far north of 42nd Street, where the city still wore most of its clean cover of snow and there was little traffic. The air was crisp and gradually Jonathan was able to rid his mind of negative thoughts, filled with the anticipation of seeing Sumner.

Sumner had recently moved out of his family's Gothic mansion on Murray Hill and into a new building called the Dakota: so named because the joke was it was so far removed from the rest of the city that it might as well be located in Dakota Territory. Sumner's parents had been shocked, not only by the unstylish address, but by the fact that their son was going to live in an apartment building. Such a living arrangement was a new fad, and they believed it was indecent to live atop other people, like honeycombed bees or tenement dwellers.

As Jonathan approached 72nd Street, his eyes travelled appreciatively over the building. Many people thought it was vulgar, but Jonathan thought it was wonderful, like a European palace, elaborately detailed with balconies, iron railings, archways and columns. Its copper roof, a fanciful creation of gables, turrets and flagpoles, gleamed in the fading evening light.

The doorman admitted Jonathan and an old woman took him up in the lift, a delicate cage of spindled wood. Sumner was waiting for him outside his apartment.

'You're here! I was getting worried,' he said, grasping Jonathan around the shoulders, smiling broadly. 'God, it's good to see you. Come in, come in! Let's warm you up with a drink.'

Inside, the drawing room was warm from the blaze in the marble fireplace. Sumner took Jonathan's coat and set about opening a bottle of champagne. Jonathan watched him, smiling. Sumner was wearing a silk smoking jacket, a rebellion against the staid suits he had to wear every day in his father's bank. Sumner was far too tradition-bound to break totally with his annoying, stuffy family, so he asserted his independence by small, impudent acts. He wanted desperately to be a true bohemian, but did not have the courage to live in Greenwich Village – so, for $3,000 a year, he had his ten-room apartment in the infamous Dakota, where his neighbours were the antithesis of his parents: middle-class people, assorted intellectuals and artists who cared more about their own lives than any notion of society.

Jonathan took a seat near the fire, his eyes ranging over the large drawing room. He wondered how any mansion on Murray Hill could be any more wonderful than this. The room was panelled in mahogany, the floors inlaid polished marble, all cast in the soft glow of the Baccarat chandelier. Jonathan stared at his friend, wondering, not for the first time, how much money he made at the bank.

Sumner handed him a glass of champagne and sat down in a chair opposite. 'So!' he said, smiling. 'How does it feel to be a hero?'

Jonathan laughed. 'For the first time, my landlady is not bothering me about the rent being late.'

'Did you really snatch the lad out from under the scythe of Death?' Sumner's eyes sparkled. He was quoting Tom's prose.

'Not in quite the vivid manner that the story implied.' Jonathan took a swallow of champagne, shutting his eyes with pleasure as the electric fizz coursed down his throat.

'Modesty will get you nowhere in this world, Jonathan, old boy,' Sumner said. 'I've always told you that.'

'I'm beginning to believe you.'

Sumner considered Jonathan carefully for a moment. 'Is something bothering you?' he asked.

Jonathan's gaze had drifted to the fire, and he looked back at Sumner, knowing he had no right to allow his dispirited mood to spoil the evening. He smiled. 'No, I'm fine. Just working too hard lately.' He leaned forward, his smile widening. 'So, you've been living all over Europe. Tell me where you've been, what you've seen. Tell me everything.'

Over dinner, Sumner told him about his life in Europe. Jonathan listened raptly, his mind making comparisons between the things Sumner described and the images that lay stored in his own imagination. The conversation went onto other subjects: about how New York was changing, about the new buildings and bridges going up, the streets being paved. Sumner complained that New York had no soul – one of his favourite themes.

'They're always tearing something down here to replace it with something new. New York is so utilitarian,' he said. 'It's nothing like London or Rome. Or Paris. Now, there's a beautiful city. Every bridge, every building, every view is designed to enthrall the senses. Let me tell you about Paris . . .' And Jonathan listened, entranced.

The conversation drifted to other subjects, and eventually to the *Herald*. Sumner was curious about a new column the paper had recently begun, one devoted entirely to social etiquette.

'It's ludicrous, really, the *Herald* taking its readers to task for their bad manners,' Sumner said. ' "One must never talk loudly at the dinner table . . . A gentleman should never stare impertinently at a lady." ' He laughed. 'Who reads that rubbish?'

'Shopgirls who dream about marrying into Mrs Astor's List of Four Hundred,' Jonathan said, 'men who aspire to better their position.' Men like me, he thought. He finished his wine and leaned back in his chair. The good food, splendid surroundings and Sumner's company had restored his good humour. He smiled across the table at his friend. 'You forget, good breeding doesn't come naturally to everyone.'

'So now we must have manuals for it . . . *comme il faut*,' Sumner murmured, smiling. 'Oh, Jonathan, if people only knew how utterly boring it all is!' He leaned forward suddenly. 'Shall I tell you what it's like to go to dinner at Mrs Astor's? First, you must arrive precisely at seven. Once, my parents and I got there early and we had to sit in our carriage outside for five minutes.'

Sumner took a draught of his brandy. 'Before dinner, everyone is served exactly one small glass of Jack Rose and exactly one canapé. You don't dare ask for more. The dinner conversation consists of thoughtful discussions of food, horses, yachts, balls, marriages and whomever it is this month they are snubbing. No politics or art. They won't discuss an artist unless he's been dead for fifty years.' Sumner paused. 'Dinner lasts exactly two hours, and at half past ten the old bird rises, and that's our cue to leave.' He drained his brandy and sighed. 'This is the gilded circle to which the *Herald* readers aspire to belong? This is the gilded cage from which I aspire to escape.'

The room was quiet for a moment. Then came the muted sound of someone playing the piano in the apartment next door. Jonathan swirled his brandy in his glass, feeling pleasantly satiated. When he looked up, Sumner was staring at him thoughtfully.

Jonathan looked down at his glass. The sound of the piano stopped suddenly and the room was quiet again. The mantel clock chimed eleven times and, for the first time that evening, Jonathan's thoughts turned towards the unpleasant prospect of returning to his flat downtown.

'Something *is* bothering you,' Sumner said. 'What is it?'

Jonathan hesitated. Suddenly, he knew he had to let out his frustration, get it out of his system somehow. Sumner was his friend, the only person he could really talk to. 'I'm going to quit the *Herald*, Sumner,' he said.

'But I thought you enjoyed your work?'

'I do. That is, I love newspapers,' Jonathan said. 'But I can't stay there any longer. I look at myself in the mirror and I see this face . . . it's not mine, it belongs to all those men at the *Herald* who've been doing the same job for decades. I see myself, years from now, looking just like them.'

He went onto tell Sumner his concerns about the state of the *Herald*. 'I'm going to try my luck at the *Times*,'

Jonathan said. He leaned forward suddenly, his eyes bright with intensity. 'I have – *ideas*, Sumner. I want to make my mark somewhere. Right now, I feel . . .' He jumped to his feet and began pacing. 'I feel like my life is at a standstill! My mother told me once that the greatest sin in life was not to live it to the fullest. I don't want to end up old and eaten up with regrets. So I'm going to do whatever it takes to change my life.'

Sumner was sitting motionless in his chair, holding his glass, staring up at him. 'I envy you, Jonathan,' he said softly.

Jonathan stared back, thinking his friend was drunk. But he could see through Sumner's spectacles that his gaze was steady.

'I envy you,' Sumner repeated. 'You can be whatever you want to.'

'I'm the one who's envious, Sumner,' Jonathan said. 'I've always been envious of you. The life you lead, the places you've been – your manners, for God's sake.'

Sumner shook his head slowly. 'None of it's important. What's important is what *you* have – the courage to do what you really want to do.'

There was something in Sumner's voice, a wistfulness that Jonathan had never heard there before. The room was silent again. But then, Sumner's face broke into a sudden grin. 'And besides that, you're a goddamn hero,' he said.

Jonathan laughed heartily. 'I don't think that would impress anyone.'

'Oh, you'd be surprised!' Sumner stood up suddenly, staggered slightly, then started towards the drawing room. 'Let's go!'

'Where?' Jonathan asked, smiling, as he reached for his coat.

'I think it's time you met the Countess.'

Jonathan paused. He didn't have to be told who the

Countess was. Everyone knew that she was the most celebrated madam in New York. The 'Countess' was really Ann Curtis, who had once been the mistress, or *femme entretenue*, as she preferred to say, of a French aristocrat. When her beauty had faded and she was abandoned, Ann Curtis had returned to New York and, using money she had pilfered from the aristocrat, opened a brothel just off Park Avenue. Only the city's most powerful and richest men were admitted; it was like an exclusive fraternity, whose entrance came only by invitation.

'The Countess adores heroes,' Sumner said, throwing a silk scarf around his neck. 'Come on. Let's go.'

But Jonathan stood fixed to the spot. 'I really don't think . . .' he began. 'I'm not really dressed for it tonight, Sumner.'

Sumner paused, understanding Jonathan's embarrassment. 'Wait here,' he said. He disappeared into another room and returned with an overcoat, top hat and another white silk scarf. 'We're the same size,' he said, thrusting them at Jonathan.

'Sumner, I couldn't—'

'Nonsense.' Sumner tossed Jonathan's old overcoat on a chair, then helped him into the other coat, wound the scarf around his neck and handed him the top hat. 'If it makes you feel any better, it's last year's style. Now, let's get going.'

They took Sumner's carriage over to the East Side, but when they came to the side street where the brothel was located, they found it blocked by snow and an abandoned wagon. Sumner sent his driver on his way, telling him they would walk the rest of the way. It was a fashionable neighbourhood, and the street was still bordered by unsullied drifts. Jonathan walked along, conscious of the caress of the silk scarf against his cold cheek and of the comfortable weight of Sumner's soft

53

cashmere overcoat on his shoulders. As he walked silently down the centre of the street at Sumner's side, he was struck by the beauty of the gaslights, which cast a pale yellow glow on the huge white drifts.

'This looks like a street in St Petersburg,' Jonathan said.

'You've never been to Russia,' Sumner said, laughing.

'Oh yes, I have,' he said softly, 'many times. In my mind.'

From the outside, the brothel looked like any other sedate house. Once inside, Jonathan hung back slightly as Sumner was greeted by the Countess. She led them to a private drawing room and offered drinks. A man was playing a piano softly and an array of stunning women lounged like cats on the furniture. They eyed Jonathan with interest. Ignorant of whatever etiquette might be at work, Jonathan watched Sumner for a clue, but Sumner was occupied already with a small blonde woman. Jonathan observed them, amused by his friend's bravado. Sumner, who was always so shy among women of any class, had drawn the prostitute on his lap, while she made soft sounds in his ear.

Jonathan averted his eyes and sat on a sofa, drinking a brandy. There were several other men present: older men, obviously of wealth and position. He saw a wedding band on the hand of a bald man and found himself wondering about the man's marriage. Back in Dryden, he had known many men and women who clung to each other only because life on the farm was so harsh – marriages of survival. Only lately had he begun to deal with the idea that his own parents had had such a marriage. He glanced back at the bald man who was leading a woman upstairs. Surely, this man's wealth left him free to marry a woman he could love, yet here he was. Jonathan felt a surge of pity for the man. What was a marriage, after all, without love and passion?

The other men left, and Jonathan glanced around the room at the remaining women. He suddenly became acutely aware of the absurdity of the situation, sitting there in the close, perfumed room, the only man fully clothed among six nearly naked women, who were watching him with a predatory detachment. But there was a power in it that he found very arousing. Finally, his eyes locked on those of a woman sitting across from him. As if on cue, she rose and slowly came over to him. She was tall with dark-brown hair and a voluptuous body, ill concealed by a light-green robe of thin velvet. She stood before him, gazing down at him with dark, kohl-rimmed eyes, then smiled and held out her hand.

Jonathan followed her out of the drawing room, up the curving staircase. The bedroom was cold, the fire in the grate burned down to embers and a window left half open. There was a pillow of snow on the sill.

'I like it cold,' she said. 'I hope you don't mind.'

He turned at the sound of her rich voice. She was leaning against the closed door, staring at him. As she swayed slowly towards him, the cold made her nipples press against the green gown that rippled over her like water. Jonathan stood still, mesmerized. Judging by the faint lines near her eyes, he guessed her age to be near forty and he was pleased; his two sexual experiences had been with women his own age, and neither woman had matched him in desire. He had long been curious to see if an older woman would bring more imagination and intensity to sex. She slipped off her robe, revealing a lush and rounded body. He wondered suddenly if the prostitute somehow sensed his inexperience and wondered too, crazily, how much this encounter would cost.

Sumner, Sumner . . . I'm always in your debt, he thought, with a small smile.

She pulled off his jacket, waistcoat and tie. He closed

his eyes and felt her cool fingers run down his bare chest, and then her warm tongue retracing the line up to his ear. He felt himself growing hard, and all thoughts of Sumner and money suddenly vanished. Grabbing a handful of her hair, he pulled her head back, kissing her roughly, and she pulled away slightly, smiling. 'Is that how you want it?' she asked.

He kissed her again. The cold pricked his bare skin and he shivered, pulling her soft body closer. A sudden picture of Marion flashed into his head and then was gone, like a glimmer of light.

He pulled back to look at the woman. 'What's your name?'

'Ellen.'

'My name is—'

Her fingers touched his lips. 'I know who you are,' she whispered. 'I read about you in the newspaper.' She slipped his pants down and took him in her hands, her dark eyes flitting quickly down over his body. 'What a beautiful man you are,' she murmured.

He stared at her eyes, which had a hard sheen. 'You're a hero, aren't you?' she said.

He nearly laughed. 'Yes,' he said.

She moved her hips slowly against him, her lips moist and warm on his neck. 'Well, then, you can have anything you want,' she said.

Jonathan never returned to the brothel or saw the woman again. Sumner would have taken him, he knew, but he would not have felt right to ask. He preferred to keep it as a memory of one extraordinary night. It had been nothing like his other sexual experiences. It had been a total immersion in the senses. No matter what he wanted, Ellen had obliged, and her willingness emboldened him, made him seek the edges, both tender and dark, of his own sensuality. It had left him transformed. To have possessed a beautiful woman, to have had his every desire indulged, to be so perfectly syncronized with another body, had been intoxicating. He knew the feeling was an illusion, that it came only because Ellen had been paid handsomely to create it. But he was left with the conviction that he could find that passion again with a woman he cared about, and that such a blending of the physical and spiritual would be transcendent.

He went to bed with other women, trying to recreate the intensity, but he couldn't. When he dreamed of the night, as he often did, the woman in it never looked like Ellen. Strangely, she sometimes resembled Marion. But most of the time she had no face at all.

Late in May, Jonathan was called into Roscoe's office. 'I got a cable from Alexander Profitt,' he said. 'It's about you.'

Jonathan sat there, in silent surprise, waiting.

'Seems he's been reading your stuff and likes it. It was your blizzard stories that really caught his eye.'

'Well, maybe I can ask you for a raise now,' Jonathan joked.

Roscoe didn't smile. 'He wants you for his newspaper in Paris.'

Jonathan sobered quickly. 'Paris! What did you tell him?'

'I cabled him that it was out of the question, that you were indispensable.' Roscoe paused. 'Here's what he cabled back.'

Jonathan took the yellow paper that Roscoe offered and read it.

I WANT NO INDISPENSABLE MEN ON MY NEWSPAPERS. STOP. FIRE HIM IMMEDIATELY. A. PROFITT

Jonathan looked up at Roscoe, stunned. For a moment, he could think of nothing to say. On one hand, the news was almost a relief. His interview months earlier at the *New York Times* had yielded only a promise that a position would open in a few months, but Jonathan had grown tired of waiting. Now he had been fired and would be forced to find a new job, but he was also furious at being treated so nonchalantly by this faceless man Profitt.

'That bastard,' he murmured. 'He doesn't even know who I am. Roscoe, what right does he—'

Roscoe pushed an envelope across the desk. 'This came for you this morning.'

Jonathan examined the contents of the envelope, and looked up at Roscoe in bewilderment. 'It's a steamship ticket – to Calais. And a train ticket to Paris.'

'When Profitt wants something, he gets it,' Roscoe said. 'You're to report to him at the *Paris Herald* in eight days.' He cleared his throat. 'We've got a rush on a passport for you. You sail tomorrow morning. You'd better get home and pack.'

Jonathan stared at the tickets, at the words Cunard Lines . . . Calais . . . first class. How had this happened? Somehow, Profitt must have seen his stories, or maybe even heard about his ideas for improving the *Herald*. Whatever, he had been impressed enough to call him to Paris. Jonathan's hand was trembling slightly.

'My God, Roscoe,' he said, 'I'm going to Paris.' He smiled, and it grew into a laugh. 'Paris, Roscoe! Do you know what that means? I'm finally going somewhere. I'm going to goddamn Paris!'

Roscoe's face remained solemn. Jonathan jumped up from his chair and paced around the office, laughing, pausing to re-examine the tickets in disbelief. Then he stopped, finally seeing the expression on Roscoe's face. He realized suddenly that Roscoe was going to miss him, not just as a reporter but also as a special ally, and that he was going to miss Roscoe.

Roscoe pulled his flask out of a drawer and took a drink. 'You'd better get going,' he said.

Jonathan nodded. He started for the door, then paused. 'Thanks, Roscoe,' he said. 'For everything.' He smiled again, unable to repress his joy. 'I'm going to Paris, Roscoe! How about at least wishing me well?'

Roscoe carefully replaced the cap on the flask. 'I wish you well, Jonathan. I know you'll do good. Just watch out. I know Profitt. I worked for him for years.' He paused, his eyes locked on Jonathan's. 'Watch out for yourself around him. He's a son of a bitch. A seductive son of a bitch.'

Jonathan shook his head, smiling. 'Don't worry about me. You just watch that rotgut. It'll kill you some day, my friend.'

Stuffing the tickets in his breast pocket, Jonathan went through the newsroom, his steps quickening with each stride.

Chapter Five

With a laboured screech of its brakes, the train made its way down the hillside and Jonathan pressed his forehead to the window. For the last two hours, the train had snaked slowly through a dark gorge. Now it was emerging into a flat valley of such contrasting beauty that he wondered for a moment if the train had not somehow magically slipped out of France and into a different country.

A plain of grey-green fields lay before him, speckled with wild flowers and grazing animals and flooded with an intense white sun. Beyond the fields, Jonathan saw a glimpse of azure and silver, ringed with red tile roofs.

'Antibes!' A voice called out from the corridor. '*L'arrêt prochain, Antibes.*'

Jonathan grabbed his guidebook and searched the map. Antibes was the last stop before Nice. He was nearly there. He turned back to the window eagerly. Everything about France was so new; though he had been in the country for only two days, his head was overflowing with strange sounds, smells and sights. He pushed the window open and the air rushed in at him, full and warm, with a faint aroma of spices and salt spray.

He sat back in his seat, overwhelmed suddenly by the fatigue of travel but also by the abrupt turns his life had taken in the last ten days. After spending a week crossing the Atlantic aboard the steamship *Carinthia*, he had arrived in Calais and, following Alexander Profitt's cabled orders, immediately left for Paris on the famous Train Bleu. The luxury accommodation that had been arranged for him on both trips filled him with awe and further whetted his curiosity about what lay ahead. He knew that Profitt was an eccentric, but why was he lavishing such treatment on an unknown employee? Surely his work in New York had not been that extraordinary – or had it?

But thoughts of his self-importance had been quickly dashed when he had arrived at the *Herald* office in Paris and discovered that not only was Profitt not there, but no one seemed to be expecting him. Finally, an editor was found who acknowledged that Profitt was on holiday on his yacht in Beaulieu-sur-Mer, near Nice, and that Jonathan was to report to him there. Jonathan accepted a train ticket with consternation and left at once for the Riviera.

Now, as the train pulled into the station at Antibes, he wondered what awaited him in Nice. He picked up the letter he had started to his father. He had been forced to leave New York so hastily that there had been no time to tell him of his plans, so he had relayed them by cable from the steamship with a promise to write. As the train pulled out and headed up the coast towards Nice, Jonathan concentrated on finishing the letter.

'And so, Pa,' he wrote, 'I am now on a train, which takes me to a place I've never been, to a future I cannot know.' He paused, pen in air, gazing out at the sea. 'I am surrounded by the unfamiliar, Pa,' he resumed. 'And I feel that my life is finally, truly, beginning.'

He finished the letter just as the train pulled into Nice. After collecting his luggage, he found a carriage to take him to Beaulieu-sur-Mer. The village was only a short distance from Nice, but it was late afternoon by the time the carriage left him on the quay. Jonathan stood there, stunned by the sight of the lone yacht sitting at anchor out in the cove. Its sheer size and beauty told him that it was the *Lysistrata*, Profitt's steam yacht. It was more than 250 feet long, with a smokestack and mast rising amidships, and it glowed a cream colour in the softening afternoon light. The quay was deserted except for a few fishermen; apparently, no one was waiting for his arrival in Beaulieu-sur-Mer either. Finally, Jonathan arranged for a fishing boat to take him out to the yacht.

As the boat pulled up to the *Lysistrata*'s side, two crewmen eyed him suspiciously, but Jonathan explained in broken collegiate French that he was expected. They helped him aboard and disappeared.

Jonathan stood on the deck, alone amid his bags. The sky was coming alive with the sunset, and it was quiet, except for the lapping of water against the yacht. Out of nowhere came the muted sound of music and a feminine laugh.

'Now what am I supposed to do?' Jonathan muttered, glancing around. Annoyance over Profitt's ill manners, exacerbated by fatigue, had displaced his excitement. Finally, he saw a man coming towards him, small and bald, with a harried expression. He was dressed formally for dinner and was clutching a leather portfolio.

'Mr Caras, I presume?'

'Yes. I'm expected by Mr Profitt.'

'Yes, I know. I'm Ernest Brookes, Mr Profitt's private secretary.' He thrust out his hand.

Jonathan shook it with a smile. 'You don't know how glad I am finally to know someone is expecting me.'

'Yes, well . . .' Brookes flipped open the portfolio, then looked back at Jonathan with a tight little smile. 'Mr Profitt and his guests are gathering in the salon for drinks.' He glanced at Jonathan's bags. 'We dress for dinner on the *Lysistrata*. But if you have need of anything, I can supply it for you.'

Jonathan did not miss the man's hint that he might lack the proper clothes. He met Brookes's eyes. 'I have everything I need.'

Brookes beckoned to a nearby servant. 'This man will show you to your cabin. You can join Mr Profitt's guests in the salon whenever you wish.' He closed his portfolio, turned sharply on his heel and was gone.

As he dressed for dinner, Jonathan tried to recall all he knew about Alexander Profitt. Beyond the newsroom stories of womanizing, hard drinking and high-spirited escapades, he realized he knew little. He remembered that Profitt had been raised and educated in France, taken there at a young age by his socialite mother. Alexander Profitt had grown up spoiled and given to debauched behaviour. Gradually he matured enough to be entrusted with the running of the *Herald* upon his father's death. But, still smarting over how he had been ostracized in New York, Alexander Profitt remained an expatriate, content with the diversion of his new English-language Paris paper.

Drawn by the sound of music, Jonathan found his way to the main salon and paused at the entrance. The salon was exquisitely furnished in antiques and lit by chandeliers. A man was playing a grand piano in a corner and a light sea breeze came through the open windows, sending the white silk curtains and the fronds of potted palms swaying to the music. There were about twenty guests, the women dressed in pale gowns and jewels, the men in stark black and white formal coats. The scene struck Jonathan as absurdly beautiful. Surely, he was not on a boat moored at some tiny French fishing village, but in the drawing room of one of Mrs Astor's Four Hundred in New York.

He moved slowly around the salon's perimeter and,

from a waiter's tray, took a fluted glass of champagne. He sipped the drink, watching the crowd, his eye drawn immediately to one man standing in the centre of the circle. He stood tall and erect, exuding a powerful charisma. Jonathan knew instantly it was Alexander Profitt.

Profitt was a striking man, in his mid-thirties, with sharp features, black hair and dark eyes that had the hard, reflective glow of obsidian. Unlike the other men, he wore no beard or moustache; when he laughed, his wide mouth revealed large white teeth and his face creased up, reminding Jonathan of the mask of comedy he had once seen on a theatre poster.

He had a compelling voice, sonorous with a soft accent that spoke of a foreign place but no particular country. Jonathan watched closely, eavesdropping as Profitt related a story about his trip to London for Queen Victoria's Diamond Jubilee. He was obviously in a merry mood and firmly in control of his enthralled audience. He proceeded without pause to relay other accounts of his travels and finally launched into a recollection of his participation in a horseless-carriage race from Paris to Amsterdam. He drank liberally from his constantly replenished glass, his voice growing steadily louder and his gestures more expansive. After a while, Jonathan realized that the man's commanding posture was not what it seemed. The evening had not yet progressed to dinner, but Alexander Profitt, the man who had summoned him to France and who held his future in his hands, was already roaringly, stunningly drunk.

Jonathan turned away. His eyes met those of Ernest Brookes, who came over to him. 'I think I should introduce you to Mr Profitt now,' he said. They joined the circle around Profitt and Brookes waited for a lull. 'Mr Profitt, may I introduce Mr Jonathan Caras,' he said. 'He arrived only this afternoon.'

Profitt stared at Jonathan, his dark eyes searching his face for some clue to who he was. Embarrassed and annoyed at being forgotten yet again, Jonathan fought back his urge to prompt Profitt's memory. Let him damn well figure it out, Jonathan thought testily.

Profitt extended his hand, which Jonathan shook. 'Mr Caras,' he said smoothly. Then he smiled broadly. 'Have you met my other guests?' He continued with cursory introductions of the others, and Jonathan caught a few of the foreign names and their titles. Then Profitt turned away towards a pretty woman and began yet another tale.

Jonathan stood listening respectfully, as long as his anger would allow, and finally excused himself to no one in particular. The full weight of his fatigue suddenly bore down on him, and he wanted to do nothing but go to bed. He glanced around the room, at all the laughing people and at Profitt, wondering if he dared breach etiquette and not go in to dinner.

What the hell? he thought. No one will miss me. He set his glass down and slipped quietly out of the salon. Back in his cabin, he lay awake for several hours, listening to the laughter and music, until he finally fell asleep.

He woke very early the next morning, ravenous with hunger. He dressed quickly and, noting that it was just seven, went up on deck. The day was already brilliant with sunshine, reflecting off the deep-blue water, and a strong breeze was blowing over the bow of the yacht. He made his way towards the stern, looking for a servant who might fetch some coffee. When he reached the aft deck, he stopped in amazement.

There, ensconced at a table under a fluttering white canopy, was Alexander Profitt. He was dressed in crisp white trousers and a pale muslin shirt, opened at the neck to reveal a tanned chest. The table held his half-finished breakfast and heaping piles of newspapers and other documents, which overflowed onto the deck. On a nearby chair a white cat lay curled in sleep. Profitt was reading a newspaper and, sensing Jonathan's presence, looked up.

'Ah, Mr Caras,' he said. 'Good morning.'

Jonathan cleared his throat. 'Good morning.'

'Splendid day, isn't it?' He smiled. 'Have you had your breakfast?'

'No.'

'Well, no one else is up and about yet, so the buffet has not been set out, I'm afraid. It was a rather late night. Would you care to join me?'

'Thank you.' Jonathan came to the table and sat opposite Profitt, trying to hide his surprise. Profitt summoned a servant and ordered breakfast as Jonathan discreetly examined the papers strewn across the table and deck. Most of them were cable dispatches from the New York and Paris offices, and there were several editions of both newspapers – marked up in red and blue pencil – together with various reports on press times, staff workload and output and other assorted mailings. Another bulging mail sack lay nearby.

'I've ordered you some mutton chops and eggs,' Profitt said. 'I hope that's enough.' He stroked the cat, which arched its back at his touch.

'That's fine, sir.'

'Well, I know you missed dinner last night. Quite a good meal it was, too.' He was looking directly at Jonathan.

Jonathan shifted in his chair. 'I was very tired from my trip. I'm sorry if I—'

Profitt smiled. 'Of course, you must have been exhausted. No apology needed.' A servant brought a silver pot, leaving it before Profitt, who poured Jonathan and himself some of the steaming coffee. 'So, how was your crossing from New York? No bad weather, I trust.'

Jonathan remembered suddenly an odd piece of newsroom lore, that Profitt was obsessed with weather reports. 'It was quite calm,' he said, wishing he could recall some meteorological detail to plump up the conversation and make more of an impression. Profitt's self-possession, in light of the face he had presented last night, was unnerving. 'We did encounter a squall on the third night, however,' he added hopefully.

Profitt picked up a newspaper and tossed it before Jonathan. 'See this column?' He pointed to a report headlined HERALD STORMS, which gave details of all storms approaching Europe from the Atlantic. 'The weather is more important than politics, social events, sports or anything else to my readers. People are on the move today, travelling the world. That's why I give them the reports from the Channel, Dover, the great capitals and all the resorts, from Aix-les-Bains to Zurich.' He smiled. 'We're quite popular in the hotels.'

Jonathan smiled, wondering if the man was serious.

'Some day,' Profitt said, 'you'll have to tell me all about the great blizzard. I read about your act of heroism. And your own story, of course. Elegant writing, yet very human. He went on to quote a paragraph from Jonathan's story, with an accuracy that amazed Jonathan.

Jonathan set his cup down. 'I'm flattered that you remember my story, Mr Profitt.'

Profitt levelled his gaze at him. 'I've read every story you've ever written for my newspaper, Mr Caras.'

At that moment, breakfast arrived, and with it, Ernest Brookes, bearing yet more cable dispatches. Profitt excused himself and as he and his secretary worked, Jonathan ate in silence, watching them, his disbelief at Profitt's lucidity growing. Profitt was succinctly issuing orders for the Paris and New York staffs, exhibiting a thorough knowledge of both operations. There was no sign of the loquacious drunk who had charmed the glittering crowd last night with hyperbolic tales. This was a man calmly in charge of himself and his empire.

After half an hour, Profitt turned back to Jonathan. 'You'll have to excuse me – I have some more work to attend to.' He rose. 'Feel free to partake of any of the *Lysistrata*'s services, Mr Caras. We have a games room, a Turkish bath, or, if you'd like to go ashore, just ask one of the servants to arrange a carriage.'

'Thank you, Mr Profitt.'

Profitt started to leave, then turned back. 'On second thoughts, I could do with a little trip myself. Why don't we meet back here after lunch and we'll go ashore together?'

'I'll look forward to it, sir.'

Profitt smiled slightly. 'It will give us a chance to get to know each other. I like to know the men who work for me.' His smile lingering, he turned and left, the white cat hastily following in his wake.

Just after lunch, Jonathan returned to the aft deck where Profitt was waiting for him, dressed in a crisp, white linen suit. A small boat took them ashore where a carriage awaited. 'Come along. I'm going to show you my favourite place,' Profit said with a smile.

As the carriage pulled away, Jonathan wondered, with some excitement, if they were going to the famous casino in Nice he had heard about. But it soon became obvious that they were headed away from the coast and up into the hills. The carriage climbed upwards on a series of hairpin turns with vertigo-inducing views of sheer cliffs. The day was hot and sunny. Jonathan was uncomfortable in his wool suit. Profitt, on the other hand, looked unfazed as he chatted on about the local flora, fauna and history.

After an hour, the carriage pulled into a village,

identified by a small signpost as La Turbie. It was a poor, rundown place, with a nondescript square and a handful of shops. The carriage pulled up before a café.

'We're here,' Profitt announced. 'Let's have a drink.' He jumped down and Jonathan followed, glancing around. The café was nothing more than a dusty little clearing under the plane trees, with an old wooden table and two benches. Why in the world, he wondered, had Profitt wanted to come to this godforsaken place?

When seated, Profitt rapped on the table to get some service. A man appeared at the open door of the inn and, recognizing Profitt, lumbered over. He was a brutish man, with burly forearms and an ample gut, restrained by a stained apron. Profitt politely asked for something in French. The man left and returned with two glasses of pale pink liquid. Profitt held out a five-franc note, which the man took without a word and disappeared.

'You're thinking that five francs is a lot of money for an aperitif,' Profitt said, smiling. 'It probably is, but the man makes this stuff only for himself, and it's quite a bracing little elixir on a hot day. Try it.'

Jonathan did so, and was surprised at the liquor's refreshing tang. 'You've been here often, then?' he ventured.

'Yes, I discovered this village several years ago while exploring.' Profitt leaned back in his chair. 'It's a dreadful little place, isn't it? Like the end of the world.'

Jonathan wanted to ask Profitt what the attraction was. But before he could speak he saw, out of the corner of his eye, someone standing just inside the café door. It was a girl, watching them with intense curiosity. As she moved out of the shadows he saw her clearly. She was about sixteen and stunningly beautiful, her hair, piled haphazardly on her head, so blonde that it glimmered white in the sun. Then, just as suddenly as she had appeared, she was gone.

Jonathan looked back at Profitt, but could not tell if he, too, had seen her. He must know about her, Jonathan thought. Surely she is why he comes to this place.

'Let's have another,' Profitt said suddenly. And he rapped on the table and called out in French. This time, the girl came forward, bearing the two glasses. Jonathan watched her, transfixed. She was small but, even though she was covered from her neck to her feet by a plain dress and apron, he could tell she had the lithe body of a woman. It was her face, however, framed by wisps of straight silky hair, that was spellbinding. It was childish, with full pink lips the colour of the strange liquor. Her large eyes, the same grey-blue as the heat-hazed sky, were hooded with dark lashes. Her skin was so white as to appear translucent, and she had a spray of faint freckles across her nose.

She noticed Jonathan looking at her and stared back. In that moment, something passed between them. In her eyes, Jonathan thought he saw a sense of recognition. He felt the same uncanny sensation, as if he had somehow known her before, or as if he were staring into a mirror and seeing inside himself. It was mesmerizing and deeply disturbing.

Profitt said something and she turned her gaze to him with some reluctance. They exchanged a few words in French and she left. Jonathan continued to stare at the inn door. Finally, he looked back to Profitt, who, he realized, had been watching him in amusement.

'You find her attractive?' Profitt asked, smiling.

'She's quite pretty,' Jonathan said cautiously.

'For a *villageoise*.'

Jonathan took a quick drink.

Profitt laughed heartily. 'These villages are filled with such girls, most no better than sluts, Jonathan. Beauty is a common commodity here.' He paused, sensing

Jonathan's embarrassment. 'Drink up. I have something I want to show you.'

They left the café and walked through the village, which was larger than it first seemed, spreading out in a labyrinth of twisting, shadowed streets no wider than alleyways. After a while, they entered a grove of cypress trees and then emerged in a clearing, out in the blinding sun once more. Jonathan was astonished to see, looming before him, an ancient stone monument. It rose hundreds of feet into the intense blue sky, but a good portion of it had fallen away into crumbled piles. Obviously, it had once been an architectural wonder, but most of it had been destroyed by time and the elements.

'Strange,' Jonathan murmured, raising his hand to shield his eyes. 'It looks like a Roman ruin.'

'That's exactly what it is,' Profitt said. He began to walk slowly around the monument and Jonathan followed. 'In the sixth century BC,' Profitt said, 'the road through this village was the Via Julia, which ran from Gaul to Rome. This monument, the Trophée des Alpes, was built for Augustus Caesar, who conquered the local hill tribes.

Jonathan glanced at Profitt, struck by the reverential tone of his voice.

'It's not so much a monument to a man as a monument to a glorious empire, and a golden moment in history,' Profitt continued. He had stopped and was staring up at the crumbling pillars.

'An empire,' Jonathan said with a smile, 'that crumbled under its own excesses and illusions.'

Profitt glanced at him, and, after a long moment, smiled. 'Yes, I suppose that's true.' He looked back up at the white pillars. 'But while it lasted, what power, achievement and grandeur there was!' He pressed his palm flat against a mossy pillar. 'You can still feel the heartbeat of the moment, right here in the stone. Go on, try it.'

71

Jonathan hesitated, then put his hand on the old stone. It was warm from the sun. He turned to look back at Profitt, who smiled slightly, then walked out towards a grassy terrace, sitting down on a stone bench, his back to Jonathan. Jonathan pulled out a handkerchief and wiped it across his sweating brow. His head throbbed with the heat, the thin air and the buzz of cicadas, and he felt dizzy. This strange, decaying place, that woman in the café, and even Profitt, with his odd, mystical musings, had conspired to produce in him feelings of unease. He stared at Profitt's back. Why had Profitt brought him up to this place? Just to stand in the hot sun and stare at relics? Why had he asked him to come to Beaulieu-sur-Mer in the first place? Profitt seemed to have taken a nebulous interest in him. But why? What was expected of him?

Jonathan started towards Profitt. It was time, he decided, to find out.

Profitt was gazing out at a breathtaking panorama of the Mediterranean and its coastline. Far below, Jonathan could see the roofs of the village and he could even make out the *Lysistrata*.

'Mr Profitt,' Jonathan said, 'why did you want me to come here?'

Profitt looked up at him. 'When I meet a man who is going to work for me, I like it to be outside the newspaper office. I like to see him out of his element, before he becomes just another by-line.'

'But why did you bring me to France?' Jonathan persisted.

Profitt paused. 'Sit down, Jonathan.' He did so, perching on the bench next to Profitt. Profitt's gaze wandered back out to sea. 'The world looks incredibly beautiful from up high, doesn't it?' Profitt said.

'Yes, it does.' There was a silence, filled with the metallic music of the cicadas. Jonathan stared at

Profitt's angular profile, waiting.

'What year is it?' Profitt asked.

Jonathan hesitated, puzzled. 'Eighteen ninety-seven,' he answered.

'Eighteen ninety-seven. A new century is almost upon us, Jonathan,' he said, without looking at him. 'An exciting new time, our own golden moment in history. The world is changing, and we're going to see all kinds of wonderful new things. Trains will go faster, horses will give way to machines, men will fly. Lights will glow brighter, women will grow lovelier and music will become sweeter. We're entering a golden era, Jonathan, an age in which there are no limits to what a man can do or how beautiful life can be.' Profitt turned towards him. 'I want my newspaper to reflect that,' he said, 'so I need men who understand. I've seen things in your stories that tell me you do. I can see it in the way you handle yourself. I know your background, I know you came from nothing. But I can see you're a man of ambition, education – and grace.'

Jonathan held Profitt's eyes steadily.

'I can see just by the look of you that you're not an ordinary man.' He paused, smiling. 'Or rather, I saw it in the faces of the women last night.' He paused again, looking out over the sea for a moment before his gaze returned to Jonathan. 'You have a great future, Jonathan Caras. A future that I can make happen for you.'

Jonathan stared at the man before him, a figure in fine white linen, bathed in the blazing white light of the sun. Was it the man, his words or the magic of the moment that he found so compelling? He didn't know. But he suddenly felt all doubts vanish, burned up in the flash-fire of his own dreams, a fire ignited by Alexander Profitt.

'I'll do my best,' Jonathan said finally. 'You won't be disappointed.'

73

Profitt smiled. He rose suddenly and looked out towards the *Lysistrata*. 'It's getting late. We'd better start back.'

They retraced their steps back to the village, where the carriage stood waiting in the square. Jonathan glanced at the door of the café, hoping for some sight of the blonde girl. He wondered, with a slight smile, if she had been an apparition; if, rendered senseless by the sun, he had somehow imagined her. The whole day had assumed an unreal quality. The only thing he was sure about now was that Alexander Profitt, for whatever reason, saw him as some sort of spiritual comrade, and that such a relationship could only be advantageous. He wondered what position on the newspaper Profitt had in mind for him. Whatever it was, he would undoubtedly soon be in a position to put his ideas about newspapers to the test. Already, he had begun to fantasize, with some anticipation, about the shape his life in Paris was going to take.

'My God, look at those animals!'

Jonathan looked towards Profitt, who had paused, one foot on the carriage step, and was staring across the square at a farmer who was herding two cows down the dusty street.

'Look at them,' Profitt repeated, pointing. 'They're magnificent!'

Jonathan watched in amazement as Profitt jumped down and went over to the farmer. He couldn't hear the exchange between the two men, but after a moment, Profitt returned, smiling broadly.

'I knew it!' he said. 'They're Alderneys. I had one stalled aboard the *Lysistrata* once, and have been searching for another. I've just arranged to buy one. Their milk is the gods' very nectar!' He jumped exuberantly into the carriage. 'What time is it?' he asked Jonathan.

Jonathan pulled out his pocket watch. 'Nearly four.'

Profitt frowned slightly. 'Listen, Jonathan, my good

man, I must get back to the ship. Would you mind remaining behind and arranging for the animal's transport?' Before Jonathan could speak, Profitt thrust some money into his hand. 'Pay the old man and save enough to hire a carriage back. And whatever you do, make sure that cow arrives on board without harm.'

Jonathan stood there, stunned. He looked down at the wad of bills, then back at Profitt, who seemed oblivious to the absurdity of his request. 'Mr Profitt –' Jonathan began.

'Driver, let's get going,' Profitt ordered.

Jonathan jumped back out of the way, and the driver urged the horses out of their lethargy.

'I'll see you at dinner,' Profitt sang out as the carriage pulled out of the square.

Jonathan stood there, clutching the money, watching the carriage disappear down the road in a cloud of white dust.

Chapter Six

Aboard the *Lysistrata*, time went by indolently, the days drenched in sun, the nights in alcohol. For three days, Jonathan awaited an order from Profitt to return to Paris and begin his job at the *Herald*, but Profitt, except for his early morning interludes with Brookes, seemed to have nothing on his mind but the pursuit of pleasure. By the fourth day, Jonathan felt restless, like a pampered prisoner, and his thoughts kept drifting back to the strange village and the girl in the café. Profitt had dismissed her as a country girl, yet Jonathan thought she had a natural sensuality that was much more arousing than the artificial beauty of the women aboard the *Lysistrata*. He grew obsessed with the idea of seeing her again.

Finally, after lunch on the fourth day, he arranged to return to La Turbie. He reached the village around two, and the square was empty in the shimmering heat. A sign on the café door proclaimed that it was closed. He stood staring at it for a moment, debating whether to knock, but he knew that a foreigner making vague inquiries about a girl would be suspicious. How could he possibly explain why he was here? He wasn't sure himself. He didn't even know the girl's name.

He surveyed the empty square, surprised by the depth of his disappointment. He decided to go to the Roman ruin to wait on the chance that the café would be open later. He started off down a narrow street in the direction he remembered Profitt taking, but he soon became lost. He wandered slowly through the dark, cobbled alleyways, trying to get his bearings, but each turn took him down another unknown path. And it seemed that not a soul was alive in the village to help him. Finally, in growing frustration, he halted in the middle of a narrow street and pulled out a handkerchief to wipe his brow. It was quiet, except for the mewing of a cat.

Then he heard it. Music. The faint sound of someone playing a piano, a strange melody that wafted in and out on the breeze. He began to walk towards it.

It grew louder, a slow, beguiling song, punctuated with little pauses and trilling notes. He followed the music until it stopped suddenly. He turned a corner and found himself in a small, sun-filled courtyard, enclosed on three sides by sagging old buildings, shuttered against the heat. But one large second-floor window was open, and he looked up.

There, in the window, was the girl from the café. She was standing in profile, wearing a white camisole and petticoat, her silvery hair piled atop her head, her chin held elegantly high. She stood motionless, as if striking a pose, with one slender white arm resting lightly on the top of a ladder-back chair.

Jonathan did not move or breathe. Caught in the full force of the sunlight, she seemed to him like some ethereal being, framed in an aureole of white light. The music started again, and she began to move her arm in a languid arc up over her head. Then she closed her eyes, bending gracefully backward from the waist, like a willow branch yielding to someone's touch. She came up slowly, in time to the music, and bent her body forward and to the side. Jonathan moved closer and watched her, entranced. He could see the sheen of sweat on her pale skin and the press of her breasts against the damp white cotton.

The music ended and she paused, relaxing now. Jonathan heard her say something to someone out of sight, and she laughed lightly. Then, suddenly, she turned towards the window and saw Jonathan watching her. For a moment, her face registered mild surprise; then a look of recognition came to her eyes. She made no move to cover herself, but stood there, looking back at him.

Suddenly, an old woman in black appeared in the window. She saw Jonathan, unleashed a barrage of angry French at him and pulled the girl away from the window, closing the shutters with a bang. After a few moments, the music resumed.

Jonathan stared up at the shutters. Then he looked quickly around the courtyard, but there were no doors. She had slipped away from him again. He remained in the courtyard a few more minutes until the music stopped. Then, reluctantly, he left and tried to find his way back to the square. By accident, he emerged instead at the clearing where the Roman ruin stood. Still feeling agitated, he decided to sit for a while and collect his thoughts. He stayed there for nearly an hour, gazing out over the sea, thinking about the girl. He wasn't a superstitious man, but he was coming to believe it was fated that he would never know who she was; yet his feeling that she somehow belonged in his life remained as strong as the first time he had seen her. Finally, he rose. It was getting late and Profitt expected him to be prompt for dinner.

After a while, he managed to find his way to the square. As he was climbing into the carriage, he noticed that the café door was now open. He got down and went to sit outside. When no one came out of the café, he rapped on the table, as Profitt had done.

After a moment, the blonde girl appeared at the door. Jonathan stared at her, his heart beating wildly. She came towards him tentatively, wearing the same drab dress and apron as on that first day. She paused, her blue-grey eyes locking on his, then, in a soft voice, asked him what he wanted.

Jonathan started to ask, in his feeble French, for a glass of the liquor he had sampled before, but he was filled with such a sudden nervousness that he couldn't think of the words.

'Your French is terrible,' she said in English. She smiled, almost shyly.

'You speak English!' Jonathan said, incredulous.

Her smile grew. 'Yes. Quite well, don't you think?' There was a long pause as she contemplated him, a touch of perplexity knitting her brow. 'I've seen you before,' she said. 'You were here several days ago with the gentleman in the white suit.'

'Yes.'

'And this afternoon . . . you were watching me.' There was no sense of invaded modesty in her eyes. In fact, her expression was bold, almost proud.

'Yes, I was,' Jonathan replied softly.

She held his gaze for a moment longer, brushed a strand of hair off her face and glanced at the café door. 'What would you like, a drink? Some food?' she asked, reverting to a neutral tone of voice.

'Your name,' Jonathan said. 'I just want to know your name.'

Her eyes widened. For the first time, she seemed self-conscious. She glanced again towards the door and wrapped her arms around herself, as if chilled, even though the air was still warm. She looked back at Jonathan. 'Cendrine,' she said softly. 'Cendrine LeClerc.'

'Cendrine LeClerc,' Jonathan repeated, as if trying

out the sounds. He smiled. 'My name is Jonathan Caras.'

It took a moment, but finally she returned his smile. It had the effect of making her look less ethereal, more human. And more sexual, Jonathan thought. He was filled with a sudden desire to touch her. Alexander Profitt's remark about village beauties, 'some no better than sluts', echoed in his thoughts. He wondered if she were a virgin but immediately pushed the thought aside. He had not come back here with the intention of seducing her, yet he was unnerved by the feelings she was arousing in him.

'Cendrine!'

Her head whirled towards the door, and Jonathan also turned to the source of the booming voice. He saw the burly man standing there, then looked back at Cendrine. Her expression was defiant, yet fearful. The man called out an angry order that Jonathan did not understand, shot Jonathan a contemptuous look, then disappeared.

'I must go,' she murmured and moved away.

Jonathan reached out and grabbed her wrist. She pulled away instinctively, her body tensing, but he held firm. 'I want to see you again,' he said. He paused, knowing how mad he must sound. 'I'm leaving here soon,' he said more softly, 'and I have to see you again. Please.'

She pulled back slightly, her expression confused.

'Please,' he repeated softly.

She looked hard at him and suddenly he felt her relax. 'All right,' she said, 'tonight, at eleven. At the Trophée. Do you know where it is?'

He nodded, then let go and she pulled her hand away, rubbing her wrist. With a glance back at Jonathan, she went quickly to the café and disappeared inside.

Jonathan returned to the *Lysistrata* in time for dinner, but he was quiet throughout the meal, preoccupied with his thoughts of meeting Cendrine. The evening began to take on a particularly hedonistic mood, but Jonathan knew his absence would be noted if he tried to leave. After dinner, everyone returned to the salon for dancing; Jonathan remained apart from the crowd, discreetly consulting his watch at frequent intervals.

At one point, he wandered over to the man playing the piano, who greeted him with a polite smile. 'May I play something for you, sir?' the man asked.

Jonathan paused. 'Do you know what this tune is?' And he hummed, as best he could, the melody he had heard coming from Cendrine's window.

The pianist gave him a look of surprise, then proceeded to play the mysterious melody. 'You mean this, sir?'

'Yes, that's it,' Jonathan said. He closed his eyes. 'It's beautiful.'

'I don't get many requests for Glazunov,' the pianist said. 'This is from a ballet called *Raymonda*.'

'A ballet?' Jonathan murmured.

At that moment, Profitt appeared at his side. 'Good Lord, James, can't we have something a bit more lively?' he said to the pianist with a laugh. 'You're putting us all to sleep.'

The pianist launched into a peppy popular tune. Jonathan saw that Profitt was looking at him with an amused expression. 'You've been rather quiet tonight, Jonathan,' he said. 'You're not becoming a recluse, are you?'

'No, sir. I'm enjoying myself greatly.'

'So where did you take off to this afternoon?'

Jonathan did not think he had been missed. 'I took a carriage to Nice,' he said. 'I wanted to see the casino.'

Profitt's expression didn't change. 'Perhaps I've kept you here too long. I think you should return to Paris soon.'

Jonathan didn't blink. 'Whatever you think best.'

'Too much of this country sun is bad for a man.' Profitt patted Jonathan on the back and sauntered off.

It was well after ten by the time Jonathan was able to steal away from the party. Once ashore, he ordered the carriage driver to travel quickly to the village. He ran all the way to the ruins, afraid that he would arrive too late, afraid that Cendrine would not appear at all.

He arrived at the clearing out of breath. Then he saw her, sitting on a pile of crumbled stone in the moonlight, dwarfed by the monument's huge silhouette. She saw him coming and rose. For a moment, neither of them spoke. They stood awkwardly staring at each other.

'I didn't think you were coming,' Cendrine said finally. 'I was about to leave.'

'I'm sorry, I couldn't get away.' Jonathan could think of nothing to say. Finally, he gestured towards the stone bench. 'Would you like to sit down?' he asked.

She turned and walked slowly ahead of him across the grass. He was struck by how smoothly she moved, her back straight, her head high. She held herself regally, like an aristocrat. She raised the hem of her dress slightly to sit down and he noticed that she was barefoot. An aristocrat, he thought with amazement, living in an end-of-the-world village. He sat down next to her.

'Are you a friend of the man in the white suit?' she asked.

Jonathan wasn't sure how to answer. 'I'm a guest on his yacht,' he said.

She was looking down towards the sea, a limitless expanse of black bordered by lights. 'He's been coming here for three years now,' she said softly. 'Once I went down to Beaulieu to see his yacht up close. He must be very rich.'

Jonathan hesitated. The last thing he wanted to do was talk about Alexander Profitt.

'Why were you watching me this afternoon?' she asked suddenly.

The question surprised him. She was facing him; even in the dark he could see her eyes, intense on his. 'It was an accident. I lost my way.' He paused. 'No, that's not true. I was watching you because I thought you were so beautiful. The way you moved . . . it was beautiful.'

'You liked it?' She smiled. 'You liked my dancing?'

'Dancing?'

'Yes,' she said eagerly. 'I'm a ballet dancer.'

Jonathan paused, perplexed. 'Ballet?' he said. 'I . . . I've never seen ballet before.'

Her smile faded. 'Then how could you know that my dancing was beautiful?'

He realized that he had somehow hurt her feelings. 'But it was!' he said quickly. 'I didn't know what it was, but it moved me. It was beautiful, truly it was.'

Her eyes searched his face, then slowly her smile returned. It was a shy smile, but touched with great pride. Ballet? Jonathan thought. How could it be? How could this young girl in a strange, isolated village be a ballet dancer? He knew hardly anything about ballet. He had seen a theatre poster in New York advertising some dancers in Oriental costumes with Russian names striking gymnastic poses but had assumed it was just some novelty act. What could that possibly have to do with the lovely movements he had seen Cendrine do in the window?

'How did you become a ballet dancer?' he asked.

She laughed. 'Well, I'm not . . . yet. But Madame Kchessinskaya is teaching me.'

Jonathan smiled. 'Madame Kessi . . . Chessa . . .'

Cendrine laughed again. 'Kchessinskaya. She's an old Russian lady.' She grew more sombre. 'She was a wonderful dancer. She performed in all the great theatres – the Maryinsky in St Petersburg, the Teatro alla Scala in Italy, the Théâtre de l'Académie in Paris. She travelled the world, and people loved her for her dancing.'

Jonathan gazed at her, uncomprehending but entranced. 'How in the world did Madame Kchessi . . . an old Russian woman end up in a French village?'

Cendrine told him Madame's story, then looked out at the sea. 'She started teaching me when I was eleven,' she said softly. 'She has taught me everything I know – my English, some Russian and, of course, ballet. She has taught me about the world. I've never been able to pay her for the lessons. But she says I am a hard worker and that I have a natural gift.' She looked back at Jonathan. 'Some day, I will be a famous ballet dancer. I will be rich, and I will come back and pay her back everything I owe her.' She looked away again. 'She is the only reason I will ever come back here.'

He was moved by the innocence of her dream and puzzled by the fierceness of her last words. 'But this is your home,' he said.

She continued to stare down at the lights lining the coast. 'No,' she said. 'I want to get away from here.' She looked back at him. 'There is a wonderful world out there, a different world, and I want to see it, smell it, taste it and touch it. I don't want to die here without ever having lived.'

As he stared into her eyes, Jonathan had the same odd feeling of looking into a mirror, of seeing himself, of hearing his own thoughts. He could hear, too, in her voice, his own mother's words.

'Why are you staring at me like that?' Cendrine said. Her eyes narrowed. 'You think it's not possible for someone like me to have such a dream?'

'No, that's not true—'

'What is wrong with wanting a better life for yourself? If God gives you a gift, why can't you use it to make your dreams come true?'

She seemed on the verge of tears. Without thinking, Jonathan reached over and took her hand. 'Nothing is wrong with dreams. Everyone has them,' he said.

She looked down at his hand covering her own. 'What are yours?' she asked.

He hesitated. He thought about telling her about going to Paris as Profitt's protégé, and how one day he would own his own newspaper. But in the light of the naïvety of her dream, he couldn't. Distant though his own dreams were, they were still achievable. He was a man, with an education and a proven skill, who could make his own way – but she was a woman, stuck in a poor village, who had been filled with romantic notions by an old woman. She had no chance of escaping this place and achieving her dreams. She would marry, have children and die in this village, much like the women did in Dryden. He felt suddenly saddened. As drawn to her as he was, he knew that when he left this place their paths would never cross again.

'My dreams are very much like yours,' he said gently.

She smiled, then looked away, out at the sea, lost in a reverie. He stared at the perfect curve of her throat.

'Why did you agree to meet me here tonight?' he asked softly.

She turned back towards him, her smile fading. 'I don't know. I can't explain it.' She searched his face. 'I shouldn't be here. I don't know you. Yet.'

He sensed that she would allow him to kiss her, and as much as he ached to, he was afraid he would not be able to stop once he touched her. Simple village girl or not, he had no right to impose himself on her. Yet he wanted her, desperately.

With a sudden movement, she pulled her hand away. She rose and backed away slightly. 'I . . . I have to go now,' she whispered.

'Tomorrow . . . I must see you again tomorrow,' he said urgently.

She took two more steps back. 'No, I can't.'

'Please, Mademoiselle LeClerc—'

She turned quickly and ran across the grass.

'Mademoiselle!'

Jonathan rose, but she was already gone, lost in the shadows of the ruins.

The next morning, Jonathan rose early after a fitful night. Cendrine possessed his every thought, and he knew that somehow he had to see her one more time. He was about to arrange to go ashore when Profitt announced that everyone was going to a luncheon at a Monte Carlo beach club. The festive luncheon dragged on until late afternoon, when a rainstorm finally drove everyone back to the *Lysistrata* to dress for dinner. During cocktails, when Profitt declared that a night at the casino in Nice was planned after dinner, Jonathan could barely contain his disappointment. He would have to wait until the next day to try to see Cendrine again.

Just after dinner, when Jonathan was in his cabin dressing to go to the casino, a servant knocked. He handed Jonathan a small folded note.

'Who sent this?' Jonathan asked, staring at the plain paper.

'I don't know, sir. A boy in a fishing boat brought it just moments ago.'

Jonathan opened the note. It was from Cendrine, a hastily scrawled plea that he meet her at the Trophée as soon as possible. Jonathan considered telling Profitt but decided against it, instead leaving his cabin quickly and finding a crewman to take him ashore.

It was nearly ten when he arrived at the ruins. When he reached the clearing, he stopped short. It was empty. There was a full moon, and the crumbling monument

86

was bathed in an eerie light. A brisk wind was blowing up from the sea; the long-fingered shadows of the swaying cypress trees danced across the grass.

Then he saw her emerge from behind a column. She came swiftly towards him. Her hair was streaming loose behind her and he could see her face, stark white in the moonlight. Without a word, she came up to him and fitted herself against his body, burying her face in his chest.

It surprised him so much that at first, he didn't move. Then his arms surrounded her, pulling her closer. He closed his eyes, the feel of her body against his overwhelming him.

After a moment, she looked up at him, her eyes unnaturally bright. He wanted to believe it was with passion, but there was something darker there.

'What is it?'

'I knew you'd come,' she said.

He felt her trembling. 'What's wrong?' he asked, alarmed.

She buried her face against him again. 'Everything's all right,' she murmured. 'I knew you'd come.'

Something had happened. Something had frightened her terribly. He felt a sudden surge of protectiveness for this woman he barely knew, a woman he wanted desperately. His hand cupped her head tenderly.

She looked up suddenly. 'Make love to me, Jonathan,' she whispered.

'What?'

'Make love to me, please.'

'Cendrine!'

The brightness in her eyes had grown harder and she pulled out of his embrace, holding his hands. She began to back slowly away, pulling him towards the shadows. 'Please,' she whispered.

He resisted, and she pulled harder. 'Please, Jonathan. . .'

He allowed her to guide him into the shadows of the ruin and over to a large, flat stone. He felt as if he were in a dream, yet all his senses were stingingly alive. He could hear the wind in the trees, feel the cold, hard surface of the stone against his palm as he guided her down on it. He could feel her hands warm at his throat as she undid his collar and the buttons of his shirt. He could smell the salt air and the earth, still damp with the rain. And when he finally kissed her, he could taste her.

He undressed her as slowly as his excitement would allow, his desire fighting with his guilt. She was so young, and he was taking advantage of her. But the sight of her bare, white body, luminous in the moonlight, inflamed him. She made no sound when he kissed her breasts, but when he finally entered her she uttered a small guttural cry and arched her back.

He tried to be gentle, but her arms clasped him with a strength that surprised him. 'Hold me,' she whispered. 'Hold me. Hold me.' She repeated it like a chant over and over, then slipped into a soft stream of French, strange words that he could not understand.

A flood of warmth came over him, that wonderful feeling of being taken in and held by a woman, and he felt the engulfing intensity he had felt that night at the brothel. But this time it was different, coupled now with a great, mysterious tenderness. He tried to go slow, but suddenly he could not hold back, and he wanted only to lose himself in that dark warmth deep inside her. With an abrupt move, he lifted her light body off the cold stone and onto his hips. She cried out, and he saw a glimmer of fear cross her face.

'Don't be afraid,' he whispered. 'I won't hurt you.'

She wrapped her arms around his back and her legs around his hips, clinging to him.

'I won't hurt you . . . I won't hurt you . . .' he

murmured. He crushed her to him, and cried out with a violent release.

After a few moments, he opened his eyes, and the darkness of the clearing swirled back into his consciousness. Her arms were still locked around his back, her face buried in his shoulder. Overhead, he could see the moon scuttling between the dark clouds. He felt the stone cold against his bare skin and the strands of her hair on his cheek.

She was trembling, but still she would not release him, her arms, her legs, all of her holding him tight. He stroked her hair. Slowly, her arms loosened around his back and he felt her body relax. He kissed her shoulder, and her lips moved against his neck.

'This is how it should be,' she said softly. 'I knew it.'

He realized, after a moment, that she was crying, and he held her gently, feeling contrite over his lack of will and the savage way he had taken her. She had been a virgin after all, and he should have refused her. But he had been unable to stop himself, and it was over now. He couldn't take back the act. He didn't want to.

She raised her head to look at him. 'When. . .'

'Tomorrow,' he said. 'I'll come back tomorrow.'

It was quiet. He could hear the rush of the wind through the cypress trees, but the sound seemed to come from the surge of his own blood through his heart.

He was awakened the next morning by a low purring sound. It took him a moment before his eyes focused on the surroundings of his cabin and his ears picked up the sound as coming from machinery of some kind. Then he realized that his bed was rocking gently.

He sat up, fully awake. The yacht was moving! He jumped out of bed and dressed quickly, then raced up to the deck, where he drew up short at the sight of Beaulieu-sur-Mer slipping away.

'No,' he said softly. He went slowly to the rail, staring out over the water. He didn't hear Profitt come up beside him.

'Good morning, Jonathan.'

Jonathan turned towards him. 'We're leaving,' he said. 'Why?'

Profitt gave a small shrug. 'I felt like taking the party to Greece.'

'Greece,' Jonathan said, absently.

'No, it's off to Paris for you. We're stopping off in Portofino. You can catch a train from there.' Profitt gave him an easy smile. 'It's time you got to work on that wonderful future I promised you, don't you think?'

Jonathan resisted the urge to look back at the coastline.

'Jonathan?'

'Yes, of course,' he said quietly.

Profitt gave Jonathan's arm a brotherly clasp. 'We'll have a drink together before you leave,' he said. With a look towards the coastline, he thrust his hands in the pockets of his jacket and sauntered off.

Jonathan waited until Profitt was out of sight before turning back to the sea. He stood there, gripping the railing, staring up into the dark-green hills above Beaulieu-sur-Mer until they vanished from view.

Chapter Seven

The wind howled against the window, sending the shutters banging against the house and Cendrine closed her eyes, trying to blank out the sound. It was the mistral, the cold wind that blew down from the north. Its relentless wail was maddening, and it always made her feel trapped.

Bang . . . bang. Bang . . . bang. Finally, she jumped up from the bed, threw the window open and struggled to pull the shutters closed. It was noon, but the closed-up attic room felt as dark and confining as a coffin. Cendrine pulled her shawl over her shoulders and began to pace. Four steps from one wall to the other. Four steps and turn. Four steps and turn.

Finally she stopped. Glancing at the pile of fabric lying on the bed, she thought of trying to resume her sewing, but she couldn't concentrate. Reaching under the mattress, she pulled out a copy of *L'Art et la mode*. The issue was a year old, but that did not diminish any of its magic. She sat down on the bed and turned to her favourite illustration. In the dim light, she could barely see it, but she knew every line of it. It was of a man, handsome and dark-haired, smiling as he walked under a canopy of trees with a woman in a Parisian park. The man looked just like Jonathan.

Jonathan . . .

Months later, the memory of their night together was still there, embedded in every pore of her skin, alive in every breath she took. His face, so stark in the moonlight; his eyes, so intense, like the blue flicker in a flame, as he looked at her; the feel of his body, hard and smooth, giving off an energy and heat that seemed to penetrate and warm her own body; the way he held her, the way he touched her. The way he made love to her. It had scared her, yet made her feel strangely protected at the same time.

Making love . . .

That was how it was supposed to be. Cendrine closed the magazine and set it aside. She rose and went to the window, pushing aside the curtain. Down in the courtyard she could see her mother wrapped in a heavy shawl, her thin arms moving rhythmically as she scrubbed out an oak barrel. She was only thirty-four years old, yet she looked like an old woman. She had been seventeen when she maried. The same age I am now, Cendrine thought.

A moment later, her father appeared, climbing out of the cellar with another barrel on his shoulder. It was September, and the barrels were being readied to hold the wine that he produced each year from his small vineyard. She stared at him, feeling her stomach twist into a knot. With Jonathan, she had learned what making love was; the thought of her father doing the same to her, defiling what had been something beautiful, made her sick. She prayed that he would remain content only to touch her. She could bear that somehow. As long as that was all he did, she could survive.

She had learned to survive by relying on the sheer force of her imagination. Whenever she heard his steps on the stairs, she forced herself into a trance, shutting her body down, letting her mind float, leaving the untouchable core of herself free to drift until it was over.

After three years, she had perfected the process. She would will her mind to go blank, turning it into an empty white expanse so something good and clean could move in and replace the ugliness. Her imagination was stored with powerful images to help her. She thought of Madame in her *Giselle* costume, of the sound of the piano, of moving to its music. She pictured the beautiful things she knew: a field of lavender, the feel of the sun on her neck. She pictured the blue water of the sea, and the long white yacht that anchored in Beaulieu. Sometimes, she thought of a warm summer night. The wind whispering in the trees. The ruins looming like benevolent ghosts in the moonlight. And a stranger who was not a stranger.

Jonathan . . .

Cendrine closed the magazine. Jonathan . . . You said you'd come back, but you didn't. Why did you make a promise that you couldn't keep? Jonathan . . . Jonathan Caras. I know nothing about you except your name. Who are you? Where did you go?

The wind raised in pitch suddenly, and there was a crash in the courtyard below that made her jump. Cendrine heard her father yelling at Roland. She shut her eyes tight and cupped her hands over her ears.

She dropped down on her knees on the floor beside her bed. Her fingers pulled at a floorboard until it finally gave way. Reaching into the hole, she withdrew a stocking weighted with coins. She spilled them out and counted them frantically.

Not enough . . . Not enough.

Madame had promised her that when Cendrine turned eighteen, she would write to her friend at the Paris Opera to inquire about a position with the ballet company. To pay for the trip, Cendrine had begun to keep the extra centime or sou that customers left on the tables in the café. Sometimes, when her father had passed out from drink, she stole a few coins from his purse.

Cendrine sat back on her legs, staring at the coins. Not enough. And it was nine months until her eighteenth birthday.

'Cendrine!'

The bellow from below rose above the wind. She darted across the room and opened the window and the shutters. 'What do you want?' she called out.

Her father looked up at her, the wind swirling the dust around him. 'I just wanted to know where you were,' he said. His eyes held hers a moment longer. It had been four months since he had last come up to her room, and the dread of his next visit was eating her up inside. She knew suddenly that tonight he would come.

She shut the window and backed away, gathering up the coins, dropping them quickly into the stocking and slipping it back in its hiding place. She picked up the magazine, carefully smoothing the pages, and slid it back under the mattress. Then, pulling the shawl tighter, she went downstairs.

The wind beat frantically against the window. Cendrine lay still in her bed, her ears attuned to the usual noises of the night. Suddenly there was a sound outside her door and she tensed. She sat up slightly in the bed, her eyes straining to see the door. It opened slowly, and the smell of wine filled the small room.

Her father closed the door and came forward. Cendrine lay rigid on the bed. She closed her eyes, readying herself as usual. But after a moment, she opened them again. Her father had not moved. He was standing over her, staring at her. She was immediately terrified. Something was different this time. Then she watched in horror as her father undid his belt and unbuttoned his trousers. She saw the white gleam of his legs in the moonlight and drew back against the wall, every muscle tensed.

He came towards her quickly. Before she could react, she felt the weight of him on the bed and her nightgown being thrust up, then his hand grabbing her thighs, pushing them apart.

'No!' she screamed. 'No! No!'

With one quick move, she reached beneath her pillow and pulled out a kitchen knife, slashing crazily at the air. It wasn't a person above her any more, it was shadow. She felt a hard blow on her face, but she kept lashing out in the dark, crying and screaming, again and again and again. Suddenly, the shadow fell back and there was a crash as her father fell hard against the dresser. She jumped out of bed and ran through the door, stumbling down the stairs. Down in the moonlit kitchen, she paused, leaning heavily on a table, trying to get her breath. She stood there, her eyes locked on the door, her heart pounding in her chest. After a moment, a shadow appeared in the door and with a cry, she raised the knife.

'Cendrine! What's wrong?' It was Roland, hair tousled by sleep but eyes wide with shock as he saw the blood on her nightgown. 'What happened, Cendrine?'

She stared at him, unable to speak. A second later, her mother appeared behind him. Cendrine lowered the knife and began to sob hysterically as Roland started towards her.

There was a crashing sound and Cendrine screamed as she saw her father staggering down the stairs. Her mother and Roland watched in paralysed shock as Gustave LeClerc stumbled into the kitchen, his shirt open, his pants hanging loose. He was bleeding heavily from a gash in his arm. He stood there, wavering slightly, staring at Cendrine, then took a step towards her, whispering her name.

She raised the knife over her head. 'Don't touch me,' she said, her voice low.

He took another step.

'Stop!' she screamed. 'No more! No more! You touch me again and I'll kill you!'

Stunned, Roland took a step closer to his mother. Cendrine stole a quick look at their faces, and she could see that her mother understood. Her mother knew! How could she have known and let it happen? Roland's eyes darted from Cendrine, to their mother and then to their father. His body went rigid with hate, and he stood there, tensed like an animal ready to attack.

Her father looked at Cendrine, then at Roland. The small kitchen was silent except for the wail of the wind outside. Gustave LeClerc stared down at his bloody arm and reeled slightly, falling against the table. Then he stumbled to the door and flung it open. The wind filled the kitchen, and he staggered out into the dark.

Cendrine stood there, still holding the knife above her head. Her arm began to tremble violently and she let out a sob as the knife clattered to the floor. It was quiet again, except for her mother's weeping.

Cendrine ran by her and up the stairs, ignoring Roland calling out her name. She was in her room, stuffing the last of her clothes into a bag, when Roland burst in.

'Where are you going?' he asked anxiously.

'Away! Far away!'

'Cendrine, you can't leave!'

She didn't look at him. 'I have to, Roland. I have to get away!'

'I'll protect you, Cendrine! He won't hurt you again. Please, don't leave.'

She heard the tears in her brother's voice and stopped. She turned to face him. 'Please understand, Roland. If I don't leave, I'll die here.' She was crying, struggling to stay in control.

'I'll come with you,' Roland said.

Cendrine wiped her eyes. 'No!' she said. Then, more softly, 'No, Roland. I don't know where I'm going yet.' She glanced around the room in confusion, shaking her head. 'I don't even know what I'm going to do. But when I have a place to live, when I have money, I'll send for you.'

She stared at him for a moment, then pulled him into her arms and held him tight. He buried his face in her neck and she pulled back to look at him. 'You must stay for a while,' she said.

Roland's eyes brimmed with tears, but he simply nodded.

She touched his cheek. 'I'll get word to you as soon as I can through Madame. And I'll send for you . . . and mother.' She glanced towards the dark stairs. 'But now I have to go, before he comes back.'

'But how will you live?' Roland asked.

She knelt down and prised up the floorboard. Roland watched wide-eyed as she withdrew the stocking. 'I have some money,' she said. 'Not much, but it will have to do.' She slipped the stocking down the bodice of her dress and put on her cape and hat, picked up her small bag and turned to Roland. She hesitated, her eyes filling with tears, then kissed him.

'I'll send for you, Roland,' she whispered. 'I promise.'

And with a final glance around the small room, she was gone.

Cendrine sat on the stone bench in the soft pre-dawn darkness, her bag at her feet on the wet grass. The edge of the sky was turning grey and the mistral whipped the tops of the cypress trees overhead. She sat watching the details of Beaulieu-sur-Mer take shape far below.

She had just come from Madame Kchessinskaya's home. She had awakened the old woman and told her what had happened, explaining that she was going to Paris. When the old woman could not deter her from her plan, she handed Cendrine a small purse of money. 'Take it. You'll need all you can get,' she said, when Cendrine tried to protest. Then she went to her desk and wrote something quickly. She pressed a piece of paper into Cendrine's palm and kissed her cheek. 'This is a letter to my old friend, the *régisseur* at the Paris Opera. Go to him. He will help you.'

Now Cendrine sat, staring down at the sea. She touched the bodice of her cape; the money in the purse was a reassuring lump beneath her clothes. She could feel, too, her heart beating as if it would burst – with fear, but also with wonderful anticipation. The mistral, *le sacré vent*, once a sound of imprisonment, now seemed a benevolent current ready to lift her away to freedom.

It was time to go. She rose, smoothed down the skirt of her black dress and adjusted her straw hat. She picked up her bag and turned, looking up at the crumbling columns and then down to the smooth stone where she had lain with Jonathan. Taking a deep breath, she crossed the clearing.

Soon she was walking down the dusty road that led out of the town. The sky was brightening with the light of the day and she walked briskly, a solitary figure in black, her skirt billowing in the wind. She passed the sign that said La Turbie and didn't look back.

Chapter Eight

Cendrine stood in the middle of the street, gazing up at the ornate façade of the Paris opera house. Its broad steps led up to the majestic arched entrance and its white columns rose to the sky, where the late-afternoon sun glinted off the gilded crest of the domed roof.

A wagon rattled by, nearly knocking her down and bringing her back to her senses. She clutched her bag to her chest and looked around the Place de l'Opéra. It was a whirlpool of motion and noise – people, carriages, dogs, horses, vendors. It was madness: terrifying, overwhelming, wonderful madness.

Paris. Nothing had prepared her for the reality of it, not Madame's stories, and certainly not her own imagination. So exaggerated were her ideas of the city's elegance that she had half expected the streets to be like shining ballroom floors, and every woman to be walking along in silk petticoats. She had quickly discovered that the dusty streets were filled with dung and that many people were shabby. But there was such excitement in the air! She looked back up at the opera house. It was Paris!

She pulled out the letter Madame had given her and stared again at the name. Maurice Foucret, the ballet master. 'Go to the theatre before two, before rehearsals begin,' Madame had said. 'When he finds you are my student, he will give you a position.'

She put the letter in her pocket. It was nearly four. Tomorrow, she thought. I'll come back tomorrow.

With a final glance at the theatre, she started off down the Boulevard des Italiens. She didn't know where to go, and she was tired and hungry, despite her exhilaration. The train had taken more of her money than she had expected, and unsure of what things might cost in Paris, she had bought only some bread and an apple to eat later. She walked on, searching for a hotel. A woman passed by, and Cendrine turned to turned to watch her, her eyes greedily taking in all the details of the woman's costume. Her dress was of a fine green silk, with a full skirt drawn up in the back and long, tight sleeves that rose in a puff at the shoulders. Her veiled hat was a fanciful creation, a dove sitting in a nest of feathers and bows. Cendrine turned and walked on, more slowly now, her hand self-consciously pulling at the collar of her cape. She had made her black dress herself; she was a good seamstress and had copied the design from one in *L'Art et la mode*. But her heart sank as she realized it was outdated and clearly labelled her as a provincial.

She turned down a narrow side street, where a group of boys stopped their noisy game as she approached. One of them pointed at her and the others giggled. She lowered her head and walked more quickly, but they were following her now. Her face began to burn with humiliation as she concluded they were making fun of her clothes. Then, suddenly, they raised a chorus: '*Elle est gentille parce-qu'elle est belle!*'

They scampered behind her, chanting the same words. Finally, she realized they were not being insulting. They were calling her beautiful! She swung around and blew them a kiss. The boys stopped, fell into a spasm of giggles and ran away, their chant echoing in the street. Smiling, Cendrine continued on.

Finally, she came to a small hotel. She went in and approached the man behind the desk. When she asked how much a room would cost, he stared at her, taking in her dress and her provincial accent. He told her two francs per night in advance. Cendrine paused, having no idea if the price was fair, and agreed to pay for three nights. The man watched her as she pulled her purse from her bodice and carefully counted out the money.

The small room, on the top floor, was spartan but clean. Cendrine unpacked her bag, placing the purse under the mattress. She set the bread and apple on a small table before the window, then went back to her bag and withdrew a pair of worn pink shoes, wound in pink ribbons. She set them carefully down on the table next to the food. She stripped down to her petticoat and camisole and washed in the small china basin, then carefully blotted the dust off her black dress and smoothed the ribbon of her hat. The sun was setting as she finished and she opened the shutters to let in the fading light.

A cool evening breeze wafted in from the window, bringing with it the sound of someone playing a flute. She shivered, looking out at the pink sky and grey rooftops, then sat down and picked up the apple. Her gaze wandered to the ballet shoes; she reached out and ran one finger over the scuffed satin.

'Tomorrow,' she said. She took a bite of the green apple. It was crisp and sour, and she closed her eyes in pleasure.

At ten minutes before two the next afternoon, Cendrine stood before the stage door of the opera house, clutching her ballet shoes. Taking a deep breath, she opened the door and went in. She paused in the dank, dark hallway; seeing no one, she made her way through a labyrinth of corridors. From somewhere above, she heard the faint sound of a piano. She followed it up some stairs to an open door at the end of a hallway. At the door she paused, her eyes widening.

It was a large hall with a soaring ceiling. A gauzy white light streamed through the tall windows and reflected off the mirrored walls. Bathed in its glow were a contingent of women, slender pale women in white tarlatan dresses, their hair parted and sleek against their heads, their faces and bodies radiant with health and vigour. The light made their dresses look transparent, and it seemed even to pass through them, rendering them ethereal.

Cendrine stood, awestruck, staring at the dancers. Slowly, she became aware of other details: a man sitting sleepily behind the piano spreading pâté on bread; thin men in tights and tunics lounging against a railing on the wall. Her eyes locked on the railing and her pulse quickened. A practice barre! She had always had to use a chair in Madame's home. Her eyes swept over the hall. This was a real studio! And these were real dancers!

'What are you doing here?'

Cendrine spun around. A short, bald man was glaring at her. 'I'm the stage manager here,' he said. 'What do you want?'

Cendrine withdrew the letter from her pocket. 'I'm here to see the *régisseur*,' she said, trying to keep her voice even. 'I have an interview for a position.'

The man eyed her suspiciously. 'Wait here.' He went into the hall to speak with a tall man standing near the piano. He came over to her, his pale eyes sweeping over her quickly.

'I am the *régisseur*,' he said. 'What do you want?'

Too nervous to speak, she held out the letter. He read it, his thin face expressionless. 'I know no Madame Kchessinskaya,' he said flatly, looking up.

Cendrine blinked. 'But you must. She danced for you, M'sieur Foucret. It was many years ago, but—'

'Foucret?' The man frowned, then shook his head. 'Oh yes, M'sieur Foucret. He died years ago. I'm sorry, mademoiselle, I can be of no help to you. I have no positions open.' He refolded the letter and held it out.

Cendrine stared at it for a moment, then took it. She glanced beyond him at the figures in white whispering and watching her in curiosity. They began to blur into one blinding glare of white light. She was dimly aware of the tall man turning away. A moment later, he clapped his hands; the music began and she saw a cloud of bodies, floating in unison.

The little bald man glared at her. 'You'll have to leave now,' he said, and slammed the door in her face.

Cendrine turned and walked away, her fingers gripping the pointe shoes.

For the next two days, Cendrine did not emerge from the hotel room, too sick with defeat and despair to do anything but sleep. Finally, driven by hunger, she went down to a café near the hotel and had some coffee and bread. She had no idea what she was going to do; she only knew that she could not go back to La Turbie. She watched a woman cleaning a table and thought idly that she would find temporary work in a café – it was, after all, the only thing she knew how to do. She had about fifty francs left, enough to find lodging and get started. Then she would think of what to do about the future.

When she returned to the hotel, the man at the desk stopped her and said she had to pay if she intended to stay on. Telling him she would, she went upstairs to get the purse. But it was not under the mattress. Frantic, she tore the room apart, searching for it, but it was gone. She ran downstairs and confronted the clerk, who denied all knowledge of the theft. Finally, he told her that if she could not pay, she had to leave.

Half an hour later, Cendrine stood in front of the

hotel, her bag in hand. She looked to her right, then to her left, not knowing which direction to take. Finally, she turned to the right and began to walk. Her one thought now was money; she had to find work. She passed several cafés, but they were too grand and intimidating, with bustling waiters. She kept going. She stopped in several smaller cafés, but none needed help – at least not the help of a girl from the provinces.

The afternoon dragged on and so did her fruitless search. It was nearly dark and the air was chilled by the time she made her way down to the river. She saw another café, a rundown place, and wearily went in, prepared for another rejection. The owner told her he had no openings, but, seeing her despair, gave her the name of a café run by a friend on the Boulevard St-Michel on the Left Bank. 'You might have better luck over in the student quarter,' he told her.

It was pitch black by the time Cendrine made her way past the Louvre. The night was quickly becoming cold and dreary and a fog was creeping in. Suddenly, the city that had seemed that morning so full of life and promise had taken on a melancholy and lonely cast. The black Seine flowed silently beneath her feet as she crossed the Pont des Artistes and the canal boats cast sickly green lights on the inky water. The massive hulk of Nôtre Dame loomed ghostlike, its towers lost in the mist.

On the Left Bank, Cendrine spotted two shapeless forms sleeping under the arch of the bridge amid scurrying rats and she quickened her step along the quay. Down by the river, the streets were crooked and cramped and an evil mix of odours pierced her nose. The lamps stuck to the walls of the houses were meagre beacons, creating shadows that seemed to quiver with life.

Cendrine turned into a narrow dirty stret, the Rue du Haut-Pavé, which twisted to a similar street. She stopped and looked around, her heart beating. She was lost in the maze of streets. Suddenly, she saw someone coming. She gripped her bag, her pulse racing. The figure emerged from the mist, an old man bundled in rags bent low, searching for cigarette butts in the gutter. He spotted her and came forwards with his palm outstretched, his eyes glittering malevolently. 'Mademoiselle, can you help a poor unfortunate?'

With a cry, Cendrine ran from the beggar, running blindly through the twisting streets. Finally, she emerged into a wide square. She paused to catch her breath and saw two newspaper vendors shivering under the gas lamps, trying to sell the remaining copies of their last edition. There were other people on the street, and the lights from the cafés burned more reassuringly through the fog. She spotted the sign for Place St-Michel and let out a gasp of nervous relief. Giving her bag a hoist, she started up the boulevard.

It was Saturday night, and Boulevard St-Michel, unlike the rest of the city, was teeming with life. The lights of the cafés, brasseries and cabarets beckoned warmly and the kiosks were aglow. The street was crowded with laughing and singing students and vendors. A flower girl called out plaintively, selling violets and roses; a crawfish vendor displayed his neat platter of little red *écrevisses*. When Cendrine passed by a chestnut vendor, the savory aroma of the nuts roasting on the brazier made her stomach churn with hunger.

She walked slowly on, searching for the Café d'Harcourt. Finally, she found it and paused at the window. Inside, it was a writhing mass of noisy humanity, waiters yelling orders over the din. Tentatively, she pushed open the door and was assaulted by the conflicting smells of perfumes and food. The room was crowded with tables of students and their female companions, playing dominoes, drinking, laughing and

105

telling stories. From a far corner came drunken singing; in another corner, a black man and a delicate blonde man were engaged in a drinking contest while a large woman with wild red hair urged them on. And in the middle of the room, a woman was dancing, her white legs gleaming above her short stockings as she punctuated her dance with high kicks. Her audience shrieked with laughter and tossed coins at her feet.

Cendrine stared at the woman, and then at all the others. What strange creatures they were! Wonderful creations of clothes and paint, with wicked eyes, so different from the elegantly remote women in *L'Art et la mode*. Cendrine saw a man behind the zinc bar and went over to him.

'I was told you might have a position open,' she said, raising her voice above the commotion.

The man paused from his chore of wiping glasses and looked her over. Cendrine did not like the lewdness in his eyes, but she was too tired, hungry and desperate to care. She needed a job. She stood straighter, thrusting her chest out slightly.

The man's mouth turned upward beneath his moustache. 'I'm sorry, little one, I have nothing for you. Perhaps you can come back some other time, hmm?' He turned back to his glasses.

Cendrine stood there for a moment, then closed her eyes. When she opened them, the room started to revolve and the noise became a pounding in her head. The room was warm but she felt suddenly chilled and dizzy and looked around for a vacant chair. Spotting one near the bar, she quickly dropped into it and leaned her head back, closing her eyes.

When she opened them, the owner was standing before her, holding a glass on a saucer. He set it before her.

'Drink this,' he said.

She looked at the amber liquid and up at him. 'I . . . can't pay,' she stammered.

'Don't worry.' He walked back behind the bar.

She raised the glass to her lips and took a sip, grimacing as the bitter liquid burned down her throat. She forced herself to take another drink, then another – the liquor worked its cure quickly on her empty stomach and finally she felt the chill inside her subsiding. But the fear and despair remained as a knot in her chest.

What am I going to do? she thought, staring at the buoyant crowd. Where will I go? For a second, her thoughts turned again to La Turbie but she quickly pushed them aside. She would never go back there. She would die here first before she would go back. Roland's face floated into her mind. Somehow, she had to stay here, to make a better life for herself and Roland – she had given him her word. An image came suddenly to her mind: the figures lying among the rats under the bridge. She shuddered, wondering where she was going to spend the night.

'Well, here's a new face.'

Cendrine looked up. A man was standing over her, holding a glass, smiling. He was young, with his hair parted and combed forward, wearing a cutaway coat and a bright red cravat.

'I've never seen you here before,' he said, wavering slightly. Someone vacated a nearby chair and he dropped into it, pulling it close to Cendrine. Wedged against the wall, she could not back away. 'You're quite pretty,' he said, reaching up and flicking the brim of her straw hat, 'in a simple sort of way. How would you like—'

Suddenly, someone grabbed his collar and yanked him back with such force that his eyes popped. It was a large, red-haired woman, the one who had been sitting with the black man. She glared down at the young man. 'Leave her alone, René!' She smacked him on the top of his head.

'Ow! Marcelle, you cow!' he exclaimed.

'Go away,' the redhead said, frowning. 'Let us be.'

The young man skulked off and the redhead slipped into the chair, shaking her head. 'He's a beast,' she said and clucked. 'No woman is safe from him. That is why I had to rescue you.'

Cendrine stared at the stranger in disbelief. The woman was about thirty, with a wild nest of flaming red hair beneath her hat. Her face was good-looking in a sturdy sort of way, but also exotic, powdered and rouged, with eyes outlined in kohl.

'Thank you for rescuing me,' Cendrine said softly, unable to take her eyes off the woman's face.

'Well, we women must stick together,' the stranger said. She held out her hand. 'I am Marcelle Derval.'

Cendrine took the woman's hand. 'I'm Cendrine LeClerc.'

Marcelle looked at her quizzically. 'You're not from here, are you?'

There was something kind in the strange woman's face that made Cendrine relax. 'No, I come from a village near Nice.' She paused. 'You can tell?'

Marcelle laughed, causing Cendrine to blush self-consciously. 'Oh, I'm sorry,' Marcelle said gently. 'I'm not laughing at you. It's just that a Parisian can always tell an outsider. You could live here for the rest of your life, my little Cendrine, and still be taken for an outsider.'

'But I want to be Parisian. I want to fit in here.'

'Ah, you should not be so eager to change,' Marcelle said with a smile. Her hand covered Cendrine's. 'You have a . . . quality about you that's very pleasing.'

Cendrine looked down at the woman's hand and wondered, with a start, if she were a lesbian. Madame had told her about such things – about women who loved only other women – but it didn't seem possible. Slowly, she pulled her hand away.

Marcelle smiled and turned to the bar. 'Arnaud! Two cognacs!'

The drinks were brought. Marcelle took a sugar cube, dipped it in the cognac and began to suck on it, her eyes on Cendrine. Cendrine quickly took a drink and grimaced.

'No, this way,' Marcelle said. She dipped the cube and held it up to Cendrine's lips. Cendrine stared into the woman's green eyes for a moment, then took a tiny bite of the cognac-soaked sugar. It tasted better – sweet, bitter and warm. Her head was beginning to swirl with too much drink and too little food. Through the fuzziness of her fatigue she began to wonder what would be worse – spending the night under the bridge with the rats or in a bed with Marcelle.

She felt the pressure of Marcelle's arm against her own and pulled away slightly. Marcelle laughed. 'Oh, Cendrine,' she whispered, 'you think I am . . . *une gouine*. I'm not trying to seduce you. I can see you need a friend, that is all. Paris can be a harsh place if you don't know your way around. It's difficult for a woman alone to survive here.'

Cendrine sighed with a mixture of relief and exhaustion. 'Yes, I'm finding that out,' she murmured. 'I don't know what I'm going to do. I have nowhere to go and no money. I don't know why you're being so kind to me.'

Marcelle dipped another sugar cube and sucked on it. 'Well, shall we say I am interested in you . . . professionally?'

Cendrine tensed. Was the woman a prostitute, a madam looking for converts? She had heard, too, about the city's brothels.

'I am an artist,' Marcelle said. 'Ah, that's a lie. I am

109

only a student at l'Ecole des Beaux Arts.'

'An artist!' Cendrine exclaimed. 'I didn't know a woman could be an artist.'

Marcelle smiled ruefully. 'It's not easy. I'm the only woman in the school. I was once a model there . . . before I became too old and shapeless.' Her eyes danced over Cendrine's face. 'When you came into the café, I was watching you. You have a fine body. You move well. I thought, now there is a natural model!'

Cendrine was speechless. A model – what did that mean? What kind of work was it? 'Do you get paid to model?' she asked.

'Oh, yes. About thirty francs per week. But the best ones can earn even more, especially if someone becomes your patron and wants to paint you exclusively.' Marcelle paused. 'I've known models who started when they were just six and kept going until their bodies betrayed them. It's hard work . . .'

Thirty francs a week! Cendrine heard nothing more. She could earn thirty francs a week just for sitting before an artist! It sounded grand and romantic. And it would be a way to get started, a way to survive until she could dance. She touched Marcelle's hand. 'Do you really think I could do it?' she asked.

'Of course,' Marcelle replied. 'Ah, if I had your face and body I could have been rich by now!'

'How do I get started?' Cendrine asked, excitedly.

'Every Sunday morning at the school, all the models present themselves for consideration. Only a few are hired, but I'm sure you could make it. Do you have a place to stay?' When Cendrine shook her head, Marcelle smiled. 'You can stay with me for a while if you like.'

Cendrine was speechless with gratitude. There was something about this woman that she liked and trusted. 'You're being so kind to me,' she said finally. 'How can I repay you?'

Marcelle smiled. 'You can pose for me – me and no one else. At least until some rich man discovers you and keeps you as his own.' She paused. 'Tomorrow, I will take you to the school.'

For the first time that day, Cendrine smiled. She glanced around the café, which now seemed more inviting, somehow less foreign, than before. She picked up a sugar cube, dipped it in the cognac and sucked on it.

'Tomorrow,' she murmured.

Chapter Nine

The morning was cold and rainy, and the small crowd gathered in front of l'Ecole des Beaux Arts stood with hunched shoulders waiting for the iron gates to open. As Cendrine and Marcelle approached, all eyes turned their way. There were five men and two women, all poorly dressed, and they stared at Cendrine suspiciously.

'Don't pay any attention to them,' Marcelle said. 'They're Italians and come here to make their living as models. It's very competitive. They don't like new faces.'

Before Cendrine could answer, the gates opened with a groan and the crowd shuffled across the courtyard and into the imposing grey building. Cendrine followed Marcelle upstairs to a studio. It was a large room, its walls rendered dingy with age and the dust of artists' charcoal. One wall was composed entirely of windows, which let in the gloomy light. There was a black coal stove in one corner, which heated the room to an unbearable stuffiness, and in the centre of the room was a raised circular platform, surrounded by dozens of easels.

Marcelle took Cendrine to a corner where the other models waited. Many had already taken off their coats and hats and were now talking or smoking with studied nonchalance. Suddenly, the door burst open and the room filled with young men, talking loudly, laughing, shoving each other into the easels. A moment later, another man entered, scowled at the others and clapped his hands, calling for silence.

'That is the *massier*, the leader of the students,' Marcelle whispered to Cendrine. 'He conducts the inspection.'

'He decides who will be hired?' Cendrine asked.

Marcelle smiled oddly. 'Not exactly. It is the students who really decide.'

Cendrine looked back at the boisterous students, a few of whom were rudely pointing towards the models with leering looks.

'Let's begin!' the *massier* shouted. 'First candidate, come forward, please.'

Someone pushed past Cendrine and walked calmly to the middle of the room. Cendrine's eyes widened. It was one of the Italians; except for his beard and a cane, he was completely nude. He mounted the platform and stood there proudly, poised like an aristocrat. His skin had an unhealthy grey cast, but his body, stripped of its layers of fat by poor nutrition, was a beautiful sculpture of planes and angles.

As shocked as she was by the man's nudity, Cendrine could not take her eyes off the man. The students jeered and made cutting remarks, but the Italian stood there with great dignity. Finally, the *massier* called for a vote and hands went up. The man was accepted and stepped down.

A woman came forward next. She was fat and her flesh jiggled as she got up on the platform and struck a pose that sent the students into a tirade of cruel taunting. Cendrine's heart began to beat rapidly and she felt a trickle of sweat make its way down her back beneath her dress. Last night, Marcelle had told her what to expect, stressing that she would have to take off her clothes. But she had never imagined it like this – in front of dozens of bluntly outspoken, cheering men.

The room was becoming stifling, but she couldn't even bring herself to take off her coat. The parade of models went by and the taunts of the students rang in her ears. So far, only the bearded Italian had been accepted. Finally, there was only one woman and herself left. The other woman went forward. Cendrine grabbed Marcelle's hand.

'I can't do it,' she whispered.

Marcelle looked at Cendrine's ashen face. 'Yes, you can.'

'I . . . I can't go up there, Marcelle. They'll laugh at me.'

Marcelle pointed to the woman on the platform, who was bringing shrieks of laughter from the students. 'See that woman? She is trying to pose like some painting she has seen in the Louvre. That's why they are laughing at her. She is not natural, not real.' Marcelle reached up and took off Cendrine's straw hat. 'This is a game they play with all new girls. It's a ritual and you must endure it.' She smoothed Cendrine's hair down over her shoulders. 'Just go up there and be yourself.'

'I'm afraid to take off my clothes,' Cendrine said.

Marcelle smiled softly. 'I know. It was hard for me the first time. Just imagine you are somewhere else, doing something else that makes you happy.'

'Who is next?'

Cendrine's eyes went to the *massier* and back to Marcelle, who saw the terror in them. 'Think of the money you will earn,' Marcelle whispered. 'That is what you want, isn't it?'

Cendrine bit her lip. 'Yes, that's what I want.'

Marcelle took off Cendrine's coat. Cendrine stood rigid, allowing Marcelle to unbutton her dress. There

114

was no dressing room, no screen, nothing to shield her from the relentless stares of the students. She willed her mind to blank it all out, their eyes, their jeers, their whistles. She thought only of the money and how it would buy a new life for her and Roland, how it would buy her time until she could dance.

She was vaguely aware of Marcelle's hands slipping off her petticoat and camisole. She heard the wild applause of the students as the last of her clothing came off. Marcelle gave her a gentle shove and, as if in a trance, Cendrine walked naked to the centre of the room. Trembling, she mounted the platform and looked out over the room, at the blur of faces that were not really faces at all, just anonymous eyes and mouths. She stood there motionless, not knowing what to do.

'But she has no tits!' someone called out.

'Maybe she left them at home!' answered another, to raucous laughter.

'You're wrong! They're the perfect size!'

Cendrine felt herself grow hot from blushing and held back her tears as the torture went on. The students closed in around her, shouting out arguments about her figure. One man claimed her waist was too long, another said her legs were too thin while someone else hotly took the other side.

'She's like a statue! Why doesn't she move!' someone yelled.

'She's just like my wife!' another called out, which set off riotous laughter. The room was hot and claustrophobic and Cendrine wavered, feeling suddenly as if she would faint. She glanced towards Marcelle, who was frantically pantomiming a pose, urging her to do anything but simply stand there.

Cendrine closed her eyes. She tried to remember some of the posing tricks Marcelle had taught her last night, but nothing would come. The mocking chorus echoed in her head and she fought back the tears. I *will* do this, she thought desperately and willed her mind into a white blank so the images could move in.

She imagined she was in the rehearsal studio at the opera house, bathed in the white light, wearing a gauzy dress. She imagined she was one of the dancers she had seen moving in time to the sound of the piano. As she opened her eyes the faces before her mutated into an audience, their jeers into applause. Slowly, she raised her arm above her head, tilted her head to a pleasing angle and extended one leg in front of the other. She was back in Madame's apartment now, listening to the old woman's commands, moving her body through the basic ballet positions: *efface, croise, écarte* . . . She moved slowly, holding each pose for a few seconds before moving to another . . . *à la quatrième, à la seconde* . . . just as Madame had taught her. It was as natural and effortless to her as breathing.

Slowly, the raucous noise lessened as the students began to watch her. A few called out insults, but others drowned them out. Everyone was watching her. After a few minutes, the *massier* jumped onto the platform and Cendrine stopped abruptly, coming out of the trance. She stood there benumbed as he called for a vote. Every hand in the studio shot up in quick assent.

The *massier* turned to Cendrine. 'You are hired,' he said matter-of-factly. 'You will begin right now.'

The students applauded wildly. A few squinted up at her lewdly, but most had already retreated behind their easels.

'Try that last pose you did,' the *massier* told her.

Dazed, Cendrine looked around the room. Finally, she found Marcelle in the crowd, who was looking up at her with approval and perhaps just a touch of envy. Hesitantly, she assumed a pose and the *massier* nodded his approval. She looked at the students. Their faces,

116

towards her, were now intense with concentration as their arms worked quickly over their canvases and sketch pads. The room grew quiet except for the soft beat of the rain on the windows and the scratching of charcoal on paper. Cendrine stood very still on the platform as the eyes of dozens of men caressed her. Slowly, her shame and embarrassment began to recede as she realized the men's eyes held nothing dark or threatening. There was nothing in them but an oddly detached, passive adoration.

It felt strange to be able to affect men in this way, to be the object of worship but to be in command at the same time. It felt . . . powerful. She glanced at Marcelle, who was also busily sketching. This is how it must feel to dance, she thought suddenly, to feel an audience respond to you.

She pulled herself up taller. Yes, this was how it must feel.

The winter months slipped by, and Cendrine's life fell into a contented pattern that revolved around the art school and the attendant stream of life along the Boulevard St-Michel. Cendrine shared Marcelle's apartment, wanting to save as much as she could in preparation for Roland's arrival. She had sent him a letter, care of Madame, saying that soon she would have enough money for them to get a room, enough to enrol him in the art school. At Marcelle's suggestion, Cendrine paid for much of her share of expenses by posing for Marcelle and the apartment soon became filled with sketches and oil paintings of Cendrine.

At the art school, Cendrine quickly became a favourite. Her only rival for the students' affection was a woman named Jacqueline, a tempestuous brunette who had reigned as the supreme beauty for years but was now getting on in years. In the student cafés, hot debates raged over the various attributes of the two women. Jacqueline was renowned for her voluptuous dark beauty, but Cendrine was worshipped for her grace and her strange, chameleonlike quality that assured no two drawings or paintings of her ever looked alike. Once, when Cendrine was modelling, Jacqueline had swept proudly into the studio, radiant in expensive silk and creamy lace petticoats, and gaily begun overturning easels, laughing at the havoc she caused. The students had greeted her happily, dancing around her like puppies as she flicked off their hats with her parasol. Cendrine wondered jealously how Jacqueline managed to dress so splendidly on just thirty francs a week – until Marcelle explained that she was the mistress of a wealthy American businessman. It was no surprise when Jacqueline finally announced her marriage and retirement.

But few models were so lucky, Cendrine quickly learned. Most did not last long. The plainer ones were unable to withstand the students' merciless criticisms; some became the companions or wives of students or artists. And then there were those who just disappeared, engulfed by the whirlwind life of the cafés.

Like the other students, Marcelle was a frequent habituée of the cafés, and Cendrine was often tempted to join her. After an exhausting day in the dreary studio, the cafés were like a ray of sunshine. But she seldom went along. She had no intention of ending up like other models she had seen, huddled in the cafés with their shabby clothes and drawn faces.

'But you're nothing like them,' Marcelle told her. 'You could be more famous than Jacqueline! Why, you're just as clever as she is. You could easily find a rich man to keep you.'

They were sitting on the terrace of the Café d'Harcourt, the same place where Marcelle had come to

Cendrine's rescue nine months before. It was a balmy summer evening and the boulevard was packed with rollicking students.

'I don't want to be someone's mistress,' Cendrine replied. She had told Marcelle of her plan to be a dancer, but she suspected that Marcelle thought it was a folly in the light of her easy potential as a model.

'You never even allow yourself to have fun!' Marcelle persisted. 'You could have any man!'

'But I don't want *any* man, Marcelle,' she said with a smile.

Cendrine had grown to love Marcelle, but there were still confidences she could not share with her. How could she explain to her friend – a woman who enjoyed the company of many men with casual abandon – that she thought of only one man, a man who existed only in a dream?

Jonathan . . . Jonathan Caras. Just a name.

'A woman needs to be in love,' Marcelle said, surveying the men walking by. 'Love keeps a woman fresh.'

Two young men tipped their hats at Cendrine and Marcelle sighed, then reached up and cupped Cendrine's face in her hands. 'By now, I know this face as well as my own. It can't lie,' she said. 'It is the face of a woman in love. Yet you have no man!'

Cendrine pulled away. 'No, no man,' she repeated softly. She looked out over the passing parade, then closed her eyes. Just the memory of one – a memory that won't go away.

It was September, a year since Cendrine's arrival in Paris. The evening was too rainy to go out, so Marcelle had stayed in to work on a painting that had been giving her trouble and Cendrine willingly agreed to pose. The large atelier was warm and cosy from a fire burning in the grate and was filled with the smell of brewing coffee. Cendrine, lying nude on a sofa before Marcelle's easel, listened to the rain beating on the large north windows, feeling pleasantly sleepy.

'You moved again!' Marcelle called out.

'Sorry,' Cendrine murmured.

Suddenly, Marcelle threw down her brush in disgust. 'I can't get it right! I have no talent!'

Cendrine propped herself up on one elbow. She had been through Marcelle's tantrums of doubt before. 'Yes, you do,' she said gently. 'Just look around this room.'

'You only say that to make me feel better!'

'I'm not the only one who thinks so.'

The walls of the room were filled with canvases of Cendrine's face and body in every imaginable pose, with dozens more stacked in corners. Recently, Marcelle had sold one of the paintings, a portrait of Cendrine's face caught in a melancholy mood, to the owner of a gallery. Marcelle was proud of her first sale. It was rare for a student to sell a painting.

Marcelle smiled, somewhat pacified. 'I suppose you're right. But I don't think he would have bought it if he had known I'm a woman. He knows only that there is a great undiscovered painter named M. Derval.' She laughed and went over to pour herself and Cendrine some coffee, bringing the steaming bowl over to Cendrine, who took it but did not drink. 'You've been sad lately,' Marcelle said. 'What's wrong?'

Cendrine sat up, looking at Marcelle with a small smile. 'I think I'm jealous of you. You are doing what you really want to, Marcelle. I still am not.'

'Perhaps you should go again to the opera.'

'I've tried twice. No one will even see me.' She put the bowl aside. 'I'm beginning to think it will never happen, Marcelle. I will never be a dancer.'

Marcelle started to say something, but there was a

knock at the door. The two women exchanged glances.

'It must be the landlord demanding the rent again,' Marcelle said, as Cendrine pulled on a robe. Marcelle went to the door and opened it. A strange man stood on the threshold. 'Well – what do you want?' she demanded.

Cendrine looked across the room at the bedraggled man, standing there in a wet coat and hat. There was something familiar about him. Suddenly, with a small cry, she ran across the room and flung herself into the man's arms.

Marcelle watched in stunned silence as the two embraced. Finally, Cendrine turned to Marcelle, laughing and wiping her eyes. 'This is my brother,' she said, beginning to cry again. 'This is Roland!'

The young man took off his wet hat and Marcelle immediately saw the resemblance. 'Well, don't just stand there dripping on my doorstep! Come in,' she said, with a smile.

Tentatively, Roland came in, one arm still wrapped around Cendrine's waist. His eyes travelled slowly over the atelier, pausing on each painting of Cendrine.

Cendrine's joy was uncontainable. 'What are you doing here? How did you get here? How did you know where to find me?'

Roland's blue eyes came back to rest on her face. 'I asked Madame where you were living. I had to come.'

She stared at him for a moment, then pulled him into an embrace. 'Oh, Roland, I've missed you so!' She pulled away and searched his face. He was obviously exhausted, but she saw something else in his face; it looked much older, with a sharper edge. Had it only been a year since she saw him? 'Why did you come, Roland?' she asked. 'I told you I would send for you.'

'I had to come,' he repeated.

'How did you get here?'

He wiped his wet hair off his forehead. For the first time, Cendrine noticed the filthiness of his coat; realized also that he was much too thin.

'I walked, found rides with people when I could,' he said, his voice toneless. 'I slept in barns, by the side of the road.' He paused. 'I had to come, Cendrine.'

'But what about mother?'

'She's dead,' he said flatly.

For a moment, Cendrine said nothing. Her mother – dead! It was a shock, but yet it wasn't. For too many years, she had seen it coming in her mother's eyes. 'How?' Cendrine asked softly, her eyes filling with tears.

'He did it,' Roland muttered. 'He killed her.'

Cendrine stared at her brother. The muscles in his face were clenched. Cendrine touched his arm; his entire body was tensed, quivering like a taut bow. 'You're shivering,' she said. 'Let me take this wet coat.'

Marcelle, who had been standing silently nearby, sprung to life. 'I'll get you some coffee,' she said, and hurried away.

Cendrine helped lift the heavy wet wool coat off Roland's shoulders, then guided him over to the sofa. He sank down on it wearily, closing his eyes, and she sat down next to him.

'What happened, Roland?' she asked softly.

'I went to Beaulieu on an errand. When I got home, she was just lying there, in bed. I thought it was strange . . . she never slept during the day. Then I saw she wasn't moving.' He drew in a deep breath. 'I went and got old Benois and he said her heart had given out.' Roland opened his eyes and looked at Cendrine. 'But he's not a real doctor. He knows horses, not people. She didn't die from a bad heart. He killed her, Cendrine. He killed her.'

His eyes, under the haze of tears, were hard and cold. She could think of nothing to say. It broke her heart to see Roland this way, so bruised by hate. They had both suffered so much at their father's hand, but she had been able to numb the pain with the balm of her imagination and dreams. Roland, however, was different – his emotions lay closer to the surface. And that was where his pain was now, a raw wound for all to see.

'It's over, Roland,' she said softly. 'He can't hurt us any more. He can't hurt mother, or me. Or you.'

His blue eyes gazed back at her. The tears were now held in check, and the hardness remained, but there was also love and trust. The boy she had left behind in La Turbie was gone, but her brother was still there. 'You're not angry I came?' he asked.

'Of course not. Why would you think that?'

Marcelle came over to the sofa and handed Roland a bowl of coffee. He took it but did not drink. He glanced up at Marcelle, his eyes taking in her wild hair and smock spattered with oil paints, then returning to Cendrine. 'I thought you would be angry at me for intruding. You have your own life here in Paris now.'

Cendrine took his hand. 'You're my brother, Roland. You're part of my life.' She glanced at Marcelle. 'You can stay here with us.'

Marcelle nodded and waved a hand. 'There's plenty of room, as you can see.'

Slowly, Roland's eyes swept over the room, over the dozens of paintings. His gaze lingered on the nearly finished painting on the easel, the one of Cendrine laying nude on the sofa. He stared at it for a long time. 'I thought you were a dancer, Cendrine,' he said finally. 'Madame told me—'

'I am!' Cendrine said quickly. She pulled the folds of her robe tighter across her chest, resisting the urge to look away. 'I will be.'

Roland continued to stare at her questioningly until finally, to her relief, he closed his eyes and wavered, seeming on the verge of falling asleep where he sat. Marcelle took the bowl from his hand. Cendrine pulled a shawl off the back of the sofa and stood up. 'I'll explain tomorrow,' she said quietly. 'You need to sleep now.'

Without a protest, he stretched out on the sofa and closed his eyes. Cendrine draped the shawl across his shoulders and watched him as his breathing slowly deepened into sleep. She gently pushed his hair back from his forehead.

'I love you, Cendrine,' he murmured.

She bent down to kiss his cheek. 'I love you, Roland.'

Chapter Ten

Cendrine frowned at her reflection in the mirror, then pinched her cheeks, bringing two spots of pink to her pale face.

'Why don't you just use some of Marcelle's paint?'

Hearing the disdain in Roland's voice, she turned to where he lay sprawled on the sofa, but decided to say nothing. She turned back to the mirror, watching him in the reflection.

She was getting tired of his moods, but didn't know how to combat them. From the start Roland had found it hard to adjust to life in Paris. Soon after he arrived, she had used her influence to enrol him at the art school, paying for it out of her modelling wages. But he found everything overwhelming – the city, the school, especially the other students. One afternoon he had burst into the apartment, livid with rage; the older students had teased him, stripping him naked and forcing him to fight a duel with paint brushes. Then they had roughly cleaned him with turpentine, given him a franc for a bath and sent him home in a smock. Cendrine told him it was only the teasing that all new students had to endure, but he would not listen.

'They make fun of me. I don't fit in here,' he said.

'You will, Roland. Give it time,' she answered.

She didn't know that *she* was one of the reasons the

students made fun of him. Roland had never said anything, but finally she had discovered it herself by accident. One morning, she was called to substitute for another model. She undressed and assumed a pose on the platform. Suddenly, she spotted Roland. He was standing motionless beside his easel, staring at her. She stared back in shock. It hadn't occurred to her that he might be in the class; life drawing was usually for the advanced students. She saw his eyes travel quickly over her body, then back up to her face. In that instant, she saw in her brother's expression a strange mix of fascination and deep embarrassment. As he caught her eye, he reddened fiercely and retreated behind his easel. Cendrine heard a whispered comment from one of the other students, followed by a titter of laughter. Roland threw down his charcoal and slipped out of the room, the snickers of other students following him.

That night, he did not come home for dinner. He never mentioned the event, and neither did Cendrine, but it hurt her that the brother with whom she had, as a child, shared a bed now looked at her with shame in his eyes.

'Roland, why don't you come with me tonight?' she said, turning from the mirror to face him.

'I want to read,' he murmured.

'Roland, you need to get out.' There was no response, so Cendrine grabbed the book. 'Like it or not, you're going to be my escort tonight,' she said. 'Marcelle has arranged—'

'You know I don't like her crowd.'

She bit back her anger. 'Roland, please! It will be fun. We need a little fun, I think.'

He looked up at her solemnly. 'All right,' he said, 'we'll go have fun.'

They met Marcelle and her crowd at the Café

d'Harcourt. Marcelle was already in high spirits, as were the six others in her party. Cendrine greeted them but waited for Marcelle to introduce the strange man sitting next to her. He was small and thin, with a ruddy face and bright darting eyes like a bird. He was obviously not one of Marcelle's usual beaux.

'Cendrine, this is M'sieur Harrison,' Marcelle said. 'He's from a place called Kansas – arrived only a week ago.' She slipped her arm through Harrison's. 'We met at a party.'

'*Enchanté, mademoiselle . . . je suis*—' he began hesitantly.

'I speak English, Mr Harrison,' Cendrine said.

'Oh, what a relief!' He smiled broadly. 'You don't know how lonely a man gets for the sound of his own language.'

Someone ordered drinks, and while Harrison drank, his eyes darted over the raucous crowd. Marcelle leaned over to Cendrine. 'He's a horrid little man, isn't he?' she said in French, glancing at Harrison. 'But he could be helpful. I've been thinking about trying theatrical design, and he's the new musical director at the Folies-Bergère.'

Cendrine stared at the American, whose eyes were riveted on a drunken woman dancing nearby. 'He's slumming,' Marcelle went on. 'He wants me to show him "the real Paris".'

At that moment there was a crash as the dancer's boot hit a gaslight, shattering the globe. Harrison, his shoulders dusted with glass, cowered in his chair. 'How can we really shock him?' Marcelle said, shaking her head. Suddenly, they looked at each other. 'The Soleil d'Or!' they exclaimed simultaneously.

The party moved outside. As they walked, everyone was in a merry mood; even Harrison was beginning to relax, chatting away in English to the attentive but uncomprehending Marcelle. Cendrine walked slightly behind the others with Roland, who trudged silently along, hands in pockets.

'You could at least be polite,' Cendrine said after a while.

'Polite? To *these* people?'

Cendrine grabbed Roland's sleeve, pulling him to a stop. 'Why are you insulting my friends?' she asked. 'What's wrong with you lately?'

'Nothing.' Roland stared at the pavement.

Cendrine touched his cheek. 'You've changed, Roland.'

He pushed her hand away. 'You're the one who's changed!'

'Cendrine! Are you coming?' Marcelle called out.

'In a moment!' Cendrine turned back to Roland. 'You're angry with me. And ashamed. I saw it in your face that day in the studio. That's it, isn't it?'

Roland met her eyes. 'Yes, I'm ashamed of you,' he said, his voice tinged with anger. 'You said you were going to be a dancer. You said we'd have a life together – a good life. Yet you stand up there naked, all those men staring at you . . .' He looked around quickly and shook his head, shutting his eyes. 'This is ugly. This city, Marcelle, what you do for money . . . it's all so ugly.'

She stared at him for a moment. 'How dare you?' she whispered. 'If it weren't for Marcelle, I'd be dead. And as for my work – I do it so I can support myself, give us a place to live, pay for your classes.' She took a deep breath. 'Do you think I enjoy it, Roland? Standing there in the heat or the cold, standing for hours until my muscles burn with pain?'

He looked away.

'It's all I can do, at least for now,' she said. 'And if you don't like it – or my friends – then you can leave.' She

128

turned sharply, leaving Roland alone. After a moment, he followed.

Marcelle led the others to a narrow little street, the Rue Galande, coming to a halt in front of a low arched doorway with a bright red door. A gas lamp, hanging askew overhead, illuminated a sign that read 'Le Cabaret au Soleil d'Or.'

The Cabaret of the Golden Sun. Its grand name was ironic; it was one of the most infamously tawdry cafés in Paris. Suddenly, a figure sprang from the shadows and, with a cry, fled to the street. Everyone stared at the retreating woman and Harrison laughed nervously.

'Is this place safe?' he asked Cendrine.

'I've never been here,' she said. 'But if you intend to know the real Paris, you must have some courage, Mr Harrison.' She smiled, feeling suddenly sorry for the little man. 'Stay by my side,' she said, threading her arm through his.

When they pushed open the doors, a suffocatingly warm gust of air, heavy with the fumes of beer, wine and tobacco, hit their cold faces. For a moment, Cendrine could see nothing because of the haze, nestled against the ceiling like fog and fed underneath by small streams of fresh smoke. The room's dirty bare walls were relieved only by a few sketches and a meagre light came from three gas burners, reflected in a mirror at the end of the room. It was crowded with an odd assortment of people. Many were women, but they were nothing like the exotic butterflies of Café d'Harcourt. These were the true bohemians, who adhered to no social rules other than those they themselves created in their dirty little hole twenty feet below the street.

Marcelle led everyone to a table and ordered beers. There were cries of recognition as the next performer, Madame Leroux, took the stage. She delicately flicked the ash from her cigarette, laid it aside, then dipped a finger into a glass of yellow liquid and used it to moisten her thin red lips. '*Il était une fois*,' she began. 'Once upon a time . . .'

The room was as silent as a crypt as she went on with her recital in a sweet, calm voice, to a soft piano accompaniment. The story was sad and impassioned; even the waiter stopped to listen. Cendrine quietly interpreted the words for Harrison. Madame Leroux finished to tumultuous applause.

'I don't understand,' Harrison said to Cendrine. 'That woman did nothing but tell a story.'

'Talented storytellers are prized,' Cendrine said.

'Doesn't hurt that she's pretty,' Harrison said with a chuckle. He was well into his third beer. 'Marcelle says you're an artist's model,' he said abruptly.

'Yes.'

'Does it pay well?'

'Enough.'

'You don't mind taking your clothes off in front of men?'

'They're artists, Mr Harrison. They don't see a woman's body the way other men do.'

Harrison laughed. 'Just the same, it can't be an easy life. A pretty girl like you . . . you could do better. Be a storyteller, maybe. At least you could keep your clothes on.'

Cendrine caught Roland's eye. He didn't understand the conversation, but she saw disapproval in his eyes. 'I won't always be a model, Mr Harrison,' she said. 'I'm a dancer.'

He drew back. 'A dancer! Well, well,' he said softly.

Cendrine knew she should ignore him, but his patronizing attitude was annoying. 'You've heard of the ballet?' she said.

'Of course.'

'That is what I do,' she said, 'ballet.'

'Are you good at it?'

'Yes, I am.'

Harrison picked up Cendrine's glass of beer and gulped it down. He smiled drunkenly. 'Well, we have dancers at the Folies.' He reached for her hand. 'Maybe I could put in a word for you.'

His hand was hot and sweaty and she slowly withdrew her own. 'No, thank you,' she said.

They stayed in the café until it closed at two. Outside, the crowds were dispersing as the cafés and cabarets fell silent. As they walked along, Harrison, now in the full flush of his drink, began to sing 'My Wife's Gone to the Country, Hurrah! Hurrah!' his voice echoing through the empty streets. 'What's next?' he asked Cendrine eagerly. 'I'm famished!'

'There's nothing open this time of night, Mr Harrison,' Cendrine said. 'By law, everything closes at two.'

Harrison stopped suddenly in the middle of the street, sniffing the air. Then he trotted towards a *boulangerie*. Its windows were shuttered tight, but the fragrant odour of baking bread wafted out into the street. 'Open up! We want to buy some bread!' he called out, banging on the shutters.

'We'd better get him some food or we'll all get arrested,' Marcelle said, pulling Harrison away from the shop. 'I suppose we could try the market.' She glanced around, looking for a cab.

At that moment, a ponderous shape came lumbering around the corner; it was a horse-drawn vegetable cart, piled high with produce, on its way to the Halles Centrales, the city market.

'Let's hitch a ride!' Harrison called out and bounded towards the cart. After some haggling, the driver, half-asleep on his perch, finally agreed to Marcelle's request – transportation for five sous a head. They clambered atop the heap of vegetables and the driver urged the big Normandy horses onward.

After a while, Harrison grew impatient with the slow progress and began to throw carrots at the plodding horses as Marcelle howled with laughter. The driver protested and told Marcelle that he would charge Harrison two sous apiece for each carrot thrown. Laughing, Harrison flung carrots from the cart as the driver kept count in a loud and menacing voice.

'Look at that fool,' Roland muttered.

Cendrine looked at Roland, then at Harrison, then back at Roland hunched among the cabbages. 'Well, you look pretty foolish yourself, sitting there like a radish in a salad,' she said, and started to giggle. 'A rotten little radish, all shrivelled up and pinched-looking!' Her giggle grew into a laugh, and she pointed a finger at him, tears streaming down her face. Roland looked at her in indignant astonishment.

Cendrine laughed so hard, she fell back against the vegetables. Roland blinked, then reluctantly smiled. The smile grew into a laugh and soon he was lying next to her, helpless with laughter.

Finally, they stopped and lay there, breathless.

'Oh, Roland, it will get better,' she said softly.

He sighed and looked up at the stars. 'I'm not like you, Cendrine,' he said softly. 'I don't fit in here.' He paused. 'I've been thinking that maybe I should go away.'

'Go away? Where?' she asked, surprised.

'I don't know. America, perhaps.'

Cendrine sat up to look at him. She saw suddenly how much he had changed, his body filling out, his face losing its softness. He was, she realized with a small ache, no longer the boy who needed her protection; he was becoming a man, and there was a new, inevitable distance between them. She embraced him suddenly.

'Don't leave, Roland,' she said. 'You belong here with me. You can't leave. I need you.'

She felt his body tense and he pushed back to look at her. 'All right, Cendrine,' he said, his voice sad and resigned. 'I'll stay . . . for now.'

She pressed her cheek against his. Over his shoulder, she saw Harrison watching her and after a moment, he crawled over the cabbages to sit near her.

'You know,' he said softly, 'I meant what I said earlier. I can help you.'

Her mind was still on Roland. Her patience with the drunken American had worn thin, and she felt suddenly tired, longing for home. 'No thank you,' she said quietly, moving away.

He smiled slightly. 'Oh, it's not what you think! I mean, you're a beautiful woman.' His smile turned sheepish. 'But I don't really find you attractive. I really prefer men.'

Cendrine stared at him in shock, then looked away, feeling foolish. She looked over at Roland, who was watching her protectively. Harrison began to chuckle. 'I suppose it's good your brother doesn't speak English or he'd think I'm trying to seduce him, too.'

Cendrine smiled. 'Oh, Mr Harrison, I'm sorry. I thought—'

'Quite all right.' He paused, glancing towards Marcelle. 'I have another confession. I'm not really the Folies musical director, I'm only the pianist. But I can help you. If you come to the theatre tomorrow, I'll get you an appointment.'

Cendrine shook her head. 'I really don't think there's anything for me to do in a music hall, Mr Harrison. I've heard what those places are like – dirty and vulgar.'

'But the Folies is different. Or will be. It's just come under new management – two Algerians who are changing it into a revue of music and dance. Very classy it'll be. That's why I was hired. I'm quite a marvellous classical pianist.'

Cendrine stared at Harrison. 'Do you really think—'

'If you really are a dancer, then you should be dancing,' Harrison said with a shrug. 'So will you let me help you?'

'Why would you do that, Mr Harrison?' Cendrine said. 'You barely know me.'

His face creased up in a forlorn smile. 'Well, you're the first person who's been even remotely kind to me since I got here,' he said. 'You don't know how hard it is being a stranger in Paris, far away from home.'

'I know, Mr Harrison,' she said quietly.

His dark eyes became liquid. 'I suppose,' he said, 'that I must seem a pretty ridiculous figure . . . a real bumpkin.'

'Bumpkin? I don't know the word.'

'A country boy. I must seem pretty simple to a sophisticated Parisian like you.'

Cendrine tried to picture what she looked like, sitting there amid the cabbages, and her lips tipped up in a smile. 'Not at all, Mr Harrison. Not at all.'

Chapter Eleven

The sounds of hammering and sawing echoed through the theatre as Cendrine stood in the middle of the stage. She looked out at the workmen crawling like ants over the balconies and seats, installing new chairs and draping red velvet for the opening of the new Folies-Bergère next month.

Her eyes came to rest on the knot of four men dressed in suits, arguing in the fourth row. Then she looked to her left and right, at the fourteen other women waiting for the audition to begin. Most were taller and more voluptuous than she; all seemed less nervous. Cendrine clutched her ballet shoes to her chest, trying to slow her heart, and sighed in relief when she saw Harrison come down an aisle holding some sheet music. He gave her a smile of encouragement as he took his place behind a piano off to one side of the stage.

A murmur arose among the other women. 'There she is,' someone whispered.

Cendrine saw an old woman emerge from the wings. She knew from Harrison's description that this tiny woman was Mariquita, the ballet mistress. Swathed in her grey shawl, she looked like a little pigeon. She carried a lorgnette in one hand and a Spanish fan in the other, which she wielded like a staff of authority as she walked up and down the line, inspecting the women.

135

'All right, let's begin,' Mariquita barked. Harrison began to play something at a slow tempo. 'Turn to your right and walk,' Mariquita said. 'In a circle, please. Just walk.'

Puzzled, Cendrine walked in a circle between two other women. The parade continued for several minutes, with the old woman calling out instructions as the men in front watched. Then, Mariquita ordered them to stop. 'Raise your skirts, please.'

Cendrine glanced down the line and saw the other women holding their skirts up to their thighs. She quickly did the same. After a moment, Mariquita said, 'That's enough. Thank you.'

The four men and Mariquita put their heads together and after five minutes, Mariquita pointed to three women. 'The rest of you are excused. Thank you for your time,' she announced.

Cendrine stood dumbfounded, then looked at Harrison, who was smiling broadly. The audition was over and she was one of the three who had been singled out. But for what? She had not danced one step of ballet.

She soon discovered she did not need to. During the next month of rehearsals, she learned that at the Folies-Bergère, dancing was just another form of popular entertainment. As a Folies dancer, Cendrine would be expected to perform in what were euphemistically called 'ballets' but were actually elaborately costumed posing designed to give peeks of legs and bosoms. As the rehearsals went on, Cendrine wondered increasingly how the new Folies-Bergère could possibly succeed.

But it did – flamboyantly. The revised revue opened and shows were sold out. Critics came and wrote sneering reviews, but suddenly everyone wanted to go to the Folies – even the rich, who normally did not frequent music halls.

But the new Folies-Bergère was nothing like the other seedy music halls that dotted the neighbourhood around the opera. It was a beautiful place in itself, a palace of pleasure, with a sumptuous colonnaded lobby, a ceiling tented in red striped cloth and tassels and comfortable leather chairs in the front rows for the best clients. The promenade, an area behind the box seats, quickly became an infamous meeting place. There, customers could have a drink or simply watch the wondrous human parade: bejewelled Indian princes in pink turbans sipping liquors with Turkish officers in plumed helmets; elegant homosexuals; Gibson girls with bared white shoulders; luxurious prostitutes with predatory eyes, who walked in pairs, fanning themselves, trailing a powerful perfume of sweat and the scent of dying corsage flowers.

As compelling as the offstage show was, the one that went on every night onstage was even more extra-ordinary. The programmes featured the best singers, musicians and comics that Europe had to offer, along with American sharpshooters and boxers, snake charmers, mimes, Gypsy bands, and even a Zulu dance troupe.

But women – the most stunning collection of women on earth – that was what really drew the crowds. Women like Lona Barrison, who appeared with a whip and a cigarette wearing a corset, a strawberry-blonde wig and a monocle. Women like the bosomy Emilienne d'Alençon, who performed with pink-tinted rabbits. And women like the voluptuous Spanish dancer La Belle Otéro, whose jewel-encrusted costumes made her look as if she were dancing beneath a shower of pulverized chandeliers.

The Folies women were a magnet for the wealthy and titled gentlemen who came to the theatre. Having a Folies star or even a chorus girl as a mistress became the latest status symbol. All the dancers had their admirers, and they accepted the flowers, gifts and invitations with great expectations for their futures. It was not uncommon for a man to install his Folies pet in a fine apartment, with servants and wardrobe and all bills paid.

Within weeks of the opening, Cendrine discovered that she, too, had become an object to be pursued and won like a prize. Men sent her flowers and notes, but she did not respond to them. It was like the art-school life all over again and she watched as dancers were abandoned as soon as a prettier girl came into the chorus. She wanted no such distractions. The Folies was just another temporary stage in her life, one step closer to the Paris Opéra.

So she avoided the men who lined up each night outside the stage door, and concentrated on improving her dancing. Every morning, she arrived a half-hour early to give herself a full barre of exercises before the others showed up. Mariquita started rehearsals with a ballet class, but it was too rudimentary. Fearing that her body was growing stiff and her skills weak, Cendrine begged Mariquita to give a real class. Mariquita was sympathetic, but claimed there was no time. 'And what good would it do?' the old woman sighed, gesturing towards the yawning, inattentive chorus girls. But finally Mariquita gave in, and often stayed late to give Cendrine personal instruction. This closeness to Mariquita soon made her an outcast among the other dancers, who were also suspicious of her rejection of the men. But Cendrine didn't care. She didn't need their friendship – or a man's financial protection.

Sometimes, she would watch a girl sweep out of the dressing room on her way to a fine restaurant, wrapped in a new fur cape, and she felt a little envious. And sometimes she ached for a man's touch. Her dreams were charged with fevered visitations from dark

strangers who stroked her and kissed her and crept away
with the morning light.

But as her first summer with the Folies approached,
Cendrine found herself sinking into a depression. She
had been turned away three times at the opera already
and with each failure, her disappointment had deepened. The opera house was barely two miles away from
the theatre, yet it seemed that the chasm between the
two places was growing wider each day.

Cendrine and Marcelle strolled arm in arm down Rue
Richer, coming to a stop before a bank of posters
adorning the front of the Folies-Bergère.

'Well, look here,' Marcelle chuckled, pointing to the
names, listed from top to bottom. 'La Belle Otéro has
moved up above Fragson. Wonder what she had to do to
get that.'

Cendrine shrugged. 'She's a star, Marcelle.'

'Ah, she's overrated! I don't see why men are so wild
for her. She's fat! And she can't dance. Not like you.'

'You've never really seen me dance, Marcelle. No one
has.'

Marcelle cocked her head in mock indignation. 'I'm
insulted! I come to this drafty theatre every Saturday, a
woman alone, enduring those horrid old men in the
promenade pinching my derrière, just to watch you! If I
say you can dance, you can!' She waved a hand towards
the poster. 'You'll be up there one day . . . soon!'

Cendrine smiled and pulled Marcelle towards a nearby
alleyway. 'Come on, I'm late.'

Entering the stage door, they left the twilight of the
sultry summer evening behind and descended into the
stifling catacombs of the backstage area. In the large
communal dressing room set aside for chorus girls,
Cendrine quickly stripped off her clothes and took her
place at one of the mirrors. The room was saturated with

the musky, mingled scent of perfume and sweat. Clothes lay strewn about like wilted flowers. The young women, stripped to their waists, gossiped and complained about the heat as they did their faces and hair, the gaslights casting pools of liquid gold on their shining arms and breasts.

Marcelle sat at Cendrine's elbow, dabbing at her face with a handkerchief. 'I hate Paris in the summer,' she muttered. 'Why don't we go to Deauville?'

'I have to work, Marcelle,' Cendrine said as she pinned up her hair. 'Besides, I can't afford it.'

'You could . . . if you wanted to.'

'I don't want to.'

Marcelle shook her head. 'Oh, Cendrine, I don't understand you! That man who sent you flowers last night – he'd take you to Deauville if you asked. Now if I were you, I would—'

'Well, you're not,' Cendrine said sharply. She saw the look on Marcelle's face and sighed. 'Marcelle, I'm sorry. It's this heat – it makes me crazy. Forgive me?'

Marcelle smiled. 'Oh, of course.' She stood up, and checked her reflection, adjusting her hat. 'I think I'll go up to the promenade. Maybe I can find a young man to buy me a cool drink.' She kissed Cendrine's cheek. 'Dance well, little one. I'll see you after the show.'

After Marcelle was gone, Cendrine picked up another handful of pins and began to push them into her upswept hair. She felt terrible for being so irritable around Marcelle lately. The heat was just an excuse; her bad temper actually came from a growing despondency. Yesterday, once again, she had failed to get into the opera audition; this time, she was so disappointed, she had not even bothered to tell Marcelle. She stared at her reflection, the laughter and chatter of the other women flowing around her. Next month was her birthday. She would be nineteen, an age when most dancers were beginning their prime years. She stared at herself, blinking back her tears. Too late, much too late to start. Time was running out.

Three sharp knocks sounded on the door, the stage manager's traditional signal that the curtain was imminent. The others streamed towards the stage. Cendrine wasn't in the first number, so she lingered at the mirror until she was alone.

A moment later, a flustered Mariquita hovered into her view. 'Take down your hair,' the old woman ordered. 'I need you to replace Nathalie.'

Cendrine spun around. 'Why?'

Mariquita grabbed a white costume off a nearby screen. 'She didn't show up tonight. Here, there's not much time.'

Cendrine stared at the costume, a long, flowing tuniclike gown. 'But Madame, Nathalie's so much taller than I am. I can't wear her costume! And I don't know the routine!'

'Just watch the others. You're clever. You can do it.' And she was gone.

With a sigh, Cendrine took down her hair and slipped the costume over her head. It fell down over her body in feathery folds, the neckline too low, the hem dragging on the floor. Cendrine belted it with the thin gold sash, fitted the gold braid headband over her forehead and headed to the wings.

Cendrine did not feel like performing, but it was not a difficult dance. The six girls executed slow-motion poses, like a frieze on a Greek vase, against a multicoloured backdrop created by projectors. In Nathalie's spot at the end of the line, Cendrine was able to mimic the others' movements. It was hot, and she could see little flashes of white out in the audience as people fanned themselves with their programmes. The routine went smoothly, even though she had a struggle to keep the too-large tunic from slipping off her shoulders.

The music ended to tepid applause. Cendrine let out a sigh of relief and started to follow the others offstage. At mid-stage, she tripped over the hem and threw out an arm to brace herself against the stage to break her fall. When she stood up, a gasp rose from the audience. The gown had pulled down to reveal her breasts.

Cendrine froze. For one horrible, silent second, she stared out over the black expanse of the pit. She glanced into the wings and saw the stage manager standing with his mouth hanging open. Many a pretty bosom had been promised on the Folies stage, but not one had yet been bared.

Cendrine looked out over the murmuring audience, then back at the wings, and saw Mariquita. 'Do something!' the old woman hissed, waving her arms. 'Dance!'

Her heart beating rapidly, Cendrine looked back out over the dark auditorium. She could make out the faces of those in the front row. Some of the women were shielding their eyes behind fans, but the men were watching her intently, many smiling. She slipped the gown back up; slowly, she walked towards the lip of the stage, where the projector lights caught her full force, bathing her in multicoloured beams. Raising her arms, she glanced down at the dumbfounded conductor and he sprang to life, wiping his brow, flipping the pages of his score and raising his baton. The orchestra began to play a segment from the overture.

It was a waltz. Cendrine briefly closed her eyes, taking deep breaths to calm her frantic heart. She began to dance: slowly at first, standing in one place, just moving her arms, then bending her pliant back, feeling the music course through her chest, up through her arms and out of her fingertips. She picked up a panel of the gown in each hand and spread them out behind her like white wings.

Finally, she began to move her legs, first in small delicate steps, then into graceful sweeps through the coloured beams of light. She leaped and spun, letting the colours play across her body, making up the movements as she went. When the music finished, it took her a moment to stop. She opened her eyes, as if emerging from a trance, her breath coming in short gasps, the filmy costume pasted to her sweaty body.

She stared out over the darkness. The theatre was as quiet as a cathedral: a dense, overwhelming quiet that grew and stretched for ever. Cendrine felt her face grow warm and she ran offstage.

She rushed through the wings and down a staircase, towards the sanctuary of the dressing room. Then she heard a strange noise, a low rumble, like thunder chasing her down the corridor. She stopped to listen, but it was a moment before she realized what it was. Applause! Applause punctuated with wild cheers. She wiped a stream of sweat off her face and leaned back against the wall, flattening her palms against the brick. She tilted her head back, closed her eyes and laughed, a quick burst of nervous energy. Then she laughed louder, and brought up her arms to hug herself. It was applause – and it was for her.

The next day, the reviews told of the 'mysterious apparition', 'the sensuous shade who was a refreshing cool breeze wafting through the fetid air of the Folies-Bergère Theatre.' No one, however, had taken the trouble to find out who she was.

It was Oliver Thayer, the *Herald*'s arts critic, who finally, inadvertently, gave her a name. 'This sylph is an artist among the mere entertainers of the Folies-Bergère,' he wrote. 'To see her dance is like watching a delicate white moth playing in the light. One can only hope we will see "La Phalare" again.'

And so Cendrine became La Phalare – the White Moth. It was not the most exotic stage name, yet it so suited the way she moved that no one questioned it – certainly not the shrewd owners, who quickly made room for their new sensation on the programme.

Cendrine expanded her original dance into a sophisticated act. With Mariquita's help, she choreographed little ballets to classical music that Harrison selected. She wore her pointe shoes. She found new ways to manipulate the coloured lights and added blowing fans, mirrors and veils to enhance the optical illusions. Though she never bared her breasts again, she kept the loose, tuniclike white costume.

Thayer became her greatest admirer, writing that, through her mix of dance and light projectors, she was 'a sublime synthesis of art and industry, a perfect symbol of our age.' He came to nearly every performance, often coming backstage, sometimes with rich, curious friends, but usually alone.

Within three months, Cendrine's salary was raised to 18,000 francs a month. And on the playbill outside the theatre, the name La Phalare glistened in the boldest and largest of letters.

Chapter Twelve

It was late afternoon, and the *Herald* newsroom was quiet. Jonathan sat slumped in a chair, the latest edition of the newspaper in his lap. He had just come from the train station, after spending three months on assignment in Germany, and had not even bothered to stop off at his apartment. He knew from experience that there would be no point.

He rubbed his hand over his eyes and unloosened his collar, thinking about the past year. At first, it had been exciting; as a correspondent for the *Paris Herald*, he was assigned to a new city every few months. But after a while the novelty had worn thin, and he grew to dread the arrival of the cable from Paris ordering him to catch a train to a new city. Since he arrived in Europe, he had been stationed in five different cities – Aix-les-Bains, St Moritz, Grindelwald, Trouville and Baden-Baden. They weren't capitals of commerce or politics; they were wealthy resorts, playgrounds for the rich. And Jonathan was not a reporter; he was a chronicler of trivial pursuits, a social columnist.

Now he had been called back to Paris again for a new posting. He sighed and picked up the newspaper, searching for his latest dispatch. He found it on page two, with a headline that read SHOOTING IN SCHWARZ-BACH: EMPEROR WILLIAM ENJOYS TWO DAYS' BAD

SPORTS. It was a story about Kaiser Wilhelm's hunting party, but it had been rewritten to stress the emperor's bad luck in deference to Alexander Profitt, who liked to take digs at the monarch who had once socially snubbed him. The story carried no name, just the usual 'From Our Special Correspondent' line. After more than a year, Jonathan had yet to get his first by-line.

He tossed the paper aside with anger. 'Correspondent' – what a worthless title! There were dozens of other 'correspondents', all, like himself, stationed at various European resorts. Their assignment was to supply gossipy 'letters' about the social activities of the rich and titled. The *Herald* was filled with the vapid, relentlessly cheerful accounts: TROUVILLE TEMPTATIONS, DELIGHTS AT AIX, GRINDELWALD CLIMBING, BITS FROM BADEN. The pay was a mere $10 a week, and the only good thing about the job was that the correspondents stayed in grand hotels, thanks to owners hoping to curry favour in the *Herald*.

The correspondents were a motley bunch: aging reporters past their prime, educated men whose greatest talent was social grace, a few alcoholics, and several young turks eager to impress Profitt and gain a permanent spot in the Paris office. Jonathan supposed that he was lumped in with the latter. His keen eye for detail and descriptive powers made his reports better than those of the others, but he hated the work. And he felt betrayed. Alexander Profitt had led him to believe he had a bright future on the *Herald*, yet he was still writing about grouse shoots and horse shows. And he had not heard one word from Profitt.

He thumbed through the *Herald*, shaking his head. There was, he thought ruefully, no newspaper on earth quite like the *Paris Herald*. It was a newspaper that reflected the world through the very peculiar slant of one man. Within the last decade, newly rich Americans had

146

discovered the pleasures of travelling abroad, and Paris was their Mecca. Alexander Profitt ingeniously offered them a newspaper that catered to their interests, and the *Herald* office itself, on the Rue de l'Opéra, had become a home from home for the Americans. As soon as an American alighted from his train or steamship, Vuitton trunks in tow, he would hurry to the *Herald* and sign a register. The names were published each day, a declaration that the new arrival was ready to be embraced by the European social lions.

As for the *Herald* itself, it was an eccentric hotch-potch of news and nonsense. Because Profitt could afford his own cable, the *Herald* was able to skim off the cream of the dispatches that poured in from around the world, often being first on the Continent with the latest news. But the *Herald* was also filled with the trivial. News of the Boer War in South Africa shared the front page with stories about a dock fire in Hoboken, the successful trial of a new German zeppelin, and a duel between the Count of Turin and the Prince Henri d'Orléans.

There were financial reports from Wall Street, the Bourse and the London stock market. There were columns devoted to the European monarchy, yacht movements, sports and cycling. For women, there was fashion, the arts and 'What the Doctors Say'. Profitt's fascination with technology was reflected in stories about radio, aeronautics, motorboating, about the Metro that was being built under Paris's streets and the new automobiles appearing atop them. It was news – but news only as defined by the parameters of Alexander Profitt's privileged world.

Jonathan's eyes lingered over Profitt's beloved weather column. The report for Paris, predicting a 'splendid fall day,' was accompanied by the usual silly drawing, this one of a chisel-chinned young man posing blithely with a tennis racket.

Jonathan's gaze wandered to the windows. Had it been a sunny day? He hadn't even noticed on his ride from the train station. He rose and went to the window, looking down on the Rue de l'Opéra two stories below. Watching the strolling people and clattering carriages, he thought again how little he knew about Paris. He had come to Paris bursting with a desire to steep himself in the city of Sumner's beguiling tales, but he had no sense of the city at all. To his frustration, he still had only the most rudimentary knowledge of French. What did the music of Paris's language sound like to a tutored ear? What secrets could the city reveal to a man who knew its *quartiers*? What did a splendid autumn day in Paris look like? What did it smell like? He tried to push the window open, but it would not budge.

'These windows haven't been opened for years. I think someone painted them shut during the reign of the last Louis.'

Jonathan turned at the sound of the familiar voice and saw Harry Parkyn, the city editor. He hadn't seen Harry in months; they communicated by cable.

'How are you, Harry?' Jonathan said, with a smile.

Harry came forward and dropped his coat on a chair. 'Not bad, not bad,' he said. 'Things have been blessedly quiet around here this week. Profitt's in Versailles.'

Jonathan nodded. He knew that Profitt kept a home in Versailles, in addition to an opulent apartment on the Champs-Elysées. Even when he was in Paris, Profitt seldom ventured into the *Herald* building. He worked out of his apartment and kept in contact through an army of messengers who travelled the streets by bicycle in green and gold uniforms.

Harry eyed Jonathan. 'You look dreadful,' he said.

'I'm tired, Harry.' Jonathan leaned against the window frame, his gaze involuntarily going back to the street.

Harry nodded in empathy. He had begun as a correspondent eleven years ago, the year Profitt had started the *Herald*. He was about forty and Oxford-educated, one of the handful of London men hired by Profitt, who liked the way the British wrote. 'I was sorry to have to call you back,' Harry said.

'Where am I off to this time?'

'Geneva.'

'Well, I'm moving up,' Jonathan said wryly.

'The boy just dropped off your ticket. You're on the ten-o'clock train tonight.'

Jonathan turned back to the window. Harry let a moment or two pass, then picked up his coat. 'Let me buy you dinner, Jonathan,' he said. 'You look as if you could use a decent meal. We'll go to La Gavroche. It's a fine evening to eat outdoors.'

Jonathan smiled slightly. 'Yes, I suppose it is.'

A short while later, they were seated on the terrace of a bistro just off the Champs-Elysées. As Jonathan ate, he half listened to Harry's small talk, his eyes wandering restlessly over the fashionable cavalcade on the avenue. The sun hovered above the horizon, as if reluctant to relinquish a grand day. The streets were filled with top-hatted men in shining black carriages and couples strolling arm in arm. There had been a dog show in the Tuileries that afternoon and women were proudly promenading their pets down the avenue, a few of the canines sporting collars and coats that matched the elaborate dress of their mistresses.

One woman in blue caught Jonathan's eye. She was blonde and rather small, and he thought suddenly of Cendrine. How many times in the past year had he thought of her? Hundreds, thousands . . . every time he saw a woman with blonde hair. Often at moments like this when he felt alone. He knew it was absurd, that he had no reason to miss her, that the night they had spent together was only a chance encounter, but he couldn't get her out of his mind. Since he left America he had met hundreds of women – beautiful, rich, luxuriant creatures – but he found himself always comparing them to Cendrine. It was ludicrous, really – Cendrine was a cipher compared to the women he had encountered. His experiences among the rich during the past year had made him understand why Profitt had dismissed her that day in the village. Among the upper class, the ideal of feminine beauty was clearly defined. A world-class beauty was tall and statuesque, with dark eyes and dark hair: queenly women like the Comtesse de Grehfulle or Jenny Churchill or the regal Amazons in the drawings of Charles Gibson. Cendrine was small and pale, a sylph composed of air, not earth. No man of taste would give her a second look. Then why can't I get her out of my mind? Jonathan thought.

The blonde in blue disappeared from his view, and he turned back to Harry, who was talking about politics. 'Harry,' he interrupted, 'I need a few days off before I go to Geneva.'

'Jonathan—'

'I've got to go to Beaulieu, Harry. It's important. There's someone there I have to see.'

'I'm sorry, Jonathan. Profitt wouldn't allow it.'

Jonathan slumped back in his chair, staring out over the avenue, while Harry refilled his glass. 'This person you must see in Beaulieu . . . is it a woman?'

Jonathan nodded absently.

'So you do have a lady in your life after all,' Harry said, smiling. 'I was beginning to wonder. What's her name?'

'Cendrine.'

'Ah, a blonde, pale as the moon.'

Jonathan looked back at him, puzzled. 'How did you know?'

'Cendrine – it's a derivation of *cendré*, which means ash-coloured.' He took a gulp of wine. 'A Cendrine is nearly always a blonde.'

They were silent, both watching the lamplighter make his way slowly up the avenue, depositing pearls of soft light in the violet sky.

'I'm truly sorry I can't give you the time off,' Harry said.

'Maybe it's for the best.'

'It is, Jonathan, believe me. At this point, you don't need the distraction that a woman would bring. You must concentrate on your vocation, your future.'

Jonathan shook his head. '*Future*? Good lord, Harry, you read the stuff I send back! What future is there in reporting that Prince Edward bought eight Tyrolean hats at Marienbad?'

'You're a gifted writer, Jonathan. You're the best I've seen.'

'You know something, Harry – you're right.' Jonathan leaned forward. 'I'm the best damn writer on this newspaper, but so far that hasn't meant a thing. Well, I've done something to change that. Soon, real soon, one of two things is going to happen. I'm either going to get the assignments I want – or I am going to get fired.'

Harry frowned slightly. 'What did you do?'

'I wrote Profitt a letter and mailed it at the station.'

'A letter? But . . .'

'Listen, don't mention anything to Profitt. He'll find out what's in it soon enough.'

'Do you mind telling me what you said?'

Jonathan drained his wineglass. 'I said that I wanted to be based in Paris,' he said evenly. 'That I want the title of senior correspondent. That I want my name as well as a by-line to all my stories and that I want a $30 weekly raise. And I want to cover real news – the best assignments.'

Harry was staring in astonishment. 'Anything else?'

Jonathan looked squarely at Harry. 'I gave Profitt some suggestions on how to make the *Herald* a better newspaper.'

Harry shook his head slowly. 'I don't think that was prudent, Jonathan,' he murmured. 'You'll offend him.'

'Offend him!' Jonathan threw up his hands. 'Alexander Profitt hasn't said one word to me in the last year. I don't know if the man even likes my work!'

'It's how he does things.'

Jonathan started to say something, but bit it back. 'I'm sorry, Harry,' he said, 'I have no right to take out my anger on you. It's just that . . .' He paused. 'When I was on his yacht, he acted differently towards me. He treated me almost like a friend, as though he really cared about my future.'

Harry began to twirl the stem of his glass between his fingers. 'Let me tell you something about Profitt, Jonathan. I've worked for him longer than anyone else, but even I don't pretend to understand him. I can't tell you why I've survived and so many other men have not. He operates totally by whim, one moment treating a man like a lifelong comrade, the next like a stranger.' He paused. 'Yet there's something about him. Men are drawn to him, and want to work for him. If you left tomorrow, there would be ten others lined up for your job.'

Jonathan sighed in frustration. 'I just want to get ahead, that's all.'

They were silent for a moment, then Harry smiled. 'A letter to Alexander Profitt,' he mused. 'Well, the men who advance at the *Herald* do so by drawing attention to themselves in one way or another and your letter will undoubtedly do that. I wish I had the nerve to tell the man what I think. But I play it safe, content with my modest rank. Ever wondered why he hires so many Englishmen? It's because we don't have far to go home once we're fired.'

Jonathan smiled, shaking his head. 'You're humouring me, Harry, trying to get my mind off my anger.'

Harry sobered. 'No, I understand your anger. But you have to understand Alexander Profitt. To him, everything's a game. He plays . . . with his yachts, his sports, his women, his newspapers and his employees. And that's all we are to him, Jonathan – employees. You must never forget that.'

Jonathan didn't respond. Harry tossed some francs on the table. 'Come on. It's getting late and you've a train to catch.'

The Beau Rivage was the best hotel in Geneva, a sumptuous palace overlooking Lac Leman. When Jonathan arrived in his room, a letter was waiting for him. For one crazy moment, he thought it was from Profitt, but it was an invitation to a reception for the empress Elizabeth of Austria, the young wife of the aging emperor Franz Joseph, who was staying at the hotel. As usual, it was not addressed to him, but to the faceless person known as '*Herald* Correspondent'. He attended the affair, dutifully recording the details of food, dress and the guest list for the *Herald*.

The next morning, when he went down to the lobby to cable his dispatch, he encountered the empress's party, leaving for a steamship excursion on the lake. By rote, he pulled out his notebook, and trailed behind the party at a discreet distance as it made its way to the dock.

Suddenly, there was a scream and a flurry of motion. He saw a figure in billowing pink silk fall on the ground – a strange man in dark clothes stood over her. 'Her Majesty's fainted!' someone cried.

Jonathan rushed forward. Two men in the empress's entourage had grabbed the strange man and were roughly leading him away while the empress lay motionless, her attendants surrounding her. A crowd from the hotel began to gather; three men pushed forward, shouting for everyone to stand back. There was a gasp of horror from the crowd as the empress was laid on a stretcher and Jonathan's eyes went instantly from her white face to the red stain on the pink silk of her bodice. The stretcher was whisked up to the hotel and the crowd erupted in turmoil.

Out of the corner of his eye, Jonathan saw a spot of pink on the landing. It was a parasol, dropped by the empress. He stooped to retrieve it, then went swiftly up to the hotel.

The empress died an hour later. She had been stabbed in the heart, the wound going unnoticed at first in the confusion. The assassin was an Italian man, an anarchist who called his act a 'blow against the oppression of the aristocracy'. Jonathan spent the rest of the day and night gathering all the facts, writing of the stupefaction that came over the city as the news spread, and of the thousands of people who took to the streets in protest. He filed the story late that night and went to his room, but was unable to sleep. He sat up all night in a chair by an open window, staring out over the lake.

Early in the morning, a messenger brought up a cable. It was from Harry.

CONGRATULATIONS, SENIOR CORRESPONDENT. STOP. HURRY HOME. STOP. SPOT AWAITS ON PARIS STAFF.

Jonathan sat in the chair, the cable in his hand, staring vacantly into the distance. At last he was going back to Paris – on his own terms.

Chapter Thirteen

Jonathan took his usual table in the back of the bistro and ordered a dinner of mussels, onion soup and wine. The bistro was a simple place, right around the corner from his small apartment just off the squalid Les Halles market, but he liked eating his meals there. It was an interesting place from which to observe the people of the city he was finally coming to know.

It had been more than a year since he returned from Geneva. He had been given a succession of choice assignments and had distinguished himself as the *Herald*'s top reporter. The work had renewed his enthusiasm, but he had still not heard one direct word from Alexander Profitt and no answer had come to his letter. He knew he shouldn't let Profitt bother him; after all, he had been given what he wanted, including a sizeable raise. But he still found himself wishing for some acknowledgement from Profitt.

The owner came over to greet Jonathan, who started to pull out money to pay his bill. But the man smiled broadly. 'It's on the house. Tonight, we are all celebrating.'

The bistro was very crowded now, filled with boisterous people. Jonathan took out his watch. It was only seven on New Year's Eve and already the party had begun. With a sigh, he snapped the watch closed.

Perhaps that was why he felt so inexplicably restless. It wasn't Profitt – it was the fact that it was New Year's Eve, and he had no one about whom he really cared to help him celebrate the occasion. Harry had invited Jonathan to a party, which was tacitly acknowledged as a gathering for the bachelors who had nowhere else to go. Reluctantly, Jonathan had finally decided it was better than being alone, so he had dressed in his best suit and gone out to dine. But it was still too early to think of going to Harry's party.

He made his farewells to the owner and his wife and left. Outside it was cold, but the streets and cafés were filled with people celebrating, a prelude to the madness that midnight would bring. He wandered the streets, eventually making his way down to the quay. A light snow had fallen earlier in the day and a portion of the Seine near the Pont Neuf had frozen over, a rare event that had brought out even more people. Dozens of people were gaily sliding over the ice, and Jonathan leaned on the bridge, watching the police who were trying in vain to stop them.

He found himself thinking suddenly of the farm, wishing he were home with his father, his uncle Jake and Marion. It was the last evening of 1899; the century was ending and a new one was beginning. The twentieth century! It should be a night to remember, but it did not feel like anything special at all.

He headed down the quay and crossed the Tuileries, where the statues brooded under cloaks of snow and the iced branches of the trees clicked eerily in the wind. He walked on, not paying attention to where he was going. Finally, he paused and looked up; as if by rote, he had walked to the *Herald* building. He checked the building clock. It was only half past eight: still too early for Harry's. He went upstairs.

The newsroom was nearly deserted; most of the men

had been given the evening off. The room was quiet, lit by the globes of the gaslights. Jonathan sat down behind his desk, his ears attuned to the laughter and noise that filtered up from the streets below. The only other sound came from a typewriter in one corner; it was Oliver Thayer, the arts critic, finishing a review. Thayer was in evening dress, obviously on his way to a grand party somewhere. Jonathan watched him in idle fascination. The man was grotesque – fat and squat, with a pocked, pumpkinlike face absurdly accented by a Vandyke beard on his chin and a pince-nez balancing on his upturned nose. Despite his appearance. Thayer was the most influential critic in Europe. His writing had given him entry to the city's elite, and he enjoyed an access to Profitt denied other employees.

Thayer finished typing and rose, marching over to a young copy editor and tossing the review on the desk before him. 'I expect this to appear exactly as I have written it,' he said.

The editor looked up and caught Jonathan's eye. Thayer followed the man's gaze. He gave Jonathan a polite nod, picked up his top hat and cape and trudged out, leaving the newsroom silent once more. Suddenly, the hush was broken by a laugh – a woman's laugh – and Jonathan turned sharply.

There at the door stood Alexander Profitt, his arm around the shoulders of a woman. She was magnificent, tall and dark, swathed in a long white cape, glistening with crystal beads and trimmed in ermine tails. Profitt was resplendent in black and white tuxedo, a top hat and a voluminous black cape that revealed a slash of red lining when he moved. Jonathan could not take his eyes off them. They were radiant and glamorous; and the dim newsroom seemed filled with light and perfume.

Profitt did not see Jonathan sitting in the corner. He went directly to the young editor and asked for Thayer's review, which the man timidly produced. Profitt perched on the edge of a desk and began to read it. After a moment, he smiled slightly and handed the review back to the editor. 'I want that fourth paragraph changed,' he said mildly. 'Where Mr Thayer has written "Miss Anthony's performance was flawed", change it to "Miss Anthony's performance was flawless". Do you understand?'

'But Mr Thayer said—' the editor replied meekly.

'Just do as I say, Mr . . . Mr . . .'

'Crowes, sir.'

Profitt stared down at him. 'Crowes. Have a good evening, Mr Crowes.'

He went back to where the woman waited and they turned and started for the door. Suddenly Profitt spotted Jonathan and paused. He stared at him for a moment, then told the woman to wait in the hall. Profitt came over to Jonathan's desk and Jonathan got to his feet.

'Mr Caras,' he said, 'what a surprise!'

'Mr Profitt.'

'What are you doing here? I gave everyone the night off. You should be out celebrating.'

Jonathan glanced at his desk and grabbed a story about the upcoming World's Fair that he had been working on yesterday. 'This piece was troubling me. I just wanted to go over it.'

Profitt held out his hand. 'Let me see it.' He gave it a cursory read and handed it back. 'It's excellent. Your work is always excellent.'

'Thank you.' Across Profitt's shoulder, Jonathan caught the eye of Crowes, who was watching them with intense curiosity.

'I suppose,' Profitt said, 'that I should have taken the trouble to tell you that before now. But I believe that the best men do not need the false support of idle praise. Praising a man suits no purpose, I've found.'

Jonathan held Profitt's eyes. 'Praise can be useful, sir, if applied judiciously.' He paused. 'There's a saying, "You can tell the character of every man when you see how he receives praise." '

'Ah, yes . . . Horace.'

'It's Seneca, I believe.'

Profitt stared at Jonathan for a moment. 'Well, you certainly know your classics.' He smiled slightly. 'So, Mr Caras, how do *you* receive praise?'

'A man must always first consider its source. And then believe only half of it.'

'More wisdom from Seneca, I take it?'

'No, from my father.'

Profitt laughed. There was a tap on the glass of the newsroom door; the brunette was motioning impatiently for Profitt to join her. Profitt turned to Jonathan. 'Well, I must go.'

'Have a good evening, sir.'

Profitt took a few steps, then turned back. 'Mr Caras – why don't you come with us?'

Jonathan could only gape. 'Where?' he stammered.

Profitt smiled. 'Maxim's. I'm hosting a party for a few of my friends to see in the new year.' Before Jonathan could say a word, Profitt picked up his coat and tossed it to him. When Jonathan did not move, Profitt said, 'Of course, if you have other plans . . .'

Jonathan shook his head quickly. 'No – nothing important.'

'Good!' Profitt clapped him on the back and they started for the door. 'You'll be my special guest, Jonathan – if I may call you Jonathan?'

'Of course,' Jonathan said, stunned. As Profitt led the way out of the newsroom door, Jonathan glanced back over his shoulder. Crowes sat behind his desk, clutching the review, his mouth hanging slack with amazement.

Outside, Profitt's carriage stood waiting, a handsome

black rig with brass lights. The driver, in black, gold-braided livery, jumped down to open the door. Jonathan climbed into the cab and was surprised to see another woman waiting. She was bundled in dark fur and her face was obscured by a delicate veil, but he could see she was pale with red hair. She gave Jonathan a curious smile as he tentatively sat down next to her, while Profitt and the brunette took the seats opposite. With a start, the carriage took off down the street.

Profitt introduced Jonathan to the two women, then he and the brunette began to talk in French about a dinner party they had attended recently. The other woman sat silent. Feeling out of place, Jonathan said nothing. What could he offer to the conversation? Why in the world had Profitt invited him along? He sat motionless, acutely aware of the slight pressure of the woman's shoulder against his own.

'You know, Alexander, you've made us late for your own party.'

It was the redhead who had spoken, in melodious, accented English. 'Why did we have to stop at your office tonight?'

'I had to read a review by Mr Thayer,' Profitt said. 'I have a friend who has a small role in the opera. I just wanted to make sure that Mr Thayer was . . . fair to her.' He looked at Jonathan and smiled slightly. 'Do you like the opera, Jonathan?'

Jonathan felt the women's eyes on him. 'I've never seen one, sir.'

Profitt shrugged. 'Most are dreadful. I enjoy the ballet portion, however. The women are enchanting.'

'Yes, ballet is quite beautiful,' Jonathan said.

'You've seen it?' Profitt asked, surprised. Jonathan hesitated. 'Only once.'

Profitt was looking at him with interest. 'Tell me, Jonathan, what do you think of Mr Thayer? Do you think he is a good critic?'

Jonathan paused. His experience of the arts was limited. He had gone to a few concerts with Sumner and had once visited a museum in New York, but otherwise his exposure was limited to what he had read in newspapers and books. In his thirst for knowledge he had read most of Thayer's columns and found them hard to understand and self-important. Yet he knew Profitt prized Thayer as the most powerful critic in Europe. Did he dare give Profitt his opinion?

'I don't know a lot about the arts,' he said slowly, 'which is why I read Mr Thayer's work. But whenever I finish one of his reviews, I feel like I've learned too little about the particular art and too much about Mr Thayer himself.'

For a moment, the cab was silent. The brunette, who did not understand English, looked bored, but the redhead was waiting for Profitt's reaction. He burst out laughing. 'You're absolutely right, Jonathan,' he said. 'The man's a pompous ass. But he has amassed a certain amount of power – the power to destroy some people's lives with his pen.'

'Why did you order his review to be changed?' Jonathan asked.

'I didn't want to see my friend's feelings hurt.' Profitt's smile lingered. 'And sometimes Mr Thayer needs to be reminded of what real power is. He works for me. I control him. And I control the *Herald*, which is the most powerful newspaper in Europe, much more powerful than one little critic.'

He paused, his eyes levelled at Jonathan. 'No one tells me what to do. That is *real* power, Jonathan – being free of other people's influence and whims, having control of your own destiny. I believe in having everything on my own terms: the *Herald*, money, life . . .'

He glanced at the brunette. 'Everything,' he said.

'Even love. Especially love.'

Jonathan stared at the man sitting opposite him. Before he could say anything, the carriage pulled to a stop. 'Ah, we're here!' Profitt announced. 'Come, ladies, let's celebrate!'

The moment Jonathan stepped inside Maxim's, he was assaulted with a barrage to his senses that left him stunned. He had heard about the place, of course, but nothing, not even his experiences at exclusive resorts, had prepared him for the palace of whimsy and luxury that was Maxim's on New Year's Eve. He followed Profitt and the two women up a grand staircase of gold, carpeted in soft red. The mirrored walls pulsated with light and gilt and the decor was alive with the voluptuous images of nature – painted vines curling up the glass ceiling, sconces shaped like rose petals, metal railings twisting across balconies like wild rose briers. And the smells and sounds! The air was heavy with scent, sandalwood, patchouli and other sultry aromas and the silvery mewing of violins provided an undercurrent for the flow of laughter and the soft pop of champagne corks. Elegant men glided by with fantastic women on their arms, women in shimmering silks and jewels, with flowers and plumes in their hair.

Jonathan stood speechless. Everywhere he looked, he could see himself, reflected back a dozen times in the mirrored walls – a bewildered, bedazzled young man in a plain black suit surrounded by a kaleidoscope of colour.

'Jonathan, this way.' Profitt grabbed his arm. As they made their way across the main dining salon, Profitt stopped often to greet people, bestowing kisses on women's cheeks, claps on men's backs. Finally, they came to a private dining room, filled with small tables draped with heavy white linen and set with small shaded lamps. It was crowded with more celebrants, who pulled Profitt and the two women eagerly into their embrace.

162

Profitt kept a firm grip on Jonathan's arm. 'Sit at my table,' he said, indicating the spot to his right on the banquette. The brunette sat on Profitt's left. The red-haired woman slipped into the seat near Jonathan and he turned to her. She was wearing a black velvet gown with a plunging neckline and an impressive diamond choker; unveiled, she was, as he had imagined, quite striking.

'I am Hélène,' she said, smiling coyly and entwining her arm through Jonathan's. 'Why don't we get some champagne, hmm?'

Jonathan stared into her blue eyes, wondering suddenly if she were a prostitute, positive that she knew he was an impostor among all these rich men. But what did it matter? Tonight, he thought, I am at Maxim's, a guest at Alexander Profitt's table. It is New Year's Eve, and I am going to celebrate! He caught the eye of a waiter. '*M'sieur,*' he called out boldly, '*champagne pour mademoiselle, s'il vous plaît!*'

The waiter nodded respectfully and brought a bottle, presenting the label for Jonathan to examine as Hélène laughed and snuggled closer.

The evening flew by in a blur of wine, food and laughter. Jonathan sat quietly for the most part, enjoying Hélène's attention and observing the party through a sweet haze of champagne. He watched Profitt moving among the others, amazed at the man's capacity for drink and revelry, and taken aback by his larger-than-life vitality.

Finally, Profitt came back and sat down. 'Well, are you enjoying yourself?' he asked, smiling.

'Yes, sir. Immensely.' He felt slightly drunk.

'Splendid!' Profitt poured more champagne for himself and for Jonathan. 'I like my friends to enjoy themselves!'

Friend? Jonathan picked up his glass and looked

directly at Profitt. 'You consider me a friend?' he asked, smiling. 'You haven't spoken a word to me since we were in Beaulieu more than a year ago.'

Profitt leaned back in the banquette, considering Jonathan with a small smile on his lips. Jonathan's smile faded as he realized the arrogance of his words. 'Forgive me,' he said, setting down his glass. 'The wine has apparently given me too much courage.'

Profitt continued to stare at him, smiling. 'Yes, I'd say so.' He paused. 'You're not afraid of me, are you, Jonathan?'

Jonathan looked into Profitt's dark eyes. 'Should I be?'

Profitt took a gulp of champagne. 'All my other men are. It's considered the prudent course.' He raised his glass again, draining it. 'I'm tired of prudent men, Jonathan. I admire men of courage, men who show that they are willing to risk the consequences.' He smiled. 'Your dispatches as a correspondent, for instance – your sense of disdain, your irony was exquisite. And that letter you sent me . . . quite remarkable.'

Jonathan took a deep breath. 'I have ideas, Mr Profitt, ways to make the *Herald* a better newspaper.'

Profitt took a drink. 'Yes, that one about sending the paper out to incoming steamships by tugboat is good, very good. We tried it with the *Bretagne* before it docked, you know. The passengers nearly rioted trying to get their hands on a copy. Being without news for a week during the crossing does that to a man.'

Jonathan grinned as he picked up his glass to drink.

'But some of your other notions,' Profitt went on, 'well, they're a little naïve.'

Jonathan set down his glass carefully. 'Naïve?'

'Like your suggestion that we cut down on our coverage of monarchs and royalty. I believe you said "in these modern times, it seems a waste of precious columns to write about such frivolous people".' Profitt was looking straight at him now. 'You're wrong, Jonathan. You will learn that Europe is a different place from America. Here, kings, czars and princes still hold sway. We don't consider them frivolous.'

Jonathan looked away, embarrassed, as Profitt finished off his glass. 'You know, Jonathan,' he said quietly, 'sending that letter was foolish. I should have fired you.'

Jonathan sat silent.

'But it was also an act of great courage,' Profitt said. His smile widened. 'I think, Jonathan, that you have genuine courage – but we need to put it to a real test.'

He rose suddenly and went to a nearby table, bending low to talk to another man, who laughed heartily while the others buzzed in excitement. Profitt raised his arms and pleaded for everyone to be quiet. After a moment, the music stopped and everyone looked up expectantly.

Profitt surveyed the room, smiling. 'My friends! Mr Childers has issued a challenge that I cannot refuse – a coaching contest, from the Place de la Concorde to the Arc and back!'

The room erupted with shouts and laughter. Everyone began to move towards the door, and Profitt came back and stood over Jonathan. 'I'd like you to ride with me,' he said.

Jonathan looked up at Profitt towering over him, grinning. There was the challenge, right there in his glittering dark eyes. He knew that he could not refuse. 'I'd be honoured,' he answered.

Soon after, everyone was gathered near the obelisk in the Place de la Concorde, a drunken party holding champagne bottles and cheering on the four men. It was snowing lightly and there were many people out in the streets. The curious crowded around, watching as the two carriages were positioned side by side. Profitt climbed atop the driver's seat, stumbling once; after a moment's hesitation, Jonathan climbed up and sat beside him. The horses, made fretful by the revellers, reared slightly, their breath making clouds in the still, cold air. Jonathan pulled up his coat collar and shivered, as much from apprehension as the cold. Surely Profitt was too drunk to handle the carriage?

A man stood before them holding a red silk scarf. The horses pawed the ground; Profitt threw his cape over his shoulder and picked up a whip, gripping the reins in his other hand. Jonathan wiped the snow from his eyes and glanced at the two men in the other carriage. 'What should I do?' he asked Profitt.

The red scarf waved. 'Hold on!' Profitt called out.

The carriage took off with a violent jolt that nearly threw Jonathan off the seat. Recovering, he gripped the small handrail as the two carriages raced out of the square and down the Champs-Elysées. The avenue was broad but dotted with other carriages and pedestrians, and Profitt steered among them, urging the black horses on with his whip.

Jonathan held on for his life, his heart pounding. The world whirred by in a blur of motion, broken only by the flash of a terrified pedestrian's face or the dark outline of a dodged wagon. The carriages raced down the avenue, barely slowing to make the turn around the Arc de Triomphe, and started back at breakneck speed. Slowly, Jonathan's fear eased and a giddy exhilaration took its place. His pulse was racing and his eyes and face burned from the stinging snow and wind. He glanced at Profitt, who was half standing, laughing and cracking the whip, his black and red cape swirling behind him. Jonathan stole a look at the other carriage, which was inching ahead as they neared the Place de la Concorde.

'He's beating us!' Jonathan cried out.

'Never!' Profitt yelled back. He brought the whip

down sharply and the horses gave a final surge. The carriages careered down the avenue, with Profitt crossing into the square just ahead of the other carriage, letting out a joyous whoop of laughter. In the next split second, a figure appeared in the street in front of them – Profitt jerked the reins and the carriage spun to the left, just missing the man. The carriage grazed a lamppost with a savage jolt and Jonathan was lifted into the air, landing hard on the street. For a moment, everything was black.

When he regained consciousness he looked around and immediately saw the overturned carriage. The horses were standing, unharmed, but there was no sign of Profitt. Jonathan struggled to his feet and ran to the carriage.

Profitt was sprawled on the ground, unconscious. Jonathan dropped to his knees. There was a deep gash on his forehead and a rivulet of blood stained his white collar and tie. The others, who had witnessed the accident from across the square, formed a circle around them, speechless with shock and fear.

'Mr Profitt,' Jonathan said urgently. He gave his cheek a sharp slap, and Profitt's eyes fluttered open; he frowned slightly, then grimaced, his fingers touching the cut on his forehead. 'Are you all right, sir?' Jonathan said.

'Yes . . . yes . . .' Profitt sat up and looked around and then back at Jonathan. 'Did we win?'

'Yes, I believe we did, sir.'

Profitt's face creased into a smile, then he roared with laughter. Jonathan helped him to his feet and he turned to Childers, who had been standing by, his face stricken. 'Childers, my good man,' Profitt said, 'you owe me ten thousand francs!' The others burst out laughing; Jonathan was pushed aside, and he stood watching Profitt in the centre of it all, glorying in the attention.

Suddenly, a great noise arose, as if from out of the thin, cold air: cheering, the banging of pots and pans, firecrackers. The bells of La Madeleine began to ring, and soon all the other churches in the city joined in the cacophony. It was midnight. The new year. The new century!

For a moment, everyone was motionless, listening; then there was a frenzy of laughter, kissing and embracing. Jonathan stood slightly apart from the others, watching. He shivered, suddenly aware of the cold. Feeling an arm weave through his, he turned to see Hélène, who reached up and took his face in her gloved hands, kissing him on the lips. '*Bonne année, cheri*,' she murmured.

A second later, he felt an arm around his shoulders and turned to see Profitt smiling broadly, brandishing a bottle of champagne. With a deferential smile, Hélène moved aside.

'Happy New Year, Jonathan,' he said, and held out the champagne.

Jonathan stared at Profitt, at his splendid face streaked with blood, and into his eyes, glittering with a seductive black fire.

'It's a new era, my friend,' Profitt said softly. 'And a new beginning for you.'

His eyes still locked on Profitt's, Jonathan took the bottle, tipped it to his lips and closed his eyes as the golden liquid burned down his throat. 'Thank you, Mr Profitt,' he said.

Profitt smiled. 'It's Alexander,' he said. 'From now on, call me Alexander.'

Chapter Fourteen

The final notes of Debussy's music floated through the theatre followed by a wave of applause. As the curtain came down, the crowd rustled to life. Jonathan followed Alexander and Oliver Thayer through the lobby and out into the cool night air.

'Well, Oliver, what did you think?' Alexander asked as they started down the boulevard.

'Romantic rubbish,' the art critic said with a sniff.

'And you, Jonathan?' Alexander said. 'What did you think of *Pelléas et Mélisande*?'

Jonathan pulled on his white gloves thoughtfully. 'I liked it. It was . . . romantic, but not sentimental, like Wagner.'

'You're developing a discriminating ear,' Alexander said.

'Only because you've given me the opportunity, Alexander. Thank you again for inviting me to sit in your box.'

'It's all part of the educational process,' Alexander said, waving a hand in dismissal.

They walked on, with a relaxed sense of purpose born of routine. That was what it had become for the three men in recent months: a routine. Alexander and Oliver had been attending opening night of the opera together for years. One evening, Alexander had invited Jonathan to join them, and Jonathan soon found himself a regular member of their exclusive little fraternity.

As they turned up Rue Laffitte, Oliver launched into a droning critique of the opera, which Alexander finally interrupted with a sharp little laugh. 'Oliver, you're such a bore!' he said. 'You have such disdain for the new! Anyone can see just by looking at you that your taste is all in your mouth!'

The critic's face reddened slightly at the reference to his weight, but he did not look at Alexander. 'As I was saying,' he began again, in a low voice.

Jonathan walked on silently, his eyes downcast. He felt the familiar wave of discomfort and he hoped the evening was not going to take a bad turn, as it sometimes did. He had learned never to know what to expect between Alexander and Oliver. Some nights they were cordial; but on other nights, there was an unpleasant tension between them. In the office he had seen Alexander arbitrarily change Oliver's copy; at social affairs, he had watched as Alexander, after too many drinks, made some cruel quip about 'his esteemed critic'. Oliver took all these slights calmly, presenting a publicly stoic face in which could be read the condescending message: 'We must forgive Alexander when he's had too much wine.' It was obvious Alexander held Oliver, as his social inferior, in some contempt; it was obvious too that Oliver resented Alexander's refusal to acknowledge him as an equal. Yet something held these two men together. What in the world, Jonathan wondered, could it be?

Finally Harry Parkyn, who knew where all the *Herald*'s skeletons were buried, provided the answer. He explained to Jonathan that when Alexander first came to Paris with the idea to start an expatriate newspaper, he had lacked the necessary capital and been forced to find investors. Oliver Thayer's father – a British entrepreneur with social ambitions – had offered money on condition that his son be given a position as the arts critic. Gradually, Alexander had been able to buy out his other partners, but Oliver, whose father had since died, refused to sell back to Alexander the interest he had inherited.

Jonathan glanced over at Alexander, who was now heatedly debating the opera's merits with Oliver, and remembered Alexander's remark about Oliver that night in the carriage on the way to Maxim's: 'He works for me. I control him.' But that wasn't entirely true. Oliver Thayer controlled a sizeable piece of the most important thing in Alexander's life – the *Herald*. Thus the unseemly alliance between the elegant Alexander Profitt and the disagreeable Oliver Thayer was forged. Through his association with Alexander, Oliver had become a member of Paris' social elite, *le gratin*, and Alexander had gained back a certain control over Oliver, knowing that a wise man held his friends close and his enemies even closer.

Jonathan often wondered about his own role in the alliance. He sometimes thought that Alexander had brought him in simply as a buffer. At times he felt used, but he couldn't bring himself to tell Alexander that. Not after everything Alexander had done for him.

As the three men walked on, the opera debate raged on; as Alexander's opinions grew more vociferous, he shifted into French, which Oliver took up without missing a word. Occasionally Jonathan was able to catch the conversational drift, but as it floated maddeningly away he sighed in frustration. Finally he gave up listening and lost himself in his own thoughts. The French would come, he knew. He was getting better at it every day, thanks largely to the tutor Alexander had hired for him. The tutor, the trips to the opera and the museums – it was all part of what Alexander called 'the educational process', which had started on New Year's

Eve well over a year ago. The week after that, Jonathan had been given a substantial raise in salary. His biggest assignment came when Queen Victoria died and he went to England to cover the state funeral and the coronation of King Edward. His stories were so far superior to those carried by other newspapers around the world that Alexander gave him carte blanche to cover whatever he wanted.

Alexander's support also extended into Jonathan's private life. Jonathan had become a regular dinner guest at Alexander's apartment and at his lodge in Versailles. At first, he had expected to be ignored by Alexander's friends, just as he had been aboard the *Lysistrata* – but he had been accepted, especially by the women. For the first time, the women he had admired for so long from afar were actively seeking his attention. Four months ago he had begun to call on a young American socialite, Lucille Wendall, whom he had met at one of Alexander's dinner parties.

Lucy . . . lovely Lucy. The daughter of a prominent New York banker, she was eighteen, tall, beautiful – and brunette, her shining hair the colour of the last leaves of autumn, wet with rain. She was sophisticated, with a quiet dignity, and he had pursued her carefully, within the dictates of social convention. He knew he couldn't treat her like any other woman he had ever met. She was not an ordinary woman; she was something refined and remote, like those young goddesses who had first bewitched him in college.

As he walked along the street, Jonathan's eye strayed to a shop window and he caught his reflection – or rather a fleeting glimpse of a tall figure in top hat and cape. It still unnerved him, seeing this elegant man in the glass. He saw, staring back at him, a man who would not now be out of place on a tennis court in Ithaca, a ballroom in Saratoga Springs or a salon in New York. Under

Alexander's tutelage, Jonathan had learned about clothing – how to buy it and, more important, how to wear it with confidence. Alexander had also helped Jonathan secure an apartment in a prime neighbourhood; it was nothing as grand as No. 82 Champs-Elysées, the ornate white building where Profitt lived, being a humble apartment on the nearby Rue Washington. But with its four well-furnished rooms, electric lights and steam-heated running water, Jonathan thought it was spectacular.

Clothes, wine, food, fascinating work that brought him a small amount of prestige, a finer home than he had ever known – not to mention Lucy's affection – he had it all, simply because Alexander Profitt had decreed it. The quick events of the last two years had left Jonathan breathless. He had moved from Alexander's employee to friend, and now it was clear to those at the *Herald*, and in Paris' social circles, that Alexander Profitt had become Jonathan Caras's patron.

Jonathan pulled his scarf tighter and glanced over at Profitt. Scarcely a day went by when he didn't wonder why Alexander had singled him out for attention. It was obvious that the older man enjoyed his company, and Jonathan certainly had come to value his friendship, especially since the other men at work now shunned him. Only Harry had remained friendly. 'The others are jealous,' Harry told him. 'I've seen it happen before, though I've never seen Profitt take such a personal interest in a man. You might as well enjoy it while it lasts.'

Alexander came to a sudden halt. 'Look, Oliver, Gaston's gallery is still open. Let's go and see what odious things he's pawning off as art.'

Jonathan followed the other two into the Bernheim Jeune Gallery and watched the owner greet Alexander and Oliver effusively. As the two men slowly circled the room, commenting on various paintings, Jonathan trailed behind. As they approached one . particular canvas, Jonathan stopped, his eye immediately drawn to it. Oliver and Alexander, after a cursory comment, moved on, but Jonathan remained.

The painting, executed in oils, pictured a road lined with cypress trees under a night sky. The moon and stars shone with exaggerated radiance. With its swirling brush strokes and thick paint, the bold blue-and-green composition was like nothing he had ever seen in any museum. It drew him in, making him feel as if he had seen the place before, as if he had been under that same moon and trees before. Suddenly he realized what it reminded him of – the ruins at La Turbie.

Jonathan stared at the painting transfixed, unaware that Alexander and Oliver had returned to his side.

'Do you like it?' Alexander asked.

'Yes,' he said quietly. 'It has such . . . passion.' He looked down at the small card below the painting, which read: '*Road with Cypress and Stars*, Vincent van Gogh. 1890.'

Oliver heaved a great sigh, took off his pince-nez, cleaned it with a handkerchief and placed it back on his nose. 'Well, some people are wild about the man's work, but I can only laugh,' he said. 'They say he was intoxicated with colour. He must have been – because he certainly couldn't see straight enough to paint.'

Alexander turned to look at him. 'I agree with Jonathan, Oliver. It does have passion. Look at that colour.'

'Delighting in colour for the sake of colour, squeezing globules of ultramarine or vermilion on a canvas, does not make a man an artist,' Oliver said with a shrug.

'I wish I could afford to buy it,' Jonathan said.

'Well, if you must buy something, put your money in an Impressionist,' Oliver said. 'You can pick up a Renoir for a couple of thousand francs.' He started towards the door.

Jonathan glanced at Alexander, who laughed. 'Come on,' Alexander said, 'the gallery's closing. Let's go to supper.'

They were nearly out of the door when another painting caught Jonathan's eye. It was much smaller than the first one and was propped up on the floor in the corner unframed, almost hidden by several other canvases. It was a portrait, and something about it was oddly familiar. He took a step closer, then he froze.

Cendrine! It was her face. Pale skin, silvery hair, grey-blue eyes. The expression was not as he remembered; it was wrong somehow. But it was Cendrine. He knew it. He crouched down, pulled out the painting and gently brushed away the dust, his fingers lingering over the rough texture of the paint.

Alexander, by this time outside the gallery, called out his name. 'Jonathan! For heaven's sake, come along! We're famished and the man wants to close up and go home.'

Jonathan looked up into the face of the gallery owner. 'Please, m'sieur,' the old man said softly. 'It's late and my wife is impatient. Perhaps you could come back tomorrow?'

Jonathan looked out of the window at Alexander and Oliver, who were already halfway down the street. He slid the painting back in its corner, stood up and brushed the dust from his hands. With a last look at the portrait, he ran to catch up.

The next morning, Jonathan was standing outside the gallery before the owner appeared. He waited impatiently as the man unlocked the door, then dashed in, going straight to the portrait, holding it up and tilting it to get the force of the morning light.

'Where did you get this?' he asked the owner.

The owner shrugged sleepily. 'I don't remember. I've had it for a long time.'

Jonathan glanced at the name in the right lower corner: M. Derval. 'Who is the artist? Where can I find him?' he asked.

'I have never met him. I bought it through a friend at the art school.'

'I have to have it,' Jonathan said urgently. 'How much is it?'

The gallery owner's eyes widened in surprise, then narrowed quickly as he calculated an easy sale from the crazy American. 'I'll let it go for five hundred francs.'

Jonathan knew it was too much, but he didn't care. He withdrew his purse and quickly counted out the money. 'Now tell me how to get to the art school,' he said.

At l'Ecole des Beaux Arts, it took Jonathan a while to elicit the necessary information from the instructor who had sold the painting to the gallery owner; he was leading a class and tried to brush Jonathan aside. But Jonathan would not be deterred. 'Just tell me where I can find this artist Derval,' he said.

'I don't know a M'sieur Derval. Look, I'm busy. Maybe if you come back tomorrow when the *massier* is here – he knows all the students.'

The man started to walk away, but Jonathan grabbed his arm. 'I must find the artist!' he demanded. Several students looked up from their easels, and Jonathan released the man's arm. 'Listen, if you don't know the artist, maybe you know the girl who modelled for the painting.'

Jonathan tore the brown paper off the canvas and the man's eyes softened as they travelled across the portrait. 'Oh, it's Cendrine,' he said. 'Not a good likeness – the mouth is wrong. But it's Cendrine.'

Jonathan's heart stopped. 'You know her?' he whispered.

176

'She modelled here at the school.'

'*Here*? She's here?' Jonathan's eyes swept the room.

The man shook his head. 'She's been gone several years. I don't know where she went. I heard a rumour that she got married and moved to America.' With a shrug, the instructor turned back to his students.

Jonathan stood, momentarily dazed. Then he glanced around the room, at the curious faces, and finally up at the nude woman standing on the platform in the centre of the room. Clutching the portrait, he turned slowly and left the studio.

He went directly back to his apartment and stood in the middle of the small parlour, holding the portrait. Eventually, he slid it behind a bureau and, without taking off his coat, slumped into a chair, sitting there unmoving, staring at the far wall.

After an hour, he rose slowly and went to the bureau; pulling out the canvas, he turned it around and stared at the face. The instructor was right; it was a poor likeness, inexpertly rendered. But it was Cendrine.

He looked up, surveying the small room, then went to the fireplace and removed a gold-framed hunting print from above the mantel, placing the unframed canvas in its place. He stepped back to look at it, surprised by how deeply the picture moved him. During the last year, he had not given Cendrine much thought: true, she had occasionally floated into his mind as a sweet remembrance but, for the most part, he had succeeded in suppressing his obsessive memories of their night together.

At least, he had until he saw the painting. Now she was with him again, as surely as if she were in the room. He could smell her, taste her, touch her. And he knew he wanted her just as much as he had the first time he saw her.

He braced himself against the mantel and leaned in

177

towards the portrait, staring at the tricks of pink, grey and blue oils that composed Cendrine's likeness.

'Where are you?' he whispered.

Two weeks later, Jonathan received an invitation to stay at Alexander's lodge in Versailles. Having packed his bags he waited, as usual, for Alexander's coachman to pick him up, but when the bell rang he was surprised to open his door and see Oliver Thayer.

'Oliver, what are you doing here?' Jonathan said. 'I thought you were going to London.'

Oliver shrugged. 'The weather's dreadful, and I can't abide the sea crossing. So I decided to ride along with you to Alexander's for the weekend.' He paused. 'May I come in?'

'Oh, of course. Forgive me.' Jonathan stood aside and Oliver came into the apartment, his eyes wandering over the furnishings. 'Make yourself comfortable,' Jonathan said. 'I'll fetch my luggage.'

When he returned from the bedroom, Oliver was standing at the fireplace, staring at the portrait of Cendrine. Thayer turned and smiled slightly. 'What a charming little place you have here, Jonathan,' he said. 'Did Alexander help you find it?'

'Yes,' Jonathan said. 'He's been a great help to me. Like a good friend. Or an older brother.'

Oliver cocked an eyebrow. 'Yes, I dare say.' He walked slowly around the room, his fingers grazing the curved back of the sofa and the draperies. 'You know, Jonathan,' Oliver began, 'I'm rather glad we'll have this chance to drive to Versailles together. It will give us the chance to get to know each other better.' He picked up a book, examined its title and set it down again. 'I admire your writing. It is the writing of an intelligent man . . . a man seeking his voice. I have a feeling we could become quite good friends.'

Jonathan was unsure what to say. He couldn't see himself getting close to Oliver. 'I'd like that,' he said.

'Where did you get this?' Oliver asked, flicking a hand towards the painting.

Jonathan hesitated. 'At some little gallery near the art school.' He crossed to Oliver's side, a sudden question filling his mind. 'Have you heard of the artist?' he asked.

Oliver brought up his glasses to examine the name, then shook his head. 'I hope you didn't pay much for it – it's not very good. What in the world made you buy it?'

Jonathan looked at the painting. 'The woman reminds me of someone I once knew,' he said. He stared at the painting a moment longer, then turned his attention back to Oliver. 'We'd better get going.'

He went to the door, opened it and picked up his bags. Oliver studied the painting for a while longer, then finally came to the door. 'It's a strange painting,' he said. 'I can't decide if she's happy or sad.'

Jonathan glanced back into the apartment. 'Happy,' he said softly, as he shut the door. 'I always think of her as happy.'

Villa Vignon sprawled over forty wooded acres just outside the village of Versailles. The chateau itself was spacious enough to accommodate thirty guests – and the fifteen cats that Alexander kept in residence there. Alexander had scheduled a flurry of activities to entertain his twenty guests during the week, with a cotillion planned for the weekend. Jonathan knew many of the other guests, but he spent most of his time with Lucy, who was also staying at Vignon with her aunt.

During the week, Jonathan and Lucy strolled through the gardens and visited the cathedral in the old town. As for the more strenuous activities – cycling, lawn tennis or shooting – Lucy was content simply to sit, carefully coiffed and dressed, and watch Jonathan. He was amazed to note she changed her outfits five, sometimes six, times during one day.

For the cotillion, she appeared in a magnificent gown of pale-blue silk and Argentan lace by the house of Worth, her lush hair upswept and decorated with pink tea roses, which had to be replaced every hour in order to look fresh. She was the most beautiful woman at the party – and she knew it. Her dance card was filled.

Finally, when she floated into Jonathan's arms, she was beaming. 'I was beginning to think you had forgotten about me,' she said, smiling coquettishly.

'I haven't been able to get near you,' Jonathan replied.

'I'm simply trying to make you jealous,' she said. 'All week, you've been so . . . so preoccupied.'

He looked at her in surprise. 'I'm sorry, Lucy, I didn't realize.'

She smiled and pressed her cool cheek against his. 'I've scratched out the rest of my card,' she murmured. 'For the rest of the night, I'm yours.'

As he guided her across the floor, Jonathan pondered her observation. It was true that he had been feeling distracted all week; it was the painting of Cendrine. Its presence in his apartment had thrust him back to another place and another time and he was flooded with memories of her. Being with Lucy all week had simply made his yearning for Cendrine all the more intense. It was irrational, he knew, but the painting had become an obsession. He was obsessed with a woman who, for him at least, no longer existed.

The music ended, and he guided Lucy to the perimeter of the room. Before they had a chance to speak, Alexander appeared in the centre of the ballroom and announced a change in the entertainment. Servants wove through the murmuring crowd, handing out small fencing foils, each fitted at the tip with a huge powderpuff.

'And now, a contest!' Alexander proclaimed, brandishing a glass of champagne. 'Every young lady will fight a duel with the gentleman who is next on her dance card!'

There was a flurry of excitement and giggles as the men and women paired off. A ruddy-faced young man presented himself before Lucy; before she could protest, he pulled her onto the dance floor and assumed an exaggerated *en garde* position. Jonathan watched as Lucy, looking very uncomfortable, raised her foil and poked it towards the man tentatively. Soon, the room was awash in rollicking laughter as the mock duels progressed. The men's faces grew redder; several of the women got into the spirit by lifting their hems and lunging gracefully, the powderpuffs bouncing harmlessly off the starched white bibs of the men's shirts.

Jonathan watched the duellists, a small smile tipping his lips. 'This is inspired, Alexander!' he said when Profitt arrived at his side.

'I had to do something to loosen things up,' Alexander said, finishing his drink.

Jonathan's eyes drifted back to Lucy, who cast him a pained smile as she deflected the young man's thrust. 'Perhaps I should go and rescue Lucy.'

'No! That's exactly what she wants you to do.' Alexander took two glasses of champagne from a waiter and handed one to Jonathan. 'You know, she's becoming very fond of you.'

Jonathan glanced at him but said nothing.

'Her mother sent her to Europe to find a husband. One with a title,' Alexander said.

'Maybe you could promote me to editor,' Jonathan joked.

'I don't think that's the kind of title that would interest Mrs Wendall,' Alexander said wryly.

'Her parents are coming from Venice next month to

take Lucy home,' Jonathan said quietly. 'She wants me to meet them.'

Alexander laughed. 'So that's what's been bothering you! You're worried that they'll find you inappropriate. It wouldn't do for pedigreed Lucy to bring home a stray.'

Jonathan turned to glare at Alexander, but his anger evaporated when he saw Alexander's drunken, but nonetheless genuinely sympathetic, smile.

'My dear Jonathan,' Alexander said, 'you're a better man than anyone in this room. So don't let the opinions of snobs bother you.' His smile softened. 'You know I'll do anything to help you, even if it means courting the insufferable Wendalls to vouch for your honour. Just don't let it bother you. While you're under my roof, I want you to be happy!'

Jonathan nodded. He took a drink of champagne and looked back out at the dance floor; Lucy had given up the duel and was coming towards him. Suddenly he saw Cendrine's face; he blinked rapidly and the image disappeared.

'Jonathan . . .' Alexander's velvet voice, fruity with the smell of wine, was close. 'Promise you'll be happy?'

'I promise, Alexander,' Jonathan murmured.

Jonathan flipped idly through the programme, then swivelled around in his front-row seat, scanning the audience.

'You're restless. Aren't you enjoying the show?'

Jonathan turned to Oliver. 'Yes,' he said, 'but I don't see why you dragged me away from Lucy's party to come here tonight.'

'The glorious Miss Wendall is a spoiled debutante. You mustn't let her exert too much power over you, dear boy. Besides, I thought you'd enjoy the Folies.'

'I didn't think you liked dance-hall entertainment. Oliver,' Jonathan said distractedly.

'Normally, I don't. But as I told you, this next act . . .

well, I think you'll find it quite extraordinary.'

Jonathan was about to consult his programme, for details, but as the lights dimmed and the music began, he turned his attention to the stage.

A backdrop was painted to resemble a blue, cloud-filled sky; projectors cast gold light upward across the stage. A gentle ripple of music rose from the pit as a woman in white stepped on stage, arms held in a graceful oval above her head, the silk folds of her sleeves concealing her face. She faced the audience and slowly unfolded her arms. Jonathan's heart stopped as Cendrine began to move. He watched as she swept through the shafts of light, a flower floating in the breeze. His head buzzed with faraway sounds, and his heart began to beat fast, ever faster, filling his throat with its pounding. Eight minutes passed, a suspended eternity. And then, suddenly, her act completed, the stage went dark and she disappeared.

A tumultuous roar brought Jonathan back to his senses. He became aware of a dull ache in his right hand and looked down to see the white ridges of his knuckles gripping the now crumpled programme.

'Jonathan? *Jonathan*?'

He drew in a quick, shallow breath, blinking his eyes, and turned towards Oliver, whose small mouth was turned up in an odd little smile. 'Are you all right?' Oliver asked.

Jonathan managed to nod. He looked towards the stage. The curtain had come down and the audience were streaming up the aisles.

'You look like you could use some air,' Oliver said.

Outside, in the cold December night, Oliver paused, watching the dispersing crowd, as Jonathan stood numbly, still too stunned to move.

'It's her, isn't it?' Oliver said. 'The woman in the painting.'

Jonathan stared at him. 'How did you know?'

'I wasn't sure,' Oliver said with a shrug. 'But from your reaction, I guessed my suspicions were correct.'

Jonathan glanced back at the theatre. The lights of the marquee blinked off.

'You know her, don't you,' Oliver said.

'I did . . . once,' Jonathan replied softly.

Thayer considered him thoughtfully. 'Well, we'd better get back to Lucy's party.' He raised his arm to signal a passing hansom cab, humming a tune from the show. When the cab pulled up, Oliver got in, but Jonathan hesitated.

'Oliver—' he began.

Oliver smiled. Reaching over, he pulled the cab door shut. 'I'll tell Miss Wendall you've fallen ill,' he said.

Jonathan thrust his hand through the window. 'Oliver . . .' he began, 'thank you.'

Oliver stared at Jonathan's hand for a moment, then took it in a limp handshake. 'The pleasure is mine, dear boy.'

As soon as the cab pulled away, Jonathan walked quickly around the building to an alleyway, where several young men were lingering around the stage door, stamping their feet against the cold. Jonathan waited with them impatiently. Other women emerged, but after forty-five minutes, Cendrine still had not appeared. Afraid he had missed her, Jonathan went back to the front of the theatre – but it was dark and locked. When he returned to the stage door, the other men were gone and he slipped inside.

He found the warren of dressing rooms, but each one he entered was empty. Finally he saw a light coming from a room at the end of a corridor and went quickly towards it. A soft, feminine voice floated out to him. Cendrine's voice.

Her voice was followed by a man's low tones that

caused Jonathan to stop short outside the open door and withdraw into the shadows, his heart hammering. Then, taking a deep breath, he presented himself square in the light.

Cendrine was seated before a mirror, dressed in red taffeta, her pale hair upswept. The man was standing behind her, fastening a necklace against the white skin of her neck, then bending low to murmur something, his silvery moustache grazing her ear. She smiled, a small smile of indecision, and touched the necklace tentatively. She turned to look up at the man, but glimpsed Jonathan standing in the doorway and froze.

For a moment, her expression was puzzled. Then her eyes widened and her hand moved to her throat as the colour drained from her face.

The silver-haired gentleman, seeing the shock in her eyes, glanced up, his face making a quick journey from surprise to irritation. 'Sir, you must have lost your way,' he said imperiously.

Jonathan didn't even look at the man. He saw only Cendrine's face, staring at him; in the three-panelled mirror behind her, her profile was reflected back to him countless times. He felt a sting of tears in his eyes.

'Cendrine,' he said, 'it's me. Jonathan.'

Chapter Fifteen

Cendrine rose slowly, her eyes locked on Jonathan's face. She extended one hand towards the table to steady herself, and the silver-haired man put a hand on her waist to help her.

'My dear, what is it?' he asked.

She stared dumbly at Jonathan until, exasperated, the man turned to Jonathan with a scowl. 'See here, young man,' he said firmly, 'I don't know what your business is here, but you've obviously upset Mademoiselle—'

'It's all right, Georges,' Cendrine said softly. 'I know him.'

The man's gaze travelled slowly from the stranger standing at the door to Cendrine. He could see in her face something more than simple shock; she looked as if a light had come on inside her. His hand fell from her waist.

Cendrine turned to him. 'Georges, I . . .' she began.

He retrieved his top hat and cape from a nearby chair, and bent over to kiss Cendrine on the cheek. 'Perhaps I should go. I'll see you tomorrow evening,' he said. With a final hard look at Jonathan, he left the dressing room.

For a long time, it was quiet. Finally, Cendrine glanced away, nervously smoothing the folds of her red gown, and when she looked back at Jonathan, she wore a new expression – one of wariness. 'How did you know I was here?' she asked softly.

'I didn't,' Jonathan said, his throat suddenly parched. 'I didn't even know you were in Paris until tonight.'

There was another long silence. Jonathan had a sudden vision of Cendrine lying on the stone in the moonlight; he wanted simply to take her in his arms. But her grey-blue eyes were like a barrier.

'You were so beautiful tonight,' he said. 'When you danced.'

'Thank you,' she said, raising her chin slightly. Then she folded her arms. As if she is trying to distance herself from me, Jonathan thought. How stupid, to think I could just barge in here like this, expecting everything to be the same!

He took two steps towards her. 'Cendrine,' he said softly, 'I never thought I'd see you again.'

'It's been a long time,' she said slowly. 'Four years . . . five years?'

She was staring at him intently, as if waiting for him to say something, but his mind was a mad tangle of emotions, and he didn't know where to begin. Another image flashed into his head: Cendrine walking barefoot across the grass. What in the world could he say to her? Five years ago, she had been a simple village girl. Now she was standing here before him, a dazzling woman in an elegant red dress and a ruby necklace. She was the same Cendrine – his heart ached at the very sight of her – but she was also fundamentally different. She was no longer a *villageoise* and he certainly couldn't treat her like one. He realized suddenly that he would have to begin again, as if their one night together had never happened.

'Would you . . .' he said softly, his voice faltering, 'would you do me the honour of dining with me tonight?'

It was a moment before she answered. 'All right,' she said, her voice giving nothing away. He watched as she slowly pulled on her long black gloves, then handed him a heavy black velvet cape with a fur collar. When he placed it over her shoulders the spicy warm aroma of her perfume made him close his eyes. Without a word, she walked ahead of him out of the dressing room.

They said nothing to each other during the short ride to the Café de Paris, the landmark restaurant that was a favourite of the after-theatre crowd. Jonathan followed Cendrine through the crowded main salon, thankful that he had listened to Alexander's advice to cultivate at least one maitre d' in Paris; he wanted very much to impress Cendrine. They were led to one of the elegant private rooms and her eyes swept over the room, with what seemed to Jonathan a feigned nonchalance.

'Have you ever been here?' he asked.

'Of course. Many times,' she said quickly.

As Jonathan ordered, Cendrine watched him carefully out of the corner of her eye. 'Your French has improved,' she said.

'I've had a good teacher,' he replied. He was staring at her, unable to help himself as he hungrily took in every detail of her appearance: her silver-blonde hair, swept up in an elaborate hairdo and adorned with a black egret plume that curved down towards her neck; the fine ridge of her collarbone, exposed by the décolletage of the gown; the soft, shifting shadows created by the play of light across her bosom as she breathed.

'So what is it you do here in Paris?' she asked.

The coolness in her voice was like a splash of water, bringing him back to earth. 'I'm a writer for the *Herald*,' he said. Her gaze remained impassive, so he added, 'You remember the man with the yacht? He is the owner and a friend of mine.'

'How nice for you,' she said distantly, and picked up the champagne glass. Jonathan watched her, mesmerized by the subtle rippling motions in her neck as she drank. She lowered the glass and ran the tip of her tongue over the full pink pillow of her upper lip. It was a guileless gesture, but he felt himself growing hard with arousal, and he quickly looked away.

'What do you write about?' she asked.

He looked back at her, trying to get himself under control. How in the world was he going to get through the evening? For him, it was as if the last five years had magically vanished; she had never really been out of his life. But for her, the lost time was irrelevant. She had obviously forgotten about him. 'I write—' He stopped. 'No,' he said, 'I want to hear about you.'

For the first time, she smiled. 'I am a dancer,' she said.

A smile came slowly to his lips. 'You told me you would be a ballet dancer, and you did it!'

He saw her smile fade slightly, but she quickly covered it with a light laugh. 'I am La Phalare,' she said, leaning back on the banquette in a provocative pose. 'I'm quite famous, you know. Everyone – princes, kings, tourists – everyone who comes to Paris comes to see La Phalare. King Leopold himself once came backstage to tell me how much he adored La Phalare.'

Jonathan watched her carefully. Her gaiety, her suddenly seductive manner, had a touching bravado to it; he could glimpse beneath her veneer of sophistication the young girl standing in the sunlight, moving to the piano music. He focused on a silky filament of her hair that had escaped its pins and fallen over her temple. Very slowly, he raised a hand to touch it.

At that moment, a small army of waiters appeared and Jonathan pulled back. The waiters began to deposit silver dishes before them with a theatrical flourish that made Cendrine smile.

'I can't eat all this,' she said.

'I didn't know what you liked, so I ordered everything,' Jonathan said with an embarrassed laugh.

189

When the waiters had left, he pushed his own plate aside. 'Tell me more,' he said softly.

So she did. Over the next two hours, she told him about how she had come to Paris, about the modelling job, and about the Folies-Bergère. Helped along by the champagne, she seemed to relax, and she even asked him questions about his own work. But her demeanour remained distant, and Jonathan noticed that not once had she even said his name. His thoughts turned to the silver-haired man in the dressing room; he suddenly wondered if Cendrine was romantically involved with him. Of course, that was it! Cendrine was the man's mistress, and she had agreed to come to this dinner only as a polite gesture.

The thought distressed him immeasurably and he stared at her, his heart sinking. God, how stupid I am! he thought. Her life has not stood still for four years! The one night we had together is nothing but a memory for her. I'm – *I'm* nothing but a memory for her.

'Another bottle of champagne, m'sieur?'

Jonathan looked up at the waiter. 'No,' he said quietly. 'That will be all, thank you.'

Cendrine sat silently while Jonathan signed the bill. Outside, they paused on the pavement. It was late, and the few people still on the streets hurried along to escape the cold, damp December night. Jonathan turned to Cendrine, who was gazing at him, her chin pulled down into her fur collar.

'I'll call a cab to take you home,' he said.

'No,' she said quickly. 'Could we walk for a while?'

'All right.' They turned west on the boulevard, walking without words, their shoulders barely touching.

Cendrine skidded on a patch of ice. 'Here, take my arm,' Jonathan said softly. When she slipped her arm through his, his heart jumped in his chest; but the despair remained, enhanced by his fevered imagination, which had conjured up a vision of Cendrine with the man, their bodies intertwined in bed. They walked on, heading up the broad expanse of the Boulevard Haussman and Jonathan felt Cendrine shiver.

'You're cold,' he said. 'Let me call—'

'No, I want to walk.' They went on in silence for several more blocks. Cendrine's shivering grew more pronounced, and Jonathan began to feel the cold creeping under his clothing, but he said nothing. Except for a vegetable wagon heading towards Les Halles, the streets were quiet. A fog moved in, covering the tops of buildings and streetlights, bringing with it a misty rain.

'You know,' Cendrine said suddenly, 'we talked about so much tonight. But we didn't talk about us.'

Her words were so surprising that he almost stopped. 'I didn't think you wanted to,' he said.

She made no answer, but her grip on his arm tightened. He looked over at her, but her eyes were trained straight ahead.

'I assumed . . .' he said hesitantly, 'that man in the dressing room . . . that you and he—'

'Georges is a fine gentleman,' she said quickly, and she paused. 'He is a good friend.'

The image of the ruby necklace against Cendrine's neck – vivid red against white – flashed through Jonathan's mind. He felt a piercing stab of jealousy mingle with the other emotions that Cendrine had stirred within him – the shock at seeing her again, the renewed hope, the doubt and the undercurrent of arousal.

'A friend who gives you expensive jewellery,' he murmured.

He regretted the words as soon as they were out. Cendrine pulled her arm from his and turned to face him. The pale yellow light of the streetlight made her skin look ghostly. 'How dare you?' she whispered.

'Cendrine—'

'How *dare* you?' she repeated, the words issuing forth in three white plumes in the cold air. Her eyes became fiercely bright. 'After five years . . . how dare you say that to me?'

Jonathan saw then that the brightness in her eyes was not from anger – she was trying not to cry. 'Cendrine,' he said, 'I'm sorry. I didn't mean . . .'

She was crying now, small sobs that caught in the back of her throat. Jonathan reached for her but she pulled away and covered her face.

'Why didn't you come back?' she whispered. Her words were muffled by her gloved hands, and at first Jonathan didn't understand. But then she lowered her hands and met his eyes. 'Why didn't you come back?' she repeated. 'You promised you'd come back.'

Suddenly, he understood. Five years ago, he had made a promise to her and he had broken it. Five years ago, he had taken advantage of a naïve girl, and then abandoned her: at least, that's how it had seemed to her. There was no way he could possibly explain to her what had happened. There was no way he could explain that he had never forgotten her. After what had happened, why would she believe him?

'I couldn't come back, Cendrine,' he said softly. 'I woke up and the boat was leaving . . .'

She looked away, pulling her cape tighter.

'I've never forgotten that night,' he said.

'I don't believe you,' she sobbed, blotting her eyes with her gloved hands.

Slowly, her crying lessened. When she looked back up at Jonathan, there were faint tracks down her white cheeks where her face powder had been rubbed away. Her lips were blue with cold and her hair was damp with mist, the black plume curving limply against her cheek. She was shivering violently.

Jonathan took her by the shoulders. 'Come with me,' he said.

'No,' she said tonelessly. 'Just take me home, please.'

Jonathan glanced quickly around the street, looking for a cab, but it was deserted. 'Please, Cendrine,' he said urgently, 'please come with me. There's something I have to show you.'

She closed her eyes and nodded. Jonathan took her arm and guided her quickly through the foggy streets.

By the time they reached his apartment on Rue Washington, their clothes were sodden. Cendrine's teeth were chattering, and she seemed drained of will. She allowed Jonathan to guide her into the apartment; once inside, she waited, slumped against the door, until he lit a lamp near the door. The apartment was cold and he hurried to the fireplace and quickly tossed a log into the grate. 'This will only take a moment,' he reassured her, his fingers trembling as he waited for the match to catch the kindling. 'The heating system in this building doesn't always—'

He turned to look up at Cendrine and stopped in mid-sentence. She was standing by the door, staring up at the painting above the mantel.

He rose, watching her face as she took a few steps towards the fireplace, her eyes never leaving the painting.

'That's what I wanted you to see,' he said softly.

She was standing next to him now, staring at the painting, her eyes brimming with tears. 'Oh, Jonathan,' she whispered, and turned to him. He reached up to wipe a tear off her face but her hand closed over his, their fingers intertwined. She closed her eyes, waiting for his kiss. Her lips were cold, so cold against his, and he gently kissed first one, then the other, holding them in his own, as if to warm them. Then her mouth opened, and he felt the warm, surprising flick of her tongue, which brought a moan out from deep in his throat. Her hands reached round the back of his neck and she pressed her body against his.

He pushed himself from her with great effort. 'I love you, Cendrine,' he said. 'I never stopped loving you.'

She glanced up at the portrait, then back at Jonathan, slipping off the heavy wet cape and pulling off the gloves. She reached up to take the feather and the pins out of her hair, combing her fingers through her damp locks, pulling it down over her shoulders. When she slowly turned her back to him, he realized she wanted him to unbutton the red dress. He stared at the long row of tiny buttons, hooks and bows, and had the absurd feeling that he had just been presented with a beautifully wrapped gift which he might somehow damage. Like last time, he thought crazily, remembering how brutal he had been that night in the ruins.

Jonathan threw off his own coat and jacket. Slowly, with trembling, clumsy fingers, he worked on the delicate buttons till finally the dress fell in a hush of red taffeta on the hearth. Her wet hair dripped down her bare back, dampening the white lace of her petticoat, but it was her tiny waist, constrained by the corset, that made him grow hard with desire. He hesitated, and she turned her head, a small smile on her lips.

'Untie me,' she said softly.

He reached for the laces, but his hands instead encircled her waist and he leaned his hips in to her, moving against her, burying his face in her neck. She gripped the edge of the mantel for support, arching her back toward him. Her breath became shallow. 'Untie me,' she whispered.

His fingers wrestled with the laces until she was free. Then she turned to him, bare to the waist, except for the ruby necklace. She unbuttoned his shirt; when she moved herself against him the feel of her breasts,

194

warmed by the fire, made him dizzy. The urge built inside him to take her, just as she stood there before him.

No, no . . . not like before, he thought. He took her hand and led her towards his bedroom. The room was cold, and he turned back the bed, gently guiding her down onto it. He quickly undressed, and when he turned back to the bed, he paused. A square of light, thrown off by the streetlight outside his window, illuminated her face. She was smiling.

He fitted his body next to hers and she pulled the covers over him, shivering. 'It's so cold,' she whispered.

'I'll warm you.'

He went slowly, kissing her lips and her neck, feeling her nipple grow hard beneath his tongue and her fingers pressing deeper into his back. He wanted to go slow, but suddenly, she would not let him. She raised her hips to take him in, but he pulled back.

'No, Cendrine, not yet.'

He kissed her again, travelling over her body with light brushes of his lips – her neck, her breasts, her stomach. He heard her moan lightly as he kissed the inside of her thighs, his tongue lingering in her downy blonde hair. He stopped suddenly, pushing himself up.

'Cendrine, look at me,' he said softly.

She stared up at him. 'Now, Jonathan, now . . .'

She enfolded him in her wet warmth. He felt her legs wrapped around his back, holding him, pulling him inside her, deeper and deeper. He watched her face, framed in the square of pale white light, lips parted, eyes glistening.

She cried out; a shudder went through her body and he felt a quick stab of pain, her nails raking across his buttocks. But then came nothing but a violent release, wave upon rolling wave, and he collapsed onto her, grasping her to him.

It was a while before he became aware of the cold drifting over his back, and the burning tracks left by her nails. Other sensations filtered back: a distant clatter of a wagon outside; the smell of the smouldering fire in the other room; the tickle of her lips moving against his neck.

She was saying his name over and over, so softly he could barely hear it: 'Jonathan . . . Jonathan . . . *je t'adore* . . . Jonathan.'

He raised himself up to look at her. Cendrine was smiling, her face streaked with tears. The ruby necklace lay like drops of blood against her white neck. His hand closed over the necklace, and he rolled the cold stones between his fingers. Then, with a quick tug, he pulled it off and threw it aside.

Chapter Sixteen

The train pulled into the Gare de l'Est with a piercing screech, coming to a stop with a great sigh of steam. Jonathan waited on the platform, searching the crowd of disembarking passengers. Then an excited smile spread across his face.

'Sumner! Over here!' he cried out.

Sumner spotted him and they met and embraced heartily. 'God, it's so good to see you!' Jonathan exclaimed.

'It's been too long – five years,' Sumner said, smiling broadly. His eyes travelled over Jonathan's elegant suit. 'You've changed, old man. Acquired a bit of style!'

'Just a little.' Jonathan clasped Sumner's arms, taking in Sumner's natty overcoat and smart hat. 'And you, thank God, have not changed at all!'

They embraced again, laughing. 'Well,' Sumner said, 'let's find a porter and be on our way.'

During the carriage ride to the hotel, they talked without stopping, catching up on news of each other's lives. Jonathan apologized for not writing more often, but Sumner himself had been too busy during the last two years to dash off more than the briefest note. A year ago, his father had been incapacitated by arthritis, and Sumner had taken up his role as head of the bank.

'I'm now running one of the most powerful banks in

the country . . . *noblesse oblige*,' Sumner said. The words were said with a smile, but Jonathan sensed a sad resignation in his friend's voice. 'By the way, Jonathan,' Sumner added, 'our biggest competitor is Manhattan Capital – owned by a fellow named Henry Wendall.' He smiled. 'The girl you wrote to me about some time ago – Lucy – she's his daughter, isn't she?'

'Yes,' Jonathan murmured, his thoughts focusing for a moment on the girl. He had not seen her in three months, since the day he saw her off on the train to Calais. It had been just a month after Cendrine had come back into his life, and though Jonathan had never mentioned Cendrine, Lucy had sensed that something had changed. 'Perhaps it's best I'm going home,' she told Jonathan with a smile as she kissed him goodbye. 'A man can grow tired of a woman if she's too available!' Nevertheless, she extracted a promise from Jonathan that he would write, and then she was gone.

'Well, that's quite a family tree – or should I say thicket – you've decided to climb,' Sumner said with a laugh. 'The Wendalls are a rather brittle bunch, old New York money gone to thorn and bramble. God knows, you'd provide some fresh seed.' When Jonathan didn't laugh, Sumner's face fell. 'Sorry, old man. No insult intended.'

'And none taken. To be honest, Mr and Mrs Wendall didn't exactly welcome me with open arms when I met them.'

'Well, I'm sure your Lucy will win them over on your behalf,' Sumner said. 'I'll look forward to meeting her some day.'

The carriage pulled up in front of the Ritz. 'So what time will you be back for dinner?' Sumner asked. 'I know this wonderful restaurant nearby that—'

'No,' Jonathan interrupted, 'I'm going to take you to dinner for a change. In fact, I'm going to show you a side of Paris you've never seen, old friend.'

Sumner cocked an eyebrow. 'Now what could you possibly show me? I know this city like the back of my hand!'

'So I'll show you the front,' Jonathan said, laughing. His smile lingered. 'Besides, there's someone I want you to meet.'

The curtain came down on the Folies revue and as the lights came up, Jonathan turned to Sumner. 'Well, what did you think of her?' he asked eagerly.

'She's exquisite,' Sumner whispered, 'absolutely exquisite.'

Jonathan smiled. 'I'm in love with her, Sumner.'

Sumner's mouth dropped open, but before he could say a word, Jonathan sprang to his feet. 'Come on, we'll go backstage!'

In the dressing room, Jonathan introduced his friend to Cendrine. Sumner was quiet, staring at the racks of exotic costumes and the parade of chorus girls giggling in the corridors, his eyes lingering on Cendrine, who had dressed for dinner in a gown of white satin, trimmed in black feathers. His wonder grew when he was introduced to Marcelle, who met them for dinner at the Café de Paris. But by the second bottle of champagne, Marcelle and Sumner were laughing and chatting away merrily in French.

As they left the restaurant, Sumner pulled Jonathan aside and, a little drunk, whispered, 'This Marcelle – I've never met a woman like her! She's a savage but such good fun!'

'I thought you'd enjoy her,' Jonathan said, smiling. 'And I think you'll enjoy the little tour of Paris she's arranged.'

They could not find a cab, so Marcelle announced blithely that they would go on the bus. Sumner looked sceptical, but when a small, horse-drawn omnibus pulled up, he gamely climbed up the ladder behind the others to the upper deck. The driver cracked his whip and the heavy machine rolled on towards Montmartre.

'This is the best way to see Paris on a Sunday night,' Marcelle said, taking Sumner's arm. The bus took the narrowest side streets; below them an intimate view of Paris's domestic life presented itself in a panorama of open windows, with dinner tables spread for the evening meal.

At the steep gradient leading to Montmartre, the bus paused while another horse was added. Then the laden vehicle crawled slowly up the hilly streets, past hawkers, street singers, bright restaurants and noisy cafés. Finally, the bus reached the summit, and everyone got out. Marcelle led the others down a dim street and up a long flight of steep steps, its length marked by glowing lamps. At the top, they all paused, panting.

Spread out far below was the great, shining sprawl of Paris, untold numbers of lights and lamps stretching to the horizon, where they seemed to melt into the moonlit, starry sky. All the landmarks were visible – Nôtre Dame, the opera house, the Pantheon, Les Invalides, and the thrusting frame of the Eiffel Tower, its revolving searchlight shining like a comet, its tail spreading through the night. Directly above them, a maze of rafters, beams and scaffolding fretted the sky – the skeleton of the unfinished Church of the Sacré-Coeur.

Sumner, his mouth slightly agape, turned slowly in a circle, taking in the vast, entrancing scene. 'I never . . .' he stammered. 'It's so . . .' His eyes came to rest on Cendrine, who was leaning back contentedly against Jonathan, enfolded in his arms.

'It's beautiful. That's what you're trying to say,' Jonathan said.

They stood for a moment longer, then Marcelle exclaimed, 'Enough of the view! The night is wasting away!' and pulled Sumner off towards the stairs.

Marcelle took them on a tour of all the brightest cafés; after three hours, Sumner had lost count of how many drinks he had consumed and how many places they had visited. Finally, Marcelle took them to a nondescript cabaret frequented by the famous 'poet of the gutter', Aristide Bruant. As they entered the gloomy room, Sumner's eyes widened as he saw a man standing on a table. He was slender, with black hair falling over his shoulders beneath a black slouch hat, and his trousers were tucked into his black boots.

The man glared down at Sumner and began to recite in a sonorous voice, *'Tous les clients sont des couchons . . . la faridon, la faridon donne . . .'* The audience let out a raucous howl.

'He's calling us pigs!' Sumner whispered to Marcelle indignantly.

'Bruant calls everyone a pig,' Marcelle shrugged.

They found a table and ordered beers. When they were brought, the waiter barked, 'Pay up!'

With an irate snort, Sumner quickly tossed some francs on the table. 'What a disgusting man!' he muttered, as Jonathan and Cendrine laughed.

Bruant had jumped to another table, and began a racy poem about the chastity of women. Suddenly, a fight broke out in one corner of the room: but Bruant, his eyes glittering, simply raised his voice above the din.

'Good Lord, I've had enough! Let's leave!' Sumner said, getting to his feet. Jonathan and the others rose quickly and followed him out of the door.

'What a dreadful place!' Sumner exclaimed.

Marcelle and Cendrine went into a spasm of giggles, and even Jonathan could not suppress his smile. 'Where's your sense of adventure, old man?'

He put his arm around Sumner's shoulders and they walked on through the crowded streets. Finally, they paused before a sedate-looking house.

'After M'sieur Bruant, I thought you'd like to go to church,' Marcelle said to Sumner mischievously, and they entered the Café du Conservatoire. The interior was like a miniature Nôtre Dame, with a vaulted Gothic ceiling, stone walls and statues of saints and candles in niches. Sumner took off his hat reverently, and Jonathan laughed. The room was crowded with people, cleaner and more prosperous than those in Bruant's place, who were listening, spellbound, to a distinguished-looking man with tear-filled eyes reciting poems about religion and aesthetics to a soft piano accompaniment.

Sumner sat quietly between Marcelle and Jonathan, sipping his drink; a reflective, melancholy look had slipped into his expression that was not lost on Jonathan. When they emerged back out into the street, Jonathan pulled him aside. 'Sumner, is something wrong?'

Sumner shook his head. 'No, of course not!'

Cendrine appeared at Jonathan's side. 'Marcelle wants to go dancing,' she told them.

'Then we will,' Jonathan said, kissing her lightly, and she ran ahead, leaving Jonathan and Sumner to trail behind. The two men walked on silently for a few minutes.

'Jonathan, I have some news I didn't tell you,' Sumner said. 'I'm getting married.'

Jonathan stopped, grabbing Sumner's arm. 'Sumner, that's wonderful!'

Sumner smiled, but even through his glasses, Jonathan could see the misery in his eyes. They resumed walking, several paces behind Cendrine and Marcelle, who were laughing gaily, their mingled perfumes drifting back on the night breeze.

'Her name is Katherine,' Sumner said. 'I've known her since we were children. She's a wonderful girl . . . a wonderful girl.' His eyes were on Cendrine and Marcelle.

Jonathan waited.

'I don't love her, Jonathan,' Sumner said softly. He drew in a deep breath. 'I mean, I *love* her, but I'm not . . . she doesn't . . .'

His voice trailed off, his eyes still on Cendrine's back. 'Cendrine's wonderful, Jonathan,' he said softly. 'You're wonderful together. I can see it.'

Jonathan hesitated, not wanting to flaunt his own brimming happiness. 'I love her so much, Sumner,' he said.

Sumner turned to him, staring at him for a moment. Then his face lit up with a huge, sudden smile. 'You'll come to my wedding, won't you?' His voice had resumed its bright tone. 'It's in late September, in the city.' He rolled his eyes. 'My mother, of course, is turning it into a circus!'

'I'll be there, Sumner,' Jonathan said.

His friend waved his hands towards the crowds and cafés. 'We're coming to Paris on our honeymoon. Maybe I can show Kathy some of your bohemian haunts!' He laughed. 'On second thoughts, I don't think she'd quite understand M'sieur Bruant the way I did!'

They had arrived at the Moulin de la Galette, a popular ballroom which pulsated with laughter, lights, movement and lusty music. The promenade surrounding the dance floor was crowded with pretty girls and strolling, smooth-faced boys. Out on the floor, a can-can was raging and bystanders were throwing lumps of sugar, egging the girls on, while tired waiters dodged through the fray with glass-laden trays.

They found a table and ordered beers. Sumner watched the girls incessantly, tapping his feet to the music.

'Let's dance,' Cendrine said to Jonathan.

'Like that?' He laughed. 'I wouldn't know what to do!'

'I'll show you!'

Cendrine pulled Jonathan towards the dance floor. Sumner watched them closely as they danced a happy quadrille, their laughter floating above the music. He finished his beer and when Jonathan and Cendrine returned, he ordered another round.

'Oh, Jonathan, you dance like a donkey,' Cendrine said with a giggle, dropping onto the bench.

'You'll pay for that insult,' Jonathan vowed and laughed, pulling her to him. Sumner watched as they kissed, then averted his eyes, embarrassed but envious of their openness. His gaze drifted around the room, at the couples kissing in corners, and out of the nearby doors towards the garden, where others embraced closely under the soft glow of Chinese lanterns swaying from the trees.

The band switched tempos, drawing Sumner's eyes back to the dance floor. They began to play a waltz. The dancers hesitated, then a few tried to bend to its rhythm, but the results were awkward, the men holding their partners woodenly. All the fun had suddenly vanished.

'Look at that,' Marcelle sniffed, with a wave of her hand. 'The French simply cannot do the waltz!'

'Then we will have to show them how!' Jonathan declared, jumping to his feet, grabbing Cendrine's hand.

'Oh, Jonathan, I don't know how,' Cendrine cried.

'I'll show you,' he said softly.

Jonathan led Cendrine to the centre of the dance floor. For a moment, they stood facing each other, smiling; then Jonathan placed his hand firmly at Cendrine's waist, and she put her left hand in his, picking up the hem of her gown in her right. They moved slowly at first, forward and back, forward and back. Then Jonathan began to turn her, and she picked up his rhythm. Soon, they were carving huge, graceful circles across the floor – round and round they went, their eyes never leaving each other's faces. The bandleader saw them and, with a smile, picked up the tempo; the crowd parted, stepping back to watch in admiration.

Suddenly, the tired little band sounded livelier, the lights glowed brighter, and a gust of cool air wafted in from the garden, sending the lanterns and women's skirts swaying. Sumner watched entranced as Jonathan and Cendrine swooped gracefully around the room, lost in the world of each other's arms.

Chapter Seventeen

Alexander leaned back in his chair and lit a cigar. 'So are you going to tell me what you've been up to lately?' he asked.

Jonathan twirled the stem of the glass between his fingers. 'I've been very busy, Alexander, and I had a friend visiting from New York. I'm sorry I couldn't come out to the lodge last month.'

'Or the month before that.' Alexander poured a generous amount of brandy into Jonathan's glass. The parlour was quiet except for the crackle of a fire in the hearth. A maid came in to clear away the dinner plates, and Alexander waited until she had left, concentrating on the amber tip of his cigar, before he looked back at Jonathan. 'Well, I'm extending another invitation that I will not allow you to refuse,' he said with a smile. 'I'm hosting a masked ball at Vignon next month, on Bastille Day. Everyone will be there. You'll come, won't you?'

'Of course.' Jonathan cradled the fragile crystal glass in his palm. He took a sip, feeling the hundred-year-old liquor slide down his throat, and considered his next words carefully, wondering how much to reveal. Without realizing it, he had distanced himself from Alexander. There was no room for anyone in his life now except Cendrine. When he was with her, he didn't want to leave; when he was away from her, his only thought was to see her again. His work had taken him far from Paris in recent months: to Delhi to record the coronation of King Edward as Emperor of India; to the Balkans to cover the ethnic unrest; to Belgrade in the wake of the assassination of King Alexander and Queen Draga. He did his work with the usual excellence, but always he ached to return to Cendrine. When he was in Paris, he went every night to the theatre to see her perform and would wait for her backstage, jealously guarding her from admirers. Then he would escort her home. She had recently taken a small but fashionable apartment on Rue La Perouse in the sixteenth arrondissement, living there with Roland, and she was proud of the fact that she could afford to pay for it out of her own salary.

As his obsession with Cendrine deepened, jealousy had thrust up its first shoots and the apartment, in his imagination, had become a trysting place for faceless lovers. One night, after dinner, she had asked him not to come in, begging fatigue. He had returned an hour later to stand in the street, staring up at her bedroom until the light went out. He preferred bringing her back to his own apartment, where they ate late dinners alone, made love in his bed and fell asleep in each other's arms. Sometimes he woke alone to find she had crept out silently at dawn; when he questioned her, she laughed. 'I love you, Jonathan,' she said, 'but a woman sometimes needs her own time and her own place. I need to go to dress fittings or to rehearsals. I need to buy a new pair of gloves or meet my musical director. Sometimes I just need to walk alone in the park.'

He didn't understand. The only thing he understood was the desire he could see in other men's eyes when they watched her dance or walk across a restaurant. He knew his jealousy was groundless; she never gave him reason to doubt. But he couldn't stop it – he was completely, irrationally, obsessively in love with her.

Jonathan glanced at Alexander. He trusted him, but how could he possibly explain this? How could Alexander – who had never relinquished control of himself to another person, never fallen in love – how could he understand this kind of love, this consuming madness?

'Alexander,' Jonathan said quickly, 'I feel I should explain something.'

Alexander waited, his black eyes intent.

'I've become rather involved with someone,' Jonathan said. He smiled slightly. 'Actually, I'm very much in love.'

Alexander smiled, drawing on the cigar. 'Well,' he murmured, 'I underestimated the depth of your feelings toward Lucy.'

'*Lucy*?' Jonathan blinked in surprise. 'No, it's not Lucy.'

Alexander's brows knitted in puzzlement. 'Then who?'

Jonathan wondered why this was suddenly so difficult. 'She's a dancer,' he said slowly, 'with the Folies-Bergère.'

Alexander's face was a blank for a moment, then he laughed, his large white teeth gripping the cigar. 'Oh, Jonathan, that's not very original!'

Jonathan's face grew warm and he realized he was holding the crystal glass with a dangerously firm grip. He stared into the glass, waiting for Alexander's laughter to subside. 'I'm serious, Alexander,' he said, his voice low. 'I'm in love with her.'

Alexander smiled gently, then he sighed. 'Of course you are.' He took a puff on his cigar, sending a tendril of blue smoke up to the ceiling, and chuckled, shaking his head. 'But somehow I can't picture you standing outside the stage door with all those other callow young men. Does Lucy know?'

'No, of course not,' Jonathan said quickly.

'Good. It's better that way.' He leaned back in his chair, propping his long legs up on a footstool. 'A mistress can be expensive. Is yours high maintenance or low maintenance?'

'I don't know what you mean.' Jonathan's face was suffused with embarrassment.

Alexander sighed and gave him a brotherly smile. 'Is your dancer pretty?'

'She's not just a dancer, she's a star,' he said defensively. 'La Phalare . . . you may know of her.'

Alexander cocked an eyebrow. 'Indeed!'

Jonathan sat up straighter, setting down the brandy. He felt foolish, acutely aware that Alexander was patronizing him. 'Perhaps I should be going,' he said quietly, rising. 'Thank you for dinner, Alexander, I—'

'Jonathan, sit down,' Alexander said gently but firmly. When he did, Alexander added, 'I'm sorry. I've embarrassed you.'

Jonathan said nothing and the clock on the mantel chimed nine times, filling the silence. Alexander tossed back his brandy, snuffed out his cigar and smiled indulgently at Jonathan. 'Look, it's early. Why don't we go over to the Folies and you can introduce me to your beloved? I promise to be utterly charming and not to embarrass you.'

Jonathan hesitated, then gave in. He couldn't stay angry at Alexander. They rose, and Alexander rang for the butler to send a carriage around.

'You know,' Alexander said as they stepped out into the night air, 'I haven't been to the Folies for years. This could be quite amusing.'

At the theatre, Alexander insisted on having a drink in the promenade before taking their seats in the front row. Cendrine, as usual, was the final act of the programme and Jonathan felt the familiar tingle of anticipation creep up his spine. Watching her perform never failed to arouse him; now Alexander's presence only added to his excitement and pride. He knew that once Alexander saw Cendrine dance, he would be impressed – not simply with Cendrine, but with the fact that Jonathan had captured such a woman.

Throughout Cendrine's dance, Jonathan was tense, wanting to gauge Alexander's reaction, and finally he stole a glance. But Alexander's profile in the dark revealed nothing out of the ordinary: just the same glimmer in his dark eyes, the same faintly sardonic twist to his lips.

Afterward, Jonathan led Alexander backstage to the dressing rooms. Cendrine greeted him with a tender kiss, not noticing Alexander standing near the door. She was wearing a white silk kimono, her hair spilling down over her shoulders and her face freshly scrubbed free of the heavy stage make-up.

'You were beautiful,' he whispered in her ear.

'I missed my cue,' she said and laughed lightly; then she sobered, noticing Alexander over Jonathan's shoulder, and pulled back, staring at him.

Jonathan turned. 'Cendrine, this is my friend, Alexander Profitt,' he said, smiling.

Alexander came forward, holding his top hat. Cendrine stared at him intently then slowly held out her hand; Alexander took it and kissed it. '*Enchanté*,' he said softly.

'*Mon plaisir, m'sieur.*'

'I truly enjoyed your dancing tonight,' Alexander said sincerely. 'It was unlike anything I have ever seen before.'

'Thank you,' Cendrine said simply.

For a moment, the three of them stood without moving as the noise from the corridor eddied around them. Jonathan looked from Alexander to Cendrine, wondering if either of them realized they had met before. Remembering how Alexander had dismissed Cendrine that day in the village so many years ago, he decided not to mention that previous meeting. He was surprised at Alexander's silence; it was unlike him to be less than loquacious around a beautiful woman.

Alexander seemed to study Cendrine's face, then finally turned to Jonathan. 'I must be going,' he said abruptly.

Jonathan hid his surprise. He had expected they might all go to dinner together. 'I'll see you to your carriage,' he said.

Alexander smiled at Cendrine. 'Perhaps we'll meet again some time, Mademoiselle—'

'LeClerc,' Cendrine replied.

With a polite nod, he turned and left the room.

Jonathan followed him out to the front of the theatre and waited as Alexander got into his carriage. 'I'm going to stay, if you don't mind,' Jonathan said.

'Of course,' Alexander said with a knowing smile. He leaned on the window, looking down at Jonathan. 'She's quite lovely. I can see why you've been so preoccupied.'

'I'm going to ask her to marry me, Alexander,' Jonathan blurted out.

Alexander's smile faded. 'Jonathan,' he said slowly, 'that would be a grave mistake.'

Jonathan's face fell. 'A mistake? But why?'

'She's a music-hall entertainer, Jonathan,' Alexander said firmly. 'Beautiful, certainly, but not a woman a man like yourself can afford to take seriously.'

Jonathan drew back slightly from the carriage. Not take seriously? So that was why Alexander had wanted to leave so quickly. His request to meet Cendrine had been nothing more than an amusing little joke. He felt anger slowly rising up inside him. 'I don't think you understand how I feel about her, Alexander,' he said, trying to subdue his emotions.

'Good God, man,' Alexander said, 'you have a reputation to consider, a reputation you've worked hard to earn. She's not worthy of you.'

'Yes, she is,' Jonathan replied staunchly.

Alexander sighed in exasperation. 'For heaven's sake, Jonathan, be reasonable! She's not the kind of woman men like us marry. Of course, keep her as your mistress – you'll be envied for that! But to marry her – you'd be the laughing stock of Paris!'

'I love her,' Jonathan said. 'I want to marry her.'

'Jonathan, listen to me.' Alexander hesitated, choosing his words carefully. 'Marriage has nothing to do with love. You marry a certain kind of woman, one who can elevate your position. A woman who stays quietly at your side, giving you sons – dozens of them, if that's what you want. Passion, sex, love, whatever you call it – you find that elsewhere. You don't mix the two!' He sighed. 'My God, I thought you had outgrown that bourgeois notion.'

Jonathan took another step back. 'I think you'd better be going, Alexander,' he said, his voice low.

'Jonathan, a woman like that will only disappoint you—'

'Just go. Please!'

Alexander stared at him for a moment, then his face hardened and, with an exasperated sigh, he banged on the window to get the driver's attention. 'Let's go!' he called out sharply.

Jonathan watched the black carriage clatter away, its brass lanterns shining in the night. He stood in the street until the carriage was out of sight, then went back inside the theatre.

Cendrine was dressing behind a screen when he returned. 'I'm almost ready,' she called out.

Jonathan slumped down in a chair in the corner,

unable to erase Alexander's final look of censure from his mind. He was angry and embarrassed; but he was also hurt. He looked up to Alexander, felt grateful to him – he respected – no, *loved* him – like the brother he had never had. To be rebuked so callously and thoughtlessly cut into his heart.

Cendrine emerged out from behind the screen. 'Well, do you like it?' she asked, twirling around so the ice-blue silk gown fanned out around her ankles.

Jonathan gave her a desultory glance. 'It's very pretty,' he said quietly.

She turned to the mirror, smiling. 'It was awfully expensive,' she said, 'but when my dressmaker showed me the fabric, I couldn't resist!' She frowned slightly. 'I know it's not as fine as a Worth or even a Poiret, but the design is rather unusual, don't you think?' She laughed. 'Some day, I shall own a gown by M'sieur Worth . . . no, a hundred gowns!' When Jonathan said nothing, she glanced towards him. 'My darling, is something wrong?'

Jonathan's mind was out in the street, watching Profitt's carriage race off into the night.

'*Jonathan*?'

He looked up; his eyes passed over the gown and up to her face. 'You're so beautiful,' he said softly.

Cendrine smiled and picked up her cape. 'Where shall we go for dinner tonight?'

Jonathan rose slowly, with a great effort shifting his thoughts away from Alexander. 'The Café de Paris?' he said, on the spur of the moment. He had decided, just in that instant, that he would ask Cendrine to marry him tonight. He had wanted to wait until he could afford to buy her a fine wedding ring, but suddenly it didn't matter. He would buy her the ring later. He would buy her everything she wanted. He would prove to Alexander that Cendrine was worthy of marriage, prove that given the chance, she could stand alongside any of the women in Alexander's gilded circle. All she needed was someone to show her the way. Alexander had done it for Jonathan; now, by making Cendrine his wife, Jonathan could do it for her.

Cendrine plucked a white rose from one of the many bouquets in the dressing room. 'I'm surprised you didn't ask your friend to have dinner with us,' she said. 'He's the man who used to come to my father's café, isn't he? The man with the white yacht?'

Jonathan hesitated. 'Yes, it's him.'

She smiled, slipping the rose into his lapel. 'There. Now you are properly dressed to escort me to the Café de Paris.'

As they started for the door, Jonathan's eyes surveyed the bouquets that filled the dressing room and he felt a pang of jealousy sweep through him. 'What do you do with all these flowers?' he asked.

Cendrine shrugged. 'I have them sent to hospitals. I don't like cut flowers, they remind me of death. I like to see them alive, growing in the fields where they belong.'

They went into the corridor, but instead of going to the stage door as usual, Cendrine paused unexpectedly. 'Come with me,' she said softly.

She headed quickly down a dark hallway. Jonathan lagged behind, following her through the gloomy corridors of the backstage area, wondering where she was going. Finally they emerged into one of the wings. The stage was bare, its gaudy backdrops raised to reveal the ugly brick wall, festooned with ropes and cables. It was dark, except for one single spotlight, and a breeze wafted through the stillness.

Cendrine was standing in the centre of the stage, staring up at the empty seats, her face bathed in the pale beam of light. The old boards of the stage creaked, echoing through the theatre, as Jonathan went to her. She gave him a small smile, then looked back out over the empty auditorium.

'I like it when it's like this,' she whispered. 'So quiet.'

She looked up at the balcony, the spotlight catching her eyes and making them glisten. Jonathan watched her silently.

'When I dance,' she said softly without looking at him, 'I'm listening to the music and I don't see or hear the audience. I can only *feel* them out there in the dark – I can feel their hearts beating, and their breath stirring the air around me. I can feel them responding to how I move, touching me, like hundreds of hands moving over my body.' She turned and gave Jonathan a strange smile. 'It's like when you make love to me.'

He stared at her rapt face, hearing his own heart hammering wildly in his chest. He felt himself growing hard, and wanted to make love to her right there and then. He pulled her to him, kissing her roughly, then moving his lips quickly down her neck across the tops of her breasts. She moaned and he sank to his knees, his hands going up under her skirt to grasp her buttocks and pulled her towards him, burying his face in the soft triangle of silk the gown formed between her legs. She dropped down beside him on the stage, took his face in her hands and kissed him hungrily.

He pushed away to look at her face. 'Marry me,' he whispered hoarsely.

Her lips parted in surprise. Illuminated from above by the spotlight, her face looked strange, an eerie study in white and black. Something came into her eyes that made Jonathan tighten his grip on her.

'Marry me, Cendrine,' he said.

'Jonathan—'

His fingers dug into her bare arms. 'I'll take care of you,' he said. 'You'll have everything you want. Clothes, servants, a beautiful home – I can make it all happen!' He laughed crazily. 'I love you, Cendrine. Marry me. I

215

can give you everything you want!'

She hesitated. 'Jonathan,' she said softly, 'I love you so much, but . . .'

'But?' he said urgently.

'I don't want to get married. At least, not yet.'

Her words, said so gently, stung like a slap across his face and he was so stunned that for a moment, he couldn't think. 'Why not?' he asked. 'Because I have no money? But I will—'

'No,' she interrupted softly, 'because I want to be a dancer.'

'You are a dancer!' he said and tried to pull her into his embrace – but she leaned back away from him. She sat back on her heels, bowing her head, her hands cradled in her lap. After a moment, she looked up at him.

'No – a *real* dancer,' she said. 'I want to be a ballet dancer.'

'Ballet?' he whispered, not comprehending. 'I thought you had given up on—'

'No, I still want it. More than anything,' she said firmly.

'More than me?' he said, searching her face.

Her eyes filled with tears. 'I want both,' she said.

Jonathan looked away out over the empty theatre, his heart heavy.

'*Please* try to understand, Jonathan,' she said. 'I have to try. I may not make it, but I have to keep trying. I can't marry you right now. Some day, perhaps, but—'

He looked back at her. 'When?' he asked softly.

She shook her head in confusion. 'I don't know.'

He took her hands. 'When, Cendrine? I can wait. Just tell me when.'

She shook her head, confused. 'I don't know . . . Please, Jonathan, don't pressure me like this . . . please.'

'When?'

She closed her eyes. 'In September, there is another audition at the opera. I'm going to try again. If I don't get a position . . .' Her voice trailed off.

'Three months,' Jonathan said. He took a deep breath. 'All right. I will ask you again in three months.'

He took her hand and wove his fingers through hers; he kissed the back of her hand, closing his eyes. For Cendrine he would wait for ever.

Alexander sat in the darkened parlour of his apartment, a glass dangling from his fingertips, an empty brandy decanter at his elbow. He had not moved from the chair all night, sitting alone with his thoughts interrupted only by the hourly chimes of the clock. Now it came again, five timorous rings: outside, in the still of the morning, he could hear the faint clip-clop of the milk wagon in the street. Soon it would be dawn, yet, as tired as he was, he couldn't go to bed. He rarely had trouble sleeping, but tonight he was unable to shut down the wheels of his mind.

All right, since returning from the theatre, he had been thinking about Jonathan – thinking about his absurd notion of marrying this . . . dancer. Thinking about how it would ruin him for future advancement. Thinking about himself, how he had cultivated him and helped him, and how betrayed he now felt: thinking, too, of the look of defiance in Jonathan's eyes.

Alexander's eyes drifted to the dying fire in the grate. But that's *why* you took him under your wing, he thought, because he defied you. He's not like all the other men you've surrounded yourself with all your life. He's more like you – a man who does not allow others to control his life. A man worthy of respect. Worthy of your love.

Alexander brought the glass up to his eyes, staring

through it, seeing the fireplace's glowing embers refracted through the cut crystal into slivers of gold. His thoughts turned to Cendrine. One image kept coming back to him: the sight of her floating across the stage like a dove. On stage he hadn't recognized her – that had come later, in the dressing room. She seemed so much smaller offstage; her bare face and loose hair had sent a sudden bolt of recognition through him. She was the girl in the village. The little *villageoise*.

Alexander let the glass fall. Different, but the same. Bathed in coloured lights, dressed in silk and moving like a dream – but still a *villageoise*, a *villageoise* who had somehow escaped and now had ambitions of her own. He had known many women like her, dancers and actresses who had moved up to the status of *demi-mondaine*, professional beauties who devoted their lives to the art of seduction. They knew every trick to please a man, from choosing a good cigar to prolonging lovemaking. He himself had once kept such a woman, who bewitched him simply by her incredible ability to take him whole in her mouth, teasing him with exquisite tenderness until he was exhausted by desire, then sucking him dry. He knew what power these women could yield; he knew, too, what motivated their behaviour. Money, of course, and the promise of protection. But the most ingenious ones sought marriage as a means of social elevation.

He had known several men who, naïvely believing themselves above reproach, had married their mistresses – only to find their telephone calls going suddenly unanswered, their calling cards ignored at the best homes. Their names would disappear from social lists, business contacts would wither, and inevitably the man and his pretty wife would mysteriously leave Paris, never to be heard from again.

It was something Jonathan would never understand.

Nothing in his experience could allow him to foresee what would happen, or to see Cendrine for what she really was – an artful opportunist.

Jonathan does not see it, Alexander thought. His heart is too tender, his eyes are too clouded. But I do – and I won't just sit back and allow her to ruin him.

The clock chimed the half-hour and he glanced towards the window, where the first grey light of the day was seeping around the draperies. With a weary sigh, he closed his eyes, but restless sparks of light shot across the insides of his eyelids; and amid them was Cendrine's face, shimmering in the dark.

Chapter Eighteen

The ballroom of Villa Vignon was ablaze with light. For his ball, Alexander had chosen a Louis XIV theme and ordered decorators to recreate the famous hall of mirrors in the Château de Versailles. The walls of the ballroom had been lined with long mirrors trimmed in gilt and twelve crystal chandeliers had been hung at even intervals from the ceiling. The villa had recently been wired for electric lights; but tonight only candles were used, hundreds of white tapers, softening the glint of diamonds and casting a golden glow over the complexions of the women.

Alexander watched with a bemused smile as his guests descended the staircase after being announced by a servant in blue brocade livery. Everyone had got into the spirit of the ball by wearing seventeenth-century costumes and the whole scene struck Alexander as absurd, almost grotesque in its gaudy silliness.

But he was not enjoying it as much as he had thought he would. He was still troubled by thoughts of Jonathan. A month had passed since their argument at the theatre, and they had not spoken during that time. At first, Alexander had been angry, but now he felt that Jonathan was merely being stubborn. He is young; he will come round, Alexander told himself. This infatuation would burn itself out, as such things always did.

Perhaps it had already. Still, he did wonder if Jonathan intended to come to the ball.

'Mr Oliver Thayer!'

Alexander's eyes went to the top of the staircase. There stood the critic, his fat little body stuffed into pale-blue satin breeches and waistcoat, a fluff of lace bouncing ridiculously on his chest, a white wig slipping down over his forehead. Alexander could not prevent himself from laughing at the sight. Thayer spotted him and came over.

'You have a mean streak, Alexander,' Oliver said. 'You enjoy making others uncomfortable.'

'I look just as ridiculous as everyone else, Oliver,' Alexander said, knowing that the reverse was true. Unlike the other men, he hadn't worn a wig, and he looked splendidly at ease in the seventeenth-century dress.

Before Oliver could reply, the voice atop the stairs called out, 'M'sieur Jonathan Caras and Mademoiselle Cendrine LeClerc!'

Alexander's head swivelled to the staircase. Jonathan and Cendrine stood there motionless for a moment, as every pair of eyes in the room locked on them. Alexander felt a spurt of anger shoot through him – how dare Jonathan bring her? But he felt in the same moment a sense of awe as he gazed at them. Never had he seen a more beautiful couple: he tall and dark-haired in black brocade; she small and pale, shimmering in a white wig and voluminous white satin gown. They were a study in physical opposites: so different yet so perfectly matched.

A multitude of eyes followed them down the stairs. Everyone knew that Cendrine was La Phalare; Oliver's reviews had made her a celebrity. Oliver had also discovered and divulged her beginnings in Paris as an artist's model, but had been unable to find out more. To stave off investigation, Cendrine had fabricated a background, letting it be known that she was a doctor's daughter who danced purely for pleasure, and the story only intensified her celebrity. And now here she was on the arm of Alexander Profitt's young American protégé, who only recently had been courting Lucy Wendall! Lips turned up in small smirks, eyebrows cocked in amusement. It was one thing for a man to have a discreet coupling with a flamboyant mistress, but to bring her into such an elite social arena was gauche – and certainly a slap at the host.

Jonathan and Cendrine made their way across the room towards Alexander; Profitt felt the burn of eyes in his back, but kept his face neutral. He could see in Jonathan's expression the same stubborn pride that had been there the night at the theatre, hardened now into outright defiance.

'I'm glad you could come,' Alexander said. He looked at Cendrine. 'You look beautiful, Mademoiselle LeClerc. Just like Marie Antoinette.'

'Moments before she was guillotined, perhaps?' Cendrine said, without smiling. She stood, back straight, head held proudly. It was possible she understood what was happening, Alexander thought; by all rights, she should have been intimidated. Yet she was perfectly serene and he found himself staring at her with admiration. A *villageoise*, but a courageous one. Yet an opportunist nonetheless.

'Jonathan,' Alexander said, 'there's something you and I must discuss.' He turned towards the critic, hovering nearby. 'Oliver, why don't you ask Mademoiselle LeClerc to dance?'

Oliver smoothed down his lace. 'Delighted.'

Cendrine allowed Oliver to lead her out among the other waltzing couples, but as they danced she kept an eye on Jonathan and Alexander. They had moved towards a corner and were talking in low voices; she couldn't hear them but she could see the displeasure in Alexander's face and the barely concealed anger in Jonathan's. Others were staring at them, whispering; she could feel the eyes of dancers scorch across her as they swept by.

'Ignore them,' Oliver said suddenly in her ear.

'What did you say?' she asked, pulling back.

'Don't listen to the buzz of these insects. They'll eat you alive if they smell your fear. Believe me, I know.'

Cendrine stared at Oliver. Over the past years, he had become a constant presence in her life. It was he who, with his first review, had given birth to La Phalare and made her a star. It was he who always came backstage bringing, not roses and fawning praise, but hard advice on how to improve her artistry. Although he repelled her at some basic level, she felt a debt to him and had come to feel oddly at ease in his company. Because Jonathan was so often away, she had fallen into the habit of having dinner with Oliver occasionally; once, when Anna Pavlova came to Paris for one performance and tickets were impossible to obtain, Oliver had taken her. Afterwards, Oliver had accompanied her backstage; Cendrine had glanced through an open door to see the small Russian dancer sobbing with pain as she pulled off her pointe shoes to reveal bloodied toes. 'It's a wonderful illusion,' Oliver had said gently, 'this triumph of beauty over agony.' It had astonished her that such an insight should come from Oliver; he seemed genuinely to love ballet. Eventually, she had told him of her dream of becoming a real dancer and he had listened sympathetically as had no one else – including Roland, Marcelle, and even Jonathan. Oliver Thayer was not a friend; but sometimes she felt as if he were the only person who really understood her needs.

Now she looked into his pink, round face. 'I don't think I should have come here tonight,' she said.

'Why?' Oliver asked.

'I'm not sure,' she said quietly. 'There's something going on with M'sieur Profitt that Jonathan won't tell me.' Out of the corner of her eye she glimpsed Jonathan turning abruptly away from Alexander and heading out of a door towards the garden. 'I have to go,' she said quickly.

But Oliver held her. 'Stay out of it,' he urged earnestly.

Cendrine hesitated, then relented and Oliver guided her awkwardly across the floor. 'So, you're going to the opera audition in September?' he asked hurriedly, to ease the tension.

She looked at him, surprised. 'I thought I might,' she said. She had never told him about her past failures.

He shook his head. 'You know, it's a hard life. Have you thought how you will survive? A *corps de ballet* dancer makes no money at all. It will be a bit of a comedown for La Phalare.'

She said nothing. She had thought about the good salary she would be relinquishing: thought too about the extravagances of pretty gowns and hats, the small but comfortable apartment, all the luxuries of her present life which had prevented her from saving money. She had hinted to Roland that he should get a job, but he had left the art school and had enrolled in the Sorbonne, studying philosophy. Most of his time, however, was spent lingering in cafés locked in heated political debates.

'If I get in, the money won't matter,' she said finally.

'Well, you can do what Madame Pavlova does,' Oliver said with a shrug. 'She was nothing but the illegitimate daughter of a Jewish businessman and a laundress. When she became a dancer, she found a string of rich men quite willing to protect her. Rumour has it she has seven lovers – one for each day of the week.'

Cendrine stared at Oliver. Inevitably he did or said something to disgust her.

'Oh, don't look at me that way, dear,' Oliver said. 'You look as if you're made of spun silk, but people forget how strong silk is. You're a survivor. You're also developing quite an appetite for fine things.' He glanced towards Jonathan. 'Your young man is handsome, but he hasn't a sou of his own, you know. All that he has – even the clothes on his back – he owes to Alexander's generosity.' Oliver sighed. 'On what he makes, Jonathan can barely keep himself in decent shirts. Will you be content with simple wool dresses and *vin ordinaire*?' Oliver smiled. 'I suppose you will. You love him, don't you?'

Cendrine jerked her hand away. 'Excuse me, Oliver,' she said. She wended her way through the dancers, pausing at the terrace door to look for Jonathan, but there was no sign of him. She set out through the garden, keeping to the stone path to avoid soaking her satin shoes. Finally she stopped and leaned against a stone railing, staring up at the moonlit sky. She sighed in exasperation. Damn Oliver! He could be so cruel, planting things in her brain, things she didn't want to hear. Once he told her that La Phalare's costumes had become too revealing, that she looked cheap. It stung her, but she knew he was right, and she had changed them immediately. She hated his brutal honesty and his disturbing ability to hit upon the truth; it would be hard for her to give up the money she now earned. She hated him, too, for what he said about Jonathan. What if he did have no money of his own right now? He was ambitious and talented. He had a future.

She heard the scrape of a shoe on stone and turned. When she saw the slender figure and dark hair for a moment she thought it was Jonathan; but it was Alexander, his longer, sharper face coming into focus as he approached.

He drew up short, surprised to see her. 'I was looking for Jonathan,' he said.

She straightened. 'So was I,' she said, in a low voice.

He stared at her. 'I particularly wanted to find him. We had a small argument,' he said.

She could see his dark eyes glinting. Her mind tripped back to the first time she had ever seen him, sitting in the café yard at La Turbie. She had been only twelve and she had never seen such a magnificent man: so mysterious and so intimidating.

'Was it over me?' she asked.

'What makes you think that?'

'Jonathan has been unhappy lately,' she said. 'He won't tell me what it is, but I think it involves you somehow. And me.'

He came towards her. 'All right, it *does* involve me. And you. I hadn't planned to, but I'll tell you what it is. You're the one who brought it up, after all.' His voice had become colder. 'Jonathan's asked you to marry him. I don't know your answer, but I think you should know how I feel about this whole matter.'

'It's no concern of yours,' she said, stiffening.

'Oh, yes, it is.' He took a step closer, and she resisted the urge to back away. 'I care about Jonathan, care about what happens to him. He has talent, great potential and the desire to better himself. He came from nothing, yet now he can hold his own among the very best society can offer. He has worked hard, done all the right things.' He paused, looking down his nose at her. 'I don't want to see him make a mistake.'

'Mistake?'

'I've made sure Jonathan met the right people, people of power who could help him no matter what he does or where he goes in the world. His future is unlimited.' Alexander paused. 'But you could – well – put him at something of a handicap.'

'What are you saying?' Cendrine asked, her voice quiet.

Alexander regarded her, unsmilingly. 'You're a clever woman. I don't think I need to explain this.'

'I think you do.'

'All right then. What I'm saying, Mademoiselle LeClerc, is that some people might find a woman of your profession and background unsuitable.'

Cendrine felt her face grow warm. 'I don't care what anyone thinks!'

'Perhaps not. But Jonathan does.'

'You're wrong. He loves me!' She tried to brush by him, but he blocked her way.

'Let me put it to you more bluntly. Mademoiselle LeClerc.' Alexander's face was inches from hers. 'What do you think will happen when they find out you aren't the daughter of a respected country doctor from Nantes, that you really climbed out of that hillside shithole? What will happen to Jonathan when they find out you tried to kill your own father?'

Cendrine's heart stopped.

'Your father was found unconscious in a field. He nearly bled to death because he was too drunk to find help. He told the police you tried to kill him. A friend in Beaulieu told me about it,' Alexander said. 'You know how news travels in a little town. It's almost as bad as Paris.'

Cendrine stared at him, speechless.

'I have no interest in hurting you,' Alexander said, his voice softer now. 'I just want to protect Jonathan. He can't see what will happen.'

She pushed against him, trying to escape, but he grabbed her upper arm, causing her to cry out.

'I know what you are,' he said. 'You'll do whatever it takes to advance yourself. You'll marry Jonathan and ruin him, and you won't care.'

'Let go!' She twisted, but his grip grew tighter, his fingers digging into her arm. She fought harder, pulling, and he gave her arm a violent jerk.

'Listen to me!' he hissed. 'I know what's best for him! I know what—'

'*You* know! That's what this is about, isn't it?' she said angrily. 'This isn't about Jonathan, it's about *you*, your ego. You have this idea that you've created this . . . perfect gentleman, and you can't stand the idea of him thinking for himself. You don't care about Jonathan. You only care about yourself!'

'I love Jonathan,' Alexander said.

'So do I,' she said, tears springing to her eyes.

Alexander released her arm. 'Then get out of his way.'

She stood there, rubbing her arm, staring at Alexander. Choking back the heavy lump in her throat, she wiped her hand across her cheek. Alexander's face was inscrutable in the moonlight. 'Let him have the life he's worked so hard to get,' he said softly. 'He won't have the heart to hurt you, Mademoiselle LeClerc – he'll ruin himself before he does that. It's up to you.'

She turned and started back towards the villa, taking her time, wanting to regain her composure before she found Jonathan. By the time she got to the terrace door, her face was dry, but she was still trembling. She lingered at the door, and finally saw Jonathan talking to Thayer and another man. She hesitated, suddenly unable to take a step towards him. Finally, he saw her and his face lit up, but his smile faded as he came up to her.

'What's wrong?' he asked.

'Nothing,' she said, forcing a smile. 'I went looking for you in the garden and got lost.'

He shook his head. 'I'm sorry I left you alone.' He touched her arm and she flinched as he saw the red marks, already deepening into bruises. 'My

God, what happened?' he asked.

'I stumbled on a loose stone,' she said. 'I'm fine.'

'You're certain?' His eyes were anxious.

She touched her gloved hand to his cheek. 'Positive,' she murmured, 'though I could use a glass of champagne.'

Jonathan sprang to life, delivering two glasses from a waiter's tray. They stood at the edge of the room, watching the other couples dancing. Cendrine scanned the crowd warily, searching for Alexander, but he hadn't reappeared. Her arm ached from the grasp of his fingers; her eyes burned with the threat of tears. She drank quickly, forcing the champagne down her constricting throat, and realized suddenly that Jonathan was gazing at her intently.

'Something is wrong,' he said. 'What is it?'

She took a deep breath and smiled shakily. 'Oh, it's just this place, Jonathan, and these people. It's all so grand! I feel . . . overwhelmed.'

She saw immedialtely that the lie had worked; Jonathan smiled and slipped his arm protectively around her waist. 'You're the most beautiful woman here,' he whispered.

A waltz started up; there was a moment of confusion before couples began to dance. Jonathan set their glasses aside and took her hand. 'Dance with me,' he said, smiling.

She resisted. 'I don't think—'

His smile widened. 'Dance with me – like that night at La Galette. Let's show them how it's done!'

He pulled her gently out to the middle of the shining parquet floor and put his arm at her waist. Picking up the hem of her gown, she put her hand in his, and he began to move her slowly back and forth to the lulling rhythm. Then he becan to turn her, sweeping graceful circles through the other couples.

She stared into Jonathan's eyes, wanting to see nothing else as the music welled up around her and crept inside her, its three-four time as insistent as a heartbeat.

They turned, faster, ever faster. The room was all mirror and crystal, the other dancers nothing but shards of coloured glass: blue, green, red, reflected back to her in the mirrored walls. She looked up into the brilliant white prism of a chandelier and then down to a pair of dazzling blue eyes. Dizzy, she choked back a cry – half laugh, half sob. The room kept turning faster and faster: mirror and crystal, blue, green and red.

Chapter Nineteen

Cendrine walked slowly to the barre, taking a place between two women. She intended to do *pliés* to warm up before the audition, but she was unable to move; her hand, gripping the barre, was trembling.

The door banged open and other dancers straggled into the studio, yawning and chatting. Cendrine watched them furtively. A young girl, no more than sixteen, was spreadeagled on the floor, stretching her legs, flexing and pointing her feet; across the room, a moon-faced boy in a ragged leotard scratched his crotch and slouched on the barre, gazing at her. Every face seemed to be staring in her direction.

She was tense – too tense – her body one raw nerve. How was she ever going to get through this? She had come to the opera house expecting to be turned away again, but to her amazement, the *régisseur* had told her to come in and attend the class. That was how everyone was auditioned, he explained – by taking a simple class.

A simple class. It had been so long since she had taken a proper ballet class. The dancing she did at the Folies had kept her in shape, but it was nothing compared to the disciplined movement ballet required of the body. She stood at the barre, her heart hammering, her head lowered so as to not make eye contact.

A rapping sound made her look up; a slender, elderly

man stood by the piano holding an ebony cane. 'Let's begin,' he said. '*Pliés* in first to second to fifth, the usual *port de bras* . . .'

The twenty dancers stood at attention. Cendrine put her feet heel to heel in first position and held her breath. The 'usual *port de bras*' . . . The dancers knew the routine but she had no idea what to expect. The pianist began to play and slowly, more or less in unison, twenty-one pairs of knees began to bend.

The elderly man kept time by pounding his cane on the floor, an insistent and unnerving rhythm. The *pliés* progressed to *tendus*, the subtle stretching exercises of the legs, the tempo increasing. Cendrine felt her body going through the motions, but something was wrong. She felt rigid and her legs were heavy and unwieldy.

Commands for other exercises came in rapid succession: *ronds de jambes, frappés, développés, battements*. It was familiar, just what Madame had always asked for. But it was also different, being among others, real dancers whose legs went higher, whose feet moved faster. The piano, slightly out of tune, droned on, punctuated by the cane: thump, thump, thump.

It was wrong . . . all wrong. What am I doing here? she thought dismally. I can't do this. My muscles have forgotten. It doesn't feel natural any more. I can't do this . . .

Thump, thump, thump. Tears threatened and she shut her eyes to force them back. Jonathan flashed into her mind: his body, the feel of him, as he had moved inside her that morning. He had kept her in bed late, making languid love to her, and she had arrived at the opera still wet and aching from him. Even now, she could feel him inside her, feel her body moving to match his rhythm.

The thumping noise receded as she concentrated on Jonathan, the feel of him that was still there in her body, trying to recreate the smooth cadence of their coupling.

Her body began to respond, feeling suddenly lighter and more pliant.

The barre exercises were over and the dancers moved to the centre of the floor for more complicated movements: slow adagios that tested control; pirouettes that demanded precision; jumps that called for strength and energy. Cendrine stayed at the back, getting through most of the exercises, faltering on the more complex ones. Gradually, however, her nervousness dissipated as her body and mind came alive with the challenge. She knew she wasn't as good as the others, but suddenly she didn't think about it. She was caught in the moment, lost in the sheer joy of dancing.

The thumping stopped; the class was over, and the dancers began to trail out of the studio. Cendrine glanced around, wondering what was expected of her, but no one seemed interested. I didn't make it, she thought bleakly. Then she saw the elderly man standing just outside the door talking to a large man.

Oliver Thayer! She hadn't noticed him during the class, but he had clearly witnessed her failure. She felt exposed, more vulnerable than she ever had felt on the Folies stage. She went quickly to a corner where she had left her bag.

'Mademoiselle?'

Cendrine looked up into the face of the elderly man in black. The man's wizened face was expressionless. 'It is my pleasure to offer you a contract for the *corps de ballet*,' he said tonelessly. 'The pay is fifty francs per month, for an eight-month season. Can you be here tomorrow?'

Cendrine clutched a pointe shoe, staring at him.

'Well?'

'Yes, of course,' she said quickly. 'Tomorrow.'

'Good. See the *régisseur* on your way out.' And he turned and limped away.

Cendrine stood there, too stunned to move. She saw her reflection in the mirrors across the room, a small figure in a white practice dress. The image grew blurry; she was crying and cursed herself for the weakness, but couldn't stop.

'Here, use this.'

Cendrine turned to see Oliver holding a handkerchief. She took it and wiped her eyes. 'Why are you crying?' Oliver said.

'I didn't think I would make it,' she said.

'I knew you would.'

Oliver – why was she so wary of him when all he had ever offered was support? 'I'm not as good as the others, Oliver,' she said. 'I had no way of judging myself before, but now I can see. I'm not very good.'

'True.'

She stared at him, stung by the cruel remark. 'But how—'

He shrugged. 'You got what you wanted. Does it matter *how*? You're a real dancer now, Cendrine. You can live in poverty, sacrificing for your art, like all these other half-starved children.' He struck a chord on the piano, shaking his head at the tone. 'Fifty francs a month – that would barely keep La Phalare in gloves. But if it's what you want, so be it.'

Cendrine suddenly understood. 'You arranged this,' she said.

He didn't have to answer; his self-satisfied smile told her it was true. Cendrine spun away from him, tore off her other shoe, threw it in her bag and hurried to the door.

Oliver grabbed her arm as she went by. 'Why are you angry?' he asked.

'You don't control me, Oliver.'

'I'm helping you.'

'I wanted to do this on my own!'

Oliver sighed. 'Cendrine, dear, you must be realistic. As La Phalare, you are special – but as a serious dancer, you have limitations.' When Cendrine looked away, Oliver took her chin roughly in his hand, pulling her back. 'Look at me, and listen.' She tried to slap his hand away. 'Listen!' he hissed. 'The director agreed to try you out. As a personal favour to me.'

'What does he get in return, Oliver? Guaranteed good reviews?'

Oliver shrugged. 'He wants the opera management to give his little company more attention. If I say nice things about the dancing, they might listen.'

Cendrine tried to push by, but he blocked her way. 'You've been quick to take my advice in the past,' he said. 'Do what I say now. Forget about how you got in. Just work hard, show them you can do it.' He grabbed her arm and pulled her closer. Realizing, with horror, that he was going to kiss her, she averted her face, feeling his beard brush her neck and his lips wet on her cheek. 'Make me proud,' he whispered.

She jerked her arm free. With a final angry glance at Oliver, she went quickly out the door.

'Goodbye, La Phalare,' Oliver said softly.

Jonathan sat alone on the banquette, his eyes on the door. He pulled out his pocket watch. Nearly nine. He snapped the watch shut impatiently. The Café de Paris was crowded, and a few people nodded their recognition to Jonathan as they came in, but he greeted them distractedly, his eyes always returning to the door. He tucked the watch away and his fingers went up to touch the small lump beneath his breast pocket. It was there, the ring in the small velvet box. The champagne was chilling in its sweating bucket. The special dinner ordered in advance. All that was missing was Cendrine – she was nearly an hour late.

Where was she? When she had left his apartment that morning, it was with the promise to meet him at the restaurant at eight. The audition had been at ten and she hadn't returned all day. He suspected that she had just wanted to be alone after the disappointment of the audition. He ran his hand over his chin, giving in to the mild guilt that had been with him since morning. His insistence on making love had been selfish; he knew he should have been more understanding about the audition, but he had wanted only to shield her from being hurt again. Tonight, he would console her, comfort her and help her forget about the ballet. Tonight, he was going to change her life.

Finally, he saw her at the door. She came towards him, smiling, floating across the room in a swirl of pale peach satin.

'Oh, Jonathan, I'm so sorry.' She sat down, smoothing her hair up off her neck.

He stared at her. She did not seem upset; her skin had a glow to it that didn't come from any trick of light. He felt suddenly relieved; she had already come to terms with the failed audition and was ready to become his wife. He leaned close. 'Everyone's staring at you. You look radiant!'

A waiter appeared to pour the champagne. She held up her glass. 'I feel like celebrating,' she said softly.

He picked up his glass. 'So do I.'

They drank, then he kissed her gently, the velvet box pressing against his heart. 'Cendrine, I want to—'

'Jonathan, I have to tell you what happened.'

'What?'

'This morning! What happened this morning at the audition!'

'The audition?'

Her eyes were shining. 'I'm in the ballet, Jonathan.'

He sat back in the banquette, stunned.

'I'll have to work very hard,' she said, 'I'm so far behind the others. At first, I was so discouraged – but then I realized I didn't care. I would at least be dancing while I learned! I don't want to waste a minute.' She laughed. 'That's why I'm late, I stayed at the opera all day and watched all the rehearsals.'

Jonathan could only stare at her.

'I even stayed for the orchestra rehearsals,' she said eagerly. 'You can learn so much about dancing just by listening to the music. Madame told me that once, but I never—'

'Cendrine—'

'—believed her. I knew when you danced, you used your head to count, of course. But you use your ears, too! I learned that today, listening to the orchestra. If you don't *hear* the music, how can you feel it? How can you—'

'Cendrine, stop!'

She pulled back, surprised. 'Jonathan, what's the matter?'

He shook his head in frustration; everything had turned upside down. 'I thought this was settled. I thought that tonight I would – we would—' She stared at him, uncomprehending, and he reached into his pocket and pulled out the velvet box, setting it down on the table before her. She looked at him, then picked up the box, almost reluctantly; opening it, she stared blankly at the opal and diamond ring.

'Three months,' Jonathan said. 'You told me to ask you again in three months.' He took a breath. 'Cendrine, will you marry me?'

She slowly closed the box, refusing to look at him.

'*Why?*' he pleaded. 'Why are you doing this?'

'Not now,' she whispered. 'I can't marry you now.'

He took her hand. 'But I love you, Cendrine!'

'Oh, Jonathan, why can't we just go on as we are? Why can't we just be content to love each other?'

'I want you to be my wife. I want a family!' He shook his head. 'Maybe it does sound middle-class and unsophisticated, but I don't care. I don't want you to have to work for your living. I want to do things for you, Cendrine, show you things, open up worlds for you. Make other people see you the way I do.'

She met his eyes, then slowly pulled her hand away. 'People like Alexander?'

'Alexander? I don't care what he thinks.'

'Yes, you do,' she said quietly. She looked away; when she looked back, her eyes were sad but her mouth was set in a determined line. 'You don't understand,' she said. 'You never have. You don't understand what dancing means to me. If you did, you'd never ask me to give it up.'

'Damn it, Cendrine, I know it's important to you. But for God's sake – I'm asking you to be my wife!'

'You're asking me to give up something before I've even had a chance!'

People at a nearby table were watching them. 'I don't believe this is happening,' Jonathan said quietly. 'I thought you loved me.'

Her eyes brimmed with tears. 'I do! But you're asking me to give up everything I've worked so hard for. You're asking me to choose, Jonathan!'

'Yes! I am!' he said, his voice rising.

More heads turned and Cendrine stared at the other diners defiantly until they looked away. 'The opera company is going to London in three days,' she said, her eyes trained straight ahead, 'and I'm going with them.' She looked at Jonathan. 'I love you, Jonathan, but I want to do this. I *will* do this.' The tears fell down her face. 'I can't marry you!'

She rose suddenly and before he could do anything, swept out from behind the table. As she did so, her skirt caught the champagne bucket, sending it crashing to the marble floor and spraying him with champagne. Cendrine froze for a moment, then fled towards the door; heads craned and waiters came scurrying, waving white linen towels. Pinned in the banquette by their fawning and frantic wiping, Jonathan could only watch helplessly as Cendrine disappeared.

'M'sieur, you are cut!' a waiter announced in alarm, reaching over to wipe Jonathan's hand, but he jumped to his feet, pushing the man away. 'Go away! Leave me alone!' he cried, and the waiters shrunk back. Jonathan looked slowly round him at all the faces; the dining room was quiet. 'Please, just let me be,' Jonathan said, looking up into the pinched face of the maitre d'.

Everyone backed away and Jonathan sank down onto the banquette as slowly a murmur of conversation and clinking cutlery filled the silence once more. He stared at the velvet box sitting on the table. After several long moments, he opened the box and took out the opal ring. Slipping it over the tip of his smallest finger, he stared at it, watching the light ignite the gold sparks buried in the pale blue stone.

Chapter Twenty

Jonathan had not been in a church since leaving Dryden. Sitting now in the cool stillness of the beautiful old Gothic Grace Church, waiting for Sumner's wedding to begin, he longed to feel the transporting sense of peace, but it didn't come. His thoughts were still with Cendrine.

It had been only two weeks since that night in the restaurant, but he was still so torn with confusion, anger and longing that at times he was physically ill. The previous night when he and Sumner had been alone in the library at Katherine's home, Jonathan told him what had happened.

'Well, can't you go on as you were?' Sumner asked.

'It's not enough, Sumner. I don't want a mistress, I want a wife.'

'But she, dear boy, does not want a husband.'

Jonathan shook his head dismally. 'What kind of woman does not want a husband?'

Sumner picked up a nearby copy of the *Ladies' Home Journal*. 'Listen! Listen to what they read,' Sumner said, opening to a romantic serial. ' "Ah, don't struggle, Margot dearest," he cried, "don't put me away with your words, your eyes. Confess your love for me. I am here because I heard you were soon to marry. Margot, I can't bear it; I cannot lose you. I cannot let that vulgar brute take from me all my treasures." She answered plaintively, "We were happy, Stelvio, weren't we?" . . .'

Sumner thumbed to another page. 'And here we have one Alice Preston dispensing advice in an article titled "A Girl's Preparation for Marriage": "Every girl should be taught from her early teens that some day, in the natural course of events, Love must come to her. It is her fate, her glorious fate. When Love comes, it brings in its hands the keys to a Paradise . . ." ' He tossed the magazine aside. 'Passion and puritanism, all in the same issue. Is it any wonder they are confused?'

Sitting in the church, Jonathan thought about Sumner's remark. Cendrine wasn't confused; she knew exactly what she wanted, and it wasn't marriage. But what kind of woman did not want the security marriage brought?

With a rustle of taffeta, the bridal party, a dozen women carrying cascades of roses, came gliding down the aisle. There was a surge from the organ and all heads turned. Jonathan stared at Katherine, holding her father's arm. He had met her for the first time last night, and thought she was sweet but rather plain; but now, as she looked to the altar where Sumner waited, her long face was infused with a beatific light and she looked transformed.

What kind of woman . . .?

When the ceremony was over, everyone gathered on the steps outside the church, spilling out into Broadway. Jonathan stood apart, his eyes taking in the details of the fine New York morning. The maples in adjoining Huntington Close were ablaze against the blue sky and the streets bustled with people, horses – and the new automobiles, bulky contraptions spitting out oil, smoke and smell. A new Packard sat at the curb, gleaming black and brass, the chauffeur awaiting the newlyweds as Mr and Mrs Sumner Briggs III emerged from the church.

241

A bouquet was tossed, goodbyes were shouted, and the bride and groom were ushered off in a cloud of noxious smoke.

Jonathan had been invited to the reception at the Waldorf Astoria – but suddenly the thought of a party was daunting. He began to walk, without direction, wandering for hours until he found himself at the entrance of the *New York Herald* building. He went in almost like an automaton, going up to the newsroom and staring at the dilapidated desks and cabinets. Nothing had changed, except that the gaslights had given way to electric lamps. He asked a secretary if Roscoe Barnes was in; the woman hesitated and told him that Mr Barnes had died a year ago. With a final look around, Jonathan left.

Back out on the street, he stood for a moment, disoriented and dispirited. He didn't want to go back to his hotel; he didn't even want to be in New York. He wanted to be in Paris with Cendrine, but she was in London with the ballet. He drew in a deep breath. The air had a crispness to it, a sharp smell that foretold of something to come. Winter would come early this year. Winter. Dryden. The farm . . .

Home. He would go home for a visit. He turned quickly on his heel and started towards his hotel.

Charles Caras lit a paraffin lamp and replaced the milk-glass globe as Jonathan sank into a chair opposite his father's desk, cradling a cup of coffee.

'You look tired, Jonathan,' his father said softly.

'It was a long trip up from New York, Pa.'

Charles considered him for a moment, then smiled. 'You should have let us know you were coming. It was a shock to hear the carriage and see you standing there suddenly in the yard.'

'I know. I decided very suddenly at the wedding.'

'Hannah's upset. She wanted to make you a proper feast.'

'Pancakes and home-made syrup – that's feast enough.'

The room was quiet. From outside came a rushing sound, the wind blowing through the birch trees, scattering the leaves. 'Syrup,' Jonathan smiled, reminiscing. 'It made me remember something I had forgotten. Ma used to scoop up snow, put it in bowls and pour syrup over it for Marion and me . . .'

'I remember,' Charles said.

Jonathan took a sip of coffee. 'How is Marion?' he asked. 'She hasn't written to me in a long time, probably because I was always too busy to write to her.'

'She got married last year, Jonathan.'

Jonathan lowered his cup slowly, stunned. Married . . . But why should he be so surprised? She was a loving woman. What man wouldn't want her as a wife? Mari – his little Mari . . .

'Ethan Steadman,' Charles said. 'He was a year behind you in school, remember? He's a good man, with his own farm over in Harford. You should go over there, Jonathan. She'd love to see you.'

'Maybe I will.'

'Send word first, or you'll scare the life out of her, too,' Charles said, smiling, his eyes taking in Jonathan's elegant suit and shining shoes. 'She might not recognize you.'

There was another silence. 'This life you've made for yourself in Paris,' Charles said, 'it sounds so exciting.'

'It is, Pa. I wish you could see Paris!'

Charles opened a drawer and pulled out a stack of papers bound by a cord. 'I have,' he said.

Jonathan recognized the writing on the envelopes. They were his letters, every one that he had written to his father over the last five years. He picked up the pile, noting the postmarks: Paris, Vienna, Berlin, London . . . He looked up at his father in amazement.

'You made me see, feel and smell all these places, Jonathan,' his father said. 'You've taken me all over the world with you, taken me to all the places I'll never see for myself.'

Jonathan could not meet his father's eyes; the naked sentiment in them was too overwhelming. How strange it felt to see him in such an intimate light, not as a father but as a man with dreams, his small regrets so rawly exposed! 'Why did you stay here, Pa? Didn't you ever want to leave?' he asked.

'I had responsibilities. To the farm my father left me and Jake. To your mother. To you.'

Jonathan stared at him for a long time; a question, always there but unexpressed, pushed forward. 'Why'd Ma leave?'

His father slowly took off his spectacles, folding them carefully and setting them down without looking up. For a moment, Jonathan feared he had gone too far: like the time when he was twelve and had ventured into a field that was undermined with limestone holes. He had kept moving even as the dirt crumbled beneath his feet. Now this treacherous question had been broached and there was nothing to do but keep going. 'Why did she leave, Pa?' he repeated softly.

'Because she had to,' his father said finally. He looked up, his eyes distant. 'There was something pulling at her inside. It had been there from the start, but it took me a while to see it. This place, this farm, me . . . none of it was ever enough for her.' His fingers closed around his spectacles. 'She'd go for these long walks,' he said quietly, 'walking for hours, miles away. She'd come back, her hair loose and her hem caked with mud, and I'd see it there in her face, all flushed from the wind and the unhappiness.'

'Did *I* make her unhappy?'

Charles shook his head. 'No, no, she loved you. You brought her joy. But when you went away, it returned: the same restlessness. It was as though she waited just long enough to see you on your way, then it was her turn.' He sighed, gazing off into the corners. 'She was not like other women, Jonathan. She was headstrong, with a mind of her own.' He glanced back at Jonathan. 'She wrote poems. She had no education to speak of, but she wrote these beautiful poems . . .'

Jonathan blinked. 'Do you still have them?'

Charles shook his head. 'I burned them after she left. Stupid . . . stupid . . .'

Jonathan leaned back in his chair, his throat thick with emotion.

'I tried to find her, not long after you left for school,' Charles said softly. 'Tracked her down to St Louis. She was in a restaurant with another man, wearing this dress, I'll never forget it, blue and white flowers. I was all set to charge in and put up a fight – but she looked so happy, happier than I had seen her look in a long time. So I left. Last I heard, she was in California. That was ten years ago. We're still married, legally.' He looked at Jonathan. 'It took me a long time to get over it. But I realized finally that it wasn't really me, or even this place . . . Your mother was a different kind of woman, a woman who didn't need a home, a family or even marriage.'

Jonathan raised a hand to his brow, covering his eyes. What kind of woman . . .?

It was quiet in the parlour. Charles raised his cup and took a sip of coffee. 'It's cold,' he said. 'Do you want some more?'

Behind the shelter of his hand, Jonathan shook his head. Slowly, he took his hand away; his eyes glistened, liquid in the lamp's soft glow. Charles stared at him, unsmiling.

'Pa,' Jonathan said haltingly, 'there's this woman in Paris. I'm in love with her.'

Charles' face registered his surprise. 'You never mentioned her in your letters—'

'I know. But I want to tell you now.'

For the next half-hour, Charles was quiet as Jonathan told him about Cendrine. When the story was finished, Charles was silent.

'I want to marry her, Pa,' Jonathan said. 'But she doesn't want that.' He hesitated, searching his father's face. In the dim light, it looked drawn, suddenly older.

'I can't tell you what to do, Jonathan,' Charles said softly. 'I can only tell you that some people can't be tied down and the closer you hold them, the harder they'll struggle to get away. I didn't understand that about your mother – and I lost her.'

Jonathan couldn't answer. For a long time, both men were quiet, then Charles rose, gathering up the coffee cups. 'I'll go and refill these,' he said, avoiding Jonathan's eyes.

Jonathan sat alone for a moment, his eyes travelling over the parlour, lingering in the shadowed corners. He rose and went to the kitchen where his father stood at the stove.

'She's the woman I love, Pa,' Jonathan said softly, 'the only woman I will ever love. I'm going to marry her. I have to.'

Charles stared at his son, stared at the tall man in the fine suit and shining shoes, knowing there was nothing he could say to deter him, nothing he could do to protect him. He came forward and embraced him.

'I know,' he said. 'I know.'

Chapter Twenty-One

It was near dusk and a brisk breeze was stirring up whirlwinds of brown and gold leaves from the gutters. Jonathan and Alexander walked along silently, side by side, each waiting for the other to speak.

'The sky is beautiful tonight, isn't it? Such extraordinary violets and pinks,' Alexander ventured.

'It's a fine evening,' Jonathan said.

And they walked on in silence once more, Jonathan wondering what was on Alexander's mind, wary of another argument over Cendrine. It had been months since they had spoken and it was Alexander who had requested that they meet. Seeing his friend, Jonathan realized that he had missed him; Alexander's affection and support had become a constant in his life. Without Cendrine, who was still in England, his life was pale enough, but it had been made even dimmer by Alexander's absence.

They travelled the length of Rue Castiglione and entered the twilight under the trees of the Tuileries. 'We need to talk, Jonathan,' Alexander said.

'I agree.'

'That night at the theatre,' Alexander began, 'I know I hurt your feelings. On reflection, I realize I spoke hastily – from my heart and not my head. But it was only because I want the best for you.'

Jonathan slowed his step, but said nothing.

'You know,' Alexander said, smiling slightly, 'there are people who wonder about our friendship. "Now what does Alexander see in that American? What has he done to merit his attention?" '

Jonathan stopped. 'What do you tell them?'

'Nothing. I owe no one answers.'

Jonathan looked away towards the quay; feeling Alexander's hand on his shoulder, he looked back. 'Except you,' Alexander said. 'I think of you as my brother, Jonathan. And I've missed you during these last few months.'

There was nothing false in Alexander's handsome face or in his voice, and Jonathan was moved by the unexpected intimacy. Alexander broke the awkwardness with a smile, and they walked on.

'I always wanted a brother when I was growing up,' Alexander confided, his voice lighter. 'I'm not sure – I was only four at the time – but I believe my mother was going to have another child. I remember only a dreadful night, with her screams carrying through the halls and the servants running everywhere. I presume it was a miscarriage – no one ever told me, of course. Soon after, she brought me here to live with her. My parents led separate lives, I scarcely saw my father at all. It was quite lonely living here and I wanted desperately to go home. I was convinced it would all have been different if I had had a brother.'

The sky had deepened into a purple bruise over the grey rooftops as they started across the Pont Royal. Alexander stopped and leaned on the bridge; Jonathan waited, fascinated by Alexander's remembrances.

'I grew to love Paris, of course,' Alexander said, his dark eyes dancing over the grey Seine and its necklaces of bridges. 'But there was always this emptiness.'

Jonathan stared at Alexander's profile. 'You should

marry, Alexander. Have your own children.'

Alexander shook his head, smiling. 'I'd make a poor husband and a poorer father. It's a trait that runs in my family. Besides, I have never met a woman who could accept that she would always be second in my heart after my business. Another woman they can accept – but grubby sheets of newsprint?'

The thought made Alexander chuckle. It was fast growing dark now and Jonathan could no longer see the shadings in his expression, but he could tell from the lighter tone in his voice that the private Alexander Profitt had submerged again.

'I have something for you,' Alexander said, pulling a paper out of his breast pocket. 'A token of my friendship.'

Jonathan took the stiff paper and unfolded it, struggling to read in the dying light. 'It grants you a 10 per cent share in the *Herald* company,' Alexander said.

Jonathan looked up, shocked. 'Alexander, this is no token of friendship. This is your life!'

'Yes, it is. But I'm forty-one years old, Jonathan, and I will never marry. You have become my family – you have been a friend to me when other men have only disappointed me. I love you like a brother, and I want you to share the thing I value above everything else in the world.'

'I don't know what to say.'

Alexander smiled. 'Nothing is necessary. I know your loyalty to the *Herald* is without question.' He paused. 'I would like you to take over as editor-in-chief.'

'*What?*'

'Simpson's retiring. It's your turn now. You're ready. I know you love writing, but I would like you to learn to run things. Will you accept?'

Jonathan looked at the paper in his hand with wonderment. Not only was the offer stunning, but it was surprising to hear Alexander request, rather than demand, an action. 'Yes. Of course,' he said.

Alexander smiled, letting out a sigh of satisfaction. 'Good! Let's have a drink to celebrate,' he said, taking Jonathan's arm.

When they reached the quay, Jonathan stopped under a gaslight. 'Alexander, this doesn't change anything,' he said. 'I still feel the same about Cendrine. I still intend to marry her.'

In the flat yellow light, Alexander's shadowed face was inscrutable. 'Do what you must, Jonathan.'

Cendrine stood in the wings, a towel draped across her bare shoulders, watching the beginning of the opera's fourth act. Her part was finished, so she was free for the rest of the evening.

As she started towards the dressing room, another dancer came running up. 'We're going out for dinner to celebrate the end of the run,' she announced. 'Want to come along?'

'I'd love to,' Cendrine answered.

'Oh, did you hear about Gilberte? She's getting married!'

'How wonderful!'

The other woman shrugged. 'Yes, but as soon as Legrandin finds out, he'll fire her. Well, I'll meet you outside!'

Cendrine was left alone to make her way to the dressing room. Poor Gilberte! She was such a promising dancer, but it was true that the ballet master would dismiss her as soon as he found out. He tolerated no distractions and marriage was a considerable one in his eyes. Her thoughts soon drifted to Jonathan; tomorrow, the company would return to Paris. Perhaps this separation had given him enough time and distance to think clearly . . . She closed her eyes, trying to conjure up the feeling of him. Her body missed him. *She* missed him.

Yet being away, being in London had been so exciting, so different from Paris! Everything about it – the people, the food, the sights – had been grand and new. She had enjoyed going out with the other dancers, eating curried lamb at an Indian restaurant; going to a horse race at Ascot; seeing Oscar Wilde's play *An Ideal Husband*. The month in London had not sated her thirst to see the world; it had made it grow stronger. She thought suddenly of what Jonathan had said the last night she saw him in the restaurant: 'I can open new worlds for you.'

Oh, Jonathan, she thought, that's not what I want from you. I can do that for myself. I just want you to love me.

'Miss, there's a wire for you.'

Cendrine took the envelope from the stage manager. Could it be from Jonathan? She unfolded the paper.

MUST SEE YOU IMMEDIATELY UPON
YOUR RETURN. CONCERNS
JONATHAN. PLEASE DO NOT SPEAK
TO HIM BEFORE. ALEXANDER PROFITT.

Alexander Profitt. What in the world did he want from her? She crumbled the paper and tossed it on the floor, an involuntary shiver going down her spine.

Quickly finishing her hair, she was pulling on her coat when her eye fell on the wadded paper. She bent to retrieve it; and slowly unfolding it in spite of herself, she read it again, then folded it and put it in her bag.

It was nearly midnight. Cendrine sat at a table near the window of her apartment, watching the street below. It was quiet, except for the soft tapping of a branch against the glass. A carriage came slowly down La Perouse and she tensed, but it went on by. It wasn't Jonathan.

Perhaps he had not received her message. She had left word at both his apartment and his office that she wanted to see him, but had received no reply.

Her eyes remained fixed on the empty street. No, he would come, she was sure of that. He would come believing that she had changed her mind. She closed her eyes. Was she doing the right thing? The question had haunted her since her meeting yesterday with Alexander Profitt. Was she doing the right thing by telling Jonathan that it was over?

A part of her had known for some time now that it had to end. She had known it in London. Maybe that was why she had agreed to see Alexander; she knew he would finally voice the thoughts she had been afraid to face. Alexander had been cordial, even respectful – nothing like he had been at Villa Vignon. He had told her of his plan to give Jonathan a share of his company, but only on condition that she end their affair.

'You *must* end it, Mademoiselle LeClerc,' he said. 'A man seeking to elevate himself socially cannot marry below himself and Jonathan is ambitious; he must play by the rules, however cruel they are. I know that's difficult for a woman to understand, but you must try, for Jonathan's sake.'

Cendrine opened her eyes, focusing back on the street. What Alexander would never comprehend was that she understood only too well. But it wasn't just for Jonathan's sake: it was for her own as well. Her ambitions, like Jonathan's, were subject to their own cruel rules and if she married, like Gilberte she would be dismissed from the company. Where then could she go – back to the Folies? And Jonathan had said he didn't want her to work for a living. He refused to accept that, for Cendrine, dancing wasn't work – it was life itself.

It wasn't fair. It wasn't fair that a man could control his own life, give it whatever shape he wished, while a woman had so few options. Oh, she could choose to be like Marcelle, living free outside society's bounds, using men for sex and love as men used women – but the price, as Cendrine had seen in the ravaged, lonely faces of the café models, was too high. The only other choice was marriage: trading dreams for the security of social position and family.

Family. Jonathan had told her often that he wanted children. Why was that something she had never felt the need for? Why did the sight of a baby not stir her as it did other women? Was she somehow abnormal?

'*You must end it.*' Alexander's words echoed in her head. '*You must end it because Jonathan never will.*' She leaned against the window. Alexander was right; she didn't want the life Jonathan wanted. It had to end.

She heard the screech of the gate below and tensed, sitting up straight, motionless, listening to the footsteps on the stairs and then the sound of a key turning in the lock.

Then Jonathan was standing before her in the doorway, slightly out of breath, his face expressionless. He took off his hat, waiting for some sign from her.

'I'm sorry it's so late. I only just got your note,' he said.

Cendrine rose slowly. 'Come in,' she said.

He came forward quickly, his eyes travelling swiftly, hungrily, over her face and body. 'God, how I've missed you,' he said softly. 'I didn't know you had returned, and—'

He stopped, just short of touching her. She was staring at the flowers he held in his hand: a bouquet of white roses, utterly without colour. He held them out to her, smiling, expectant. 'The last bunch, just as the vendor was closing,' he said.

Her eyes, grey and naked, held his. In that one moment she told him everything. Then she quickly looked away.

Very slowly, Jonathan's smile faded and his eyes dropped to the floor. He let the flowers fall. 'Why did you ask me to come here?' he murmured.

Cendrine turned her back to him, unable to speak.

'Tell me,' he said. 'You owe me that much, at least.'

She turned to face him. 'It's over,' she said gently. 'It's over, Jonathan. It won't work, not the way we both need it to. It has to end, and we have to go on with our own lives. We have to . . .' She paused, fighting tears. 'We have to go on.'

He stared at her for a long time. '*Go on*?' he murmured. 'Simple as that – just go on?'

She shut her eyes tight so she wouldn't cry. 'Yes.'

He shook his head slowly. 'I don't think I can, Cendrine – not after what we have had. I can't just "go on".'

'Please, Jonathan. Please . . .'

'I don't think you can either.' He reached for her and she jumped back as if burned.

'Don't touch me,' she whispered, starting to cry. 'Oh, please, don't touch me!'

He drew back and as he did, his shoulders sagged. Suddenly, everything was clear. The soft hiss of the gaslight; the gentle tap-tap-tap of a branch against glass; the sweet smell of rose potpourri sitting in a delicate bowl on the table; the fine blue veins in Cendrine's white hand, standing in high relief as she gripped the back of a chair: it all came to him now, so sharp and heightened that it was almost painful, the moment for ever burned into his senses.

'Please go.' Cendrine's whispered plea, only half-heard, brought him back to reality. He realized he was still holding the bouquet. Woodenly, he held it out, then withdrew it. 'You don't like cut flowers,' he whispered. 'I remember now . . .'

He turned slowly and went out of the door. Cendrine heard the iron gate slam and the slow retreat of footsteps in the street below.

Chapter Twenty-Two

A clamorous rattling rose up from the street below, wrenching Cendrine awake from her dream. A wonderful dream in which she was nestled in a big warm bed in her beautiful apartment on Rue La Perouse.

She rubbed her eyes, bringing into focus the room with its faded grey-papered walls and sad sticks of furniture. She closed her eyes as she realized how the dream had tricked her. She wasn't in her apartment on Rue La Perouse; she hadn't been for more than a year now. She had given up the apartment, unable to afford the rent, and had moved to this room, filled with the dust, smells and noises of the street.

The noises rose up to her now, proclaiming the beginning of another day. The old concierge dragging the dustbins through the courtyard, followed by the swooshing sounds of the women sweeping out the gutters. Then came the wail of the fishwoman, heralding a discordant symphony of wine casks being flushed and anvils being pounded. She waited until she heard the chirping sound that meant the man in the apartment below had hung his canary cage in the window, and she got out of bed.

She went to a small iron stove to light a fire. She prepared some coffee, standing near the warmth of the stove, trying to wake up. Winter was coming, she could feel it in her body.

She took her coffee to the table by the window, gazed down over the uninspiring view of grey rooftops and dirty, vine-laced windows. Normally, she tried not to dwell on her surroundings, but the mocking luxury of her dream had brought her lowered status sharply back to her. It had been two years now since she had given up her life as La Phalare, and Oliver had been right after all. She was barely existing on her wages as an opera dancer. She had sold most of the possessions that she had worked so hard to get, all her pretty gowns and costume jewellery. Yet there was never enough money, and this month, she didn't even have enough for the rent.

Cendrine glanced across the room to Roland's bed. It was untouched again. He often stayed away for a night or two, out running with his bohemian friends. But this time, he had been gone for five nights with no word. It was, she suspected, because they had had another fight, a bitter one, about his refusal to get a job. 'I won't subjugate myself to a system that rewards the rich and exploits the poor,' he yelled. She had screamed back, 'Then let your idiot friends support you, because I won't keep doing it!' She didn't regret her words; she was tired of Roland's rhetoric and revolutionary posing. But she regretted the schism that had developed between them. She needed her brother, now more than ever, and he wasn't there for her.

She went to the sink to wash, shuddering as she splashed her neck and face with cold water. Oh, how her body hurt this morning! Every bone, ever muscle ached. The strain of the last two years of dancing had taken its toll. A class every morning, a rehearsal every day, a performance every night. An endless cycle of exhaustion, pain and frustration as she tried to make up for the lost years. She would never dance like Pavlova; she had yet even to dance in a real role.

For the first time in her life, dancing was losing its pleasure. She used to feel an exhilarating fusion of mind and body whenever she danced. But now her body had become a separate thing, a mere machine that was slowly running down, deprived of the passion that had fuelled it.

Now, the thought of subjecting herself to another rehearsal in the draughty studio was unbearable. An idea came to her suddenly. A hot bath, that was what she needed, and damn the cost! She went to the apartment next door and asked the neighbour's son to go to the bathhouse on the Boulevard St-Michel. Soon after, a man lugged a zinc tub into the apartment and filled it with hot water, hauled up six flights in buckets.

Cendrine eased herself into the tub. At two francs, the bath was a luxury, but she didn't care. She leaned back, closing her eyes in pleasure. The hot water was soothing, and as her body relaxed, she let her mind float. It was dangerous, because her unbridled thoughts often turned to Jonathan. And they did now, but she let it happen.

She didn't think about that last night. She thought only about the finest moments. She thought about where he was now, wondering what he was doing. Oliver had told her he was now editor-in-chief of the *Herald*, but she yearned to know the details of his everyday existence, the wine he was drinking, the colour of his coat.

She ached to see him, but forced herself to stay away from places he frequented. Then, a month ago, standing in her usual position in the wings, she had seen him in the opera audience, sitting with Alexander and a beautiful brunette. When it became clear that the woman was his escort, she had drawn back, unable to watch.

The bath was working its magic on her body, the heat easing her hurt. She soaped her hands and ran them over her neck and shoulders. The feel of her own hands slipping over her skin made her close her eyes in sadness. Her body had once been like a vibrant voice, reminding her, as she danced or made love, that she was alive. But now it was mute. Her hands moved slowly down across her breasts, over the curve of her belly, down to the inside of her thigh. She sighed, moving to a touch that was not Jonathan's but one she tried to recreate as his.

That evening, she danced listlessly. She returned to the dark apartment and tried to eat, but could not. She thought about going to see Marcelle, but lacked the energy even to do that. She was sitting, staring out of the window, when a knock on the door interrupted her thoughts. She opened the door to see a poorly dressed man. His furtive eyes made her immediately apprehensive.

'Cendrine LeClerc?'

'Who are you?'

'Your brother told me to get word to you. He's been arrested.' He turned and bolted down the stairs.

'Wait!' Cendrine yelled. But he was gone. Rigid with shock, Cendrine stared down into the darkness. Then she sprang into action, grabbing her coat.

At the *commissariat de police*, she was led down into a dank basement, filled with noxious smells. There she saw Roland slumped on the floor behind iron bars. His face was misshapen with bruises and cuts, and he was lying very still with his eyes closed. She stood at the bars, staring at him.

'Oh Roland! What happened?' she whispered.

The guard came up behind her. 'He killed a man.'

Cendrine spun around. 'What?'

'There was a riot. Your brother and four other

anarchists stabbed one of our men.'

'Anarchist? Roland wouldn't kill anyone.'

'Call out when you're ready to come up,' the guard said.

The door clanked shut, and Cendrine turned back to the cell. 'Roland?' she said. 'Can you hear me?'

After a few moments, he stirred and opened his eyes, which focused on her unsteadily. 'Go away, Cendrine,' he murmured.

'I want to help, Roland.' There was silence. 'Talk to me, please!' she cried.

With great effort, Roland got to his feet, leaning against the wall. He stumbled towards her, bracing himself on the bars. Close up, the sight of his bloodied face made her recoil.

'Oh, Roland,' she whispered, her eyes welling. 'What happened? The guard said you killed someone. He said you—'

'It's true.'

She was stunned. 'But why?'

'They executed a man, an innocent man, whose only crime was that he stood up against the oppression of the system. It was our duty to strike back.'

The words emerged tonelessly, as if by rote. Cendrine shook her head. 'I don't understand . . .'

Roland closed his eyes. 'No, you don't. No one does. You're all blind.'

Cendrine started to cry. 'Roland, please. Don't . . .'

He sank back down to the floor. 'Go away, Cendrine.'

'I want to help you!'

'You can't. They'll find me guilty and I'll be shot.'

'No, there's got to be something we can do.' She bent down and reached through the bars to touch his cheek. He flinched and pulled away.

'Maybe you can get one of your rich gentlemen friends to bribe the judge,' he muttered. He laughed softly and

260

turned his head to the wall.

'Roland, please!' She stood up, calling his name again, but there was no answer and no movement. She was relieved to see the rise and fall of his chest; he had only fainted. She stood gazing at him for a few minutes longer, then called for the guard to let her out.

Two days later, Roland and the other men were transferred to prison to await trial. Cendrine read the newspaper accounts about the riot. The politics of the event escaped her; she knew only that Roland was going to die, and there was nothing she could do to stop it.

Sick with anxiety, she finally turned to Oliver. 'Your brother is right,' he said, 'there is nothing you can do. There have been too many assassinations and political outbursts. The public wants order restored.' Remembering what Roland had said about a bribe, she asked Oliver if it were possible. 'Of course,' he answered, 'but it takes money and the right connections. Even I can't help you this time, dear. No one can.'

But Oliver was wrong. She knew there was one person who could help. She sent a message to Alexander Profitt. By the afternoon, he sent word back, agreeing to meet her.

Cendrine arrived at the café early, taking a table by the window. It was raining, and as she sat watching the people hurrying by under umbrellas, she nervously smoothed her hair back from her temples. She toyed with a spoon and noticed that her white gloves were soiled. She pulled them off and thrust them in her purse.

She looked up to see Alexander Profitt at the door of the café. He came forward. 'Mademoiselle LeClerc,' he said politely.

'Sit down, M'sieur Profitt, please,' she said.

He slipped off his coat and took the chair opposite her. His dark eyes were dispassionate, but she could see the hint of curiosity in them.

'Thank you for seeing me,' she said.

'It's my pleasure.'

She paused, about to make conversation, but decided suddenly that her only chance was directness. She took a deep breath. 'I need your help, M'sieur Profitt,' she said firmly.

As she told him about Roland, Alexander listened, his expression revealing nothing. 'What do you expect me to do?' he asked simply.

'Lend me the money.' She waited, but he just stared at her. 'I know you don't like me,' she added, 'but you're the only person who can help my brother.'

Alexander stared at her steadfastly. 'I deplore what your brother claims to stand for, you know.'

'My brother is not a killer.'

'Nonetheless, he and others like him would like nothing better than to see men like me dead.'

Cendrine sat silent, steeling herself against crying. 'Please, M'sieur Profitt, I need your help. I will find a way to repay the money,' she said firmly.

'I don't care about that. If I do this, it will be because I feel like it.'

She stared at him. 'Then you name the terms.'

He said nothing. She held his eyes steady for a few seconds, then had to look away, the hardness of his black eyes making her feel vulnerable.

'I will help your brother,' he said, 'if you will become my mistress.'

Why hadn't it surprised her? Somehow, in the back of her mind, she had known that this was the only thing he would want. 'For how long?' she asked, staring at him.

'Until we . . . tire of the arrangement.'

She closed her eyes. 'All right,' she said.

Alexander ordered two cognacs. 'I don't want anyone to know about this,' Cendrine said softly.

262

'Nor do I.'

They stared at each other, both knowing they spoke of Jonathan. They each took a drink, Cendrine shutting her eyes as the liquor burned down her throat.

When she opened them, she saw Alexander looking at her, his eyes softer now. 'I will take care of you,' he said. 'You'll want for nothing.' He rose, drawing on his coat. He gave her a graceful nod. 'Good night, Mademoiselle LeClerc.'

Cendrine watched his carriage disappear into the rain.

A week later, Alexander sent a carriage to move Cendrine and her belongings to an elegant apartment. He set up accounts for her at the best shops and hired a small household staff. Over the next month, a continuous flow of gifts arrived. But he sent no personal messages and no indication of when he intended to exercise the intimate option of their bargain.

As the weeks dragged on, Cendrine heard nothing about Roland, either. Then, late one night, he appeared at her door. He looked around the opulent apartment with weary eyes.

'How can you afford this place?' he asked.

'I can't tell you,' she answered.

'Does it have anything to do with me?'

'No questions, Roland, please.'

'Good God, Cendrine, what have you done?' When she didn't answer, he just shook his head. There was something depleted about him, as if the anger and all his other emotions had been leached away by his imprisonment. 'I have to go,' he said. 'I have to leave the country, and I won't be back. It was part of the deal.'

'Where are you going?' she asked in alarm.

'America.'

'Oh, Roland!' She threw her arms around him, crying. He stood stiffly. Finally his arms came up to encircle

263

her. 'I'm sorry, Cendrine, I'm sorry,' he said gruffly. She extracted a promise from him that he would send word when he was settled, and then he was gone.

After Roland's departure, Cendrine felt a loneliness more profound than any she had ever experienced. During the long days at the opera, her dancing sustained her, but at night, when she returned to the coldly beautiful apartment, the isolation closed in around her. It was coupled with a growing anxiety over Alexander. Two months had passed, yet there was still no word from him. Her initial relief had long since given way to a paralysing dread. Now she wished he would come, just to get it over with.

Then, on Christmas Eve, she returned home from the theatre to find a gift from Alexander waiting for her. It was a vial of Jicky perfume from the salon of Guerlain. Cendrine held the stopper up to her nose. It was a curious scent, vaguely Oriental, smelling of lemon, spices and lavender. There was a note with it. 'Please dine with me this evening at eight.'

At seven, she sat down in the drawing room to wait. The staff had set out the dinner and silently disappeared. The wine was decanted. A fire was burning in the grate. She wore a satin gown of midnight blue, designed by Worth, her neck and arms touched by the sweet perfume. She sat motionless by the fire, staring out of the window at the snow falling softly outside.

At eight, she heard the key in the lock but did not go to the door. Alexander came to her. The severe cut of his black suit made him look taller and his face more austere than usual.

'You look beautiful,' he said. He held out his hand. She hesitated, then put her hand in his. 'Shall we go in to dinner?'

The pheasant was rare, the wine a velvety burgundy, but Cendrine tasted nothing. Alexander talked about a recent trip to London, but she heard little of what he said. She was waiting, waiting for it to be over with. Finally, Alexander fell silent.

'Do you like the perfume?' he asked.

'Yes,' she answered.

'It suits you, I think. Modern, but with an echo of something ancient.'

'You see me as a contradiction?'

He smiled. 'It's a compliment, Cendrine.'

His unexpected use of her first name was disorienting. She picked up her wine glass and took a drink.

'You *are* a modern woman,' he said. 'Not in the way of those suffragette creatures, but in the way you have recreated yourself. Yet there's still something in you of that crumbling old hill village.'

She lowered the glass. 'I thought I was just an opportunist. That's what you told me once, and you didn't mean it as a compliment then.'

'I was cruel. I didn't mean to be.'

Cendrine said nothing. Alexander stared at her intently for a moment, then reached over the table to pour more wine. 'There's a part of me that admires your ambition,' he said. 'I just didn't want to see it affect Jonathan.'

His name sent a jolt through her. 'My ambition was never directed at Jonathan,' she said. 'It was directed at dance. It still is.'

'Still, you wanted to marry him.'

'No,' she said, holding Alexander's eyes steadily. 'A dancer is not a normal person. She cannot marry. There's not enough room for both things in her life. She can love someone, but that someone has to . . . understand that he cannot be first in her heart.' She looked away.

'And Jonathan did not understand?' Alexander asked.

She didn't answer. Alexander leaned back in his chair,

watching Cendrine closely, considering what she had just said about Jonathan. Was it possible that she truly had not wanted to marry him? He could not believe it of a woman, yet there was something in her expression that made him think she was telling the truth.

'This dancing, it's that important to you?' he asked.

'Yes.'

'Well, you won't have to worry about it with me,' he said. 'I'll make no demands on your freedom. There will be no attachments.'

For the first time, he noticed the colour of her eyes. In the candlelight they were more grey than blue and without a hint of softness. He realized now he had never really looked closely at her face. His attraction to her had been limited to that one night he saw her perform, and if she had remained in his mind it was only as a fleeting infatuation with a stage illusion. Now he examined each feature of her face. Individually, they did not stir him: her eyes were too wide-set, her lips too childish, the roundness of her face too common. Yet somehow, when taken together, her features fell into harmony, producing a face of irresistible contradiction: purity and voluptuousness, fragility and strength, new and old. He had seen the same paradoxical qualities in her dancing. But what was then mere tricks of light and movement was now transformed into the sensual realities of skin, bone, hair and blood. He felt a sudden stab of arousal and gazed at her, amazed, as it coursed languidly up through his body like a drug.

He rose, holding out his hand. 'Come with me,' he said softly.

She was silent as he led her to the bedroom. He watched as she undressed, but she didn't look at him when he took off his coat and shirt. When he took her in his arms and bent to kiss her neck, he felt a tightening in her body; then her arms came up to cross his back. He picked her up, amazed at the slightness of her body, and put her in the bed. He stared down at her small breasts and slender hips; her body was the antithesis of all that he found exciting, yet he was aching with desire.

Her lips were soft and yielding when he kissed her, and her arms held him. But there was nothing behind it but a sense of duty. He kissed her harder, as if trying to extract a passion equal to what he felt, but there was nothing. He drew back to look at her. Her eyes brimmed with tears.

'I'm sorry,' she whispered.

She pulled him down and kissed him, more forcefully now but still with an emptiness. He drew back again, and took her by the wrists. He stared down at her, his heart beating fast, his body screaming out simply to take her and be done with it. But he let go of her.

He stood with his back to her for a moment, then slowly pulled on his shirt. He picked up his coat, hesitating as if he wanted to say something. Instead, he went to the door, but stopped in the doorway, looking back. 'We weren't alone tonight,' he said softly. 'In the future, I hope we can be.' Then he turned and was gone.

Chapter Twenty-Three

Alexander continued to come to the apartment on Rue Daunou every Sunday. It was always the same: he would send a polite note, arrive for dinner at eight and depart at eleven. His behaviour towards Cendrine also never varied. It was cordial, almost courtly and, after that first night, he never tried to force himself on her again. Throughout the winter, the pattern continued, and though Cendrine wondered about Alexander's lack of aggression, she gradually lost her dislike of him. Eventually, she came to look forward to and enjoy their interludes. Alexander entertained her with stories about his privileged world. He talked about politics and history, and she listened, intrigued and amazed that he seemed to find a woman a worthy listener. She was amazed, too, to discover that he wanted to know about her world. At first she had been hesitant; dance was such an insular, boring topic for a man like him. Yet he listened.

It surprised her – it was so unlike Jonathan's indifference – and, in the end, it seduced her. Alexander had come to treat her as something of an equal. She did not fool herself into believing he truly cared for her. It was a business arrangement. It was fitting that whenever they addressed each other in French, they each always used the formal *vous* instead of the more intimate *tu*. Yet gradually, she found herself liking Alexander. And finally, when Alexander led her to the bedroom, it was this fondness that allowed her to accept it. Alexander was a passionate, skilful lover. And though she missed the mystical, transporting intensity that she had always felt with Jonathan, she felt replenished by Alexander's lovemaking. Her body, which she had feared deadened, was alive. She was alive.

The intensity returned to her dancing, as she felt again the simple joy of physical movement. Then, in May of 1909, she heard that a new ballet company was coming to Paris to offer an entire programme devoted just to dance. Posters touting the Imperial Ballet of Russia, led by the impresario Serge Diaghilev, appeared all over Paris. The posters showed a delicate charcoal portrait of Anna Pavlova, but the talk among insiders was of a new sensation named Nijinsky. On the night of the performance, lines of carriages and motorcars surrounded the Théâtre du Châtelet. The old theatre had been transformed for the occasion, its walls and floors covered in red cloth, its boxes draped in red velvet. Monarchs, ambassadors, socialites and members of the arts elite filled the seats. All the prettiest young women in Paris, recruited from actresses and dancers, had been given seats in the front row of the dress circle, blondes alternating with brunettes. The effect was so striking that someone remarked it looked like a basket of fresh flowers.

Like the other opera dancers, Cendrine was given a ticket. She took her place with her cohort in the front row of the upper circle. She saw Oliver and Alexander; then Jonathan came in, escorting the same brunette she had seen him with before. She watched them in morbid curiosity until the lights went down.

The dancing made her forget everything, as she watched the passionate Russians with great longing.

Nijinsky induced in her an empathy so strong that she felt lifted from her seat. He spun and jumped, his feet beating like hummingbird wings. The temperature in the theatre seemed to rise, and at the end, instead of running after the others into the wings, he leaped. The audience gasped. The timing of the leap was so clever that only the ascent was seen, leaving an endless illusion of never coming down. There was a volley of thunderous applause.

The next morning, she arrived at class to find a knot of dancers gathered around a notice on the wall. When she read it, her heart stopped. The Imperial Ballet was auditioning for corps dancers that afternoon.

Cendrine arrived at the audition half an hour early. In the dusk of the backstage light, she saw the Russian dancers just finishing their rehearsal. Cendrine watched, her eyes riveted to Nijinsky. Finally, the pianist stopped and the dancers faded into the wings. Cendrine caught snippets of their Russian, and was momentarily transported back to La Turbie, back to Madame Kchessinskaya's apartment. To her surprise, she found that she could understand some of the language – the dancers were talking about how ravishing Paris was.

A man called out for auditioners to come forward. He was thin and looked high-strung, wearing a tunic that made him resemble a fencing instructor. There were fifteen dancers, most of whom Cendrine recognized from the opera, including two talented soloists. But even their presence did not bother Cendrine. This time she felt confident, not as at her audition for the opera years ago. Somehow, seeing this wonderful company, being among these splendid Russian dancers, she felt curiously at ease, as if she had come home. Or as if a part of home was there with her – Madame at her side, calling out the steps, counting out the beats, encouraging her.

After it was over, the thin man came up to her. He

introduced himself as Michel Fokine, the ballet master.

'How old are you?' he asked.

She hesitated. 'Twenty-seven.'

'Not young.' His eyes held hers. 'But you have a passion that the young ones lack. I can use you.'

That night when Alexander came to the apartment, she told him she had been accepted by the Russian ballet. Alexander listened in silence.

'Oh, Alexander, I can't tell you what this means to me!' she said. Giddy with happiness, she threw her arms around his neck and kissed him. After a moment, they pulled back, both surprised at her impulsive ardour. She went to the table to pour a glass of wine. 'It's my chance, finally,' she said softly. It was a moment before she could turn to face him and hand him the glass.

His dark eyes scanned her face. He took a drink, reconsidered and drained his glass. She poured him another. 'The company is returning to St Petersburg soon, I suppose,' he said, his voice neutral.

'No,' she said softly. 'Diaghilev wants to form a new company. He wants to move it to Monte Carlo.'

He turned to look at her. 'Monte Carlo?'

'He can't raise the money he needs in Russia. He wants to create a company, based in Monte Carlo, but with seasons in London, Rome and Paris.'

Alexander took another drink of wine, then walked slowly into the drawing room and sat down before the fire. Cendrine went to his side, but he didn't look up.

'You said this was to last until we tired of the arrangement,' she said softly. 'We made a bargain, Alexander, and I will hold up my part of it. You could stop me from going.'

He looked at her. 'No, I couldn't,' he said. 'It's the most important thing in your life, Cendrine, just as the newspaper is the most important thing in mine.' He paused. 'That's why this has worked. We understand that about each other.' He looked back at the fire. 'Consider your obligation fulfilled.'

She raised her hand to touch his head but stopped, her fingers poised just above his dark hair. Glancing around the drawing room, at the marble and gilt, at the silk-covered walls that at times had felt like a cage, she felt a strange mix of exhilaration and sadness.

Alexander was silent for a long time. 'Monte Carlo?' he said softly. 'The *Lysistrata* has been in Denmark for repairs, but I was thinking of taking her down to the Riviera this July. May I come to see you?'

'I'd like that very much,' she said softly.

In Monte Carlo, Cendrine spent the rest of the spring and summer in a blissful state of fatigue as the company prepared for its first season. Exciting new ballets were being created by Fokine, and the corps dancers, a group drawn from six nationalities, were being drilled by the Italian master Enrico Cecchetti to unify their divergent styles. Cendrine could feel her technique expanding by the day.

In July, Alexander sent a carriage to Monte Carlo to bring Cendrine to the *Lysistrata*, docked at Beaulieu. Alone on the yacht for three days, they slipped easily back into their relationship, sharing their experiences and Alexander's bed. On the morning Cendrine was to return to Monte Carlo, Alexander took her up the steep roads, back to La Turbie. Silently he watched her as she walked slowly through the dusty streets, her face set like stone. Her expression remained unchanged when she came to the boarded-up café, and even when the baker next door told her that her father had died five years before. It was only when she went to see the old Russian woman that Cendrine seemed to become human again, emerging from the apartment with a tender smile and brimming eyes. And when she led Alexander to the ruins of the Trophée des Alpes, he saw her face change again. As she gazed at the crumbling stones, her eyes became distant and dark with some unvented emotion.

When the company came to Paris for its first season, Alexander sat in the opening-night audience, watching Cendrine. She was lost in the anonymity of the corps – except to his eye. He wondered if Jonathan, sitting at his side, could pick her out, but he said nothing. He glanced at Jonathan, who was whispering to Lucy, sitting on his other side. Jonathan never mentioned Cendrine and, from all appearances, he seemed to have got over the affair. Lucy, it seemed, was pre-eminent in his heart; every time she came to Paris, they were together, and the previous autumn Jonathan had gone back to New York to visit her.

The lights went up for intermission, and Alexander and his escort followed Jonathan and Lucy out to the lobby. Alexander watched as Jonathan talked with the Belgian ambassador and the director of the Comédie Française, feeling a small surge of pride. How far Jonathan had come! He had ripened physically, his once raw sexual appeal now honed to a commanding presence. He had matured intellectually, his storehouse of experiences and his clout as editor of the *Herald* giving him a special cachet.

His eyes went to Lucy. Of course, Lucy did not appreciate Jonathan's artistic soul, but what woman could truly understand a man's inner currents? The marriage would be a good match for Jonathan, the Wendall family name the crowning touch to assure his social standing for ever. Lucy would be good for him in a way that Cendrine never could have been.

Jonathan brought Lucy over to Alexander. 'You've been staring at us rather strangely, Alexander,' Lucy said with a smile. 'What have you been thinking?'

273

'That you make a handsome couple.'

'Well, perhaps soon we'll make it official.'

Alexander looked at Jonathan with a surprised smile. 'Do I sense an engagement in the making?'

A bell announced the end of intermission. 'Let's go to our seats,' Jonathan said quickly, smiling.

'He's been awful, Alexander,' Lucy said with a laugh. 'He's practically forced me to take the initiative—'

'Lucy, we agreed not to announce it yet,' Jonathan said.

Alexander kissed Lucy's cheek and embraced Jonathan. 'Wonderful!' he said. 'Of course, you'll have use of the *Lysistrata* for your honeymoon!'

The lights dimmed, and they were forced to hurry to their seats before anything else could be said. As the next ballet began, Alexander sat back in his seat, his gaze going to the stage. He watched the group of women in white tulle, focusing on Cendrine. Even from this distance, he could see her expression of radiant happiness. There were moments when he felt a small stab of guilt over keeping his relationship with Cendrine from Jonathan. But everything had worked out so well – what did it matter now?

He felt his senses suddenly sharpen with anticipation, thinking about the dinner he would share with Jonathan and Lucy at Maxim's and the bed he would share later with Cendrine. He glanced around him, smelling the mingled aroma of expensive perfumes, seeing the discreet glimmer of diamonds in the dark, hearing the sweetly melancholy strains of Fauré's music. And he wished that, somehow, everything could stand still, for he was certain that, at that moment, the world had never been more beautiful.

Chapter Twenty-Four

Cendrine finished her warm-up exercises and joined the other dancers on stage. The sounds of the orchestra tuning up drifted backstage, and many of the dancers began to pace nervously. There was something strange in the air tonight, a tension that had never been there before.

Cendrine parted the curtain wide enough to peek out at the packed theatre. The audience felt it, too. Over the past few years, Parisians had come to expect surprises from Diaghilev and his Ballet Russe de Monte Carlo. And tonight, there would be another work choreographed by Nijinsky, who had already shocked everyone with a scandalous ballet the previous year. No one had been prepared for what they had seen that night on stage – the famous dancer, dressed like a satyr, holding himself prone above a silk scarf, erotically mimicking the motions of lovemaking!

Word had spread that tonight's premiere would be even more titillating, and the theatre was packed with socialites, students and artists. Cendrine peered at the mixed crowd, at the shabby suits sitting amid the osprey plumes and tails. Tonight she would dance her first solo, and her emotions were swinging between elation and dread. Finally, she had a leading role, but in all her dreams, she had never imagined it would be in such a hideous ballet.

Le Sacre du printemps – The Rite of Spring. The endless rehearsals had gone badly, and the movements – turned-in feet and slumped postures – were grotesque, the exact opposite of what her ballet training had taught her to do. Even the music sounded bizarre, not music at all, just shrieking notes. They had rehearsed only with a piano, under the relentless gaze of the composer, a pinch-faced Russian named Stravinsky. And the costume, a sack dress and leggings with leather straps, made her feel unglamorous and downright ugly; the whole ballet was ugly.

Nijinsky had tried to explain the role to her: '*You're a Russian peasant, a girl chosen to be sacrificed, who must dance herself to death to appease the gods.*' But she didn't understand. She knew only that her turn had come, and she felt nothing in her heart for what she was supposed to do.

'Are you all right?'

Cendrine turned. Nijinsky stood before her, his pale face more forlorn than usual.

'Yes, I think so.'

'Passion,' he said softly.

'What?'

'It's about passion. Not the kind poets talk about, but the violent passion of struggle.' And he was gone. Cendrine looked bewildered after him.

Out in the audience, Jonathan sat quietly in his seat, the programme in his hand, seeing nothing but Cendrine's name. Since Oliver had told him that she had joined the Ballet Russe, he had gone to many of the performances and watched her, managing to keep his feelings in check. But tonight the sight of her name on the programme listed as a soloist had unleashed the pent-up emotions. It felt as if a wound, which he had thought long since healed over, had begun to hurt again. He was proud for her, yet his own sense of loss was

276

unbearable. He felt himself sinking into a sadness, a refrain running in his head. What if I hadn't made demands on her? What if . . . what if. . .?

'Jonathan, look, there's Diaghilev!'

He turned to Lucy, whose eyes avidly scanned the audience. Her fingers wove through his, and he glanced down at the engagement ring. What if . . . what if. . .?

The lights went out and the murmur fell to a hush of expectant silence.

The curtain rose to reveal a strange scene, a wasteland dominated by massive stones. The dancers, dressed like peasants, sat in calm groups. The music began quietly as a strange plaintive cry, and the audience rustled nervously. Then the dancers began to move, with bent knees and stooped postures. Confused, the audience began to hiss and boo.

A sudden driving chord made Jonathan jump in his seat. The dancers began to stomp around the stage. The music became savage, with squawks, shrieks and terrifying arpeggios. The movement turned brutal, the boys attacking and carrying the girls away. Jonathan was entranced and repelled at the same time; it was so primitive, yet fascinating.

The audience were shouting and whistling now, though some were applauding, mainly the students in the balconies. Jonathan looked around him and was astonished to see fights breaking out. He felt Lucy's hand grip his.

When he looked back to the stage, he froze. There was Cendrine, standing in the middle of a group of women. Even in the shapeless costume and black wig, he knew it was her. The cacophonous music and the shouting faded as he watched her. She looked tentative, almost fearful, just as all the other dancers did. When she began to move, he watched transfixed. There was nothing lovely in the way she moved, and he didn't understand it, yet the passion of it pulled at him.

Finally the curtain came down and the lights went up, but the shouting continued. Police were hauling away some of the loudest demonstrators.

'Jonathan, this is horrid! I think we should leave,' Lucy pleaded, pulling at his arm.

Before they could move, the lights went down again for the second scene. There was a thunderous drum roll as the curtain rose to reveal the setting of a sacrifice, bathed in blood-red lighting. The shouting, whistling and booing resumed even louder than before. As the Chosen One, Cendrine stood in mid-stage, the strange music surging around her. She stood trembling, her feet turned in, holding her hands under her right cheek. It was a poignant pose, and Jonathan felt an inexplicable sting of tears in his eyes.

Suddenly the theatre seemed to shudder and shake, as if in the throes of an earthquake, and pandemonium broke out as the audience rioted. Fights raged in the boxes. One elegant woman slapped a man who was clapping. Men challenged others to duels. Jonathan saw the music critic of the *New York Times* fall to the floor after being beaten on the head by a young man behind him.

Improbably, the performance went on. The conductor, his face beet red with indignation, urged the orchestra forward as the music swelled towards its climax. Jonathan saw Diaghilev standing in the front row, yelling, 'I beg you! Let them finish the performance!'

On stage, the dancers, unable to hear the music, were looking to the wings where Nijinsky was frantically yelling out the counts. Jonathan watched Cendrine as she went through her final violent dance of death. Suddenly, the two men in the row in front jumped up to block his view. They began to fight, and the people around them scrambled frantically to get out of the way. Jonathan heard someone scream. One of the men tumbled over the seat and on top of him, jolting him to the floor, where his body became wedged between the rows. He brought up his arms to shield his head as feet scrambled over him. He heard a rush of sound, screaming and shrieking noises, but he didn't know if it was the orchestra or the audience.

Finally he was able to pull himself to his feet. He was dazed and his mouth was bleeding. He looked around for Lucy, but she was gone; so was Alexander. On stage he could see the dancers whirling, caught up in a maelstrom as the violent music raced on. Nothing looked real any more. It all looked like a nightmare, a vision of the whole world cracking apart. He saw Cendrine fall to the floor as the music reached its slapping crescendo.

The lights came up and he stood there for a moment, his hand gripping a seat to steady himself. The curtain had come down, and he was vaguely aware of people crying, arguing, struggling out of their seats and into the aisles. One thought filled his head, the sight of Cendrine falling down. He had to find her.

He pushed his way past the other people trying to get out of the row. Having made his way back to the wings, he drew up short at the sight of the sweating dancers, who, in their costumes and garish, streaked make-up, stared at him like grotesque dolls. He lurched across the stage, looking for Cendrine, calling out her name. He reached the other wing and froze.

There in the shadows were Alexander and Cendrine. He was holding her as she cried against his chest. Jonathan watched as he took her chin and tilted her head upward, but he couldn't hear what Alexander said. He saw Cendrine nod, and when they kissed, Jonathan staggered back as if he had been stabbed.

'No,' he whispered. Then he shouted, 'No!'

Cendrine and Alexander both turned towards him. Before either of them could react, Jonathan lunged at

Alexander. The force of his attack threw them against a piece of scenery and they fell to the floor. Cendrine screamed as Jonathan's fists shot out at Alexander's face, again and again.

At last two men pulled Jonathan off Alexander's chest. Alexander lay unconscious and bleeding as the men held Jonathan's arms.

'Get up, goddamn you! Get up!' Jonathan shouted.

Cendrine dropped to the floor at Alexander's side, and Jonathan struggled to free himself from the men's grasp. 'Get away from him!' he shouted. 'Get away from him!'

Alexander's eyes opened. After a moment, helped by Cendrine, he struggled to prop himself up on one elbow. His eyes focused first on Cendrine, then on Jonathan standing over him, his chest heaving, his eyes flashing, his white shirt splattered with blood. 'Jonathan,' he whispered.

'You have nothing to say! Nothing!' Jonathan yelled. His eyes darted to Cendrine. 'You . . . how could you do this? Why him? Why?'

She stared at him, her face foreign-looking in the heavy make-up. Her eyes filled with tears, and they fell silently down her face.

Looking at her, Jonathan felt his body go limp as the last of his energy drained away. He realized suddenly that until tonight, everything he had ever felt for her had remained there, living inside him. He had tried to bury it, but it was still there, and it had all come flooding out when he saw her on stage. But now he saw something in her face that told him that it was over. That strange, mystical, wonderful bond between them had been broken. It was gone.

He looked at Alexander. Everything was gone.

Jonathan jerked his arms free of the men and wiped the blood from his mouth. He wanted to walk away but he couldn't stop looking at them.

'I loved you,' he whispered, his voice hoarse. 'I loved you both so much.'

He closed his eyes and turned away. When he opened them, he saw Lucy standing nearby, her hand at her throat, her eyes wide. He took several steps towards her, looked at her white face and, wavering slightly, walked by her out of the wings. Lucy looked down at Cendrine and Alexander, then turned to follow him.

It was an hour before dawn and the *Herald* office was still dark. Alexander stood at the glass doors, looking at the empty newsroom, then pushed the doors open and entered. He went slowly past the desks and tables until he reached the partitioned office at the end of the room. He stared at the name on the door spelled out in neat gilt letters – JONATHAN CARAS. EDITOR-IN-CHIEF – before going in. He turned up the gaslight over the desk, and the details of the office came to life: piles of newspapers and books, wire reports, maps, a tray holding the remnants of a half-eaten meal, a pair of gold cufflinks, cast off for the comfort of rolled sleeves. The debris of a working editor.

He sat down at the desk, idly shifting through the wire reports, finally picking up one to read it. He heard a sound and looked up. Jonathan was standing at the door. Alexander stared at his stony face, waiting for him to say something.

'You've come back,' Alexander said finally. 'After what happened last night, I didn't think you would.'

Jonathan came into the office. 'I came back only to get my things,' he said flatly. He withdrew an envelope from this coat. 'But as long as you're here, I might as well give you this. Save myself the postage.' He tossed the paper on the desk.

Alexander did not pick it up. He knew it was a resignation letter. 'Jonathan,' he said, 'it doesn't have to be this way.'

'Yes, it does,' Jonathan said curtly.

'I want you to stay here with the *Herald*.'

'I can't work for a man I don't trust.'

Alexander's eyes went to the envelope. He was very tired. His head was throbbing, and he reached up to touch the heavy bandage on his left cheekbone. 'You don't by any chance keep a bottle in here somewhere?' he said. 'I could use a drink.'

Jonathan just stood there rigid. Finally he said flatly, 'Your face – how bad is it?'

'You broke my cheekbone. You could have warned me you have a right like Carpentier, you know.'

Jonathan stared at Alexander for a moment, then moved to a closet to gather some items of clothing. When Jonathan opened a drawer at the desk, Alexander touched his arm. 'Jonathan, please, let's talk—'

Jonathan jerked his arm away. 'There's nothing to say. I'm leaving. I'm going back to New York with Lucy tomorrow.'

'Jonathan, listen, I know how you must feel about me right now, but you can't leave Paris and your life here. Your future, everything you've worked for is here—'

'I've had enough,' Jonathan interrupted, 'enough of Paris and your beautiful life. And of you.' He paused. 'It's over, Alexander. Do you understand? It's all over.'

Alexander looked searchingly at Jonathan for a moment. Pushing the chair back from the desk, he turned it towards the window. He stared out at the eastern sky, a velvet curtain with a hem of pale grey. It was June, he realized suddenly, 1 June 1913. A Sunday.

'Did you read the latest dispatches?' Alexander said quietly, staring out of the window. 'The Balkans are at war again. And there's a report that says shipbuilding is up sharply. Everyone's going crazy arming themselves, but no one knows what for.'

Jonathan stopped going through the drawers for a

moment, then resumed.

Alexander turned back to face him. 'Jonathan, there's work to be done here. The *Herald* needs you. And you need it.'

Jonathan shook his head. 'I'm going home.'

Alexander closed his eyes as a spasm of pain hit, then opened them again. 'Look, I know there's nothing I can ever do to set things right between us again. But you don't have to cut yourself off from the most important thing in your life.' He paused. 'Go home – but as the editor of the *New York Herald*.'

Jonathan stared at him in disbelief. 'There's no reason,' Alexander went on quickly, 'that you can't do it. You still have your percentage, and you always told me the *New York Herald* could be a great newspaper, that it just needed a good man to turn it round. Well, go do it.'

Jonathan could only stare.

'Do it, Jonathan,' Alexander said quietly. 'I'll give you every resource you need, complete autonomy. And you'll never have to see me again. I promise.'

Alexander waited. He could see in Jonathan's face the emotions fighting inside.

'All right,' Jonathan said finally.

Alexander closed his eyes. When he opened them, Jonathan was still looking at him with a stony expression. 'I won't ask that we shake on it,' Alexander said.

'Goodbye, Alexander,' Jonathan said flatly. Without waiting for an answer, he turned and was gone.

Alexander heard the newsroom door slam. Slowly, Alexander rose and turned out the gaslight. He stared vacantly out of the window. Morning had come, grey with the promise of rain.

Chapter Twenty-Five

Jonathan picked up the proof of the *New York Herald*'s front page. The headlines, as usual, were ominous. The Germans were mounting a massive offensive on the western front. Another bombing on Paris had left thirteen dead. Jonathan stared at the date: 31 September 1917. More than three years of war, and still there was no sign that the end was near.

He set the proof down and rubbed his eyes as the fatigue of the last few days washed over him. He had not been home in two days, catching snatches of food and sleep at the office as the staff laboured to keep up with the latest war developments.

It was a near-impossible task these days, with his staff heavily depleted by the draft. So many men had left and were now fighting in places that to Jonathan were just pinpricks on the map in his office. He glanced out at the newsroom, his eyes coming to rest on a woman sweeping the floor. Try as he might, he could not get used to the sight of women doing men's jobs – running the trams, hauling ice, directing traffic. It didn't seem normal. But what did these days?

Jonathan forced his attention back to work. He marked up some suggestions for changes on the page. Douglas Fairbanks appearing at a Liberty Bond rally in Wall Street would have to be moved inside to make way for a story about New York schools closing because coal rationing had caused a shortage of heating fuel.

Jonathan's eyes travelled one more time over the page, and he allowed himself a faint glow of pride. He had done much to improve the *Herald* in just five years. True to his word, Alexander had given him free rein. But the war had made money tight. The *Paris Herald*, never a profitable enterprise, had lost most of its advertising during the first year of the war, and Alexander depended on the New York operation to keep things afloat. Despite budget constraints, Jonathan was still able to give New Yorkers thorough war coverage, including an innovation no other paper in the city could offer: brown-tinted rotogravure photographs from the front. Every day, the *Herald* brought the war home with horrific intimacy. Photos of a battle-weary corporal sitting in the Argonne forest. Infantrymen, blinded by gas, lined up at a field hospital. Soldiers standing around a hole in a field at St-Mihiel, praying at a comrade's funeral. And the hellish landscape of shattered trees and bodies at Ypres, where battle had raged uselessly since July. Even the writer inside Jonathan had to concede that the best-woven words could not compete with the raw power of the images.

The photograph illustrating the Paris story showed a bombed-out shell of a building. Jonathan peered at the photo, searching for a landmark to place the scene in his memory.

'Mr Caras?' Jonathan looked up to see the mailboy at the door. 'Here's this afternoon's batch for you.'

'Thanks, Eddie.' Jonathan began to sort through the mail, and a pale-blue envelope caught his eye: a letter from Harry. It had been months since anything from Harry Parkyn had made it out of Paris. After the war had broken out, most of Alexander's staff of Britons had returned to their homes to join up, but Harry, tethered to the *Herald* by his love of Paris, stayed, and was elevated to managing editor by default. Though his own newspaper had kept Jonathan abreast of the war in Europe, Harry's letters had told him what Paris was really like now.

Harry had written about a city transformed, with shops closed and dark and deserted streets. The *Herald*, its circulation drying up and its French and British staffs disappearing, had floundered badly at first. But then, Alexander had surprised everyone by taking charge. Harry told Jonathan how one night Alexander had appeared in the office, rolled up his sleeves and taken command as he never had before. He worked in editorial or composing, even acting as a reporter, going round the city on foot. Alexander had also opened the *Herald*'s pages to help the thousands of Americans stranded in Paris when the shipping offices closed. Along with war maps and news, he published information of support groups, diplomatic notices and lists of pensions that had rooms. And he kept the *Herald*'s tone determinedly optimistic.

Still, as the influx of wounded French and British soldiers into the city grew heavy, the mood in Paris became bleak. The city endured daily bombings even after the French government abandoned Paris and moved to Bordeaux. After that, Harry's letters grew infrequent and more grim.

Jonathan was almost reluctant to open Harry's latest letter, for fear of the kind of news it might contain. When he had left Paris, he had done so in anger, with every intent to forget his life there. Yet he had found himself hungering for any word or phrase of Paris, anything that would feed his memories. The memories haunted him like the last, fading moments of a dream: the sight of the indolent Seine glimpsed through a lacy curtain of spring leaves; the lingering perfume of

Armagnac in an empty glass; the burnished chandelier glow on women's faces as they glided up the grand staircase at the opera; the sound of Alexander's silvery laughter – even that, despite everything.

Finally, he opened the letter. It was short, with the look of being hastily written. 'The Germans are only forty miles to the north now and we can hear gunfire,' Harry wrote.

> Yesterday, Alexander called us together and said we could leave if we wanted to. I tried to get him to leave, but he refused. He told me that Paris is not just the capital of France, it is the capital of the world – *his* world – and he'll never leave it. So we stay on. I fear that Paris will never be the same city you once knew. There are lines now on the old girl's lovely face.

Jonathan carefully folded the letter and slipped it inside his pocket. He rose and went to the window, his memory reconstructing the streets, buildings and bridges of Paris. Would any of it still be there when this was all over?

He looked up at the sky, where huge clouds lumbered along, doggedly withholding the snow within. He stared down at the slushy, traffic-choked streets, wanting suddenly, desperately, to be back in Paris. Why was it he had never felt at home in New York? When he had arrived back in the city, he had been determined to make it his home. But now, after nearly five years, he still felt out of step. He told himself that it was because the city had changed so much since he had first set foot in it all those years ago. It had become a jumble of mismatched buildings stretching gracelessly from river to river all the way to Harlem. Skyscrapers, they were called, crowding the very air, making the city look like . . . an extravagant pin cushion – who had called it that? Jonathan searched his memory, rubbing his temples. Henry James, it was Henry James.

The telephone rang. Jonathan stood at the window, ignoring it. Finally, he picked it up.

'Jonathan? Are you there?'

'Yes, Lucy.'

'Are you coming home tonight?'

'If I can.'

'We have guests coming for dinner. You promised me you—'

'I know. I'll try. I really will this time.'

A pause. 'At least be home in time to say goodnight to David.'

The line went dead. Jonathan replaced the receiver and returned to the window. He had forgotten about the dinner party. He didn't feel like entertaining. He didn't even feel like going home tonight; the thought of the house on Fifth Avenue filled him with dread. It was a beautiful place, a wedding gift from Lucy's parents, but it felt more like a museum than a home.

Jonathan stared out at the grey sky. It wasn't just the house; it was Lucy he was trying to avoid, and he couldn't look at her without thinking that she could read in his face what was in his heart.

When had it started? When did the emptiness begin? He thought back to the first year of their marriage. It was the last time he could remember feeling a closeness to Lucy, a bond. Perhaps it was because they had both been determined to make their life together work. Perhaps they had just tried too hard.

Desperate to put Cendrine and Alexander behind him, Jonathan had vowed to make himself and Lucy happy. With the same obsessive energy, he also devoted himself to restoring the *Herald*. The Wendalls, conceding they had to make the best of their daughter's unfortunate choice, accepted Jonathan into their social circle. Lucy took to her role as wife and hostess with a fierce energy. Soon Jonathan found himself no longer regarded as a social interloper but as the brilliant young saviour of the ailing *Herald* and, because of Lucy, a lion among New York's young socialites. When his son David was born, it was the jewel in the crown.

It was not until the third year of their marriage that Jonathan realized that he and Lucy were leading completely separate lives. It had happened slowly, gradually, both drawing further into their respective worlds and away from each other. Eventually, even sex ceased to give them a reason for coming together. Lucy had never been passionate in bed. She did not refuse him, but he felt that it always came out of a sense of duty, never with any reciprocal joy.

After David's birth, Lucy had channelled her energies into his care, and Jonathan found himself subtly cut off, not only from Lucy but from his own son. Whatever passion Lucy harboured was now given to David; there was nothing left for Jonathan. Lucy used David's difficult birth as an excuse to avoid sex until, finally, Jonathan stopped approaching her. It wasn't just the sex he yearned for; it was simple affection, the touch of another human body.

Soon after his marriage, Jonathan had renewed his friendship with Sumner, eventually confiding in him about the emptiness of his marriage. Sumner had suggested Jonathan go back to the elegant East Side brothel that they had frequented twenty years before. So it was that Jonathan now found himself as a paying member of the exclusive fraternity of men he had once pitied.

Jonathan stared vacantly out at the grey buildings, thinking of that night twenty years ago. He could remember the sensations vividly, yet he couldn't remember what the prostitute looked like. Every woman looked the same to him now – all like Cendrine.

He had thought that her memory would fade, yet it

had grown only brighter as the years went by. The larger the void inside him became, the larger her memory grew to fill it. Usually, he could control it by filling his hours with work. But during these last few weeks, even that had failed. He suspected it was because the war news from Paris was so bleak. Cendrine, Paris, even Alexander . . . all were inextricably tangled together in his memories and there was nothing he could do to escape them.

Jonathan glanced at his watch. If he was going to make it home in time for dinner, he had to leave soon. He put on his hat and coat and left, dropping the proof on the night editor's desk.

Despite Lucy's best efforts, the ambiance of the dinner party was subdued, the conversation dominated by talk of the war. The food was heavily sauced and the dining room overheated, and the effort of putting on a good performance for Lucy's sake left Jonathan with a blinding headache. His thoughts kept drifting back to Paris, and he struggled to stay focused. Finally, he could stand it no longer.

'Would you all excuse me?' he said, rising.

'Where are you going, dear?' Lucy asked.

'To say good night to David. I'll be back in a few minutes.'

He went upstairs, pausing outside the nursery. The door was ajar and he could see the nanny, a severe-faced Englishwoman, putting David in his bed. He watched her, dismayed by her brisk, efficient manner. He didn't like the woman; she was so cold. He didn't even like the idea of David being raised by a nanny. But Lucy could not be deterred from her belief that a child needed a discipline that only a professional could provide. Jonathan watched David, who was crying about having to go to sleep.

'Well, we'll have a tune, then,' the nanny said crisply. She began to clap her hands sharply over David's bed. 'My mother said that I never should play with the Gypsies in the wood. If I did, she would say, naughty boy to disobey.'

David was staring up at the nanny with wide eyes.

'My father said that if I did, he'd bang my head with a teapot lid.' Slap, slap, went the woman's hands above the bed.

Jonathan pushed open the door and the nanny turned. 'Why, Mr Caras, good evening,' she said.

'Good evening, Mrs Willetts. What was that you were singing?'

'Just a little jingle. It quiets the lad up right quick.'

'Don't do it any more.'

'Well, it's just—'

'It frightens him. Can't you see that?'

The woman's mouth pulled into a line. 'Very well, Mr Caras.'

Jonathan looked down at the boy in the bed. With his brown, glossy hair and large hazel eyes, his resemblance to Lucy was already remarkable. He had the strong, high forehead of Lucy's father. He doesn't look like me at all, Jonathan thought. What does he have of me in him? Jonathan reached in his jacket and pulled out a small biscuit he had taken from the dessert tray at dinner. He held it out to David, and the child smiled.

'Sweets are bad for his teeth, Mr Caras,' the nanny muttered.

'One biscuit won't hurt him, Mrs Willetts.'

'But Mrs Caras said—'

'Let him keep the biscuit.'

The nanny sighed in frustration and turned away. Jonathan leaned over the bed and kissed David's downy cheek. He felt the slight pressure of a pair of plump arms go up around his neck and closed his eyes. 'Good night, son,' he said softly.

'Night, Daddy. I love you, Daddy.'

At the door, he turned and looked at the nanny. 'Good night, Mrs Willetts,' he said. She muttered a good night, without smiling.

Out in the corridor, Jonathan paused, listening to the faint buzz of conversation below. The clock in the hall chimed nine times. He pulled at the stiff collar of his dress shirt and decided to take something for his headache before returning to the drawing room. But as he approached the bathroom, his eyes were drawn to the end of the long corridor, to the door that led up to the attic. He approached it slowly.

Opening it, he peered up into the darkness of the stairs. Although he couldn't find the light switch, he began to climb, slowly at first, then with more deliberation. A feeble reflection from the streetlight filtered in through a small oval window on the far wall. He saw a hurricane lamp, lifted its dusty shade and lit it. The soft light bounced off the mounds of boxes and discarded furnishings. The air was heavy with dust, but it was cold, deliciously cold. Jonathan undid his collar and yanked it off. He held up the lamp, his eyes travelling over the debris. Hesitating briefly, he picked his way across the creaking floorboards towards the oval window. He set the lamp on a table, crouched down and reached behind a trunk.

His fingers found their target and he pulled it out. It was the painting of Cendrine, covered with dust and cobwebs. Jonathan brushed them off and stared at the portrait.

A knot formed in his chest, catching him by surprise with its force. He had not looked at the portrait for five years, not since that day he had found it in the rubbish bin where Lucy had put it. He had hidden it in the attic, never intending to look at it again. But tonight, the compulsion to see it had seized him suddenly and without warning.

As he contemplated Cendrine's face, time stopped, reversed itself, and he was back in Paris, back in the gallery, seeing the portrait for the first time and reliving the terrible sense of her loss. Back then, they had lost each other and gone their separate ways, but they had found each other again. Now they were separated by thousands of miles and commitments to other people. Now he was a different man from the one he had left behind in Paris. That man – who loved the opera, who laughed at the fizz of champagne on the tongue, who danced the waltz – that man was gone.

He stared at the portrait and ran his hand over its rough surface, trying to remember the sensation of her skin. Finally, he propped it against the trunk and sat back on the floor. He dropped his head onto his folded arms, brought up his dusty hands to cover his eyes, then ran them back through his hair. He knew suddenly that he had to go back to find her.

'Fool,' he whispered. 'Fool. . .'

Chapter Twenty-Six

Maxim's was open again. The bombing of Paris continued, and most of the other restaurants, cafés and theatres remained closed. But after being shuttered for a year, the grand old restaurant had defiantly flung open its doors.

As Alexander followed Cendrine through the main dining salon, his eyes travelled over the familiar room. The sinuous Art Nouveau decor looked the same and the orchestra was playing. But the mood was different, the light more subdued, and his nose could pick up no trace of perfume. His gaze passed over the women, and he was struck by how much the fashions had changed. Clothes had become easier, less flamboyant, and no one wore corsets any more. His eyes fell on Cendrine walking ahead of him. Her loose dress floated over her curves, and he was struck by how differently she moved: her walk was freer, almost aggressive. Alexander felt a mix of mild arousal and slight melancholy. The limpid dress was provocative, yet he missed the stiff voluptuousness of the old style.

They were led to the best table in the half-full room. Paris was still empty, yet, at Maxim's, all the tables were set each night as if in anticipation of everyone's sudden return. Alexander's eyes fell on the place setting at the next table. A red rose had been placed across the plate. It was a well-known symbol by now. In the early optimistic years of the war, young aviators had blithely flown off in the morning expecting to return that evening to Maxim's for dinner. Every time one was killed, a rose was placed on a plate.

Cendrine saw Alexander noticing the rose. 'Alexander,' she said gently, touching his arm.

He looked at her. 'You're right. No talk of death or war, or even the *Herald* tonight. I promised you that, didn't I?'

Alexander ordered champagne; after he took a drink, he grimaced slightly and summoned the sommelier to give a lecture. Cendrine watched him carefully, but waited until dinner was ordered before she brought up his mood.

'Something is bothering you,' she said. 'You've been acting strange for weeks now.'

'I'm fine.' He poured more champagne.

'You're drinking too much,' she said softly.

'That is my business.'

'It's mine, too, Alexander.'

'You have no claims on me, Cendrine. Just as I have none on you. That's how we like it, remember?'

'Why are you treating me like this?' she murmured.

Alexander drank his champagne, saying nothing.

'I thought tonight would be a chance for us to just be together, to enjoy each other, the way we used to,' Cendrine said, her eyes searching his face. 'What's *wrong*, Alexander? Tell me, please.'

Alexander stared at her. Tell her? Tell her what? That he loved her? Tell her that that was the reason he had been so on edge lately. He *loved* her, and he didn't even believe it himself sometimes. He had come to the startling realization only recently, and he wasn't even sure how or when it had happened. Because so much of the city had been closed down and most people in his old social circle had fled, there had been nothing else, except Cendrine and the *Herald*, to distract him. And because the war made travel impossible, the Ballet Russe had temporarily disbanded and Cendrine was no longer dancing. During the last two years, they had spent all their time with each other. There was suddenly time – time for walks, time to sit before a fire reading to each other, time to talk. They had created an insulated little world to replace the ones that the war had taken away from each of them.

Love – he wasn't even sure what it was. Was it that he no longer had a desire to be with another woman? Was it because he felt at ease when he was with her? Was it because, after five years, he was still aroused by the sight of her body, the sound of her laugh? Was it because he felt protective of her yet strangely protected by her? Love? It wasn't love. It was need. He needed her. He had never needed anyone before.

Alexander looked away. Except for companionship, she didn't need him, that was clear. When they made love, he could sometimes see a distant look in her eyes. How could he tell her that he *knew* her thoughts were with Jonathan, especially since she had heard about his marriage? He knew that she still loved him.

Could he tell her that he felt sometimes as if he were adrift? That he looked around at the city he so loved and saw something blemished, mutated? The worlds he once knew were dead or dying. The technology he had once worshipped had brought horrible destruction. The hope for the future that he had once felt was diminished. Even the very thing that he once knew with certainty about himself – that he would never relinquish power over himself to someone – was now challenged. He needed Cendrine, and a part of him hated himself for it.

Cendrine was waiting for an answer. He picked up his glass and drained it. 'I think you should leave Paris,' he said softly.

Cendrine stared at him. 'Leave? Why? Why are you so angry with me, Alexander?'

He couldn't look into her eyes. The last thing in the world he wanted was that she should leave. Yet he knew that he needed to be away from her for a while, to regain his perspective. If he didn't, in his present state of mind, he would do something cruel that would drive her away for ever.

'I'm not angry with you,' he said. 'I want you to leave because it's too dangerous here now. When the Germans come, I don't want you to be here.'

'I'm not going to leave, Alexander.'

He took her hand. 'Please, Cendrine, don't argue with me. I know what I'm talking about. I've arranged for you to go to Switzerland. I've rented a villa for you near Interlaken—'

'Switzerland! I don't want—'

'Just until this is over. You can stay there – I'll pay for everything – and you can come back when it's safe.'

'I won't do—'

'Yes, you will,' he said. 'If you care about me, you'll do this for me. Please.'

'Alexander—'

He pulled her hand roughly. 'Do you care about me?'

She stared at him. 'Yes,' she said after a moment.

He closed his eyes, his grip on her hand relaxing.

'When must I leave?' Cendrine asked.

'Tomorrow.'

They were both silent for a moment. Alexander took a drink, his eyes trained straight ahead. There, it was done. She would be safe. And when it was all over, he would bring her back, and they would go on as before. And some day, given enough time, there would come a moment when he would look into her eyes and see himself reflected there, not Jonathan. When he looked at Cendrine, there were tears in her eyes.

'*Tu me manqueras*,' she whispered.

He stared at her, startled. In five years she had never

once used the familiar address in French in speaking to him, even when they made love.

'I'll miss you, too,' he said softly.

Cendrine stood at the window, staring out at the blustery scene outside. The waters of Lake Brienz were grey and choppy, stirred up by the wind that swept down from the Alps. Far out on the lake, she saw a small black dot and a faint curl of grey smoke rising from it. Good, Cendrine thought, her spirits rising, at least the ferry was running again. For a week now, the bad weather had prevented anyone or anything from reaching Iseltwald, the small village on the south side of the lake where her villa was located.

She watched the black dot creep closer. Perhaps Berta was on the ferry. Cendrine was anxious to see another face, even if it was the grumpy old housekeeper. And maybe the mail would come today, perhaps a letter from Madame or Marcelle, or even from Roland. A letter had reached her, forwarded from Paris, three weeks ago, from a place called Baltimore. He wrote that he was doing well and she shouldn't worry. She had written back straight away but was not sure if her letter had got through. Nor had there been any letter recently from Alexander.

Cendrine turned away from the window, looking around the villa's sitting room. It was a fine chalet that Alexander had picked out for her, in a beautiful little village far removed from the dangers of the war. But it was a lonely place. She found the taciturn nature of the Swiss hard to penetrate, and felt more alone than she ever had in her life.

She went to a desk near the fire and sat down. She picked up the letter to Alexander that she had started earlier, a faint frown creasing her forehead. She read it, then crumpled the paper and tossed it into the fire.

She watched it burn, just like all the others before it.

She picked up the pen again, wrote two words, then set it down. 'Oh, Alexander,' she said softly, 'how am I ever going to tell you. . .?'

She returned to the window. The ferry was so close now that she could make out the details of its windows and railings. She knew she had to finish the letter so it could go back that evening on the outgoing ferry. If only she could find the right words! But she knew that no matter how she tried to phrase what she had to say, Alexander would not accept it. She thought back to their last night together in Paris. He had acted so strange, as if he were suddenly trying to push her away and end their relationship. Yet he had made love to her with a tenderness that left her wondering if she knew him at all. She knew him; she knew what kind of man he was and that he wanted no entanglements in his life. After all their years together, she was sure of at least that much about him.

She leaned her forehead against the cold glass, staring at the approaching ferry.

'Oh, Alexander,' she whispered. 'How am I going to tell you I'm going to have your baby?'

As the ferry made its way across the lake, Jonathan stood at a window, watching the tiny collection of wooden buildings on the far shore grow larger. Finally, he could stand it no longer and went outside on deck. The wind stung his face and tore through his coat, but he didn't care. He had come so far, and was so impatient by now that nothing seemed to matter but finally seeing Cendrine.

He stared at the village, remembering what had happened in Paris. He had gone to Marcelle to find out where Cendrine was living, and at first Marcelle would not tell him. 'She doesn't want to see you, Jonathan,' she said. 'You forced her to make a decision she didn't want to, and now she's put you out of her mind.'

In the end, he had convinced Marcelle to tell him where Cendrine was. Now, as the ferry pulled up to the dock at Iseltwald, he wondered again at the futility of what he was doing. He had no real reason for being here. He had a completely different life in a different world, thousands of miles away. And Marcelle was right; Cendrine had made her decision. What business did he have forcing himself back into her life?

But when the ferry docked, he nearly ran to the village. In the *boulangerie*, the owner gave him directions to Cendrine's villa just west of the village. When he reached it, for several minutes he stood outside, looking nervously at it. Finally, he knocked.

The door opened and Cendrine stood before him. 'Oh, my God,' she whispered.

Jonathan stared at her. All the words he had planned in his head during the trip were suddenly gone. They just stood there, gazing mutely at each other. He had a sudden vision of the time he had appeared at the door of her dressing room at the Folies-Bergères. Then, he had been so sure of what he was doing. Now he was paralysed with the idea that it was, finally, too late.

'It's very cold,' he said finally. 'May I come in?'

Cendrine stepped aside and then closed the door behind him. His eyes flicked quickly to the living room beyond, but came swiftly back to Cendrine. Her eyes looked as grey as the autumn sky.

'What are you doing here, Jonathan?' she asked softly.

'I wanted to see you again,' he said. 'I had to see you again.'

She hugged herself as if cold. 'Give me your coat,' she said, 'and come in by the fire where it's warm.'

Cendrine took his wet coat and hat and placed them near the fire to dry. There was a long silence, painful and awkward. 'I'll make some coffee,' she said nervously, going quickly to the kitchen. He took a chair near the fire and waited. She brought a tray, poured him a large cup of coffee and then, as if looking for something more to do, knelt to prod the fire into a bigger blaze. Not once during all this did she look directly at him. But his eyes never once left her.

He noticed her plain but expensive grey wool dress and the silver brooch at her neck, and found himself thinking jealously of Alexander. He realized that her figure was rounder and that she wore her hair differently now, rolled softly up and away from her face. Her face itself was far less childish-looking, and he reminded himself that she was now thirty-seven years old.

'You look beautiful,' he said softly.

She was kneeling at the hearth, her back to him, and his words made her freeze. Then she stood up and slowly turned to face him. Her eyes were brimming.

'Don't say that,' she said, pleading. 'Don't say anything. If you say one more word, I'll . . .'

He rose and started towards her. She backed away. 'Why are you here?' she asked, shaking her head. 'Why are you here?'

'Because I have to be,' he said.

Cendrine stared at him, taking in every detail of his face. He had changed in four years. He was thinner, and there were lines in his face now, and a hint of grey in his dark thick hair. But he didn't look older so much as subdued. His eyes, his beguiling blue eyes, had lost their fire. Yet, he was still Jonathan, her Jonathan.

With one quick stride, Jonathan grabbed her arms, pinning her against the stone hearth. She gazed up into his eyes, seeing the fire suddenly rekindle in them. His lips came roughly down on hers, and he crushed her to his chest. In a flood, it all came back, all the longing and desire that he had always been able to stir in her. The incredible feeling of being caught in the moment, so aware of each sense and every part of her body. And their strange bond was there too, as powerful as the first day she had seen him.

His lips moved hungrily over her face, down her neck. His body pressed against hers, as if trying to touch every part of her at once. His arms held her in a vicelike grip, as if he were afraid to let her go.

He lifted her up onto his hips. She shut her eyes at the exquisite feel of him, hard against her.

His eyes were glistening. 'If you tell me to go—'

'No,' she said. 'Stay.'

Two days later, the wind dropped. The sky turned a vivid blue broken only by a few grey clouds. Cendrine took Jonathan to the village, where she bought tickets for the ferry. 'I want to show you my favourite place,' she said.

The ferry headed west, hugging the shore until it came to a dock in the middle of nowhere. There was nothing but a dense forest of dark-green fir trees. Another couple had got off the ferry with suitcases, and Cendrine followed them, clutching Jonathan's hand, up a path away from the dock. It was only then that Jonathan saw the old hotel, a honey-coloured, turreted monstrosity nestled in a stand of ancient fir and pine.

'Let's get something to warm up,' Cendrine suggested.

The old Hotel Giessbach was huge, with a slightly worn elegance. In the sunny dining room, Jonathan noticed that the diners were all young couples who were obviously more interested in each other than lunch.

Cendrine saw Jonathan watching them. 'Honeymooners,' she said, smiling slightly.

Jonathan looked at her, and she quickly looked down at her cup, stirring milk into her hot chocolate.

He reached across the table and covered her hand with his own, stopping the sound of the spoon against the cup. 'Are you sorry I came?' he asked.

She didn't look up. 'No,' she said.

'But?' he prodded.

She slowly pulled her hand away, setting down the spoon. 'We can't go back, Jonathan. We can't undo our lives.'

'I know,' he said. 'God knows, if I could, I would. I was a fool to make demands on you the way I did.'

They were silent. The soft sound of a couple's laughter drifted over from a nearby table. Cendrine's eyes went to the window, out to the lake below. It was a while before she looked back at Jonathan.

'Are you happy?' she asked.

Jonathan sighed. 'I love my work. I love my son.'

Cendrine could not hide her shock. 'A son – what's his name?'

'David.'

She looked out of the window again. Jonathan watched her carefully. A string quartet began to play out in the lobby. 'What about you?' Jonathan asked softly. 'Are you happy?'

She nodded slowly, her eyes still focused on the lake.

'Does . . .' Jonathan paused, the question hard to form. 'Does Alexander treat you well?'

She nodded again, shutting her eyes. Jonathan reached for her hand, and she wove her fingers quickly through his, but still would not look at him. The laughter of the couple nearby floated over to them again.

'Let's get out of here,' Jonathan said quickly.

Cendrine rose and swept by him into the lobby. Jonathan tossed some money on the table and ran after her.

He caught up with her on the veranda and helped her into her coat. He was relieved to see she was not crying. He couldn't have withstood her tears. She wound her scarf around her neck and pulled on her gloves. 'Let's walk,' she said.

303

He followed her on a path away from the hotel and into the forest. A recent snowfall made the going difficult, and the path wound steadily upward through the canyon of giant fir trees. Cendrine pressed on, silently. After a while, they emerged in a small clearing. Jonathan paused to catch his breath.

There before him was a fantastic sight – a towering frozen waterfall, fourteen different cascades, one leading down to another, glistening in the sun like a monumental crystal staircase. He stood there, awe-struck, staring upward at the waterfall and the majestic black-green trees with their epaulettes of snow, and he was transported back to another time and another place: the little glen near Dryden, and that moment so many years ago when everything was simple and glimmering with promise.

He looked at Cendrine, who was gazing at him, her face solemn. She was right, he couldn't undo his life. No matter how desperately he wanted to, he couldn't. But he was suddenly filled with the determination somehow to begin moving forward again.

It started to snow. The huge flakes fell down, settling on Cendrine's shoulders and in her hair. It was so quiet that he could hear the gentle sound of the snow as it kissed the ground.

Cendrine took his hand. 'Come with me,' she said softly.

She led him to a small building a few yards further up the path. It was a church, a rustic little place with a few mismatched broken chairs, an earth floor and a bare altar with its small cross still in place. There was a small hole in the roof and the snow spiralled down through it. They stood near the entrance, both staring at the cross for a moment.

'This is it, my favourite place,' Cendrine said softly. 'I don't think anyone uses it any more, but I come here when I feel the need. It's peaceful.' She walked slowly towards the altar and Jonathan followed.

They were silent for a long time. Then she turned to face him. 'You're leaving soon, aren't you?' she said.

'Yes. I have to.' He paused. 'But I'll come back, as soon as I can, as often as I can. The war can't last much longer and we can—'

She turned away and he stopped. 'Cendrine,' he whispered. 'I want you. And this time, it can be any way you want it to be. If that means living apart, only seeing each other when we can, I'll take it. I just can't stand the idea of never seeing you again.'

She turned back to him, her eyes brimming. 'It won't work, Jonathan. Not now.'

'Why not?'

'You wanted a wife, Jonathan. And you have one. I couldn't be a wife, not the way you wanted.'

'I know that now,' he said.

'It's too late,' she whispered. 'It's too—'

'Would you now?' he asked softly.

'Would I what?'

'Would you marry me now?'

She looked blankly at him. He took her in his arms. 'Right here, right now,' he said. 'Will you marry me now?'

'Jonathan . . .' She started to cry.

He kissed her gently. 'I, Jonathan Caras,' he began softly, 'promise to love you, Cendrine LeClerc, as long as we both may live.'

The snow spiralled down and he paused, wiping it off her face. 'Don't cry,' he said, 'please don't cry.'

He drew in a breath. 'Do you, Cendrine LeClerc, promise to love me, Jonathan Caras, as long as we both may live?'

She stared up at him for a long time, then laid her head against his shoulder.

'Yes,' she whispered.

Chapter Twenty-Seven

As Cendrine looked down at the baby sleeping in the crib, a flood of warmth coursed through her. It came every time she looked at the baby, a tenderness so terrifying it made her weak.

A daughter . . . Even now, after three months, she still couldn't believe she had a daughter. During her pregnancy she had been consumed with negative emotions. She had felt no love, no maternal feelings at all. Watching her lithe body swell, she had felt ugly and mourned her lost independence, thinking about how she would be tethered to another human being. She thought often about what her own father had done to her – and how her mother had let it happen – and she wondered how she would ever be able to feel love for a child. She lay in bed at night, her hands pressing on her rounded stomach, praying for a miscarriage. She hated the thing growing inside her, this thing that had taken control of her body and her future. It made her feel hopeless and trapped. How could she ever dance again? How could she be free ever to do anything again?

Luckily, Berta had been at the villa when Cendrine's labour began. With her usual efficiency, she had coaxed Cendrine through the difficult labour and stayed on. At first, Cendrine refused even to see the baby. But after a day, Berta brought the infant into the bedroom and laid it in Cendrine's arms. 'You can't let her starve,' she said.

The baby was so heavily swaddled that only the tiny pink oval of her face showed. She was quiet, her blue-grey eyes fixed on Cendrine. Cendrine beheld the baby, and something happened in that moment. The past fell away, the future grew dim. There was, suddenly, only the moment and the baby's eyes staring solemnly up at her. Cendrine slowly unwrapped the swaddling and examined the baby's feet and hands. Tiny, everything so tiny! She touched the spikes of soft black hair and bent her nose down to smell the skin: a smell like no other, so intensely, purely human but more fragrant than a peach.

Cendrine looked up at Berta. 'How . . .?' she asked softly.

Berta showed her how to breastfeed the baby.

Now, as Cendrine stared at the baby, she wondered how she ever could have felt anything other than love for her daughter. The baby had given her someone to take care of, a being into whom she could pour her love. For the first time in a long time, she no longer felt lonely. She had a daughter: Joëlle Christine.

Joëlle Christine LeClerc.

Cendrine reached down to touch Joëlle's hair. A new feeling rose up inside her, displacing the tenderness. It was the apprehension that came every time she thought about the fact that her daughter had no legal surname. Joëlle was illegitimate. After all these months, Cendrine still had not been able to tell Alexander about the baby. She knew that, if she asked, he would provide for the child, but she knew, too, that his commitment would never extend beyond that. He had told her often that he had no interest in a wife or family. In those rare moments when he had mentioned his own parents, she had sensed the aridity of his childhood. She knew she could not count on him to feel anything other than obligation towards Joëlle. He loved her because she had always been able to accept the limits of that love. But there was no room in his heart to accommodate the untidy needs of a child.

She stroked Joëlle's hair, wondering if it would stay dark, like Alexander's. Then she crept from the room, closing the door.

Sitting down at her desk, she wrote quickly, a short unemotional letter, simply telling Alexander about Joëlle and requesting his financial support. She was sealing it when Berta came in from the kitchen.

'Berta, I'm going to the post office,' Cendrine said. 'Joëlle's asleep. I'll be back as soon as I can.'

'Oh, I've already been, madame,' Berta said. 'I put your letters on the table in the hall. Just leave that one, I'll post it for you tomorrow.'

Cendrine hesitated, tapping the letter against her hand. With a sigh, she tossed it into the fire. Its words were too hasty and cold. She would try again later to compose a better effort. Alexander deserved at least that much from her.

She went to the hall and picked up the mail. Again, nothing from Alexander, but her heart leaped when she saw a fat envelope from Madame. The postmark on another letter – Barcelona – puzzled her. She opened it and, as she read, her eyes widened in astonishment. It was from Sergei Grigoriev, the manager of the Ballet Russe. The company was reorganizing for an appearance in England and Grigoriev was having trouble gathering enough dancers.

It's only a two-week engagement, [he wrote] but Diaghilev wants to open with *Giselle* at the Coliseum and if you can be here, I think he might give you the lead. We're meeting at the Palace Hotel in Monte Carlo on 20 September and leaving the next day by transport specially arranged by the English ambassador. Please come if you can safely find your way.

She held the letter, her heart pounding. *Giselle* . . . the role she had always wanted to dance. She thought suddenly of her body, how out of shape it was, but she pushed the thought aside. No, she would do it somehow. But she froze when she realized that it was already 18 September. The envelope was branded with countless stamps and crossed-out addresses, and the letter had taken two months to find its way to her here in Iseltwald. There wasn't enough time to get to Monte Carlo.

She ran to the kitchen and commanded the stunned Berta to pack. 'But where are you going?' the woman asked.

'London. And I'm taking Joëlle with me. Hurry, the ferry leaves in an hour!' Then Cendrine thought about Alexander, and a new plan formed in her head. After the engagement in London was finished, she would go back to Paris and tell him in person about Joëlle. It would be better that way. Surely, if Alexander saw the baby, it would be easier for him to accept her.

At Interlaken, Cendrine caught a train for Lausanne. She was forced to stay there for more than a day because trains going anywhere in Europe were so erratic. She arrived in Monte Carlo early in the morning of the twenty-second only to discover that the company had left the night before.

Exhausted and discouraged, she spent the night at the hotel. The next morning, she tried to arrange transport to London, but no one could help her. One official finally told her that although it was risky, passenger boats were still making occasional Channel crossings from Cherbourg. That night, back at the hotel, Cendrine lay in bed with Joëlle in her arms, considering her course. She was determined to get to London, but her thoughts kept returning to Alexander. She couldn't tell him; he would only try to stop her from going.

Suddenly she saw her way clear. She would go to La Turbie. She would leave Joëlle with Madame, knowing she would care for her until she returned. And she would go on to London alone.

The next morning, she hired a car and driver and set out for La Turbie. The old village looked much the same as it always had; the war had not touched it. Riding through the dusty, deserted streets with Joëlle in her arms, Cendrine was surprised by the slight melancholy she felt.

In her mind, it had always been a place of malevolence and imprisonment. She had associated it with isolation, ugliness, provinciality and poverty – and her father. But now he was dead. She found herself looking at the drab buildings and narrow sunless streets and thinking that no matter how many miles or years she had put between herself and the village, it was still a part of her. And a small part of her would always remain there.

Madame was shocked to see her, but took Joëlle without pause, cradling her to her breast. Cendrine watched Madame carefully. The woman was nearly eighty now but though slowed by arthritis, she still moved with grace and great dignity.

Madame put the sleeping Joëlle in the bedroom and went to the kitchen to make tea. Cendrine sat quietly waiting, her eyes travelling slowly over the faded red wallpaper, the bric-a-brac and photographs. When Madame poured the tea from the beautiful old Spode service, Cendrine's eyes filled with tears.

'What's wrong?' Madame asked.

'I don't know,' Cendrine said slowly. 'Something about this place . . . .' She hesitated. 'Coming back here now, at this time in my life . . . It makes me think about . . . how things have turned out.' She paused. 'It hasn't gone as I planned.'

'It never does, *ma puce*. It never does.'

Cendrine stayed as long as she could. Then, tearfully, she kissed Joëlle and Madame and left. She walked to the Roman ruins and stood for a few moments, gazing down at the Mediterranean. Then she left for Cherbourg.

The steamship departed late at night. The Channel waters were choppy, and Cendrine lay in her cabin, tired from her trip from Monte Carlo, thinking about Joëlle and fighting mild nausea as the ship pitched and rolled. Finally. She dozed off.

When the blast came, she didn't hear it so much as feel it. A violent lurching threw her to the floor. She heard the wail of a siren followed by the sound of running in the passageway outside her door: frantic voices and pounding footsteps.

She got up and started towards the door. Then came a thunderous boom, a far greater explosion than the first, that shook the ship and flung her against the wall. Her head struck the door with a violent jolt and she grabbed at the air, but couldn't keep from falling.

The lights went out, plunging the cabin into darkness. She lay crumpled near the door, unable to move. She tried to think clearly, figure out what to do, but her head was stinging with pain. She could feel something sticky and hot running down her face. Blood . . . her blood, and why couldn't she move? Her ear was to the floor and she could feel the vibrations of footsteps running past her door.

She heard the siren wailing and women and men screaming. She could feel the room moving; it was tilting at a sickening angle. And she could smell, faintly, acrid smoke.

Voices outside her door. She tried to get up but couldn't, and she began to lose consciousness. 'Help me,' she cried out. She pounded on the door. 'Help me,' she called out again. 'I'm in here! Help me!'

She heard the footsteps echoing down the passageway. 'Please!' she called out. 'Please! Don't leave me here! Don't leave me here!' Then everything went black.

Alexander set down the wire reports and leaned back in his chair, rubbing his eyes. It was after midnight and the next day's *Herald* had just gone to press. The newsroom outside his office was quiet as the handful of editors and reporters lingered, waiting for the first copies to come up from the pressroom.

Alexander's eyes focused on the bottle sitting on his desk and he reached for it. He stared at it for a second, then slowly poured the last of the cognac in his glass. There it was, the last of his best stock. He raised the glass, closed his eyes, and drank it down. He remained like that for a moment, head back against his chair, luxuriating in the narcotic, deadening effect of the alcohol.

He heard someone come in and looked towards the door. A copyboy had placed the *Herald* on his desk and slipped out. Alexander picked it up and tried to focus on the headlines. Death and destruction; war, nothing but war. But at least, for the first time, there was guarded optimism. The Germans were in full retreat across the Aisne and the British had taken back Trescault. German manpower was dwindling with each Allied hit and predictions were that the war would be over within months.

Alexander tossed the paper aside and shut his eyes. Tired, he was so tired! Yet, no matter what he did, no matter how much he drank, he couldn't sleep.

'Alexander!'

Alexander looked up, but it was a moment before he recognized Harry Parkyn standing at the door. Harry noticed Alexander's unshaven face but knew there was no point in advising him to go home. He came forward, holding out a wire report.

'This just came in,' Harry said. 'A German U-boat sank

a passenger ship out of Cherbourg. You want to remake the front page for it?'

Alexander closed his eyes. 'Do what you think best, Harry.'

Harry hesitated, wanting to say something, but finally turned and left the office. When he returned an hour later, Alexander had not moved. 'We remade the front,' Harry said. 'Thought you might want to see it.' He set the newspaper down before Alexander on the desk and left.

Alexander forced himself to sit up. He picked up the newspaper, and the headline swam before his eyes in bold black type. ALL FEARED DEAD IN CHANNEL SINKING. He didn't read the story; he knew it was no different from the countless others like it he had printed over the last four years. His eyes floated over the rest of the page and found a short list of names. For a moment, it looked like the old social registry of new arrivals that the *Herald* used to print, but then he realized it was the passenger list of the doomed ship, another list of casualties. His eyes flicked over the names.

Then he froze. His heart began to pound.

C. LeClerc.

It couldn't be . . . She was in Switzerland, far away. She was safe. It had to someone else. LeClerc was a common name. But the *Herald* had resorted to using only initials when printing casualty lists to save precious column inches.

Alexander jumped to his feet. 'Harry!' he screamed.

Harry came running. 'What is it?'

'The list!' Alexander said. 'Where's the original list?'

'What list?'

'The passenger list! The wire report! I have to see it!'

Harry took one look at Alexander's white face and ran out to the newsroom. He returned with the wire report.

Alexander grabbed it and frantically searched through

the names. Then he let out a groan and turned abruptly to the window. 'Oh, God, no! No, no, no . . .'

Harry watched in alarm as Alexander's shoulders slumped and his entire body seemed to shrink. He stood there, unsure what to do or say. It was a long time before Alexander turned around to face him.

Harry was horrified by the look of despair on Alexander's face, the black eyes glistening. Never, in all his years at the *Herald*, had Harry seen what he was seeing now – Alexander Profitt was crying. The sight left him paralysed.

'Harry I . . . I want you to do something for me,' Alexander whispered.

'Yes, of course.'

Alexander straightened slightly. He was still gripping the passenger list. 'I want you to call, send a wire, do whatever you must to get through.' Alexander paused, the tears falling down his face. 'It's to go to New York, to Jonathan Caras.'

Chapter Twenty-Eight

'Jonathan?'

Lucy came halfway down the staircase, drawing up short when she saw Jonathan standing in the hall, his head bowed, his arms braced against the wall. He was muttering something to himself, over and over.

'Jonathan? I heard someone at the door.' She stared at him in alarm. 'Jonathan, what is it?'

He looked up; his face was white, his eyes glazed. He looked at her for a moment, not seeming to see her. Slowly he straightened and started up the stairs.

'Jonathan? My God! Tell me what's wrong.'

He passed by her, climbing woodenly, and disappeared into the bedroom. She turned and followed him. When she came into the room, he was pulling a suitcase from the closet. He tossed it on the bed and went to the bureau. Lucy stood at the door, immobilized by his strange behaviour.

'Jonathan, what *is* it?' she demanded.

He pulled clothing out of drawers without seeming to realize what he was doing. Lucy saw a crumpled yellow paper on the floor by the bed and stooped to pick it up. She read the telegram twice, then looked up at her husband.

'Where are you going?' she asked softly.

For the first time, Jonathan looked at her. 'Paris,' he said, and turned away.

'Don't do this,' Lucy said.

Jonathan continued to throw clothes into the suitcase.

'Jonathan . . . I'm asking you not to do this.'

'I have to,' he said, without looking at her.

She shut her eyes tightly, willing herself to stay calm. She heard the snap of the suitcase locks and looked back at Jonathan.

'I've tried to ignore it,' she said. 'All these years, I've tried to pretend you don't think about her. But I know you do.' She paused, her throat constricting. 'I know you went to see her last year.'

Jonathan still would not look at her.

'But why now?' Lucy pleaded. 'She's dead, for God's sake. Why now?'

Jonathan closed his eyes, bracing himself against the suitcase. 'I'm sorry, Lucy,' he whispered. He looked up, his eyes brimming. 'I have to go.'

She stood straight as the tears fell down her face. 'You're obsessed,' she said. 'She's dead and you're still obsessed!'

Picking up his suitcase, coat and hat, Jonathan went quickly by her and out of the door. She turned and followed him, standing at the top of the staircase, gripping the railing.

'Jonathan!'

He stopped and turned to look up at her.

'If you go, you won't set foot in this house again,' she said.

Seeing her beautiful face, so rigid now with pain and pride, he felt his chest tighten with guilt. 'Goodbye, Lucy,' he whispered and closed the door behind him.

Jonathan stood at the door of Alexander's apartment, unable to bring himself to ring the bell. He had come there after walking for hours throughout the city. He had walked, as if in a trance, going to all the places he could

316

remember that had been central to Cendrine's life, where she had lived, worked or only visited. He had gone to the Folies theatre, which was dark and shuttered, and to the Café de Paris, which was closed. He had walked to the Latin Quarter and climbed the stairs to Marcelle's apartment, only to be told that Marcelle had moved. He had travelled back across the river to the Right Bank to look at Cendrine's old apartment in Rue La Perouse. When, at dusk, he found the street, he discovered that the block where Cendrine had lived had been levelled by shelling. He stood there for a long time, staring at the rubble.

Now, standing at Alexander's door, he could not even remember how he had got there, and he did not know why he was there. He knocked softly. At first there was no answer, and he was about to leave when the door opened. Harry Parkyn stood there.

Jonathan stared at him in surprise. 'Harry? What are you doing here?'

'Jonathan! Alexander said you would come,' Harry said. He opened the door wider. 'Come in, please. Give me your coat.'

Jonathan followed Harry into the drawing room. The room was quiet, illuminated by one lamp and the ember of a fire that had burned down in the grate. Jonathan stood stiffly in the middle of the room. The mantel clock chimed once.

'I didn't realize it was so late,' Jonathan said. 'I'm sorry.'

'Forget it. It's good to see you, Jonathan.'

The two men stood facing each other for a moment, then Jonathan clasped Harry to him in an embrace, shutting his eyes. They pulled apart awkwardly.

'Jonathan, I'm so sorry —' Harry began.

Jonathan raised a hand to silence him. 'It's all right, Harry, it's all right. *I'm* all right.'

'Sit down. You look exhausted.' Jonathan slumped down into a chair and Harry brought him a glass. Jonathan drank the liquor down without looking at it or tasting it.

'Where's Alexander?' Jonathan asked.

Harry's eyes flicked to the foyer. 'In the bedroom. He started drinking four days ago when . . .' He paused. 'When the news came, he ordered me to send you the wire. Then he left the office. I found him here, passed out, half-dead, and called a doctor. He was delirious yesterday. Thank God, he's finally asleep.'

Jonathan closed his eyes, letting his head fall back against the chair. 'Tell me what happened, Harry,' he murmured. 'Tell me everything.'

Harry shifted uncomfortably in his chair. 'There's not a lot to tell, Jonathan. She was going to London, apparently, though no one knows why. She didn't even tell Alexander. Her ship was torpedoed by a U-boat.' He paused. 'There were no survivors.'

'They're positive it was her?'

'They used the original ticket vouchers to verify the names. She purchased the ticket as Cendrine LeClerc of La Turbie. I thought that odd – La Turbie – but that seemed to be the one thing that finally convinced Alexander it was her.'

Jonathan brought up his hand to cover his eyes. Harry rose and took the empty glass that was dangling from Jonathan's other hand. 'I'll have a room made up for you,' he said softly. He started out of the room, then turned back. 'There's a memorial service tomorrow,' he said. 'Alexander asked me to arrange it. I don't think he'll be in any shape to go. The doctor has him on some pretty strong sedatives in hopes of keeping him away from the booze.' Harry paused and looked searchingly at Jonathan. 'You don't have to go if you don't want to.'

Jonathan looked up at him, his face drawn. 'I'll be there.'

The day was crisp and cool, and a brilliant white sun hung in the cloudless blue sky. Jonathan stood in the courtyard of Sainte-Chapelle for a moment, then went inside. Sunlight blazed through the walls of stained glass, flooding the chapel with rainbows. There were many people gathered; Jonathan recognized Cendrine's dressmaker, Mariquita, Harrison the pianist, artists and teachers, other dancers and musicians from the Folies. And, one far corner, Marcelle, her hair coloured brighter than ever but her face faded and drawn. Soft organ music floated down from somewhere above. Jonathan walked woodenly to a chair and sat down. He saw Ernest Brookes, Alexander's secretary, but Alexander was nowhere to be seen. Jonathan turned to face the front, where a priest was preparing for the service. He sat with unfocused eyes, his mind and body numb.

He felt an unnatural calm, a deadened feeling as if he were drugged, and he was thankful for it. The feeling had been with him since the day he left New York, and it had carried him through the five days since. After the initial shock of Alexander's cable had worn off, he had expected to be engulfed by anguish. But whenever he thought about Cendrine, the dead feeling took over, buttressing him and keeping him from tumbling into some bottomless crevasse of grief. He knew instinctively that if he fell, he would never get out again.

The service had started. Jonathan saw the priest's lips moving but heard no words come out. Out of the corner of his eye, he spotted something moving, a figure in a black suit coming down the aisle. It was Alexander. He was pale, and he moved slowly but with his back straight and head high. He took a chair one row ahead and slightly to the left of Jonathan. Jonathan searched his profile but it was expressionless, almost dispassionate. Jonathan looked away quickly.

The sight of Alexander triggered something in his brain, and suddenly, small but vivid memories flooded Jonathan's head. Colourful shards of recollection swirled around him like the light from the windows. The bells of St Madeleine on New Year's Eve. The illuminated grape lamps of the Café de Paris. Red jewels against a white throat – Cendrine's throat. A dark-green satin gown, the whisper of it when she walked. Chinese lanters at Moulin de la Galette swaying in the warm breeze. Cendrine whirling in the lights on stage. Snow on her face, a promise made in another church, another time. The touch of her lips on his chest. The deep curve of her bare waist as she lay on his bed. Cendrine kissing him, Cendrine dancing, Cendrine laughing, laughing, laughing . . .

Gone. All gone.

He closed his eyes, trying to shut it out. But the memories kept coming, bombarding him, filling his head with images, smells and sounds. His chest began to pound and his hands to tremble. He felt himself growing dizzy and took deep breaths. Falling . . . falling, he was falling. With a start, he opened his eyes.

Flowers. White flowers: a wall of them in front of him. Sprays of white flowers piled against the altar. How had ne not seen them before? He jumped to his feet.

'*Nooooooooooo!*' The word emerged in one low, anguished cry.

He ran past the astonished priest and began tearing at the sprays of flowers. He hurled the bouquets across the altar, flinging the flowers to the floor. 'No flowers!' he screamed. 'No flowers! She hates cut flowers! What's the matter with you? *No flowers!*'

Hands pulled at him and he struggled against them.

Tears streamed down his face. 'No flowers! They're for the dead! She hates them! They're for the dead!'

'Jonathan! Stop it! Jonathan!' Harry Parkyn grabbed him, restraining his arms. 'Jonathan!' Harry drew back and slapped Jonathan hard on the face.

Jonathan's body stiffened and he raised a fist to strike back. The he focused on Harry's stunned face. Slowly, he looked around at the scattered flowers, the shocked white faces and the figure of Alexander, who was standing over him.

A sob tore through his body and he closed his eyes.

Harry put his arm around him. 'Come on,' he whispered.

He started to lead Jonathan down the aisle, but Alexander stepped in front of them. 'Let me, Harry,' he said.

He took Jonathan's arm firmly and let him out of the chapel.

Out in the brilliant sunlight of the courtyard, Jonathan pushed against Alexander and staggered away. He walked unsteadily a few paces, wiping his face, drawing in deep breaths. After several minutes, Alexander approached him.

'Are you all right now?' he asked.

Jonathan turned to face him. 'Yes.'

Alexander looked at him doubtfully. 'Would you like to walk a bit? It's a fine day—'

'No,' Jonathan interrupted. He looked around the courtyard, up at the Gothic spires of the chapel and at the blank windows of the nearby Palais de Justice, anywhere but at Alexander.

'You're going to have to deal with this,' Alexander said.

'What?'

'You're going to have to learn to live without her or you'll destroy yourself.'

Jonathan stared at Alexander. 'I don't need your advice.'

Alexander sighed and looked at the ground. 'Jonathan, I didn't have to send you that cable. But I knew how much you loved her, and how much she loved you. I thought you should be here.'

Jonathan turned away. He took a few steps and sank down on the stone base of the iron fence surrounding the chapel. He shut his eyes, willing the drugged feeling to come back, to restore his control. He sensed Alexander sitting down.

'There's something I should tell you,' Alexander said. He hesitated, looking across the courtyard. 'God, I don't know how to tell you this. I've only started to come to grips with it myself in the last couple of hours.'

Jonathan heard the strange tone in Alexander's voice and turned to him.

'After I found out about Cendrine's death,' Alexander began softly, 'I sent Brookes to Iseltwald to collect her things and close the villa. He met the housekeeper, who told him that Cendrine had a child.' He paused, taking a deep breath. 'A daughter. I didn't know about it.'

Jonathan stared at Alexander in shock.

'I didn't know about it,' Alexander repeated softly.

'Where is the baby?' Jonathan asked.

Alexander shook his head. 'I don't know. I hired people to find out, but there's no trace anywhere. The housekeeper said that Cendrine took the baby with her when she left.' He paused, staring out over the courtyard. 'My guess is that the baby was on the ship, too.'

'But what about the passenger list? A child would have appeared on it.'

Alexander shook his head slowly. 'Infants don't require tickets.'

Jonathan sat there, stunned. A baby . . . a baby! His

mind raced back to the week he had spent with Cendrine in Iseltwald. 'How old?' he murmured.

'What?'

'How old was the baby?'

'I don't know.'

Jonathan was silent. It was possible the baby could have been his. He looked at Alexander, thinking that he should tell him that he had been with Cendrine. But if it was his child, why hadn't Cendrine written to him?

He was quiet for a long time. There was only one answer: Alexander had to be the father. What good would it do now to tell Alexander that he had been with Cendrine? What did it matter now?

Both men were silent for a long time. The sound of an organ could be heard faintly from the chapel.

'You can't stop looking, Alexander,' Jonathan said finally. 'If there's even a chance that—'

'She's dead, Jonathan. Cendrine's dead. The baby's dead.'

The flat finality of Alexander's voice made Jonathan look at him closely. For the first time, he saw the grief in Alexander's face. He had been so involved in his own sorrow that he had missed it. He had come back to Paris ready to blame Alexander for all his own pain, for the wrong turn his life had taken. He even wanted, in some nebulous way, to blame Alexander for Cendrine's death, so great was his need to make sense of it. But now, seeing Alexander's lined face, he couldn't do it. Alexander's anguish was as acute as his own. Alexander had loved Cendrine.

'Alexander . . .' Jonathan paused. 'I'm going to keep looking. I'm going to find the baby.'

Alexander didn't look at him.

'If I do,' Jonathan said, 'I'd like to take her back with me to the States.' There was no response. 'Did you hear me?'

Alexander's eyes glistened in the bright sun. Finally, he turned to Jonathan. 'I'm fifty-six years old,' he said. 'I'm not the father type. I told you that once, remember? Cendrine's gone, and I'm going to get on with my life.' He paused, searching Jonathan's face. 'But if you want to keep looking for . . . something that's gone, I won't try to stop you. I think it will only bring you heartache, but I won't stand in your way.'

Jonathan rose. He waited, but Alexander remained sitting. 'I have to go,' he said. He stared down at Alexander's dark hair, now streaked with grey. He wished fervently that there was some way to undo the past, erase the hurt between them and make their friendship go back to the way they had been so many years ago.

'Take care of yourself, Alexander,' Jonathan said softly.

There was no response. Jonathan turned and started out of the courtyard.

'Goodbye, my friend,' Alexander whispered.

Chapter Twenty-Nine

The car came to a stop in the dusty square, and Jonathan got out. 'Wait here,' he told the driver. With a quick look at the boarded-up café, Jonathan set out through the narrow cobblestone streets. It did not take him long to find Madame Kchessinskaya's apartment, and as he climbed the stairs, he heard a baby's cry that made him draw up short. He closed his eyes, muttering a prayer of thanks. His hunch had been right: Cendrine had taken the baby to the one person on earth she truly trusted.

He knocked and waited impatiently until the old woman came to the door. She eyed him suspiciously.

'Madame,' he said. 'I'm Jonathan, Jonathan Caras.'

Her face registered surprise, and her eyes softened. 'Oh, come in,' she said.

Jonathan took the chair near the piano that she offered, his eyes scanning the parlour, looking for the baby.

'Cendrine told me that you went to see her in Switzerland,' Madame said, settling into a chair. She eyed him intently. 'She's not here, if that's why you came. She's in London with the ballet.'

Jonathan hesitated. In his preoccupation with finding Cendrine's baby, he had not even considered that the old woman would have no way of knowing that Cendrine was dead. How was he going to tell her? 'Madame —' he began.

A baby's cry came from the bedroom. 'Oh, dear,' Madame said. She pushed herself up with effort. 'I have a girl who comes to help me, but she's lazy and doesn't always show up . . .'

She turned, holding the fussing baby. Jonathan rose, his eyes riveted to the baby's dark hair. He ventured close and gazed down at the child, looking for echoes of Cendrine in its face. 'May I hold her?' he asked softly.

Madame handed him the baby, who after a moment became quiet. 'You must have children of your own, Mr Caras,' she said, smiling.

'A son.'

'A baby needs so much attention. Too much for an old woman like me who's never had children of her own. Frankly, I will be glad when Cendrine gets back. Here, let me take her from you.'

Jonathan watched as the old woman rocked her. 'Madame, there's something I have to tell you,' he said. He took a deep breath; there was no way to soften it. 'Cendrine's dead,' he said. 'She was killed a week ago when her ship was sunk by the Germans.'

He watched the old woman's face, seeing it move slowly from shock through disbelief and into despair. Her body began to sag, and Jonathan feared she was going to faint. 'Here,' he said gently, and helped her down into her chair. Madame sat slumped, her eyes closed, cradling the baby. After a moment, Jonathan saw tears streaming down her face. He stood there, helpless, the knot tightening in his throat, feeling his own grief well up all over again.

'She was my daughter,' Madame murmured. 'My daughter . . . I loved her as if she were my own.'

Jonathan felt tears spring to his eyes. He watched the old woman rocking the baby. How could he find the heart now to take the baby away from her? For a long time, the room was quiet. Then Madame opened her eyes to look at Jonathan.

'I can't raise her,' she said, as if dazed. 'I'm eighty-three years old, I can't raise her here alone.' She began to cry, cradling the baby. 'It's not right . . . Cendrine would never have wanted her daughter to grow up here . . . it's not right.'

'Madame –' Jonathan rose. 'Let me take care of the baby.' The woman looked up at him. 'I can give her everything: the best care, an education, a family – and love.' He paused, his heart hammering. 'Please. Let me take her back with me to New York.'

The old woman stared at him for a long time. 'Cendrine loved you,' she said finally. 'I know she loved you.'

'She'll never want for anything, I promise you,' Jonathan said.

The old woman looked down at the sleeping baby and carefully tucked in the sides of the blanket. Then she held the baby out to Jonathan. He gathered the tiny bundle into his arms and stroked the baby's dark hair, thinking fleetingly of Alexander, but then only of Cendrine.

'What is her name?' he asked.

'Joëlle . . . Joëlle Christine,' Madame replied.

'Joëlle,' Jonathan repeated softly, 'Joëlle Christine Caras.'

A thunderous boom . . . then another. A flash of white light. The walls were shaking and everything was on fire, the ship was tilting, tilting. She was falling, falling down into the icy cold water.

Another boom and she screamed, screamed and thrashed out to keep from going under. But the water was holding her down, dragging her down . . . She

327

couldn't move or breathe.

'Hold her! Hold her! She'll hurt herself! Hold her still so I can get this in her!'

The nurse grabbed her arms while the doctor prepared an injection. The doctor paused, looking down into the wide, terrified eyes of the woman in the bed. 'She's out of the coma. Thank God for that at least.'

Cendrine stared up at the faces above her, panic-stricken. Who were these people? How did they get into the water with her? Why were they holding her down? She thrashed out at them blindly. Another boom, another flash of fire. Then she felt herself being pulled under the cold water, going down, drowning. Everything was going grey . . . greyer . . . to blackness.

She woke up hours later with a start, still groggy from the sedative. She saw a dim light far off in the distance but couldn't focus her eyes. She tried to scream but her throat was raw and parched. Ghostly blurs moved across her vision, and her heart hammered. Dead . . . I'm dead, she thought.

'Can you hear me?'

Words . . . she could hear someone talking to her, but it was faint. Again, the grey waters came, threatening to pull her under to the soothing blackness.

'Wake up! You must try to wake up!'

Something struck her cheek and she flinched. What was that? Who was talking? She struggled against the grey waves. The dim light returned and slowly grew stronger. A blurry thing hovered above her, and she concentrated on it.

'That's it. Fight it! Try to wake up.'

Features came into focus. A man with white hair. She heard a strange drumming sound. Rain . . . it was rain against a window. She saw the dim light and realized it was a lamp. She was not dead. She was lying in a bed in a room. Another figure moved into her vision – a woman,

328

with a round face and glasses. She focused on the glasses.

'What . . .' Her throat ached. 'Where . . . what?'

'A hospital,' the woman said softly. 'You're in a hospital. You're going to be all right now.'

'Fire . . . explosions,' she whispered.

'Dreams, and a thunderstorm last night. That's all. You're going to be all right now.'

Her body hurt. Tired, she was so tired. But she was afraid to shut her eyes, afraid the cold grey water would close over her again. Finally, she could hold out no longer; her eyes closed and she was quickly asleep again.

The woman was standing at her bedside when she woke up the next morning. As soon as she saw that Cendrine was awake, she left to get the doctor. Cendrine lay in bed, too weak to move. Slowly, with great effort, she moved her head slightly to try to get some sense of her surroundings. It was a small, sparsely furnished room, not at all like a hospital. The white-haired man came in and began to examine a dressing on her head.

'Head hurts,' she whispered through parched lips.

'A bad concussion. You've been in a coma for nearly four months.'

Four months . . . four months! She had so many questions, but she couldn't think clearly enough to ask them. She realized suddenly that the doctor had been speaking English, with an odd British accent.

'Where . . .?' she whispered.

'St Peter Port, on the isle of Guernsey.' The doctor smiled at her. 'Don't talk. I'll tell you everything in due time.'

Cendrine was propped up in the bed, waiting for the doctor. Two days had passed since she had woken up, and still the doctor had told her nothing. Her own body had told her that she was seriously hurt. Every muscle, joint and bone ached. Her right arm was bandaged, her skin showed evidence of healing burns, and her left leg was immobilized in a crude cast from the hip to below the knee. She could remember little of the ship sinking. Just the explosions, and the final tremendous jolt that had lifted her in the air and into the cold water. After that, everything was dim. She had a memory of someone in the water with her and of being dragged onto something wooden and rough. She could remember clinging to it, drifting in and out of consciousness, and she could remember the cold, the relentless cold, knifing into her body.

She shivered and pulled the blanket tighter. She closed her eyes as a spasm of pain shot through her leg. Four months! She had to get word to Madame that she was all right. She had to get back to Joëlle.

The doctor came in, and Cendrine stared at him. In his slightly shabby clothes and heavy shoes, he looked more like a farmer than a doctor. 'You seem better this morning,' he said, examining the head dressing.

'I want to know how I got here,' Cendrine said. 'And when I can leave.'

'Fishermen found you drifting, half dead,' he said as he tested her pupils with a light. 'They brought you here, and I did the best I could. This may not look like much of a place, but I am a real doctor.' His tone was defensive. He moved on to examine her arm. 'I considered moving you to a hospital in Plymouth, but the coma prevented that. And with your leg, it would have been too dangerous.'

Cendrine looked down at the cast, then back at the doctor. 'It's broken, isn't it?' she said.

The doctor held her eyes for a moment, then looked away. He busied himself preparing an injection. 'You're French, aren't you?' he said flatly.

'Yes . . .' She stared at the cast.

He gave her an injection. 'This'll ease the pain in your hip.'

Cendrine watched the doctor's face. She saw something evasive in his eyes and a knot began to form in her stomach. 'What's wrong with my leg?' she asked.

He held her eyes. 'Your hip was shattered. I did what I could.'

The words had come out so dispassionately that for a moment she thought she had heard him wrong. Then she looked down at the cast. She willed the leg to move, but nothing happened. The cast was heavy, too heavy, that's all it was. When the thing was off, she'd be able to move her leg all right. She looked up at the doctor, beseechingly.

'You might as well know now,' he said. 'You won't be able ever to use it again.'

The knot in her stomach tightened into a searing band of pain. Speechless with shock, she stared at the doctor's dour face.

'There's nothing more to be done about it,' the doctor said. 'It's better to know right away so you can get used to it.'

'No,' Cendrine said. She began to cry softly. 'No, no, no . . .'

The doctor watched her for a moment, then walked away. Cendrine turned her face to the pillow. 'No, no, no . . .' The crying grew into sobs that racked her body. At first, she didn't feel the touch on her arm. Then she looked up into the round face of the woman with glasses.

'Is there someone I can contact for you?' she asked gently.

Cendrine looked at her, the words barely registering.

'Do you have a husband?'

The woman's hand was cool on her forehead. Alexander's face floated to her mind, but Cendrine shut her eyes against it. No, he wouldn't want her now. She

331

was a cripple, and she would never allow herself to become a burden to him. She would send word to Madame, at least let her know she was safe. But what could the old woman do to help her? Cendrine began to cry again.

'Where is your family, dear?' the woman asked. 'Surely there is someone who can take care of you?'

Cendrine closed her eyes. There was no one, no one who could help her. Jonathan's face floated to her mind only to drift away. Another face took shape, growing ever clearer.

'Roland,' she whispered.

Cendrine sat on the porch of the clinic wrapped in a blanket. She could see, far off in the distance, the rise and fall of the white-tipped waves out in the English Channel. She sat there in the same place every day, facing south, towards where she imagined France to be, watching the waves for hours. Two more months had passed, and her body had nearly healed itself. But she had grown dependent on the drugs to keep the pain in her hip at bay. Yesterday, the round-faced woman, who was the doctor's wife, had told her that soon she would be able to leave and return to her life.

It began to rain. Cendrine stared vacantly at the waves. Leave – and go where? Back to La Turbie? There was nothing for her there. The two letters she had sent to Madame had come back unopened. And last week, a third had come back, this time with the message that Madame Kchessinskaya was dead. Dead . . . Madame was dead. No one knew where Joëlle was, and there was no way to find her.

Leave – and go back to what life? Back to Paris? There was nothing for her there either any more. She could never dance again. She couldn't even walk. That life was gone for ever.

A gust blew the rain onto the porch, but Cendrine didn't feel it dampening her hair and the blanket. Dead . . . Joëlle is dead to me. I am dead . . . everything is dead.

A figure was coming up the rocky lawn, up from the village. She focused on it apathetically, then let it grow blurry again. The next time she looked, she saw through dim eyes that it was a man, coming towards the porch. She closed her eyes wearily.

She heard the scrape of shoes on stone and opened her eyes. The man's coat was wet, his hair slick. She was about to look away when she saw his face. She forced herself to bring it into focus, fighting through the grey veil of the drugs.

'Roland,' she whispered.

He stood before her, not the Roland she had kept in her memories, but rather a tall, gaunt man with thinning blonde hair, a beard and cheerless eyes underscored with lines.

'Roland . . .' Her eyes filled with tears.

His eyes were riveted to the wheelchair. Finally, he knelt down beside it and gathered her into his arms. He held her tight as she cried, and when he finally pulled back to look at her it took every fibre of his will not to cry. His eyes took in her grey skin, her tangled wet hair and the blue hollows beneath her eyes. Though she was weeping, her eyes were flat and lifeless. The woman who had written to him had warned him that Cendrine had been ill, but he had not been prepared for what he now saw. His sister's beauty, her extraordinary beauty, had been ravaged. And she was a cripple.

'I'm here,' he whispered. 'It's all right, Cendrine.'

For the first time, he noticed the shabby exterior of the clinic. He could only imagine what it must have been like for her, six months alone, with no hope, in this godforsaken place. He closed his eyes, thinking about what might have happened if the woman had not been kind enough to send word to him in Baltimore . . . or if he had not come. His own life had only just begun to turn round. So many false starts, so many aborted dreams, a wife who left him and two lost years in prison for theft. He had come out resigned, vowing to give up all his grandiose schemes for success, and had found steady work as a sign painter. Then the letter had come. In the end, he had stolen the money from his boss to get to England, and he couldn't go back. But now, as he looked at his sister, he knew he had done the right thing.

'Cendrine, don't cry,' he said gently.

'Oh, Roland, you're here . . . you're here!'

He brushed the hair off her face. 'Don't cry, please.'

'You can find Joëlle . . . say you'll find her.'

'Joëlle? Who's Joëlle?'

'You'll find her . . . you'll find Joëlle and bring her to me.'

Roland looked into Cendrine's dazed eyes, his heart sinking. It was the drugs, the woman had warned him about that at least. Cendrine was not making any sense at all. But he would take care of her, he would make everything right again.

'I'm going to take you away,' he said softly.

'Away?'

'To London,' he said. It had just come into his head at that moment. He couldn't return to France or Baltimore. There never had been anything for him there; he knew that now. In London he would find work, and he would take care of Cendrine. They would make a life together again.

He pulled Cendrine into his arms. 'We'll go to London, and I'll take care of you. Everything is going to be all right, I promise.'

The August sky was hazy, and a hot breeze, heavy with

the cloying scent of honeysuckle, blew across the yard. The sweet smell, so redolent of waning childhood summers, made Jonathan close his eyes. He heard the rasp of the screen door and opened his eyes to see his father.

'We need rain,' Charles said, scanning the sky. 'It's been a bad summer.'

'Sit down, Pa,' Jonathan said. 'I have something I want to tell you.' Charles took the rocker next to Jonathan. 'I'm not going back to New York,' Jonathan said. 'I've decided to stay here.'

His father looked at him in surprise. 'What about the newspaper?'

Jonathan shook his head slowly. 'I'm going to keep my shares in it for now, but I'm turning over the editorship to someone else. It's not important. What's important is that I give Joëlle a home, a place where she can grow up normal. I want her to know you and Jake and Hannah. I want her to have a family. I can't do that in New York.'

'Are you sure about this Jonathan? You love your work.'

'I've been thinking about it ever since I got back, Pa. Being back here with you these past few weeks convinced me it was the right thing to do. I want to stay here.'

'And do what, Jonathan? You were never one to be idle.'

Jonathan squinted out at the fields. 'I've accepted a position at Cornell, Pa, in the English department. I'm going to teach.' He glanced back at his father. 'Why are you looking at me like that?'

'It's not right, Jonathan.' Charles shook his head slowly. 'I know you want to do right by that child in there, but deep down you're doing this for yourself. You've been hurt, really hurt, and you're looking for a safe burrow to climb into.' He paused, searching

Jonathan's face. 'It's one thing to want to stay if your heart is here. But if you're doing it to run away from yourself, because you're afraid to face up to things, it won't work.' He looked away. 'In the end, you'll be unhappy, and it won't work.'

Jonathan could not look at his father. He had been sure his father would be pleased, yet now he was all but calling him a coward. But before he could reply, Hannah came out. 'Well, the little one's had a cool bath and I've put her down for a nap,' she said. 'Heat's made the poor thing so cranky.'

Jonathan looked up gratefully. 'Thanks, Hannah.'

'If you don't mind me saying so, you're looking a little peaked yourself, Jonathan,' Hannah said.

'It's the heat, that's all.'

She smiled. 'Maybe you need a cooling off, too. Go for a swim. It always worked when you were a boy.'

'Swimming?' The idea struck Jonathan as irresistible. It would clear his head, just as it always did when he was younger. He glanced at his father. And maybe later he would be able to deal with what his father had said. He got up. 'I'll be back by dinner,' he said.

He went down the dusty road, thinking about his father's remarks. Afraid? What did he mean? What could he possibly be afraid of? He didn't want to live here for himself; he wanted it for Joëlle.

He quickened his stride, passing the familiar fields and fences. Afraid? He was not afraid. He just wanted to create a good life for Joëlle, and he couldn't do that in New York. Not now that Lucy had found out about the child and was divorcing him. How could he go on living there, trying to raise a child in that city alone?

He cut across a field, his pace picking up to a spring. Suddenly he was running, racing through the parched grass and over the hard ground. The sun burned on his neck, his breath came in quick gasps as he ran, the

336

sights, sounds and smells of his childhood enclosing him. Things achingly familiar yet strangely foreign.

He reached the glen, his chest heaving, and stood for a while on the rocks, trying to catch his breath. It was cool here within the green sanctuary of the pines, and quiet except for the gentle rush of the waterfall and the cry of a bird hovering far above. He stared down into the rippling water for a moment, then, with quick movements, stripped off his clothes and dove in.

The cold water washed him over, stinging his body and clearing his head. He swam back and forth across the pool with fierce, powerful strokes. His energy spent, he turned onto his back and floated, closing his eyes against the shaft of sunlight streaming down between the trees.

He heard a sound and looked up to the rocks above. A figure was silhouetted there, and shielded his eyes to see it better.

'Marion?' he said softly. 'Is that you?'

She didn't move. 'Yes,' she answered softly. She climbed down to the lower rocks, and Jonathan swam a little closer. Things so familiar, yet strangely foreign . . . She looked the same, yet subtly changed, her hair still a rich brown but now framing the face not of a girl but of a middle-aged woman. And her eyes, her soft brown eyes looked the same but with a sadness to them now. Ethan Steadman, her husband – Jonathan remembered suddenly that Hannah had told him he had been killed in an accident three years ago, and that Marion had been living alone on the farm since.

'I followed you,' Marion said softly. 'I was coming across the field to see you, and you took off down the road, so I followed you. You ran too fast and I lost you. But I figured this was where you would come.' She looked sideways at him. 'I didn't mean to spy on you.'

He was standing in the waist-high water, but felt no shame about his nakedness. All he could think about was how happy he was to see her. 'I should have come to see you before now,' he said.

She smiled slightly. 'You have a lot to keep you busy right now, I hear. The baby, I mean.' She paused. 'What's her name?'

'Joëlle.'

'Joëlle. Pretty.'

'It's French.'

There was a long silence. Jonathan had the feeling that Marion was torn between wanting to leave and wanting to stay, but he didn't know what to say to her. Everything felt off-kilter, awkward and unnatural, nothing like the way it had been when they were children.

'Well, I should be getting back,' Marion said softly.

'No, stay,' Jonathan said quickly. 'Come for a swim.'

She gazed at him for a long time, her eyes filled with a sadness that touched him deeply. Finally she smiled slightly. 'I don't have a bathing suit.'

He smiled back. 'Used to be your underwear was good enough.' When she made no move, he said again, 'Stay . . . please.'

Hesitantly, she began to unbutton her dress. Jonathan turned and swam a few yards away. He heard her splash and waited for her to swim up to him. She looked younger with her hair wet and slicked back from her face. Though she was smiling, the sadness still coloured her eyes. She swam slowly away and Jonathan followed, matching her stroke with his. They swam silently side by side until they reached the waterfall at the far end of the pool.

'I haven't been to this place in years,' Marion said.

'It hasn't changed,' Jonathan said. 'It's the same as it was that day we . . .'

Marion looked away. She swam over to a rock and propped her arms up on it. Jonathan went over to her. 'I

338

heard about Ethan,' he said softly. 'I'm sorry, really sorry.'

She looked at him, her eyes brimming. She got out of the water, stumbled across the slippery rocks and disappeared behind the falls. With one quick move, Jonathan hauled himself out of the water and went after her. He found her huddled under the fall, half caught in the downpour of water. He took her in his arms. 'Mari, Mari,' he said softly, 'it's all right. Don't cry. It's all right . . .'

She looked up at him. 'I didn't love him,' she said. 'I married him only because I couldn't have you.'

Jonathan stared at her. The water from the fall misted over her face and he couldn't tell now if she was still crying. But her eyes looked at him entreatingly.

'I loved you, Jonathan,' she said softly. 'I always loved you.' She fit her body against his. 'Oh, how I missed you.'

The sudden, unexpected pressure of her skin against his left him momentarily stunned. So long . . . it had been so long since he had felt the simple warmth and closeness of another human being, so long since he had been touched by a woman. He felt something inside him begin to crumble, breaking away in pieces. So long . . . so long . . .

The heaviness inside him grew, rising up, choking, into his throat. Memories and emotions surged up: memories of Paris, of Alexander . . . and of Cendrine. A life seen in fragments, as if it had happened to someone else long ago. Memories – and he was afraid of them, terrified of them.

The cool water rushed down over him, and he held Marion tighter. He was crying, silent tears rolling down his face. He turned his face upward, into the falling water. Drops of water, caught in the sun, falling down. Falling, falling, falling down on his face, washing everything away. Washing everything away, the memories, the tears, everything.

He buried his face in Marion's shoulder. Oh, God, he thought, help me forget. Please help me forget.

Chapter Thirty

Suddenly, it was spring. The winter had been long and hard, but then, during one moment in early March, the air grew suddenly warmer. The trees were bare against the pearl-grey sky, but there were great swatches of yellow everywhere, as if someone had splashed paint across a pencil sketch. The forsythia was in bloom, the first sign of renewal. It was spring.

Joëlle crossed the campus, heading for home. As she walked briskly along, she was humming a fragment of music, slightly off key. None of the students she passed would have recognized it as Mozart, and most would not even have taken notice of the eighteen-year-old girl. She was wearing a boy's shapeless mackintosh over a sweater and slacks, and her hair was pulled back in a ponytail. She walked with a coltish, wide stride, eyes trained straight ahead, a blue canvas bag slung over her shoulder. Only the most observant young man would have given her a second glance. Such a man would have noticed the sheen of her straight dark hair, the electric crackle in her blue-grey eyes. If he were a maths student, her high, intelligent forehead and the strong lines of her cheeks and jaw might have made him think of geometry. She was not made of the usual feminine curves; she was composed of angles, the cleanest, most elegant of angles.

Joëlle reached Cascadilla Street, where the forsythia

bushes blazed up the banks of the creek. She glanced towards the sun, low in the west, estimated it was nearly five o'clock and quickened her pace. She wanted to get home before her father did, and she knew his last class ended at four. She had lost track of time, spending the afternoon wandering, visiting her favourite childhood places. She wasn't usually given to doing such sentimental things, but that day, for some reason, it had felt like the right thing to do. She had gone back to her elementary school and sat in the playground swings. She had stood outside the old Temple Theater downtown where she had spent so many Saturdays watching westerns and listening to the pipe organ. And she had even gone down to the baseball diamond and stood at home plate, staring out at the left-field fence to the exact place where once, during an extra-inning game with a rival high school, she had hit a home run.

She had ended her journey back up on the 'ag' campus where she used to take her child's scooter to play because there was hardly ever any traffic there.

Now, as she cut across the campus, she could see that the traffic was heavier, of course. And there were things about Cornell and Ithaca that had changed. But it was still a magical place, a wonderful sanctuary in which to grow up. She had been away from Ithaca only once, yet she knew, instinctively, that it would be difficult to leave.

She reached the big Victorian house on Oxford Street out of breath. In the hall, she tossed her coat on the coat rack, sniffed the air and smiled. Pot roast for dinner. She bounded up the stairs to her room, and was changing her clothes when Marion came in.

'I thought I heard you,' Marion said, smiling.

'Sorry I'm late, Mom.'

'Did Miss Schweitzer keep you late again?'

'Nope. We finished at one.' She buttoned a chambray shirt. 'I just got to walking and the day got away from me.'

Marion's smile faded slightly. 'Oh, Joey, you're not going to wear that, are you?'

'What's wrong with it? Grandpa gave it to me.'

'You know your father hates it when you dress like a boy.'

'But I'm wearing a skirt!'

A memory popped into Marion's head of the day when the eight-year-old girl came home, sniffling and with a black eye, and proclamed that Joëlle was a sissy name and that from now on, she was 'just plain Joey'.

Marion smiled. 'Tonight,' she said, 'I think you should wear a dress. For your father's sake.'

Joey considered this for a moment, then took off her clothes. After staring into the closet for a moment, she pulled out a flowered dress. 'Did you tell Dad yet?' she asked Marion.

'I was going to this morning,' Marion said. 'But then I realized it wasn't my place. It has to come from you.'

'But you know he won't listen to me, Mom. I'm afraid he—'

'No, this is your plan, so you're going to have to face up to him. Come here, let's fix your hair.'

Joey sat down at the dressing table and Marion began to comb out her hair. She watched Joey's face in the mirror, seeing the doubt there and feeling a surge of love. Joey, the fearless, independent Joey, who never needed help with anything, needed her help now.

'You're only afraid to tell him because you don't want to hurt him,' Marion said.

Joey's eyes met Marion's. 'But how am I going to tell him, Mom? He's always wanted me to go to college here. It's all he ever talked about. How am I going to tell him I want to go to New York?'

Marion's hand paused on Joey's dark hair. 'You want to do this, don't you?'

'More than anything.'

'Then you'll find a way to tell him tonight.' She drew Joey's hair back with a ribbon. 'Don't underestimate your father. It'll be hard for him, but he'll accept it in the end because he loves you so much.'

Joey hesitated, then smiled. She drew Marion down towards her and kissed her cheek. The sudden, plaintive howl of a dog rose up from the kitchen below. 'Oh no, I forgot about Elton!' Joey said, jumping to her feet. 'I better go feed him before Dad gets home.'

At the door, she turned. 'Thanks, Mom,' she said softly. 'For everything.'

Marion smiled, then looked at the clothes scattered around the untidy bedroom and began to gather them up for the laundry basket. She spotted the blue canvas bag and emptied its contents on the bed: a rumpled leotard, tights and ballet shoes. She picked up one of the scuffed pink toe shoes and bent it gently between her hands. It gave too easily; the shank was broken. Marion shook her head and sighed – another pair used up already. The pointe shoes were expensive, four dollars a pair, the same price as those glamorous reptile pumps she had admired in the window of Rothchild's. Gladys Schweitzer had assured her Joey had strong feet and could withstand taking ballet classes in soft, worn-out shoes. But Marion didn't want Joey dancing in harmful shoes, so she had taken money out of her household account to buy new ones.

Marion sat down on the bed, holding the toe shoe. She had never quite got round to telling Jonathan about the extra expense of the shoes. He wouldn't have begrudged her the money; his salary as a professor more than covered their needs. But he would not have understood the commitment the shoes symbolized.

Marion rubbed a thumb over the shoe's scuffed satin, thinking about the day she told him that Joey wanted to take ballet lessons. He had looked stunned, as if she had hit him. And he had answered quickly that it would be just another whim, just as the microscope and coin collecting had been.

It was true that Joey had always been easily distracted, Marion thought. Growing up in a college town, with the other kids of faculty members, exposed her to such diversity that she wanted to sample everything. Even her schoolwork suffered from her restless curiosity. All her teachers said she was bright, but that she couldn't seem to focus her energy enough to make good grades. It seemed nothing – except her puppy Elton and maybe baseball – held her interest for long. Marion had tried to interest Joey in the arts, taking her to art galleries and to hear the great singers who appeared on campus – such as Paul Robeson and Marian Anderson – but to no avail. Until one day a dance troupe came, and Joey suddenly wanted to take ballet lessons. Marion was only mildly surprised when Joey showed not only a deep interest, but also a talent, for dance. She had sensed from the start that this time, things were going to be different. Joey's love of dance had risen out of something much deeper than childish whim.

Marion rose, picking up the bundle of dirty clothes, and her eyes went involuntarily up to the picture hanging above Joey's bed. A small portrait in oils of a woman with blonde hair and blue-grey eyes – Joey's eyes, but more sombre. It was Cendrine, Joey's mother.

Marion felt a small tightening deep in her stomach. Strange how the painting still affected her after all these years. For almost seven years she had lived with it, ignoring it for the most part, treating it as just another thing in Joey's room that needed dusting. But sometimes she felt its oppressive presence like an overwhelming perfume that ebbed and flowed throughout the house, never quite dissipating. The portrait had been in the basement since the year she and Jonathan had married and moved to Ithaca. Jonathan had put it there and forgotten about it. It remained there until the day Jonathan had finally been forced to bring it out, to show it to Joey.

Marion stared at the portrait, remembering that day, the day when everything in the house on Oxford Street had shifted ever so slightly, the day Jonathan had told Joey about Cendrine.

When Joey was still a baby, Jonathan and Marion had talked often about whether they should some day tell Joey the truth about her birth. Eventually Marion convinced him that, when the right time came, Joey should know about Cendrine. But Jonathan decided not to tell her about Alexander. 'It will be confusing enough just finding out about Cendrine,' Jonathan said then. 'I don't know how to tell her about a father who didn't want her.' Marion agreed it was the best course.

So when Joey was twelve, Jonathan sat her down and told her about the woman who had given birth to her, the woman who had died during the war in Europe. He told her, too, that Marion had loved Joey so much that she wanted to be her mother. Much to Jonathan's and Marion's relief, Joey seemed to accept this news calmly.

But soon after, the questions had begun. What was she like? Was she pretty? Do I look like her? Do you have a picture of her, Daddy? Why don't you have a picture?

Finally, reluctantly, Jonathan showed her the portrait. He was worried that Joey's preoccupation with Cendrine was hurting Marion, and he hoped that if Joey saw the portrait, her curiosity might be placated. Instead, it only made the questions grow increasingly complex. Did you love her? Why didn't you get married? Joey wanted to have the portrait upstairs, but Jonathan objected. Finally Marion told him that Joey needed to have some physical evidence of her mother's existence, and that they shouldn't fight it. Seeing the portrait hanging in Joey's room stung Marion, and sometimes she felt it had created a distance between her and Joey that hadn't been there before, but she said nothing. From the beginning, she had loved Joey as her own daughter, especially since she was unable to have children of her own. Seeing the portrait also sometimes made her feel jealous. The portrait was a powerful symbol of the bond that Joey and Jonathan shared, a link to each other and the past in which she had no part.

Joey's questions about Cendrine continued over the next two years, and Jonathan answered them all patiently. Listening to him, Marion sometimes thought it was painful for him, dredging up memories to satisfy his daughter's hunger to know. But sometimes, when Marion eavesdropped on their conversations, she would hear in Jonathan's words more than simple answers. Jonathan was a natural storyteller, and without realizing what he was doing, he would lapse into nostalgia and weave enchanted tales of a lost time when everything was grand and beautiful. So, in the inflamed imagination of a little girl, Paris became a fairyland, its people a race of gods and goddesses, and Cendrine a ballerina more beloved than Pavlova.

Marion picked up the other pointe shoe and carefully wound the ribbon around it. You should have seen it coming, Jonathan, she thought, but you didn't want to. From the start, Jonathan, who usually took an avid interest in whatever Joey did, had maintained that the ballet lessons were a waste of time and money. Marion recognized Jonathan's unreasonable attitude as a denial of Cendrine's memory, but she couldn't bring herself to tell him that. How could she? They had never even really talked about Cendrine, except when the subject applied to Joey.

By the time Joey turned fourteen, she had outgrown

her need to deify Cendrine's memory, and Marion felt the closeness with her adopted daughter return, stronger than ever. And there was an added reward: Marion felt a new respect from the girl, created by the support Marion had given her over the ballet classes. The portrait of Cendrine remained in Joey's bedroom, but it ceased to be an icon for Joey and a threat to Marion.

But now, as Marion stared at it, she felt the old twinge of jealousy. 'I'm no saint,' she said softly to Cendrine's likeness. 'I still wish he had never met you.'

She heard the front door open and Jonathan's voice calling for her. She tossed the laundry into the basket and went downstairs.

During dinner, Marion waited for Joey to bring up the subject of New York, but the girl nervously kept the conversation on other topics. Finally, as Marion was serving the cake for dessert, she heard Joey draw in a deep breath.

'Dad, I have something I want to tell you,' Joey said, her voice firm. 'It's important. *Very* important. And I want you to let me finish before you say anything. Don't interrupt, okay?' Joey looked up at Marion, who gave her a nod of encouragement.

Jonathan set down his coffee, smiling slightly. 'Do I have any choice?'

'I went to an audition last month,' Joey said. 'Well, Mom took me, actually. It was for a ballet school in New York.' She drew in another breath. 'They accepted me.'

Jonathan stared at her, dumbfounded. Marion stood frozen, holding the cake plates. Joey looked from one to the other, then laughed, a small laugh of nerves and excitement. 'It's a brand-new school, Dad, for professional dancers. It was started up just last year by this rich guy and some Russian man. It's so exciting! They're starting a company, too, the first real American ballet company, and I might get to be in it!'

'This is preposterous,' Jonathan said quietly, staring at Joey as if she were crazy. His eyes swung quickly to Marion. 'What's this all about, Marion?'

'Dad, listen, *please*,' Joey interrupted. 'I really want to do this, with all my heart. I've known for a while I wanted to be a dancer, and when Mom took me to the audition in New York—'

Jonathan looked back at Marion. 'New York? You took her to New York and didn't tell me?'

Marion set down the plates. 'I was going to,' she said softly, 'but I didn't think you'd let her go.'

'You're right, I wouldn't have.' Jonathan looked back at Joey, his eyes snapping. 'I don't know what you two have been up to, but I don't appreciate it. I told you both years ago that these lessons were a waste of time.'

'Dad, please! Just listen to what—'

'No, I won't listen.'

'Jonathan!'

Joey leaned across the table, her eyes bright. 'Dad, I'm not a kid. I'm almost eighteen. That's old enough to decide what I want to do. I deserve to be treated with a little respect—'

'Respect!' Jonathan's voice rose. 'Don't tell me about respect, young lady. You go behind my back, without telling me a thing, concoct some harebrained scheme, and you expect me to sit back and accept it?' He glanced at Marion. 'Well, I don't. You're not going to New York. You're not going to be a dancer. You're going to stay here and go to school as we planned.'

'As *you* planned, Dad, as *you* planned!' Joey cried. 'I never wanted to go to college. I don't even have the grades to get in! You had to pull strings to get me accepted!'

'You're smart, Joëlle,' Jonathan said, lowering his voice to regain his control. 'You could have done it yourself if you wanted.'

'But that's just it! I *don't* want it! I want to be a dancer!' Tears sprang to Joey's eyes. 'I've tried to tell you that before, but you never listened!'

Jonathan picked up his coffee, not looking at Joey or Marion. 'I don't want to hear any more of this. You're *not* going to New York, and that's the end of it.'

Joey stared at him, tears streaming down her face. She looked up at Marion, who stood silent, too stunned by Jonathan's behaviour to say anything. Joey jumped to her feet. 'I'm going to walk Elton,' she said to Marion, and ran out of the kitchen.

The screen door slammed and the house became suddenly very quiet. Marion sat down at the table across from Jonathan. 'That wasn't fair,' she said quietly.

Jonathan looked up at her. 'Now you're going to turn on me, too, I suppose?'

'No one's turning on you, Jonathan. Least of all Joey.'

'I can't believe you had a part in this, Marion. My God, what in the world were you thinking about, taking her to New York?'

'I was thinking about Joey!' said Marion angrily. 'And what would make her happy!'

Jonathan stared at her in surprise; he had never heard her raise her voice before. Her face wore a look he had never seen. There was a fierce determination in the set of her mouth, but an inexplicable flicker of sadness in her eyes.

'I don't want her to go either, but she really wants this,' Marion said softly. 'I've never seen her this way about something before. I thought it was a whim at first, but it's got under her skin; it's in her blood.'

Jonathan was silent for a long time. He looked away, towards the door through which his daughter had disappeared. 'I don't want her to be a dancer, Mari,' he said quietly.

350

'I know.' Marion paused. 'And I know why.'

Jonathan didn't look at her.

Marion drew the edges of her cardigan together. 'You told her so much about Cendrine,' she said softly. 'You filled her head with your stories, and you never saw what it was doing.'

Jonathan glanced at her, then looked back at the screen door. There was another long silence.

'All these years, you and Joey talked about her,' Marion went on, 'but you and I never did, you know. Not once.'

Jonathan looked back at Marion.

'Maybe I never really wanted you to talk about her,' Marion said softly. 'Maybe I . . .' Her voice faltered and she looked around the kitchen, everywhere but directly at Jonathan. 'Maybe I thought that if you never talked about her, we could pretend she never existed. I could pretend you never think about her.'

She paused, her eyes shining. 'But you do think about her sometimes. I know you do. And . . .' She paused again, finally looking at Jonathan. 'I was always afraid that I just couldn't match up . . . couldn't match up to a memory.'

The last words came out in a whisper, then Marion looked away. Jonathan took her hand, bringing it up against his cheek. 'Oh, Mari,' he said, shaking his head. 'That was another time, another life. It's a memory, that's all it is, just a memory. It's nothing you have to match up to. It's just a memory.' He kissed her hand. 'I love you, Mari. I love you so much. You're my life. You and Joey, both of you. You're my life. You know that, don't you? Please tell me you know that.'

Marion intertwined her fingers with Jonathan's. After a moment, she nodded.

'God, she's so young,' Jonathan said softly. 'She doesn't even know what she wants out of life.'

'She's not a baby any more, Jonathan.'

Jonathan shook his head. 'New York . . .'

'This is 1937, Jonathan. Young women are more independent today.' She wiped at her eyes briskly.

'I don't want her to go, Mari.'

'Maybe if you let her go to New York, she'll get this out of her system.'

'I doubt it,' he whispered. 'I really doubt it.'

They were silent. Marion saw his eyes drift to the screen door. 'It's a nice night,' he said. 'Let's take our coffee out on the porch.'

She shook her head. 'No, you go wait for Joey. You two have things to talk about. I'll wait for you upstairs.'

Jonathan hesitated, picked up his coffee and left the kitchen. On the veranda, he sat down in the swing, holding the coffee, staring out at the darkness. He heard a cat meow and the answering bark of the neighbour's dog. All up and down the street, warm yellow lights burned reassuringly from the neat Victorian houses, and he could hear a radio playing nearby. 'Tonight, we bring you Chapter Three of *One Man's Family*, dedicated to the mothers and fathers of the younger generation and their bewildering offspring!'

Jonathan leaned back in the swing. How pale the problems of his own family seemed compared to those of the soap-opera Barbour family! No death, scandal or missing heirs, just a headstrong daughter who wants to traipse off to the wilds of New York and throw away her life.

Jonathan set the coffee aside and closed his eyes. He had tried so hard to do everything right for Joey, Marion and himself. On that day he had returned from France with Joey, he knew he had made an irrevocable decision. With that one act, he had turned his back on his marriage to Lucy and had set off down a road on which he could never double back. But everything had turned out all right. He had built a new life, a good life. He was a tenured, respected professor, soon to be head of the department. Marion had learned to fit in with the other faculty wives and their social functions. Joey, it was true, had tried his patience at times with her lack of effort at school. But he loved her and Marion very much. Life in the big house on Oxford Street had been comfortable and full. They had been happy, just the three of them.

Jonathan's mind now tripped back over the past eighteen years, remembering the Christmases and birthdays, the big and small events. He remembered the summer the three of them had rented a cottage on the lake, and how, when it got too hot, they pulled the mattresses out onto the porch to sleep. He remembered the autumn he took Joey to her first football game, watching her delight as the Big Red Band did its half-time formations. He remembered the day he took her to watch the circus parade on State Street, and all the times they had played catch right here in the front yard. And he could remember sitting in his office upstairs, listening to her childish cry rising up to him out of the twilight as she played kick the can in the street.

Sometimes, he wondered what his life might have been like if he had never found Joey. If he had never gone to France, if he had never left Lucy. He was sorry he had hurt Lucy, but he didn't regret the end of his marriage; he understood now that it had been based on nothing more than his own pathetic need to manufacture the magic he couldn't have with Cendrine. But David – that was different. David was real. And his one regret was that in his own obsessive behaviour over Cendrine's death, David had been sacrificed. David, his son, his own flesh and blood, had been lost to him for ever.

He thought suddenly of something his father had said a long time ago. Something about holding onto people too tightly, so tightly that you drive them away. He had done that with Cendrine, and now he was trying to do it all over again with Joey.

He heard a sound and opened his eyes to see Joey coming up the walk with Elton on his leash.

She saw him and stopped. 'Dad, what are you doing out here?'

'Enjoying the night,' he said.

'It's too cold to be sitting out here,' she said.

'I know.' He paused. 'Come sit with me for a moment.'

She hesitated, then came slowly up the steps. She perched on a railing, but Jonathan patted the space next to him on the swing. 'No, next to me, please.'

She sat down on the swing. With a groan, the old golden retriever curled up at her feet. The silence was broken only by the creaking of the swing.

'I was just remembering,' Jonathan said finally, his voice soft, 'all the things we've done together. Remember when we built the tree house?'

Joey wound the leash around her hand. 'Yeah.'

'We did a pretty good job.'

'Best one in the neighbourhood.'

Jonathan glanced over at her, taking in the high curve of her forehead, the straight lines of her nose and jaw – and the determined set of her mouth. It was the last detail that made him think suddenly of Cendrine. Funny, how little Joey looked like Cendrine. But sometimes, when the stubbornness crept into her face, he could see Cendrine there so clearly. People were for ever telling him how much Joey resembled him, but he knew the truth: it was Alexander's blood that had given her her height and elegant features.

'You know what I was remembering earlier today?' Joey said softly, without looking at him. 'How you used to take me down to the station at night to watch the trains. Remember how they'd come down from

Trumansburg, braking down the hill, the wheels spitting off sparks from all the friction? You told me it was a magic dragon.' She turned to look at him. 'Magic. I believed you.'

It was quiet for a moment. 'Joëlle . . . Joey,' Jonathan began, then sighed. 'I shoudn't have spoken to you the way I did earlier.'

Joey twisted the leash between her hands, her eyes trained downward. 'Don't get mad at Mom about the audition. I put her up to it,' she said. 'She wanted me to tell you ahead of time, but I was afraid you'd forbid me to go.'

'I probably would have.'

It was quiet again, except for the radio playing next door and Elton snoring.

'Dad, I know I disappoint you sometimes,' Joey began.

'Joey, that's not—'

'I mean, about school, not getting the grades I should have. Shoot, the only thing I ever got an A in was gym.' She paused and turned to face him. 'But dancing is different. It makes me feel so good about myself. When I jump high or make a pirouette come out just right, I feel wonderful inside, so . . . competent, as if no matter what I tried to do, it would somehow work. Like hitting a home run, only a hundred times better. When I dance, it feels like a light going on inside me, this wonderful burning white light.' She paused again. 'Does any of this make sense to you?'

He was looking hard at her. 'Yes.'

She sighed. 'I really want to do this, Dad. Please, let me try it. Just let me try it.'

The intensity in her eyes was too much and Jonathan had to turn away. He felt an ache in his heart, an ache he could only recognize finally as envy.

He gazed out at the darkness. 'I don't suppose you've

given even a thought to where you'd live,' he said quietly.

'I thought I could maybe share an apartment with some of the other dancers,' Joey said tentatively, watching Jonathan's face carefully. 'Dad, does this mean you'll—'

Jonathan faced her. 'We'll give it a try, for a year.'

Joey threw her arms around his neck. 'Oh, Dad! I'm so happy!' She pulled back, her eyes bright with tears.

'Not so fast,' Jonathan said. 'Despite what you and your mother think, you're still a child. I'll let you go on one condition. I'll call Katherine and Sumner and see if they'll mind you staying with them.'

'Dad!'

'It's not negotiable, Joëlle. I won't be able to sleep at night thinking about you living in some Village rathole. You stay with your godparents or you don't go.'

A smile came slowly to Joey's face. 'Deal.'

She hugged Jonathan again, then nestled down against his side. The radio next door was silent. The street was quiet except for the music of crickets.

'Joey?' Jonathan said softly. 'How good are you?'

Her voice came back to him in the dark. 'Good, really good, Dad. I just know I am. I can't wait for you to see me dance.'

Jonathan stared out at the velvety darkness. A firefly blinked on and then quickly off again. He closed his eyes and leaned his cheek against his daughter's head.

Chapter Thirty-One

Joey pushed open the door of the delicatessen on Madison Avenue and was enfolded by the warming smell of coffee and pastrami. She went to the counter, pulling off her gloves, and gave the owner a smile.

'You look frozen to the bone,' he said to her over his shoulder as he fried eggs on the grill.

'It's five degrees above zero and the transit workers decided today was the perfect day to strike,' Joey said, patting her cheeks. 'A black coffee to go, Sammy.'

'Sit down and have some oatmeal,' Sammy said. 'You're too skinny. All you dancers are too skinny.'

'Just coffee,' Joey said. 'I'm late.'

Clutching the bag Sammy gave her, Joey left the deli. Crossing the street, she entered a nondescript building and got into the rickety lift. With a groan it made its way laboriously past the second floor, where Joey could hear a samba coming from the Tuxedo Ballroom, and past the third floor, where the whir of sewing machines spilled out of the tailor shop. The lift jerked to a stop on the fourth floor and Joey got out.

She pushed open the facing door with its small sign announcing School of American Ballet, and went quickly through the narrow hallway to the dressing room. Joey greeted the three other dancers, and quickly changed into her practice clothes. Carrying her pointe shoes and the bag of coffee, she went to the studio.

She paused at the door, struck for a moment by the sight of the sun streaming through the big windows, making puddles on the wooden floor. It was a huge room with plenty of space to move, nothing like Gladys Schweitzer's little studio back home. Joey smiled and sat down on the floor. But then, nothing about New York was like anything she had seen back in Ithaca. Everything was bigger here.

The studio was deserted. There was still half an hour before class, but she always came early to give herself enough time to warm up. It was the first hard lesson she had learned after coming to New York. There was no one – no Gladys Schweitzer, no Mom – to remind her what to do or scold her when she was lazy. She was on her own.

She put on her pointe shoes, opened the bag and smiled, shaking her head, as she saw the bagel Sammy had tucked inside. She leaned back against the wall, sipping the coffee, feeling its warmth course through her chilled body, thinking about the past year.

So much excitement. So much uncertainty. So much to learn. So much . . . everything. The School of American Ballet was a strange, new world, and at first she had been overwhelmed. The classes, based on the style taught at the Imperial School in Russia; were difficult compared to what she had been taught in Ithaca. She had to learn character dancing and go to lectures on art, music and architecture. The teachers, many of them foreign, were intimidating, especially the elegant Pierre Valdimiroff, who was once Pavlova's partner. And then there were the other students, who were all better than she was. Some had even performed before, like Harold and Lew Christensen, who had done stints in vaudeville, and Ruthanna Boris, a precocious teenager who had danced with the opera. Even those with no experience seemed better trained, like the girls who came from Catherine

Littlefield's school in Philadelphia.

Yet, from the first moment she had set foot inside the School of American Ballet, she had felt an inexplicable sense of belonging. There was an air of intense seriousness, as if everyone involved with the school and its company understood they were part of a grand experiment of historical significance.

The atmosphere came in part from Lincoln Kirstein, the man whose vision had given birth to the company and school. Joey had seen Kirstein prowling the school in his fine grey suit. She had heard about the young Harvard graduate who collected art, founded an arts magazine and wrote a novel – all before his thirtieth birthday. She had heard the story, too, about how Kirstein, while at a cocktail party in London, had enticed a young, broke Russian choreographer named Georgi Balanchivadze to come to America.

Balanchivadze was to make his name as George Balanchine.

Joey sipped her coffee, thinking about the first time she had seen the man who would become, in just one year, nearly as influential in shaping her life as her father had been.

It had been at her first class. She could remember it clearly. Balanchine had walked into the studio, a dark, slight, handsome man in his early thirties. Joey knew many of the other girls had crushes on him, but she thought that there was nothing remarkable about him. But once the class began, she understood. What she had been doing in Gladys Schweitzer's studio was nothing like what Balanchine wanted. What she had done before was mere marching on pointe and curtsying. Suddenly, this strange Russian was asking her and the others to move with crispness and speed, to make their arms and upper bodies more fluid and to devour the space around them. She had to learn to dance from the balls of her feet, never sitting in a preparation long. Suddenly, she was not merely moving; she was dancing.

It had been hard those first few months, especially since she thought Balanchine was ignoring her. But she was determined, strong and fearless, unafraid to try and fail. It was that quality that finally caught Balanchine's eye.

Towards the end of a particularly gruelling class, Balanchine had given a fast, very difficult combination of steps, and no one seemed able to do it to his satisfaction. Finally, he told Joey to step to the front. 'You try,' he said.

Joey hesitated. The combination ended with a double pirouette, and turns had always been her weakness. 'I've never been able to do a double,' she said.

'Do it,' Balanchine said.

The pianist began and Joey flew through the fiendish combination. She gitted her teeth for the pirouette, and just as her momentum carried her halfway round, she felt a whack on her behind. She spun round twice, three times, before she fell over. Balanchine helped her to her feet and smiled. 'Good.'

Joey had stared at him in astonishment. Gladys Schweitzer had never laid a hand on her; she had always affected an aloof manner. But Joey quickly discovered that such an impersonal approach wasn't Balanchine's way. When he taught, he pushed, tugged, poked and touched. It was electrifying and drove her to try daring things she had never done before.

After that, Joey became known for her willingness to try the most outrageous steps. Balanchine would often give a difficult step or combination and tell the class, 'Watch Joey.' But he had yet to offer her a position in his company.

Joey took a bite of the bagel. A few other dancers had trickled into the studio. She finished her coffee and took a place at the barre to do her warm-ups. Soon after, the class began, taught by Vladimiroff. When it was over, he came up to see her.

'I have good news,' he said, smiling.

Joey waited expectantly. Such a personal thing as a smile was a rare thing from the austere Russian.

'Balanchine wants to try you in his new ballet, *Orpheus and Eurydice*,' he said. 'He wants a young girl with dark hair, and he thinks if you work hard you might be able to do it.'

Joey stood there, stunned. 'I can,' she said finally.

Vladimiroff's smile lingered. 'Go see him this afternoon.'

Joey waited until Vladimiroff left, until the studio was completely empty. Then she let out a whoop of joy. She was in the company. Her time had finally come.

The American Ballet, Joey had learned, was not so much a ballet company as a collection of whatever dancers were available at any given time. For four years, Balanchine and Kirstein had struggled to keep their little ballet company afloat, and dancers came and went, many lured away by the money offered by revues and musicals. Finally, Balanchine had been forced to accept the invitation of the Metropolitan Opera to become its resident ballet company.

But the arrangement had quickly soured. The dancers were relegated to dank dressing rooms, and were never allowed to rehearse with the orchestra. The management nagged Balanchine about every penny he spent, and complained that the dynamic ballets he created clashed with the slow mannerisms of the singers.

By the time the opera agreed to let Balanchine stage *Orpheus and Eurydice*, rumour had it that the management was simply giving him enough rope so he would finally hang himself and his American Ballet.

During the three months of rehearsals, Joey saw nothing that led her to think *Orpheus and Eurydice* was unusual. It was not until the final dress rehearsal that she realized that this was not a normal opera; it was a revolution. The set was a surreal, hellish vision of chicken wire, dead tree branches and cheesecloth. The singers were banished to the pit with the orchestra. There was no intermission to stop the flow of ballet. The choreography, she thought, was beautiful. And she was thrilled to be dancing opposite Lew Christensen, a tall, talented, handsome blond.

On opening night, she was tense with anticipation. She wished her mother and father could have come. But they had been forced to cancel their plans to come to New York at the last minute, unwilling to leave Grandpa Charles, who had come down with the flu. Just before curtain, Joey impulsively called home from backstage. Marion accepted the collect call, concern in her voice.

'Joey? Is something wrong?'

'No, everything's fine.'

'But it's nearly eight. Isn't the opera just about to start?'

'Yeah. I just wanted to hear your voice.'

'Oh, Joey, you'll do fine,' Marion said softly.

A stagehand gave out the call for places. 'Is Dad there?' Joey asked quickly.

'Yes, I'll put him on.'

Joey shifted the phone to another ear, careful not to smear her heavy make-up. Jonathan's voice came to her through the telephone like an embrace. 'Don't tell me you're nervous,' he said.

'A little . . .'

'You've never been afraid of anything in your life.'

'Dad, I only have a minute. I wanted to tell you something. It's kind of important.'

'What is it?'

Joey hesitated. 'Remember this man I told you about, Mr B.? Well, the other day, he told me that now that I'm a professional dancer, I should change my name.

'Change you name? Why?'

'He said Joey Caras sounded too much like a baseball player.'

Jonathan's laugh came back to her, low and soft.

'I didn't want to, Dad,' Joey said. 'But everybody does it, so they sound more foreign or more glamorous.' She paused. 'So I used Joëlle. Joëlle LeClerc.' There was no reply. 'Dad? Are you there, Dad?'

'I'm here, Joey.'

She sighed. 'I hope you're not mad. I mean, that I used her name instead of yours.'

'LeClerc is your name, too, Joey, just as much as Caras is.'

'So you're not hurt?'

'No,' Jonathan said softly. 'I'm not hurt.'

The orchestra had finished its tune-up. 'Oh God, I've got to run,' Joey said. 'I love you, Dad.'

'I love you too, Joey. Dance well.'

She hung up and scurried across the darkened stage to the right wing. She heard a curious sound, like waves breaking on a shore, and realized it was the stirring of the audience, somewhere out there on the other side of the heavy curtain. And another sound, the rushing of blood in her head, pumping wildly from her heart. She thought of Sumner and Katherine out there in the vast darkness and it left her somewhat comforted. She thought briefly of the party that she would be going to after the opera. One of the ballet's patrons was throwing it for the cast. She had bought a new dress – bright red – and the highest heels she could find, the first pair she had ever owned.

The music began. She waited for her first cue, took a breath and stepped out into the lights. The next two and a half hours went by in a white haze as she became caught up in the exquisite joy of dancing. When it was over, she knew she had danced well. So she was puzzled and a little hurt when the curtain came down to only polite applause.

'Don't worry,' Balanchine told her. 'People who go to the opera know only bad ballet.'

Despite his words, Joey could not shake off her mild depression. Sumner and Katherine greeted her backstage and confessed that while they had enjoyed watching her, they thought the production was ugly. They kissed her good night at the stage door. The atmosphere at the party was determinedly buoyant, but Joey was subdued, her mind and body still filled with the experience of performing. She had loved it, and she had loved the ballet itself. Maybe the design was too strange, but why couldn't anyone see beyond it? Couldn't they see how beautiful the dancing itself was?

After midnight, someone came in with the early editions of the newspapers. The *New York Times* critic pronounced *Orpheus and Eurydice* 'pretentious dilettantism'. The verdict from other newspapers was just as dismal. Joey listened for a while, then drifted away from the crowd.

She wandered away from the salon and out into a marble hallway. She looked around at the various doors. The adrenaline that had fuelled her performance was gone and she was very tired. Her new shoes were pinching her aching feet, and she suddenly wanted just to find a place to be alone. She went down the hall; and pushing open a door, she found herself in a conservatory. The light was dim, but she could see that it was filled with orchids, hundreds of them in every colour, crowding the tables, suspended from the glass ceiling. The room was very warm, dense with humidity, and she could hear the gentle murmur of water. It came from a small fountain crowned by a stone statue of a cherub grinning as he peed down onto the lilypads below.

Joey sat down on the edge of the fountain and, grimacing, carefully took off her shoes. Her left foot bore a huge festering blister. How had she not felt it while dancing? She inspected her right foot, knowing she would soon lose another toenail. With a sigh, she hiked her dress up on her thighs, slipped her feet into the warm water of the fountain and closed her eyes. The humidity seeped into her body, easing her muscles. The gurgling of the water was lulling, peaceful. She didn't hear the man when he came in. It was the smell of his cigarette that made her turn.

He was standing near the door, watching her. She couldn't see his face, just his tall, slender figure leaning against the door, and the spiral of the cigarette smoke. She waited, peeved that her solitude had been interrupted, but he made no move or sound.

'Third door on the left,' she said finally.

'Pardon?' His voice came back to her low and deep, a little raspy.

'The party's down the hall. Third door on the left. Can't miss it.' She turned her back to him.

'I'm not looking for the party,' he said. 'I was looking for a place to be alone.'

'Well, so was I,' Joey said. 'I still am, if you don't mind.'

He didn't move. Joey sighed, shaking her head slightly. The guy couldn't take a hint. She glanced back at him. Tossing the cigarette to the earthen floor, he ground it out with his heel and came towards her, hands tucked in his trouser pockets. He was wearing a dinner jacket, his tie loose at his neck. Joey took in the details of his face – handsome, high cheekbones, thin lips and light-brown eyes – and his hair, thick and dark auburn.

She felt a catch in her throat; she hated the fact that good-looking men had the power to make her shy. That was the way it had been in high school, and her defence had been a carefully cultivated pose of indifference or a quick and cutting word that always sent the fellow away, bewildered. But this man had something about him, and she didn't really want him to go away. He was staring at her feet in the pool, or her thighs, she couldn't tell which.

'Can I join you?' he asked.

'Why not? It feels great.'

He laughed and sat down next to her on the fountain's edge. She watched him, thinking about the way her grandfather's carpenter rule folded neatly down into place. This man's body had the same efficient grace. She saw that he was definitely looking at her feet.

'They're ugly, aren't they?' she said, lifting them out of the water. She flexed them, to give him a better look at the bunions and broken toenails. 'Go ahead, stare if you want.'

He examined her feet a moment longer. 'Extraordinarily ugly,' he said. 'Were you born that way or were they run over by a bus?'

She glared at him; then she saw the smile in his eyes. She slipped her feet back into the water. 'I'm a dancer,' she said. 'Dancers have ugly feet.'

He looked at her for a moment, then smiled. A nice smile, she thought, warm, real. 'Of course,' he said. 'You were the one in the opera tonight. Eurydice. From your hair, I should have known.'

'What's wrong with my hair?' she asked.

'Nothing. It's beautiful. That part in the second act, where you climbed slowly up the mountain . . . then at the top you turned your back and you let down your hair.' He smiled. 'What a moment! I fell in love with you and your hair in that moment.'

Joey looked sharply at him, now positive he was making fun of her. But there was only the gentlest hint of a tease in his eyes. His eyes, she noticed, looked tired or unhappy; something was back there, behind the charm. She quickly estimated that he was in his early twenties, hardly old enough to have such eyes.

She concentrated on his remark about her hair, but could not think of one halfway intelligent thing to say in response. She realized suddenly with amazement that the nervousness she was feeling was attraction – sexual attraction. She drew in a breath. There was no time for that right now, and besides, she didn't have the foggiest idea of how such things went. She had never even had a real boyfriend in high school. Boys had always treated her as a friend. And all the ones she had liked were . . . well, too short.

'So,' she said finally, 'did you enjoy the opera?'

'My mother has been dragging me to operas since I was eight. But this one was nothing like anything I've seen before.' He paused, meeting her eyes directly. 'I liked the dancing. It was very moving. Very noble. Very . . . erotic.'

She felt the colour creep into her face, but held his eyes steadily. She found she couldn't look away. The air was thick and warm. She was aware of the murmur of the water and of the sensual, waxy petals of the orchids thrusting upward in the dim light. She noticed a faint sheen of sweat above his upper lip, and a tiny cut, a shaving nick.

He extended his hand. 'My name is David,' he said. 'David Savage.'

She took his hand. It was warm. 'Joëlle . . .' She hesitated. 'Joëlle leClerc.'

He smiled. 'I saw your name on the programme. It's French, isn't it?'

She nodded and, realizing he was still holding her

hand, pulled hers away. They fell silent for a moment. Then Joey lifted her feet from the water. 'It must be after one. I should be getting home,' she said softly. She tried to slip on her shoe, but grimaced when it touched the blister. As she started to get up, David rose quickly, held out his hand and pulled her to her feet. Tall, he was tall, at least six foot three. She had to look up to meet his eyes. It brought a smile to her face and suddenly she felt less nervous.

'Can I see you home?' he asked.

'All right.' She took a limping step.

'Should I carry you?' he asked.

'Oh no! God, no. Please!'

'Good. I don't think I could.' He smiled, picked up her shoes and took her arm. 'You're a big girl, you know.'

'So I've been told.'

'I like tall women.'

They were able to make their way unnoticed out of the front door. Outside, Beekman Place was deserted. They paused for a moment at the bottom of the townhouse's steps, and David frowned slightly. 'I don't have my car,' he said apologetically. 'I came with my mother and I'll be damned if I'll go back in there and beg for the keys.' He gave Joey a smile. 'Can you make it to the corner? We can get a cab at 51st.'

Joey nodded. David gripped her arm tighter and they made their way down the block. At the corner they stopped, and David paced up and down, scanning the sparse traffic. Joey watched his face, focusing on how he clenched his jaw and how his eyes snapped with impatience. She wondered if he was irritated with the position he now found himself in: he had flirted with a strange woman in whom he really wasn't interested, and now he was trapped into taking her home.

'Listen,' she said, 'you don't have to do this. I can call my—'

'No,' he said quickly. 'I said I'd see you home and I will.' He paused, looking at her. 'That is, if you still want to go home.'

She gazed at him, looking deep into his eyes, his sad-happy eyes, and felt something turn inside her. His hand, warm and firm, closed round hers.

'I have an idea,' he said softly.

He led her away from Beekman Place to a small park at the foot of 51st Street. There was nothing special about the park except its extraordinary view of the East River and, to the north, the lights of the Queensboro Bridge leapfrogging across Roosevelt Island. Joey spotted a set of swings and, with a glance back at David, headed towards it. He followed, fitting himself onto the one beside her. They sat there quietly, the groan of the swings breaking the silence.

'The bridge is beautiful,' Joey said finally.

'This is one of the best views in the city. I collect great views of New York. What's your favourite?'

Joey glanced at him. 'I've only been here about a year, and I spend most my time in the ballet studio. I haven't really seen much of New York.'

He smiled. 'Well, we'll have to change that, won't we, Joëlle LeClerc?'

Hesitantly she smiled back. 'Maybe.' She wiggled her toes in the sand and pushed off, propelling herself up and back through the soft night air. Flirting – she was actually flirting! And it felt easy and right.

'I've heard about you dancers,' David said. 'You live like nuns, devoting yourself to your art, with no room for anything – or anyone – else. Sounds pretty boring to me.'

Joey brought herself to a stop and turned to look at him. 'Oh, but it's not,' she said. 'It's exciting. To give yourself over to something so completely that you . . . you lose yourself. It's very exciting. It's hard sometimes, but I don't care. When I'm dancing, I feel I'm pouring all

369

my energy, all of myself into it. It feels like the only thing in the world I want to do. When I dance, I feel . . .' She paused, seeing his eyes on her. She felt her face grow warm.

'Go on,' he said quietly.

'I feel . . . a light inside me . . . right here,' she said softly, touching her chest. She looked away. 'I'm not very good with words. I can't explain it.'

David sat motionless in the swing, contemplating her. 'You explain it quite well,' he said quietly. After a moment, he looked straight ahead, then pushed off, swinging slowly, his face impassive. She watched him, mystified by his change in mood.

'So what do you do?' she asked.

'I just graduated from Yale. I'm writing a play.'

'A play! How exciting!' Joey said, smiling. 'What's it about?'

He didn't look at her, just kept swinging back and forth, his arms locked over the chains. 'It's not going well,' he said flatly. 'I'd rather not talk about it right now.'

It was quiet for a long time. Finally, Joey got up and picked up her shoes. 'I really have to be getting home,' she said softly. He stopped swinging abruptly and looked at her, as if he wanted to say something, but finally just rose and took her arm. They retraced their steps back to 51st Street and found a cab. It was nearly three by the time it pulled up in front of the Briggs's townhouse on Murray Hill.

David eyed the ornate Gothic building. 'This is where you live?' he asked.

'I live with my godparents,' she said, with a rueful glance at the lighted windows. 'By now, they're probably in a panic and have called my father, who may be on his way to get me.' She looked at David. 'Thank you for bringing me home.'

He gave her a charming smile. 'My pleasure.'

She hesitated, but when it was clear he was not going to say anything else, she opened the door and climbed out. She felt his hand grab hers and turned back.

'Joëlle,' he said. His eyes had that odd intense sadness to them as he looked at her. 'I'd like to see you again. Can I—'

'Yes,' she said quickly. She smiled and was glad to see that he did, too.

'Tomorrow night?' he asked.

'Yes, I'd like – oh, wait, no,' she frowned slightly. 'I promised this girl in the company I'd go to this party she's throwing. I can't tomorrow.' She brightened. 'Unless you'd like to come with me. I mean, it won't be anything like you're used to, I suppose. It's a rent party down in the Village.'

'I'd love to go,' he said with a laugh. She gave him her phone number. He still had hold of her hand. 'Good night, Joëlle LeClerc . . .'

'Good night, David.' She withdrew her hand and, carrying her shoes, went up the stairs. She unlocked the door but stayed there, watching the cab until it rounded the corner.

Chapter Thirty-Two

Lucy paused at the top of the stairway, her hand resting on the wrought-iron railing. Her eyes took in the entrance hall below, its stone arches, marble floor and carved door. Everything was perfect. Her gaze came to rest on the large arrangement of cut flowers on the French commode, and the corner of her mouth twitched. Even from a distance, she could see a faint water ring on its veined marble top. She went slowly down the stairway, pulled a linen handkerchief from her sleeve and rubbed the marble clean.

She turned to survey the drawing room on the level below. It was just past sunset, and the fading gold light streaming in from the large lead-glass windows on the west wall gave the stone walls an ochre glow. The entire drawing room, in fact, looked almost cozy. She frowned, wondering why the maid had not turned on the lights. She flicked on a wall switch and the enormous Venetian crystal chandelier flooded the vast room with blazing cold light. The feeling of intimacy vanished.

It was a room not meant for comfort. Every detail of the drawing room – from the twenty-foot coffered ceiling to the gleaming herringbone parquet floor – was calculated to humble. That was the way Lucy liked it; that was the way she had planned it when she had set out to refurbish the 25-room, prewar maisonette. 'I want it to feel like a cathedral,' she told her decorator. 'I want whoever comes in here to know they are entering an important place.'

It had taken Lucy and the decorator a full ten years to finish the project. The walls were adorned with a collection of French Gothic art. The bedrooms were furnished in eighteenth-century Venetian antiques and the baths done in African onyx and gold. And Lucy's prize, a tapestry that had belonged to Henry VIII, hung above the massive stone fireplace.

She gazed now at the tapestry with deep satisfaction. With the lights on, it could be admired. Everyone who entered would see it and know they were in the most impressive home on Park Avenue.

Park Avenue! If someone had told her when she was young that it would one day be her home, she would have laughed. She would rather have lived on Fifth, in the beautiful house of her childhood, but that was gone now, like so many of the old homes. She had moved into the maisonette shortly after her marriage to her third husband, Edwin, in 1935. Edwin had been convinced Park Avenue was the next great address.

He was right, of course. Edwin was always right about such things. He was a property speculator. Edwin had seen that the last of the great families were abandoning Fifth, their palaces being torn down to make way for department stores and office buildings. Park Avenue had become the real repository of choice for new American fortunes.

No one could call Park Avenue a pretty street. The sliver of green space in its median did little to relieve the regimented look of the buildings, which offered hardly a terrace or garden to break the monolithic monotony. Park Avenue was like a stone monument: a monument to mass-production wealth – money made from railways and widgets, mining and motorcars, property development and toothpaste.

After a number of years, Lucy had been able to convince herself that soulless Park Avenue was actually rather noble-looking in design. Likewise, she had convinced herself that Edwin Pendrick was not simply a dull man with one talent – turning vacant sites and decrepit buildings into money. She had come to see him as a solid, serious man, a protector, *her* protector.

The clock in the entry hall chimed seven times. Lucy's eyes went to the bar in the corner near the piano. She never drank before seven, and now, finally, she could have her nightly cocktail alone, the way she liked it. Edwin would be late, as usual, and the guests were not due until eight.

She made a martini and positioned herself in a chair, as artfully as a cat, slanting her legs at an attractive angle, arranging the folds of her beaded gown. It was a new gown, and she knew it flattered her still slender figure. Not that men really noticed any more. Least of all Edwin.

Lucy sipped her drink. She hardly gave a thought any more to love, romance or being admired and pursued by a man. But today, for some reason, her thoughts had been drifting, taking her back to those times in her life when such things had mattered greatly.

She had been remembering the year of her triumphant debut, and reliving her wonderful trips to Europe, with all those young men throwing themselves at her feet. Especially Jonathan – she had been thinking a lot about him. All day, as she had gone about tending to the last-minute details of her dinner party, as she had bathed and dressed, he had been flitting about the edges of her thoughts. Was it because tomorrow was her birthday and she was feeling less womanly, as if she were somehow invisible to men, now that she was in her mid-fifties? Jonathan had loved her for her beauty. That was, she had found out eventually, the only thing that he had loved about her. And it hadn't been enough to keep him from running to the arms of another woman.

She rose abruptly, and went to a mirror and stared intently at her reflection for a moment, then turned sharply away. When she raised the martini to her lips, her hand was trembling. With a cry, she hurled the glass across the room. The shatter of glass against stone echoed through the drawing room.

A servant appeared, drawn by the sound. He looked inquiringly at Lucy before bending to pick up the glass.

'Leave me alone,' Lucy said, without looking at him.

The servant retreated. Lucy stood there, her arms wrapped across her trembling body. Her eyes focused on the shards of crystal scattered across the shining parquet, and she had a vision of her own body broken in pieces, strewn across a blackness. It was a recurring vision and it always made her feel as if she were losing her mind. She was shaking; she closed her eyes, willing herself to regain control. Slowly, the vision receded and she felt a calm returning.

She reached the bar with wavering steps and made another drink. She drank it quickly, feeling the liquor extinguish the burning of her nerves.

Why, after all these years, did she allow Jonathan still to have such power over her? Why couldn't she just forget him and what he did to her? It had all happened such a long time ago, in a different time, in a different world. So why hadn't she been able just to forget?

She knew the answer. It wasn't just that Jonathan, at one point in his life, had loved Cendrine. She had known that before she married him, but believed it meant nothing. What man hadn't had his affairs before finally settling into marriage? But on that day the cable came to the house, the cable that said Cendrine had been killed, she understood that Jonathan had never stopped loving the dancer. And when he left that day to go to Paris, she had been stunned by the realization that he loved another woman, a *dead* woman, more than he had ever loved her. That day, that one day, had been a turning point in her own life. Before, her life had been like a gift, so bright and beautiful. But after, everything had been a struggle, and there had been nothing but disappointment.

First, she had had to deal with the scandal of Jonathan's desertion and the divorce. So sorry, so sorry, you poor dear . . . she could hear the pity in her friends' condolences and she could see the silent reproach in her parents' eyes. What can one expect, after all, marrying out of one's class?

Then, six months after her divorce, she had met Jay. He was charming and easy-going. He was the scion of a wealthy old-guard New York family, more interested in going to parties and racing his sloop than tending the family fortunes. His lack of ambition was like a balm after Jonathan's intensity. Her parents pressured her into a quick remarriage. For a while, it was fun being Jay's wife, hopping from El Morocco to the Stock Club with his glittering friends, dancing the rumba with deposed Europeans, seeing her picture in *Vogue* with Elsa Maxwell or Douglas Fairbanks Jr.

But she soon discovered that Jay was more adept at putting his charm to work in his role of café-society swain than as husband. As she grew tired of the clubs, he began to ignore her, leaving her at home most nights.

She was able to forgive him only because he was affectionate towards her son, David. After the divorce, she had forbidden Jonathan to see David. She shuddered, remembering the bitter and protracted fights, how Jonathan would show up at the door, pleading to see David; how she would scream at him, threatening to call the police; Jonathan's endless calls, pleading, always pleading. She had hired the best lawyer in New York to fight him. Finally the courts, ruling that Jonathan had been unfaithful to his wife and deserted his family, had granted her request that he be denied access to the boy. Then Jonathan had left New York, and she – and David – were free of him.

Jay had stepped in, filling the void Jonathan left. For all his lack of talent, initially Jay was good at playing the role of husband, and even better at playing father to David. When the boy was five, Jay adopted him.

It was four years into her marriage to Jay that she was able to admit to herself that her husband's conviviality was just a cover for his alcoholism, and it was another year before she discovered his infidelities, with members of both sexes. But Jay was discreet, so she endured it all in silence, not wanting to upset the quiet life she had created for herself and David. Then, the day after the stock market crashed on 24 October 1929, Jay took his sloop out on Long Island Sound, downed a bottle of bourbon and shot himself in the head. The boat drifted for two weeks before it was found, Jay's body ravaged by gulls.

There was little time to mourn. The Wendalls had lost nearly all their own fortune in the crash. Lucy was forced to take David and move to Detroit to live with her sister and brother-in-law. They lived well enough; her brother-in-law was a cousin in the Ford motorcar clan. But Lucy hated Detroit and its provincial social life, and found it difficult to scale back a taste used to unlimited servants, clothes, food and status. By the time Edwin Pendrick entered the picture three years later, Lucy had only one goal in mind – getting back to New York and the life she had lost.

Edwin had made his fortune in Manhattan property. He was a rough-edged man, defensive about not coming from a family of wealth, and he saw Lucy as an affirmation of his social arrival. Lucy saw Edwin

Pendrick as a financial haven for herself and David. So she took her third husband.

Now she was Lucy Wendall Caras Savage Pendrick. And she was safe. It was not the graceful, patrician life she had been born into. It was not the glamorous life she had sampled with Jay. It was a haven, buttressed by nouveau-riche money.

She kept in touch with a few of her old friends, mainly her club cronies and fellow patrons at the opera, names more likely found in the society pages than in the headlines, names of good families rather than great or talented individuals. But gradually, her life had narrowed down to the small square of Manhattan that included the Colony Club at Park and 63rd Street and her fortress home just a few blocks north. Edwin, obsessed with his work, was like a visitor to the house, but she didn't care. She didn't really want a husband. She wanted no one in her life, really. She needed no one else.

Except David. He was her light, and she had grown to need him more than she was willing to admit. How good it was to have a loving son! His affection had been like a bonus, the only compensation for getting old. Strange, but when she thought of her pregnancy now, she could remember feeling only a vague sense of maternal duty. And after David's birth, she had been content to leave looking after him to a nanny. She had loved her infant son, but in the same way she might love a precious family possession, to be cherished on her own terms. But then, everything had changed; Jonathan had changed it. On the day when he had walked out of the front door, everything had shifted. And during the next nineteen years, as her marriages failed, her own parents died and her fortune fluctuated, David remained the only constant in her life. He became the centre of her universe.

Lucy rose and went to the window. She looked down at the street below, where she could see the headlights of the cars cutting through the darkness. A cab pulled up to the kerb; she held her breath as a man got out, but it wasn't David. She glanced at the clock. He was late. Where was he?

She looked back out at the street. It hadn't been easy bringing up David. He had been a moody, restless boy with an introspective, almost secretive aspect of his personality. He ran away often, or spent too much time locked in his room reading. Lucy hated the fact that he reminded her of Jonathan. But Jay had changed that somewhat. His presence seemed to stabilize David, his gregariousness coaxing him out of his shell. By simple example, he bestowed on David social skills and the beginnings of a sense of humour. Jay was the kind of man who never tried hard at anything but often succeeded by accident. And with the same ease, he brought enough light into David's life to temper the dark moods.

David had been an adolescent when Jay killed himself, and the shock had left the boy reeling. As nonchalant a father as Jay had been, he had been the only father David had really known. And with his death, David changed, as if he had grown up overnight. He became suddenly more responsible and almost protective of her. Where once Lucy had looked at her son and seen a temperamental boy, she began to see a polished young man, a son who would make her proud. A son who was less like Jonathan and more like herself.

She sighed. Now David was grown-up. Soon, he would leave her; he would marry and have his own family. It had been bad enough when he went off to Yale, but at least that had been temporary. But soon . . . in a year, in five years, she knew she would lose him.

'Stop it,' she chided herself softly. 'He's your son. You'll never really lose him.'

She heard the door open in the entrance hall and spun around. 'David?' she called out. 'Is that you?'

'Yes, Mother, it's me.'

She went quickly to the hall, a smile lighting up her face, and drew him tight into her arms. 'Where have you been? I thought you'd never get here.'

David extracted himself from her embrace. 'Swimming,' he said. 'I went to the club for a swim.'

She reached up to push his still wet hair off his forehead. 'I don't understand this obsession of yours. Must you do it every day?'

He tried to avoid her hand but finally allowed her to arrange his hair. 'I like it. It makes me feel good to tire myself out.'

'But today? Did you have to go today?'

'Why not?'

Lucy put a hurt look on her face. 'But it's my birthday, David, and—'

David frowned slightly, confused. 'Your birthday is tomorrow.'

'I know,' Lucy said with a shrug. 'But I couldn't ask everyone to come out on a Sunday night.' Her smile returned. 'You'd better go change. People will be arriving any moment.'

'People? What people?' His mouth drew into a line and he sighed. 'I can't, Mother. I made other plans for tonight.'

Lucy's smile faded. 'Other plans? On my birthday?'

'You never mentioned a party to me. Besides, today is not really your birthday, Mother. We made plans to go to dinner on your birthday, remember? And we will – tomorrow.'

Lucy turned away sharply and went to the bar. She made another martini and took a quick drink. She turned back to face him. 'So what are these plans of yours that are so important that you can't come to your mother's birthday party?'

He searched her face for a clue to her mood. It could change so sharply, and the last thing he wanted was to provoke an outburst. 'I have a date,' he said quietly.

'A date? With whom?'

Hesitantly, David came down into the drawing room. 'Someone I met at the party last night after the opera.'

'Do I know this young lady?' Lucy asked.

'I doubt it. She's a dancer with—'

'Dancer?'

For a moment, Lucy's face registered nothing. Then the corner of her mouth began to twitch. It would not stop, and finally, she had to cover the side of her face with her hand. David had seen it before, whenever she was agitated, and he averted his eyes, knowing how self-conscious she was about the tic. He noticed the broken glass scattered across the floor but said nothing.

'She's a dancer with the ballet company,' he said.

For a moment, Lucy just glowered at him. 'I want you to call this person, David,' she said finally, her voice low, 'and tell her that you can't make it.'

David watched her carefully, bewildered. 'I can't. She's coming from a rehearsal and we're meeting somewhere. It's too late to reach her and —'

'I don't want you to be with her,' Lucy interrupted.

'What?'

'I don't want you to be with her!'

'Mother, I won't—'

'Stop! You're just like your fath —' Lucy caught herself. 'You'll stay here tonight, David, with me,' she said, more calmly. 'It's what I want. I won't listen to any more about it.'

David stared at her in disbelief. Slowly, the anger rose up inside him. 'Yes, you will listen,' he said. 'For once, you'll listen.'

Lucy turned to look at him, surprised.

'You can't just tell me to do something, Mother,' he said, 'and expect me just blindly to obey. What about what *I* want?'

He had said the words very quietly, very controlled, but Lucy's face showed her shock, as if he had struck her. 'David, don't talk to me like that,' she whispered.

'You force me to, Mother, because you never really listen to me! You always —' He stopped, running his hand roughly through his hair in frustration. Suddenly, he could no longer hold it back, and it all burst out. 'You have never listened to me. You never asked me what I want to do. It's always what you want! You make the decisions, you run my life!' He shook his head. 'I can't take it any more, Mother. I'm going to live my life the way I want, not the way *you* think I should! Starting right now, tonight!'

Lucy stared at him in astonishment. But before she could say anything, he turned and ran up the stairs.

'David!' she called out.

A door slammed somewhere in the recesses of the vast house. Lucy grabbed the back of a chair for support, lowering herself down into it. Another fight. None had yet been as bad as this one; David had never spoken to her like this. Not when she had questioned his choice of friends; not even when they had disagreed about his becoming a banker, as her father and grandfather had been. Each time they had fought, but he had always, in the end, conceded to her wishes. But tonight, something was different. Some faceless woman somewhere had come between them.

She sat there, her hand covering her eyes, until she heard a sound and looked up. David was standing before her, holding his hat, his coat draped over his arm.

'I'm going now, Mother,' he said quietly.

She just looked at him.

'I'm sorry,' he said. He hesitated, then kissed her

cheek. 'We'll have dinner together tomorrow, all right?'

She straightened. 'Fine,' she said stiffly.

He paused, unsure whether to leave. But finally, he rose and went to the door. He opened it and nearly ran into the man outside, whose finger was poised to ring the bell.

'Oh, pardon me, David my boy,' the man said.

'Oliver! Oh, Oliver, is that you?' Lucy called out.

David stepped aside to allow Oliver Thayer enough room to move his bulky body through the door. He watched as Lucy came quickly forward to embrace the man.

'I'm afraid I'm a tad early, Lucy dear.'

'Oh, Oliver, darling, you don't know how happy I am to see you! Come have a drink!'

As Lucy led Oliver down into the drawing room, David's apprehension over leaving his mother was replaced by relief. He didn't like Oliver Thayer, but at least his presence had refocused his mother's attention. He was free to leave. He closed the door, shutting out their laughter.

David reached the Biltmore Hotel still feeling depressed over the scene with his mother. He glanced up at the bronze clock. He was early, and was thankful for the extra time to get his feelings under control before Joëlle arrived.

He took off his hat and sat down on a bench, replaying the scene in his head, replaying every disagreement he and his mother had ever had. Their arguments had been growing more frequent and more vehement. They always made him realize how torn he was in his feelings towards his mother. On the one hand, he deeply resented the fact that she tried to control his life. On the other hand, he knew that she only meant to do what was best for him. And he wanted her to be happy. She had experienced enough unhappiness in her life, and he wanted to erase all that. That was the reason he had finally agreed to try banking as his career. He knew his mother was looking to him to make up for what her family had lost in the Crash. But it was draining, being the centre of her life, and it seemed that the older he got and the more he asserted his independence, the more tightly she clung.

He sighed, thinking now about how strangely she had acted, how fast her mood had shifted. That, too, had been happening with greater frequency, and he was growing more concerned about her state of mind. Two years ago, she had been hospitalized. The doctor, when pressed, had admitted that she had suffered a mild nervous breakdown. At first, David blamed himself. What had he done to antagonize her? But then he realized it had to be something deeper. It wasn't just something he had done. It could be traced back all the way to his father.

Jonathan Caras was nothing but a name to him, really. Who was Jonathan Caras, the faceless man who had crept out of his life when he was little? He wasn't even real any more.

But he was still very real for his mother. David could remember how, when he was eight, his mother had sat him down and told him the truth, told him about his 'real' father, told him that he had abandoned them both because he didn't love them. It seemed that his mother never missed an opportunity to talk about what this man, Jonathan Caras, had done to them. She made no effort to hide her bitterness towards him; in fact, she did everything she could to make sure David shared it.

At first, David had not wanted to believe her. He had only the barest of memories of the man, nothing that he could even remotely connect to the image of a father. The only concrete evidence he had had of his real father was a single letter. It had come, addressed to him, when he was eight. Lucy was out of town, so the maid had simply given it to David. When David had seen whom it was from, he had ripped it open, but he couldn't really read it. Later he showed it to Lucy, begging her to read it to him, and she tore it from his hand.

'But maybe he wants to see us,' he told his mother.

'No,' Lucy answered sharply. 'He wants nothing to do with me – or you, David. You should never forget that.'

Jonathan Caras was his 'real' father. But how real could he be? David shared nothing with the man, not a name, not a face. His mother had repeatedly told him, with undisguised satisfaction, that he bore absolutely no resemblance to him.

The only father he had ever known was Jay Savage. His main memories of him were of a slender, boisterous man, smelling of cologne and drink, who swooped in and out of his life, marking his presence with toys and laughter. A man who taught him to sail and tell jokes. But what he remembered most about Jay were his long, yawning absences. And then Jay had been gone for good.

He had loved Jay Savage, loved him fiercely or, rather, loved having this hovering masculine presence he could call 'father'. But just as his real father had done, Jay had deserted him. It was only after Jay's death that David grew to hate Jonathan Caras. He hated him for not being there, for leaving him, for not loving him enough to stay. It was then he began to believe what his mother had always told him – that it was Jonathan Caras who caused all their problems. He blamed him for having to leave his friends and go live in Detroit where he felt so lost. He blamed him for making his mother short-tempered with him. He blamed him for making her cry, for making him cry. After Jay Savage's death, it had become easy to blame that faceless man, Jonathan Caras, for all his hurts.

David sighed, his eyes travelling up to the clock. His

385

thoughts drifted back to his mother. What had happened this time to bring on her outburst? And what in the world had she meant when she had started to say that he was just like his father? Was she comparing him to Jay, just because he wanted to go out and have fun? He knew that Jay had often left her home to go out with other women, but he wasn't Jay, and it wasn't fair for his mother to compare him to him. His anger bubbled up anew. Wasn't it enough that he was working in a bank as she wanted instead of writing, the one thing he really wanted to do? Wasn't any of it enough?

At that moment, he spotted Joëlle coming across the street, and he jumped to his feet.

She was half running, half walking, her face flushed and her dark hair, caught in the wind, fanning out behind her. As she made her way through the crowd, she seemed surrounded by an aura of crackling energy that made every other person around her look dim. She looked so happy, so free, and he ached with envy. He concentrated on her, trying to push away all the dark thoughts that had been crowding around him, all the worries about his mother and his thoughts about Jonathan Caras. He concentrated on her face as it came closer. He began to feel lighter, with a slight but unmistakable undercurrent of arousal.

'Easy, let's take this easy,' he said to himself.

She drew up, out of breath. 'I'm not late, am I?' she asked. She glanced up at the bronze clock. 'I'm five minutes early! I don't believe it. I'm always late!' She looked at David and laughed. 'Well, maybe my horoscope was right and you really are going to change my life, David Savage!'

He took her hand, and though she seemed surprised, she didn't pull away. 'And maybe you'll change mine,' he said.

The rent party, in a building on West 18th Street in the

Village, was in full swing by the time they arrived. A man was stationed at the door, holding a shoe box. Joëlle waited, looking at David with a smile.

'A quarter will get us in,' she said. 'Fifty cents if you're a big spender.'

David withdrew a five-dollar bill from his wallet and tossed it in. The man thanked him profusely.

'Money doesn't impress me, you know,' Joey joked as they edged their way inside the apartment.

'Then what does?' David asked, smiling.

She looked at him enigmatically and led him through the throng of bodies. The apartment was filled with cigarette smoke and crowded to bursting point. There was laughter and heated conversations, and a few couples had carved out a spot to dance as a scratchy phonograph spewed out 'Johnny One Note'.

'Why did we have to pay to get in?' David asked.

Joey looked at him as if he were crazy. 'Well, when someone can't pay their rent, everyone gets together and pays to come to a party. The girl who rents this place used to dance with the company but had to quit, and now she's on home relief. The others, well a lot of them are working on government job-creation schemes. They're the only ones with any money. That guy over there was paid to take a census of dogs in albany. That man's an artist, he does murals. I posed for him once.'

David was looking round the room at all the people laughing and talking. 'Another world,' he murmured.

They tried to find a place to sit, but bodies were wedged in every corner. Joey finally led David out to the fire escape, but it, too, was overflowing. It led to another building, where a second party was raging just as fervently in another apartment. After about half an hour of dodging elbows. David turned to Joey. 'Let's get out of here,' he said. Joey nodded and soon they were back out on the pavement.

387

'I didn't know it would be so packed,' Joey said by way of apologizing.

'It's not exactly what I had in mind for a first date,' David said a little testily, pulling at his tie. 'I was going to take you to a nice, romantic restaurant or—'

Joey smiled. 'Oh, I know a very romantic place. Come on.'

She led him through the narrow, twisting streets of the Village. The neighbourhood was foreign to David, and he was struck by the compact, slightly faded beauty of it. He had always wanted to visit Paris – in his travels with his mother to Europe she had refused to go there – and this was how he pictured it. Rows of narrow old houses with lights beckoning warmly and the smells of food wafting on the cool evening breeze. The faint sound of a flute playing somewhere up high; a greengrocer furling his awning for the night. He felt strangely at ease, both with this place and, though he barely knew her, with the woman walking silently by his side. The scene with his mother had faded; his own cloistered, privileged world, just two miles away, had faded. He stopped abruptly, struck by the sight of the moonlight on the street.

Filtering through the fanlike leaves of the ginkgo trees, the moonlight gave the paving stones the mottled look of marble.

'Look at that,' he said, pointing. 'See how the colours move? It's beautiful.'

Joëlle nodded, smiling, and they walked on.

'You won't believe this,' David said, 'but I've lived in New York all my life and never set foot in Greenwich Village.'

'And you call yourself a collector of views,' Joey said.

He looked at her. 'I've missed some, I see that now.'

There was an awkward silence. They walked on down Bedford Street for a while, until Joey stopped before a rundown building. 'The most romantic place in New

York,' she said, gesturing.

There was no sign. David stared at the dilapidated door with distaste. Joey laughed heartily and opened the door, pulling him along. David was surprised to find himself in a bar. It was low-ceilinged and slightly shabby, cramped with tables and wooden booths. The walls were covered with faded dust jackets from books. The place smelled of paper, drink and decades of dust, as if someone had swabbed the floors of a library with beer.

David followed Joey to a booth and slid in beside her. She was watching his face with great amusement.

'Do you want to leave?' she asked.

'No. Why on earth do you think this is a romantic place?'

'Well, until a couple of years ago, this was a speakeasy. Now it's just a bar, a hangout for writers mainly,' she said. 'I know it's not very elegant, not like the places you're used to. But I thought you'd like it, since you're a playwright.'

She was looking at him eagerly, waiting for his response. He looked up at the collection of dust jackets and noticed a jacket for Eugene O'Neill's *Strange Interlude*. He met Joey's eyes, then had to look away. He was glad when a man wandered over to ask what they wanted to drink.

'Scotch straight up for me,' he said. Seeing Joey's blank look, he realized that she didn't have the faintest idea what to order, and that she was suddenly trying very hard to look old enough to be in a bar at all. 'And scotch and milk for the lady,' he added.

It was a few minutes before he could look her in the eyes. 'Joëlle,' he said, 'I lied last night. I'm not a playwright.'

'Well, I'm not twenty-one. I'm barely twenty, and I've never even been in this bar, or any bar, before. Two lies. We're even.'

He shook his head. 'It's not the same.'

The drinks arrived. Joey took a tentative sip and smiled. 'Nice! I can't taste the scotch.' She set the glass down. 'So what do you do, David Savage – if that's your real name.'

'The name is real.' He wrapped his hands around his glass. 'I work in a bank. My grandfather's bank.'

'You don't seem like a banker.' Joey took another sip of her drink, searching David's suddenly sober face. 'I liked you better when you were a playwright. You smiled . . .'

He grinned at her, taken aback.

'I think you're lying to me again,' she went on. 'You're not really a banker. Bankers don't notice shadows on pavements.'

He took a drink. 'I'm not lying this time. I'm a banker.' He paused. 'I used to write things – reviews of books I had read, descriptions of things I had seen, all these great, terribly profound thoughts I had. I put it all down in a journal.'

'Still?'

'No, not for a long time.' He looked straight into her eyes. 'I did write a play once, when I was sixteen.'

'What was it about?'

'My father.'

David fell quiet again. Joey sipped her drink, watching him. 'If you like to write, why don't you do it any more?' she asked.

He shrugged without looking at her. 'I tried once, a couple of years ago. But I don't feel things as intensely as I did when I was a kid. And it just didn't work. You get out of practice and when you sit down at a typewriter, nothing happens. It's like trying to use muscles that have atrophied. It goes . . . it just goes, and you can't get it back.'

She studied his face for a moment. 'One winter,' she

said, 'I fell on some ice and broke my leg, and couldn't take ballet classes for six months. When I finally went back to class, I couldn't do anything, and I was ready to give up.' She paused. 'But I kept working, and eventually it came back. It all came back. And I was even better than before, because I found out how much I had missed it.'

David was looking hard at her.

'You could try,' she said softly.

He wanted to escape the hold of her eyes, but was unable to look away. He realized suddenly he had been holding his breath. 'Maybe,' he said. 'Some day.'

He took a big drink of the scotch, and when he looked back at her, he felt his feet were again on the ground and he was back in control. Smile, he told himself, smile. 'But for now, I am a banker,' he said. He felt his lips curve. 'Do you feel cheated, knowing you're out with a junior bank executive from Yale instead of a starving artist?'

He was relieved to see that she smiled, too. She raised her drink in a mock salute. 'Well, it probably would make my father happy,' she said with a laugh.

For the next hour, the talk remained light. When they finally emerged from the bar, Joey was slightly tipsy. 'I've corrupted a minor,' David said jovially, 'and I'd better get her some dinner.'

He slipped his arm round Joey to steady her as they walked. But they took only a few steps before they stopped and faced each other. David's arms were round her waist. She looked up at him, then her own arms came up, tentatively, to encircle his neck. The light from the street lamp slanted across her cheek, lighting her eyes. He could feel the soft pressure of her thighs against his own. He kissed her, a kiss tasting of milk and scotch that made him feel drunk.

'I think . . .'

Her fingers moved on the back of his neck.

'I think I'm falling in love with you,' he whispered.

'Another lie?' she said.

'No. No lies, ever again.'

Chapter Thirty-Three

L ucy picked up the silver teapot and carefully filled the two porcelain cups. Using tiny silver tongs, she plucked a sugar cube out of the bowl and slipped it into one of the cups. She picked up another cube, her hand poised over the cup.

'Two – isn't that right, dear?'

Oliver smiled. 'You know me so well.'

'Well, I should after all these years.' She poured herself some tea. 'How long have we been doing this, Oliver?'

'What?'

'Enjoying our little afternoon habit.'

Oliver pursed his lips. 'Let's see . . . I left Paris just after the war began, in 1914. Good Lord, has it really been twenty-five years?'

A faraway look came to Lucy's eyes. 'Yes, it has,' she said. 'I feel so old lately, Oliver.'

'You? Old? Nonsense! You're as stunning as the day I first saw you, sitting between your parents at the opera.' He covered her hand with his own. 'You're ageless Lucy, *toujours jeune*.'

'Oh, Oliver, you always know just when to tell the truth . . . and when to lie.' She smiled slightly. 'I don't know what I would have done without you all these years. You've been my confidant, my escort, my . . .

best friend. You've—'

There was a sound in the entrance hall and Lucy turned. Oliver noticed her smile fade and looked up to see David.

'I'm leaving now,' he said.

'What time will you be home?' Lucy asked, her voice even.

'I don't know. Don't wait up . . . please.' He turned to leave.

'David—'

'Good night, Mother,' he said quietly. And he was gone.

Lucy stared at the closed door. Oliver watched with surprise as her eyes welled with tears. She plucked a handkerchief from her sleeve and dabbed at her eyes.

Oliver sipped his tea, watching her. 'You know, dear, you've been terribly emotional lately. Why, every time I come to see you, you're always on the verge. Is something wrong? Is that dreadful man making demands on you again?'

'No. Edwin sleeps at the club usually.'

'Then what is it?'

Lucy blew her nose and smoothed a hair back into place. 'It's David. I don't know what to do with him.'

'David? Beautiful, perfect David? What could he possibly do to upset you so?'

'He has a girl.'

Oliver chuckled.

'Don't laugh, Oliver,' Lucy said sharply. 'It's serious this time. It's been going on for nearly six months now.'

'Well, what can you expect, dear? He's not a monk. Young men do fall in love, you know.'

'In love?' Lucy's face became stony. 'No, I won't allow it. Not with this girl.'

'You've met her, then?'

'No. David wanted to bring her home, but I told him I

would absolutely forbid her to set foot in my home.' She paused, her mouth drawing into a tight line. 'That's when the trouble really started between us.' She sighed. 'Oh, Oliver, he's been terrible! He has continued to see her, despite my objections, despite the fact I've advised him that she's totally unacceptable.'

'Now, Lucy, what's so terrible about this one? Does she live on Staten Island? Does she have two heads?' He laughed softly. 'Is her father a New Deal Democrat?'

'Stop it, Oliver!' Lucy shot back. 'She's a dancer.'

Slowly, Oliver's face became sober. He took in Lucy's rigid face, her white fingers clutching the teacup so fiercely that he thought she might shatter it. He took the cup from her carefully and set it aside. 'Oh, Lucy,' he said, shaking his head. 'Just because Jonathan—'

'Don't!' Lucy held up her hands. 'Don't,' she repeated.

Oliver regarded her for a moment, then, with a heavy sigh, picked up his cup. It was empty. He glanced at Lucy, expecting her to refill it, but she suddenly didn't seem even to be aware of him. She had drifted off to revisit her old pain. Oliver poured himself another cup of tea, shifted his bulk in the overstuffed chair and tried to conjure up some pity for Lucy.

He couldn't, really. He knew Lucy had had her share of disappointment. Jonathan's desertion had been only the start of it. But dwelling on the past was such a colossal waste of energy; he knew that from his own experience. Things hadn't been all roses for him, either. Good God, twenty-five years! Hard to believe it had been so long. He sipped his tea, allowing fragments of the past to slip into his consciousness. The first day the bombs had fallen on Paris, he had cowered beneath his bed, so terrified that he had wet himself. He had fled the city, but not to his home in London because he was afraid the Germans would invade. Tail tucked between his legs, he had gone to New York City, landing with only what he could carry and the small amount of cash he had kept in his Paris bank account.

He had been miserable, living in the strange, inhospitable city with little money and no contacts. He felt as if he had been cast adrift, cut off from the life of comfort and influence he had known in Paris. Finally, he had landed a job with the *New York Times* as the third-string critic, paid only on a freelance basis by the column inch, sent to cover only the second-rate productions. He hated being a nonentity, outside the circle of important people, living in a city where social status and power were everything.

Then, one night at the opera, he had run into Lucy. She was alone and had greeted him like an old friend. It surprised him, considering he had barely known her in Paris. But it did not take him long to realize that Lucy was lonely. It took him even less time to understand that Lucy could be his conduit, his way back into the gilded circle. Her husband Edwin hated the opera, so Oliver became her willing escort. He was good in his new role, charming, socially adept and knowledgeable about the arts, wine and food. He knew how to ingratiate himself with women like Lucy, how to make them feel as if every word they uttered was witty, every dress they wore divine. Within a year, other wealthy matrons were seeking him out as a companion to fill in for husbands too powerful or preoccupied to fulfil social duties. His name began appearing in the society columns, his face in the pictorials. His breakthrough came when the gossip columnist Elsa Maxwell invited him to her Pet Hates Ball, where everyone came dressed as his or her favorite *bête noire*. He and Lucy stole the spotlight dressed as Franklin and Eleanor Roosevelt. Finally, when the drama critic of the *Times* died, Oliver, based on his celebrity, was able to leapfrog the other man to claim the title of premier critic at a high salary. He was back on top again. All because fate had conspired to placy Lucy Wendall in his path once more.

He looked at her now, the pity finally registering. He knew that he owed her something for his new life. But sometimes she was such a bore, like all the women he knew. Then again, what wasn't a bore these days? Nothing was the way it had been when he was young during those years in Paris. The things that once held his interest – the theatre, art, music – no longer enthralled him. He was nearly seventy now, and his main pleasures were food and drink, much to his doctor's dismay.

Well, there was still one thing that didn't bore him. It was the feeling of power he got whenever he was able to affect another person's life. He loved imagining an actor's face as he read a negative review. He enjoyed hearing that a play he had savaged had closed after two performances. He liked seeing a stage ingenue whom he had singled out get the call to go to Hollywood. It all happened simply because he deemed it so. Early in his life, he had discovered he had no real talent of his own. The point had been driven home by an English professor who had cruelly torn apart his novel before the class, saying 'the author's lack of imagination is surpassed only by his inability to manipulate his characters'.

He never wrote another book, but he did learn how to manipulate real people. They became his characters and he loved moving them around, placing them in each other's way, forcing their confrontations, watching their little dramas, just to see what would happen.

He glanced up at Lucy. He had done it brilliantly with her. What fun it had been to bring her, Jonathan and Cendrine together and then sit back and watch the explosion between the three! He shut his eyes, thinking about Cendrine. She had given him an intense, almost sexual pleasure as he orchestrated her course into the dance company. He had been saddened to hear about her death; in a strange way, he had always been in love with her.

And then there was Alexander. Well, he had never truly been able to manipulate him, but at least he still had those shares of the *Herald*. Alexander's lawyer had contacted him several times over the years about selling, but Oliver had refused. He knew that Alexander had sold Jonathan a block of stock, and he could guess how desperate Alexander was to get back majority ownership after his falling-out with Jonathan over Cendrine. Holding even that small element of control over the self-satisfied bastard had been vindication enough. He should have sold the shares years ago, but something had always kept him from doing it. Maybe he would look into it now; he really didn't care about Alexander any more. Alexander, Cendrine and Jonathan, the *Herald*, Paris . . . it was all part of the past. None of it had anything to do with his life now.

'Oliver?'

He opened his eyes.

'You aren't listening to me, Oliver,' Lucy said petulantly. 'I'm having a crisis and you're off daydreaming.'

Oliver gave her a soothing smile. 'I've heard every word you said, dear. David's a sensible young man. It's probably just a crush, he's had them before. If you ignore it, they probably—'

'No,' Lucy said firmly. 'It's different this time. I feel it. I want him back.' She grabbed Oliver's hand with such force that he almost dropped the cup he was holding in the other. 'Help me, Oliver! Help me get my son back.'

Oliver resisted the urge to pull his hand from her grasp. 'Lucy, there's nothing I—'

'You owe me, Oliver.'

Her words, said so forcefully, momentarily stunned

him. So Lucy wasn't as stupid as he thought; she knew as well as he what her role in his success had been. She probably knew, too, that she still wielded enough power in town to affect his status. He looked into her hard brown eyes, realizing that he didn't really want to have Lucy as an enemy. 'You're right, Lucy dear,' he said finally. 'I suppose I do owe you.'

She let go of his hand. Oliver set his cup down and massaged his wrist. 'What's the girl's name?' he asked.

Lucy looked back. 'I don't remember. Something foreign. Joe – Joe something. Joëlle. I don't know her last name.'

'With whom does she dance?' Oliver asked patiently. 'Which company?'

'Oh, I don't know, Oliver! For God's sake! The one with the opera, I think.'

'Balanchine's company?' A smile spread across Oliver's face. 'Well, then, you have nothing to worry about. I just heard today that Balanchine's taking them on tour to Europe. They'll be gone for a month.' He leaned back in his chair, thankful to be relieved of his obligation to tend Lucy's latest neurosis. 'Young love cannot possibly endure the immensity of both time and the ocean. I guarantee that David will come to his senses and be onto the next debutante within a week.'

Lucy's look was dubious, but then it turned vaguely hopeful. 'Do you really think . . .?'

'You raised him well, Lucy. He's been a difficult boy at times, I know. But he'll do the right thing in the end.' He shrugged. 'When the girl returns, if you still need my help, well, you know I'm always here for you, dearest Lucy.'

Lucy sighed heavily. She sat there for a moment, pensive, then reached for her tea. 'Oh, it's cold,' she said.

Oliver picked up the teapot. 'Let me,' he said with a smile.

Joey went down the stairs of the school, pausing in the foyer. She glanced at the closed deli across the street, yearning for a takeout carton of warm soup. Two classes and a rehearsal, and she hadn't had time to eat all day. She pulled up her collar and flung her woollen scarf around it before she pushed open the door.

The blast of icy November wind nearly knocked her off her feet, but she felt someone catch her and pull her back sharply. A second later, she was held tight in David's arms.

'David! You scared me,' she said.

'Sorry.' He tossed aside his cigarette and kissed her.

'My God,' she said, 'your lips are freezing! Are you crazy? How long have you been waiting out here?'

'Since five.'

'But I thought you were having dinner with your mother?'

'I changed my mind. I had to see you tonight.' He slipped his hands beneath her coat, up under the edge of her sweater.

'Cold!' she shrieked, laughing. 'Your hands are cold! Where are your gloves?'

'I don't know. I think I left them in the taxi.'

She smiled and kissed him. Even through the bulky layers of clothing, she could feel his body against her own, his fingers moving on her lower back, and it made her stomach churn. In the last six months, they had not done much more than touching, but it was getting hard to resist. She loved the feel of his hands on her skin, and now it was making her weak. 'We can't . . . stay here . . . We'll freeze,' she said, breathless.

'Then where?'

'David . . .'

He smiled slyly. His cold fingers grazed the sides of

her breasts, and she could feel him growing hard against her thigh. She glanced nervously at the people passing by, but no one seemed to notice what was happening. She was dizzy with the need to feel his fingers on the rest of her body. For months now, she had wanted desperately to give in, but something always made her pull back. With a deep sigh, she pulled back now, reluctantly.

David couldn't suppress a groan. He ran his hand through his hair in agitation. Finally, he smiled. 'You're driving me nuts. You know that, don't you?' He laughed and turned towards the street, arms held high. 'God, she's driving me nuts! Do you hear me? This woman is driving me nuts!'

A man glanced at him strangely and hurried along. Joey smiled self-consciously. 'David, I'm sorry. It's just that . . .'

He let his arms drop and looked at her, shaking his head. With a sigh, he slipped his arm through hers. 'Come on, I'll buy you dinner. I know you didn't eat today.'

He hailed a cab, which dropped them off at the Plaza Hotel. As David led her through the lobby towards the restaurant, Joey's eyes travelled over the marble, the ornate furnishings, the scurrying bellboys in their red livery, and the well-dressed women. She was quiet as David checked their coats and gave his name to the captain. After they had been seated, she leaned across the table.

'David, I'm not dressed for this,' she whispered. 'When you said dinner, I thought maybe a hamburger or—'

'You look fine.' He picked up the menu and scanned it quickly. 'The food here is very good, the duck especially. I think we should have a bottle of wine.' He looked up at Joey, who was sitting rigid, her face slightly flushed.

'Joëlle,' he said, smiling slightly. 'Don't tell me all this intimidates you.'

'Of course not,' she said crisply. She picked up the menu and frowned. 'There are no prices on this menu,' she said.

David laughed. 'There are on mine.'

'Well, how am I supposed to order if I don't know what things cost?'

'I don't want you to know. For once, I am not going to listen to you complain about how much money I'm spending on you. Besides, I'm tired of sandwiches, souvlaki and bad chianti.' He smiled gently. 'I wanted something special tonight. So humour me – just this once.'

She scanned the menu. 'I feel stupid. The only word I recognize is chicken,' she said, her voice low. 'You order for me, please.'

'Finally! You're allowing me to take charge!' David's face drew up into a delighted grin. 'You, poor starved dancer creature, are about to have the feast of your life. I have so many things to teach you . . .'

The courses flowed by in a stately procession: asparagus with truffle sauce, mussels and tiny new potatoes with saffron, a fillet of lamb with thyme. There was a silver tray with three Burgundian cheeses, and to drink, a Pommard. By the time the waiter brought out the dessert – a rainbow of poached fruit fanned out on a white china plate – Joey could only gaze at it.

'I can't,' she whispered.

'You ate everything else,' David said, smiling.

'It's too pretty to eat.' With a smile, she took a bite, shutting her eyes in pleasure. David watched her over the top of his wine glass, focusing on her lips, moist with the raspberry sauce. She finished it, then discreetly ran one finger along the plate to get the last of the sauce.

'This is sinful, David,' she murmured. 'Being in a

place like this, eating food like this, when so many people are—'

'Joëlle,' he interrupted. 'I have money. I want to spend it on you. Don't take the fun out of this for me. Please.'

She stared at him, taken aback. 'I'm sorry.'

He sighed and reached out to take her hand. 'Don't apologize. I'm the one who should be doing that.'

'But why?'

'I don't know. The way I've had to treat you – us – these last few months. Not being able to take you home, my mother refusing even to meet you.' He paused. 'Maybe that's why I wanted to bring you here – to try to make up for that.'

'I told you it wasn't important, David.'

He knew from the look on her face, though, that it was. 'I'm sorry I can't come home with you for Thanksgiving. I really want to meet your parents,' he said softly. 'Maybe I could come for Christmas?'

Joey toyed with a spoon, not meeting his eyes.

'Is something wrong?' David asked. 'You look as if you lost your best friend all of a sudden.'

'David,' she said slowly, looking him straight in the eye. 'I have to go away for a while. The company's going on tour to Europe. We leave right after Thanksgiving.'

He stared at her in shock. 'For how long?'

'Two months.'

'Two months!' he exclaimed. Other diners turned to look at him. 'Joëlle, why didn't you tell me before now?'

'I just found out yesterday.'

'But . . . you can't, there's . . . what about . . .' He collapsed back in his chair, his eyes roving vacantly across the room. He took a drink of wine, trying to calm himself. Finally, after a long time, he looked back at her. 'Two months,' he murmured.

'I have to go,' she said. She paused, her face

reddening slightly. 'David, you've been so patient with me. I know how hard it's been for you, wanting to . . . and me being kind of slow about . . .' Her voice trailed off. She cleared her throat. 'I won't blame you if you say you never want to see me again. I mean, two months is a long time, and after this dinner tonight I won't blame you if you tell me to take a hike and—'

'Shut up,' he said gently.

'What?'

'You're not going anywhere. Except to Europe.' He reached across the table to take both her hands in his. He brought them up to his lips and kissed her palms. 'I love you, Joëlle,' he said. 'I understand what this dancing means to you. I only have to watch you dance to see it.' He smiled wanly. 'So if it means I have to be second in your life right now, so be it. But not all the time, understand? Once in a while, I get to be first.'

'Okay,' she said softly. 'I love you, David.'

He kissed her palm again, then each finger, finally taking one into his mouth. It was sticky with raspberry sauce. She closed her eyes as he sucked gently on it, her lips parting slightly. When she opened her eyes, he was looking at her with undisguised desire.

'David . . .' she whispered.

His fingers intertwined with hers.

'I want to,' she said, almost shyly. 'Tonight.'

He stared at her, stunned. 'Are you sure?' he asked softly.

'Yes.'

He wasn't sure what to say. 'I don't want to pressure you, Joëlle. You know I haven't meant to.'

'I know. That's why I want to now.'

He quickly motioned for the bill and signed it. In the lobby, she waited awkwardly while he signed the register. Upstairs, she waited again, ill at ease, while David tipped the bellboy. Joey watched him go, her eyes wide.

'He knew, didn't he?' Joey said when they were alone. 'He knew because we don't have a suitcase. What did you tell him?'

'That we just got married in Cleveland and the airline lost our luggage.' When Joey's face showed her shock, he laughed softly. 'Nothing,' he said. 'I told him nothing.'

He saw her eyes flitting over the opulent suite, the French furniture, the fresh flowers, the bed. He came to her, took her in his arms and kissed her gently.

'It's all right,' he said.

'How much is—' she began.

His lips came down to muffle her words. His kiss was harder this time, and she returned it with one of equal intensity.

'Look at me, I'm shaking,' she said, with a nervous laugh. 'I don't know what to do.'

'Yes, you do,' he whispered. 'What you don't know I'll teach you. I told you before, I'll teach you.'

He guided her over to the edge of the bed and began lightly kissing her face, first on the cheeks, then her eyes and behind her ears. She moaned softly when he brushed the nape of her neck with his lips. He pulled away from her and looked deep into her eyes before reaching down to take hold of her sweater.

'Lift up,' he said, gently helping her off with it. When she started to cover herself with her arms modestly, he said softly, 'No, don't.'

He stepped back and looked at her firm breasts. 'Take off your skirt,' he said softly. Soon she was standing before him, wearing only her panties. 'My God, you're beautiful,' he said.

He quickly stripped off his clothes and led her down onto the bed. He held himself above her and looked hard into her eyes. 'Joëlle, I love you,' he said. 'I love you so much.'

'Oh David,' she said softly. 'I love you, too.'

He kissed her again, moving over her face, neck and down to her breasts. He lightly kissed each nipple, then gently nibbled on them. She let out another moan, more urgent this time. Then he was kissing her stomach and the inside of her thighs.

'Oh, David,' she sighed. 'I want you . . .'

'Soon,' he said, slipping off her panties. He reached underneath her, grabbed her buttocks, arched her up and began to kiss her soft mound. He began flicking his tongue on her sweet spot, alternating between quick and slow strokes. He felt her getting moist. 'David . . . please . . . now,' she said.

David reached down, took his erect penis and slowly guided it inside her. She let out a quick, sharp cry.

'I'm inside you, Joëlle,' he said softly. He saw a tear fall down her cheek. 'I'm inside you,' he said again.

Not taking his eyes off her, he slowly moved his hips, first back and forth and then side to side. She sighed, and he felt her body respond to his and he quickened the pace.

Suddenly he stopped and withdrew from her.

'David, what are you . . .?'

He was kissing her between her legs again. 'David,' she whispered. He continued to kiss and lick, feeling her getting wetter and wetter. Suddenly she was saying his name, over and over, and he felt her quiver, first a few quick bursts, then with more intensity.

With a quick move, he turned her over so she was on top of him. Her face showed her surprise for a moment, but then he was quickly inside her again. She closed her eyes and arched back, as their bodies moved back and forth together.

They were moving faster now, faster, faster. Then they each let out a huge cry, calling each other's name.

They lay still in each other's arms, their breath coming in short gasps. They said nothing, just gripped each other tight, as if afraid to let go.

It was near eleven when they emerged from the hotel
entrance. They paused at the foot of the steps as people
streamed around them, theatregoers stopping in for
after-show drinks, weary well-heeled tourists arriving
with Vuitton bags in tow, and an elderly couple who
emerged from a horse-drawn hansom cab with arms
round each other's waists.

David started to signal for a taxi, but Joey stopped
him. 'Not yet,' she said softly. 'A few minutes more.'
She looked back to the lobby of the hotel.

'Stop thinking about how much it cost,' David chided
gently.

'Priceless,' she whispered.

It began to snow, swirling flakes buffeted by the gusty,
cold wind. She looked at David's face and the flakes
settling in his hair. She touched his face.

'White time,' she whispered. 'It's my white time . . .'

'What's that?'

'A perfect time, your own special moment when
everything is perfect. That's what this is, David, our
white time.'

'You look sad,' he said. 'Why?'

'I don't know. Maybe because it can never be so
perfect again.'

He took her face in his hands. 'Yes, it will. I promise.'

Chapter Thirty-Four

It was very late and the living room was nearly dark. Coming into the room, Joey flicked on the light switch. Jonathan, sitting behind the desk, stirred, blinking in the bright light.

'Dad! I thought you'd gone to bed,' Joey said, surprised.

'I did. Couldn't sleep.' He sat up with a slight grimace, stretching. 'I came down here to grade some papers and must have dozed off.' He rubbed his hand over his face. 'What time is it?'

'A little past two.'

He squinted at her. 'Why don't you turn that overhead light off, Joey? It's hard on the eyes.' Joey flicked off the switch and Jonathan raised the flame of the paraffin lamp. 'You know,' he said, 'your grandfather fought me about putting electricity in this house, and even then, I couldn't get him to get rid of this old lamp.' He paused. 'Now I know why. It's kinder to the eyes . . . and the soul.'

Joey took the chair opposite Jonathan. 'I like this room,' she said. 'I like this old house.'

'So do I,' Jonathan said, his eyes surveying the room. It hadn't changed much over the years. The red brocade wallpaper had finally been replaced by a crisp print, and the hulking Victorian furniture had been recovered. But the messy stacks of books and papers were still there, his father's work, now mixed in with some of Jonathan's own.

'I'm glad we decided to spend Thanksgiving here, Dad,' Joey said. 'It's good to see Grandpa.'

'He's become pretty frail in the last year, Joey,' Jonathan said. 'Seeing you was a tonic.'

'Is that new nurse good to him?' When Jonathan nodded, she added softly, 'I miss Hannah.'

Jonathan nodded in acknowledgment and then it was quiet, except for the soft hiss of the radiator and the echoing rustle of the wind sifting through the birch trees just outside the window.

'You know, your mother's really upset about you going on this tour to Europe,' Jonathan said finally. 'You should have given us some warning instead of just springing it on us during dinner.'

Joey's eyes dropped and she began to twist her ring, a gold and sapphire rang that Jonathan and Marion had given her on her sixteenth birthday. 'I know,' she said softly. 'As usual, I didn't think. Well, I did think . . . I thought you and Mom wouldn't let me go.' She looked up. 'But I have to, Dad, I just have to. It's a chance to see the world. I mean, I've never been *anywhere*, I haven't seen *anything* . . .' Her hands carved graceful, urgent circles in the air as she spoke. 'I mean, I don't want to sound ungrateful. I loved growing up here. But New York did something to me, Dad. I want to see other places.'

Jonathan's eyes were soft as he looked at his daughter, his lips turned up in a suggestion of a smile.

'Why are you smiling?' Joey asked in surprise.

'No reason . . . no reason.'

Joey heaved a sigh of perplexity. 'I thought you were mad at me. You seemed like it at dinner.'

'I'm not angry, Joey, I was just surprised.' He leaned

forward, resting his elbows on the desk. 'And I want you to go to Europe. I know now that you can handle it. When you went off to New York, I thought you were too immature to be on your own. But you proved me wrong. You've grown up this past year.'

Joey smiled slightly and looked away.

'It makes me feel old,' Jonathan added softly.

Joey looked up. 'You're not old, Dad. You're still the handsomest man I know.'

Jonathan gave her a wry smile. 'Handsomer than your new beau? The way you talked about him tonight, you'd think he was Clark Gable and Robert Taylor rolled into one.' He laughed softly when she blushed.

'I'm sorry you couldn't meet him, Dad.'

'Maybe this spring. Your mother and I are thinking of coming to New York. I haven't seen Sumner and Katherine in years. And I've never seen you dance. It's about time, I think.'

Joey's face grew serious. There was a long pause before she spoke. 'You didn't want me to be a dancer, did you?' she said.

'I was worried about you going to New York.'

'No, it was more than that.' She hesitated again. 'I always thought that you didn't want me to dance because it made you think about . . . about my . . . Cendrine.'

Jonathan stared at her, taken aback by her perception. Joey had not mentioned Cendrine's name in years, not since her early teens, when she had discovered who her mother was. And now, hearing Cendrine's name come from his daughter, Cendrine's daughter, made him feel disoriented.

'Did you love her a lot?' Joey asked softly.

For a moment, Jonathan could not bring himself to answer. 'Yes . . . once, a long time ago,' he said finally.

He was grateful that the answer seemed to satisfy her. It was quiet again. Finally, Joey smiled slightly, a smile that grew into a yawn.

'It's late. We have to get started for home early. Go on up to bed, Joëlle,' he said softly.

She nodded and rose, stretching. She came forward and, bending low, put her arms around him, pressed her cheek against his and hugged him. 'Night, Dad. Don't stay up too late.'

'I won't. Just want to finish my work.' And she was gone, leaving the room quiet again.

Jonathan sat there motionless, staring off into the shadowed corners of the room. It had been such an innocent question – did you love her a lot? But it had unleashed a torrent of memories and emotions in him, feelings that, for so many years now, he had managed to keep restrained behind the sturdy dam of his intellect. It was not that he had never thought about Cendrine over the years. He had, but it was always with a perspective of distance that his mind supplied. But now, suddenly, he was remembering with his heart. And the intensity of it had taken his breath away.

Why now? Was it because Joëlle seemed to him suddenly so grown-up, so womanly? Was it the simplicity of the question itself? Or was it just that he was feeling vulnerable lately, much too mortal and too aware of the passage of time?

He pulled up the shawl collar of his old sweater and picked up a pen to resume work. After a moment, he put it down again.

Too often, lately, he had found himself thinking about the past, the twists and turns his life had taken. Too often he had wondered if he should have done things differently. Too often he had asked, 'What if . . .'

What if he had never gone to Paris? What if Alexander had not taken him to the café in La Turbie that day? What if he had not forced Cendrine to decide between him and dancing? What if, twenty-one years

411

ago, he had simply stayed with her in that little village on the lake in Switzerland, stayed there for ever? He had thought about it at the time, agonized over choosing between Cendrine and the life he had built back in the States. But finally he had boarded the ferry and gone home, back to New York where Lucy and David waited.

Jonathan took off his glasses and ran his hand over his eyes. David . . . how ironic that Joey's boyfriend had the same name. When Joey had first mentioned it, Jonathan had felt something go off inside him, a burst of painful memories that had not abated all during the holiday weekend at the farm. Marion had noticed his mood and asked what was wrong, but Jonathan told her nothing of his thoughts.

David . . . his son David. He would be twenty-three now. What did he look like? What was he doing with his life? Was he happy?

He didn't even know where David was. The last letter he had received from Lucy had been more than nine years ago, in 1930. The postmark had been Detroit. He knew Lucy had a sister there, but he was surprised that Lucy herself would ever live anywhere but New York. The contents of her letter contained no surprises, however. In the tersely written note Lucy demanded that he stop writing to David, and insisted that the boy wanted nothing to do with him. She added that if he persisted, she would consult a lawyer.

Jonathan had written more than thirty letters in which he had tried to explain to the young boy something even he, to this day, did not understand. How could you explain obsession? How could you explain the need to ignore your head and listen to the whispering of the heart? How could you explain why a father left his wife and son? It made no sense to him sometimes; how could he ever have expected a little boy to understand? Finally, he decided he could explain none of it, and he stopped writing. Lucy had sent back all the letters, unopened. Now they sat in the bottom drawer of Jonathan's desk in Ithaca. He had never once looked at them, but could not bring himself to throw them away.

It was guilt that finally made him give up any thought of ever seeing David again. You left him, he told himself over and over, and when you did, you forfeited any claim to him as your son. And he had built a new life with Marion and Joey.

Joey meant a great deal to him. It had never mattered that she wasn't really his child. She was his link to Cendrine and the time they had shared. She was a gift from God, an atonement for the past and for his son, both of which were lost to him for ever.

He closed his eyes, saying a silent prayer of thanksgiving. Then he turned off the lamp and went up to bed.

'Joey! Come on, you'll miss your train!'

'I'm coming, Mom!' Joey rushed down the stairs and paused, slightly out of breath, taking a mental inventory of what she had packed. She had come home to Ithaca after Thanksgiving dinner last night to pick up some extra clothing that she would need in Europe. She had spent half the night trying to decide what dresses would be right, before telling Marion that nothing she owned was right for Paris and London. Marion had forced her to choose, nonetheless, and was now waiting for her at the old Studebaker parked by the kerb. Jonathan was loading her two suitcases into the boot.

Joey hoisted her canvas dance bag onto her shoulder, ticking off its contents in her head: four pairs of new pointe shoes, a sewing kit to attach ribbons and darn the shoes' tips, extra lambswool, Band-Aids and iodine, the hammer that she used to beat the hard box of the pointe shoes into softness and the can of Fabulon floor wax that she applied to the satin to give it strength; leotards, tights, a French phrase book, and . . .

She froze. She had almost forgotten the single most important thing.

'Joey!'

'I forgot something! I'll be right back!'

She dropped her bag and ran back to Jonathan's study at the back of the house. Her mind was racing; she feared that if she missed the train back to New York, she would not be able to get her passport issued in time. But first, she had to find her birth certificate. She paused, then went to Jonathan's desk. It had to be in there with all the other family papers that she knew he kept in the bottom drawer.

She opened the drawer and riffled through the contents. A marriage certificate, a sealed will, a few old stock and bonds, a stack of old letters bound in frayed ribbon, her immunization records and some of her grade-school report cards, the sight of which made her smile. Finally, she found a faded envelope with her name written on it and eagerly opened it.

It was an official-looking document, a large, beautiful thing, printed on pale-blue paper with lovely script writing. But it was all in French. She scanned it in frustration, focusing on the words at the top: *Acte de Naissance*, and the place: Iseltwald, Suisse. It had to be her birth certificate.

Slowly, the reality of the document sunk in. She had never seen it before and now she stared at it in fascination. Her father had told her about her birth, but it had never seemed real. But here, in her hands, was the tangible proof of her past. There was her name: Joëlle Christine LeClerc. She felt a strange elation course through her as she stared at the name below it. *Nom de mère:* Cendrine Eugénie LeClerc. Mother . . . her real mother.

Then her eyes found the line below that. *Nom de père:* Alexander Winston Profitt.

She blinked in disbelief. Something was wrong. Profitt? Who was Alexander Profitt? She scanned the document several times for Jonathan's name, but her eyes kept returning to two words, *mère* and *père*.

Alexander Profitt . . . *father*?

'Joey?'

She spun around at the sound of Jonathan's voice. He was standing at the door. 'Come on, the snow's getting bad and—'

He stopped, seeing the look on her face. His eyes went to the distinctive blue paper in her hand, and then back to her face. The question he saw there in her eyes made his heart stop.

'Joey,' he said softly.

'I . . . I came back,' she said weakly, 'to get my birth certificate.' She looked dazed. 'I need . . . I needed it for my . . .'

Jonathan came to her. He took the blue paper from her trembling hand and glanced at it, then back at her, helplessly.

'Who is he?' she asked. 'Who is Alexander Profitt?'

Her eyes burned into him with such intensity that he had to look away.

'Dad. I want to know. Who *is* he?'

It took him a few moments to meet her eyes. 'He's your father, Joey,' he said softly.

She stared at him in disbelief. The colour drained from her face, and she wavered slightly as she stood there. She seemed to Jonathan to be suddenly so vulnerable, as if a breeze could knock her down, and he ached to take her into his arms. But some instinct prevented him from touching her. Her eyes filled with tears, and he let out a groan.

'Oh, Joey, I'm sorry,' he whispered.

'Why didn't you tell me?' she said.

Jonathan could think of nothing to say.

'Why didn't you tell me?' she repeated, the tears now streaming down her face.

'Joey, I . . . it just . . .'

'Why didn't you tell me you're not my real father?'

Jonathan felt the tears spring to his own eyes and he reached out for her, but she backed away.

'I wanted . . .' Jonathan searched desperately for the right words. 'I wanted to protect you, Joëlle. I thought it was the right thing to do.' He paused, trying to collect himself enough to go on speaking. 'You're my daughter, I love you . . .'

'But you lied!' she said, crying. 'You always told me I could count on you. But you lied to me! You should have told me!'

At that moment, Marion appeared at the door. She saw Joey's face and stopped short. 'Joey? What's the matter?' she said, her eyes darting to Jonathan. 'Jonathan? What is it?'

Joey turned quickly, grabbed the blue paper from Jonathan's hand and ran from the room. Marion reached for her as she went by. 'Joey! What is it?' She looked back at Jonathan, alarmed. 'What in the world is going on?' she asked.

Jonathan sank down into a chair, holding his head in his hand. 'She knows, Marion. She knows about Alexander. She came back to get her birth certificate and . . .' His voice trailed off.

Marion was too stunned to move. Finally she went to Jonathan and knelt beside the chair. His face was slack with confusion and despair. The sight of it made her own eyes swell up.

'You'd better go find her,' she said softly.

Jonathan looked up at her.

'You have to tell her the truth, Jonathan, all of it.'

It took a moment before he nodded and got up from the chair. Marion followed him to the front door. He picked up his hat and, with a final glance at Marion, stepped outside.

It was snowing lightly. He looked up and down the street but there was no sign of Joey. Then, seeing faint footprints in the snow, he started off in the direction they led. She was running, he could tell that much. Soon the prints stopped, lost in slushy snow. He stood on a corner, trying to think of the places she might have gone. Finally, he turned the corner and headed down the hill.

He reached the park and paused at the gate. There was no one in the park, not even a tobogganer. He squinted out over the white expanse. Far off in the distance, he spotted a speck of red: Joey's coat. There she was, sitting on the bleachers of the baseball diamond.

He trudged towards her. She saw him coming, but made no move to escape. She was huddled down into the collar of her coat, her dark hair wet with snow. She wouldn't look at him as he stood before her, so he climbed up and sat down beside her. He looked at her profile, her lips compressed tightly and her eyes staring fixedly ahead, and took a deep breath.

'I should have told you,' he said.

She didn't move or even blink.

'I should have told you a long time ago. You had a right to know,' he said. He took in another deep breath of the cold air. 'But I didn't. I used to tell myself it was for you, to protect you from being hurt. But it was for me, really. I was selfish.' He paused again. 'I wanted to be your father. Your only father.'

She still didn't move.

'Joey, I always loved you as my daughter,' Jonathan said softly. 'From that first day I held you in my arms, I have loved you. And I'm sorry, so very, very sorry I have hurt you.'

Her eyes filled with tears, but she refused to look at him.

'Tell me about him,' she said.

'All right,' he said.

For the next hour, they sat on the bleachers as the snow fell around them and the afternoon light waned. Jonathan told her about Alexander, about how they had met and their deep friendship. He told her the truth, as best his own feelings would allow, about how his inability to accept Cendrine's need to dance had driven her away. He told her, too, how Cendrine had finally come between him and Alexander. Joey listened without saying a word, without looking at him even once. Finally, Jonathan fell silent.

'Why didn't he want me?' she asked.

Jonathan hesitated. 'He was convinced you had died with Cendrine,' he said. 'And then, when I found you, I wasn't about to give you up. So I never told him.' He paused. 'I'm sorry for that, too.'

Joey reached in her coat pocket, pulled out the blue paper and slowly unfolded it. 'Is he still alive?' she asked.

Jonathan nodded.

Her eyes went back to the paper. 'I want to find him,' she said softly. 'When I go to Paris, I'm going to try to find him.'

He was going to try to talk her out of it, but then he saw the look in her eyes, the fierce determination, and it reminded him of Cendrine. He knew in that moment that he could say nothing to dissuade her. Every fibre of his being was shouting that it wasn't fair, that he was her real father and that it wasn't fair that he should lose her to a man who never wanted her in the first place. Even when Alexander was dead, his memory would for ever cast a shadow. Yet, a part of Jonathan understood what she was feeling. Once, he had felt the same need to reconnect with his own mother, to talk to her, to find out why she had left. As much as it hurt him, as much as it might hurt Joey, he couldn't deny her the chance he had never had.

'All right,' he said. 'But I'll write to him first.' He looked out at the snowy field. 'He doesn't even know you exist, and I think I should be the one to tell him. I'll tell him you're coming. It'll be easier for you, for both of you, that way.'

Joey still did not look at him.

He felt a tightening deep in his chest, a welling of emotion. 'I wish you weren't leaving today,' he said.

'I have to,' she answered.

He shivered, staring out at the snow drifting down from the grey clouds. He suddenly didn't trust himself to look at her.

'Dad?'

The word, that single word, made him turn.

'I love you, Dad.'

He stared at her face, at her eyes filled with tears. He pulled her into his arms, holding her as tightly as he could.

Chapter Thirty-Five

The train slowed as it approached the outskirts of Paris. Joey pressed against the window to see the old buildings with their webs of laundry stretched between them. She glanced up at the sky and squinted. The sun was bright in a brilliantly blue winter sky. It seemed wrong, incongruous; but then, so did her feelings. She was in Paris, and she should have felt only excitement. Yet it was confusion that dominated her feelings.

Another dancer leaned over Joey to peer out of the window. 'There it is! Paris!' she squealed. 'Can you see the Eiffel Tower? Oh, isn't this exciting?'

Joey was glad when the girl left, leaving her alone with her thoughts. All week, during the ocean crossing and the train ride to Paris, the same questions had been running through her head. Why hadn't her father told her about Alexander? And what was Alexander like. He had denied her existence once. Would he welcome her now, or reject her, just as he had done so many years ago? Why did she even care? Why did she want – no, need – to meet this man? Strange, strange . . . it was all so strange and still much too tender. Her mind had kept travelling back to when she was twelve, to the day when she had first found out about Cendrine. It had been a shock to find out Marion was not her mother, but she had learned to accept it. She had been able to do it finally because Cendrine was dead and thus somehow unreal.

But now, to find out that somewhere out there was a *living* parent, someone who was her father instead of the man she had known and loved all her life. She looked avidly at the approaching station, at the sign that announced Paris. Somewhere out there in all that strangeness was her real father, Alexander Profitt.

The train came to a stop. Gathering up her dance bag, she joined the other dancers in the line to get off the train. She was grateful that there would be no more time to dwell on Alexander Profitt. The rest of the day would be taken up with getting to the hotel and then to the theatre, where a rehearsal was scheduled for late afternoon. The opening was the following night, and Balanchine had left hardly a spare moment before. And then she would be dancing, and that would fill her head, leaving no room for Alexander Profitt. Later, she would deal with the idea of meeting him.

On the platform, she stood quietly among the other dancers. Her senses devoured everything around her: the harried, mustachioed, blue-coated porters weaving their carts through the crowd; the acrid smell of the dark cigarette held by a man standing nearby; the colourful mosaic of magazines in the kiosk; the bubbling brook of French eddying all around her. And the women, the famously stylish Parisian women, with their pale, placid faces, bright-red lips and carefully waved hair.

The company manager was gathering the dancers into a group so he could return their passports. Somone else was trying to collect their luggage and arrange for transport to the hotel. It was chaos, and Joey stood slightly apart, wishing it could be straightened out so she could get to the hotel and rest before the rehearsal. She was tired from the travel. Her eyes wandered idly over the crowd. Suddenly they locked on one man standing about ten feet away.

It was clear that he was watching her. He was an old man, distinguished-looking, very tall and thin. He was wearing a fine gaberdine trench coat belted around his slender waist and a slope-brimmed hat that partly shielded his eyes.

She stared back at him, unable to look away. After a few moments, he came towards her. Something in his dark eyes made her draw in her breath.

'Joëlle? Are you Joëlle?' he asked softly. His voice was velvety and tentative, his eyes were shining with expectancy. And suddenly Joey knew, and her heart stopped.

'Yes,' she whispered.

'I'm Alexander,' he said. 'Alexander Profitt.'

She looked intently at the strange man before her. She registered his thick, white hair, his long, thin nose and wide mouth; and the angular contours of his face, a face creased with age, but still striking in its patrician grace. She found herself searching for something of herself in it. She had done this once before: soon after discovering the portrait of Cendrine, she had stared for hours at it at Cendrine's round face and pale colouring, looking vainly for any resemblance. '*It's in your eyes*,' Jonathan had finally told her, '*you have her eyes*.' Joey had always believed her dark hair, height and angularity came from Jonathan. But now, as she saw Alexander Profitt, she thought she could find an echo of herself in him instead. Was it there? There in his hair or the sharpness of his cheekbones? Or was she just wishing it so. She felt as if she were seeing a reflection – distorted, as if the mirror had been broken, but still a reflection of herself. Her eyes filled with tears.

The old man blinked in dismay. 'Oh, dear, I knew it,' he said. 'I knew I shouldn't have come here without warning. It's too much of a shock.' He paused, searching her face. 'But I couldn't help myself. I just had to see you.'

He held out a handkerchief, and she dried her eyes. When she looked back at him, he was regarding her intently, as if taking her features apart, one by one, searching for something, just as she had.

'What's the matter?' she asked.

'Nothing,' he said. 'Nothing . . .'

They stood silent for a moment, surrounded by the sounds of the station. Joey didn't know what to say or do. Should she hug him, shake his hand? He seemed equally at a loss. It was such a shock. A part of her wanted to run away from this man; another part of her wanted desperately to be with him, to hear every word he had to say, to watch everything he did. All during the voyage over, she had imagined what was going to happen when she finally met him. She imagined she would feel a surge of love for this man who was her real father, and that he would take her in his arms, begging her to forgive him for not wanting her so many years ago. But none of that was happening. There was only this awkwardness and paralysing uneasiness. She had wanted desperately to be sophisticated about this, to handle it like an adult. But all the words she had so carefully rehearsed were forgotten. Suddenly, she felt as if she were ten years old.

'Let me take you to your hotel,' Alexander said.

'What? Oh, I . . . the company is . . . I mean, I have to go with them,' Joey said quickly, pointing to the others who were trailing off towards the taxi stand outside.

Alexander smiled slightly. It was the first time he had smiled, and it was as if a switch had been turned inside him. He seemed determined to put her, and himself, at ease. He took her satchel. 'I don't think they'll miss you.'

Joey hesitated.

'Please,' Alexander said. 'It would really make me happy if you'd let me take you to your hotel, Joëlle.'

She nodded and walked woodenly by his side through the crowd. A gleaming black Mercedes sedan sat waiting

423

outside and a man opened the door when Alexander approached. Joey looked wide-eyed at the car and the driver, then back at Alexander. He helped her into the car and slid in beside her. The car pulled away from the station. Joey sat motionless, her fingers lightly touching the soft leather of the seat. She felt his eyes on her but, unable to bring herself to look at him, she tried to concentrate on the sights streaming by outside.

'What hotel are you staying in?' Alexander asked.

She turned to him in surprise. 'Oh, it's called the Hotel Day-Ban. Somewhere near the theatre, I think.'

Alexander smiled slightly. 'Jean-Paul,' he said to the driver, '*l'Hôtel des Bains, sur le Rue Delambre.*' He turned to Joey. 'I can recommend something much nicer,' he said.

'All the company's staying there,' Joey said. 'I really should be with them.'

Alexander nodded and they were quiet again. Joey looked out of the window, up at the sun shining in the blue sky. She felt tears sting her eyes again but blinked them back. This is not going right, she thought, this is all wrong. It's not working. I wish I had never found out about him.

The car pulled up to the hotel. Many of the dancers were already there, just getting out of taxis or waiting in groups on the pavement with their luggage. They stared at the black Mercedes as it stopped and Jean-Paul jumped out to open Joey's door. She looked at the others, then turned to face Alexander.

'Thank you for the ride,' she said.

'Joëlle,' he said softly. 'Will you have dinner with me tonight? We have so much to talk about.'

'I . . . there's a rehearsal this afternoon. I don't know how long it will last . . .' Her voice trailed off. 'And I'm kind of tired.'

Alexander nodded. 'I understand.'

Getting out of the car, she paused. 'I'm dancing tomorrow night,' she said tentatively. 'Would you like to come?'

Alexander's face creased up in a smile. 'Very much.'

'I'll leave a ticket for you.' She hesitated. 'Goodbye.'

'Goodbye, Joëlle.'

She closed the door and watched the car as it slid away, gleaming in the sun. One of the dancers came up to her side. 'Who was *that*?' she asked breathlessly.

Joey watched the car until it disappeared around the corner. 'My father,' she said softly.

The next night, she danced the role of Polyhymnia, one of the three muses in Balanchine's ballet *Apollon Musagete*. It wasn't the lead, the role of Terpsichore, which all the young women coveted. But Joey enjoyed Polyhymnia's solo because it was fast and vivacious, allowing her to show off the things she did best. Usually, when she danced, she tried hard to impress Balanchine, who always watched from the wings. But tonight she thought about Alexander Profitt sitting out there in the audience, and found herself wanting to dance well for him.

Afterwards, just as she finished changing in the dressing room, Alexander appeared at the door. The other girls stared at the tall stranger in his austere formal dress holding a small bouquet of dark-red roses. Then their eyes, filled with curiosity, went back to Joey. She quickly stepped outside.

'These are for you,' Alexander said, holding out the flowers.

'Thanks,' Joey said, taking them, with a look back at the giggling dancers.

Alexander smiled at the sight of her reddening face. 'I'm sorry. I didn't mean to embarrass you.'

'They're just jealous. Corps girls never get flowers.'

'But you danced a solo. I thought—'

'No, I'm still in the corps.'

'Well, you danced beautifully.'

Joey looked up at Alexander and smiled slowly, shyly.

Alexander cleared his throat. 'I thought I'd try again to convince you to come to dinner with me.' He smiled. 'That is, if you're not too tired?'

She could not take her eyes off his face. 'All right,' she said softly. 'Give me a minute.' She slid back behind the door, her heart hammering.

He was waiting for her outside the stage door. She followed him to the black Mercedes, got in, and the car slipped into the traffic around the Place de l'Opéra. Joey looked up at the gold facade of the opera house, and at the fountain, artfully illuminated in the black night. Women in long gowns and furs and men in tuxedos were streaming down the steps to sleek dark cars waiting below. It all looked very beautiful.

'Are you hungry?' Alexander asked.

'Dancers are always hungry,' she said with a small smile.

'Good. I wanted to take you somewhere special, a favourite place of mine.'

They said nothing to each other during the short time it took to reach Maxim's. Joey could not conceal her awe as Alexander led her through the flamboyant lobby. Her eyes took in the gilt mirrors, the velvet walls and stained glass; she heard the violins playing and saw the waiters gliding by. She focused finally on the evening gowns of the women, all the velvets, silks and satins.

'Is something wrong?' Alexander asked afer they had been seated at a central table.

'I didn't know we'd be going to a place so . . . fancy,' Joey said weakly, unable to think of a better word. Her mind tripped back to the time David had taken her to the Plaza. She hadn't really worried then about how she looked; she had been with David, after all, who never cared what she wore. But this was Paris – a different world. Alexander Profitt's world.

'Don't worry,' Alexander whispered, accepting a menu from the waiter.

Joey was relieved that Alexander took the initiative and ordered. She listened, fascinated, to the lilting French rolling off his tongue.

'Do you like fish?' he asked her.

She nodded, thinking of the perch she caught with her father back on the farm during the summer. The thought made her start and she looked at Alexander. Father . . . She suddenly felt overcome with confusion.

'I enjoyed the ballet tonight,' Alexander said.

'Do you go to the ballet often?' Joey asked, glad to have something to talk about.

Alexander shook his head, smiling slightly. 'No, I haven't gone in years . . . years.'

The sommelier appeared and poured a small amount of wine in Alexander's glass. He tasted it and nodded. The man filled Joey's glass with the pale-gold liquid and then Alexander's. 'I didn't know what kind of wine you might like,' Alexander said. 'This is a Burgundy, a Meursault; it's light, but with a lot of life. Like the way you danced tonight.'

Joey looked down in embarrassment and picked up her glass by the delicate stem, the way Alexander did. He raised his glass slightly and took a drink. She did the same, startled by the first bite of the wine, then pleased by its dry, fruity taste.

'You don't like it,' Alexander said, clearly disappointed.

'No, no . . . I do,' Joey said quickly. 'It's just, well, I've only had wine once before. It was a Burgundy, but it was red.' She shrugged. 'I'm not very sophisticated, I guess.'

427

Alexander smiled. He was quiet, and Joey noticed the same intense scrutiny of her face that she had seen at the train station.

'You're staring at me again,' she said softly. 'The way you did yesterday . . .'

Alexander sat back slightly. 'I'm sorry,' he said. 'It's just . . . I just can't believe this. I can't believe you exist.' He paused, shaking his head.

Joey nodded, feeling her chest tighten. 'I know. I can't believe any of it either.'

Alexander took a drink of wine. His eyes came back to her face, but there was a distant look in them. 'I look at you, trying to see something of her in you . . .' His voice trailed off.

'I have her eyes,' Joey offered.

Alexander could only look at her. They were both silent as the sounds of the restaurant flowed around them. Joey fiddled with the napkin in her lap. The awkwardness had returned. For a moment, they had managed to push it aside, but now it was back, creating a gulf between them. Hopeless, Joey thought sadly, it's hopeless. We have no way to connect. He's my father, yet we have nothing to bring us together after all these years.

She looked up at Alexander and saw that he was thinking the same thing. 'Tell me about her,' she said quickly. 'Tell me about Cendrine.'

Something passed over Alexander's dark eyes and, for a moment, he seemed to leave her. 'I know a lot about her already,' Joey said. 'My fa—' She caught herself. 'I'd like you to tell me about her.'

Slowly, subtly, Alexander's expression changed. It remained distant but warmer. He looked directly at Joey. 'I was in love with her,' he began.

For the next three hours, Joey listened. Alexander told her about Cendrine's life in La Turbie, and how they had met. He didn't tell her outright that Cendrine had been his mistress, but Joey understood their relationship. He told her about Cendrine's ambition, her independence, her strength, her passion to dance above all else. He told her about Cendrine as he had known her. And as Joey listened, she began to create in her mind a new picture of Cendrine. It was not the one of her childhood, the romantic sketch of a beautiful, tragic ballerina that Jonathan had drawn for her. It was not even the more richly coloured, altered one Jonathan had given her a week ago in the park when he finally told her the truth. And it certainly wasn't the one she herself had shaped in her dreams, dreams based on the pale portrait that hung above her bed. This new picture of Cendrine was a composite of all these, a portrait of a real woman.

Finally, Alexander fell silent, pensive. He picked up the third bottle of wine and poured the last of it into his glass.

'Thank you,' Joey said softly.

Alexander finished the wine. 'It's not easy, remembering,' he said. He was silent again, toying with the glass, avoiding her eyes. 'I haven't done it in a long time. But when I received Jonathan's letter about you, I couldn't avoid it. And now, here you are, and I can't seem to stop.'

'I'm sorry . . . for causing you pain.'

Alexander looked up at her. 'No, no, it's all right. It's just difficult . . .' His voice trailed off as he looked at her in bewilderment.

Joey felt her eyes brim. She reached across the table and touched Alexander's hand. He looked at her, then quickly down at her hand covering his.

Alexander came to every performance of the ballet during its week-long engagement at the opera house. Every night, he waited for Joey at the stage entrance and they went to dinner. They talked, usually about Cendrine, but increasingly about their own lives, still sending out tentative emotional runners in their search to connect. When it came time for the company to leave, he took her to the train station. They stood awkwardly until finally, Alexander took her by the shoulders and brushed each of her cheeks with his own, gently, respectfully, in a way that spoke of some bygone graceful time. But that was Alexander Profitt, she had learned in the past week. He was a man out of time, an elegant, living anachronism. She found it beguiling but also a little sad. She looked up at him, blinking rapidly. He was still a stranger to her, yet she realized that she was going to miss him.

'I wish I didn't have to go,' she said.

'I wish you didn't either, Joëlle.'

The porter gave the final boarding call.

'Can't I stay?' Joey asked suddenly, without thinking.

Alexander stared at her in surprise.

'I could call home and ask if I could stay on a little longer,' Joey said in a rush. 'With you, here . . . I mean, if you'd want me to.'

She waited for Alexander's reaction. After a moment, he smiled. 'I'd like that, Joëlle,' he said, 'very much indeed.'

Joey grinned and then impulsively hugged Alexander. He was so stunned that at first he did not return the embrace; then his arms came up, tentatively, to encircle her.

Late that night, Alexander sat alone in his library. Joey was asleep in a guest bedroom, but he was still wide awake, reliving the feel of her impetuous embrace. Why had it unnerved him? Was it because it was so unexpected, such an innocent display of affection?

Affection – that was one thing he had not been

prepared for from her. When the letter from Jonathan had come, it had shocked him to his bones. Cendrine's child was alive! And she was coming to see him. He had had so little time to prepare himself, and, in the end, there had been no way to do so. A part of him had expected to see a child at the station that first day, a small, blonde, pale child, a miniature version of Cendrine. To see, instead, a tall, dark-haired, beautiful young woman had been a great shock.

Alexander raised himself up slightly in the chair and reached for the brandy on the table at his elbow. But his hand grazed the bottle, sending it clattering to the floor. Through hazy eyes, he stared down at it, expecting to see its contents spilled on the carpet. But it was empty . . . empty? He had drunk the entire bottle and could not remember doing it.

He sank back into the chair, seeing Joëlle's face again; seeing Cendrine's sombre blue-grey eyes looking back at him from a stranger's face. No, not a stranger. Cendrine's daughter – his daughter. Why hadn't Cendrine told him?

He closed his eyes, his mind clicking back over the years to the last time he had seen Cendrine, the night he had told her he was sending her away, the last time they had made love.

He ran a hand over his eyes. It wasn't easy, remembering. It never had been, not once in over twenty years, remembering everything he had lost so many years ago. But that was what the drink was for, to stop the memories. It always worked, given enough of it. But tonight it wasn't working. It couldn't work against something tangible, something as real as Joëlle.

How was he going to be able to withstand her presence in his life? He had barely made it through the past week. A part of him had found joy in her, but another part of him, the part that always, inevitably, dominated, the part of him that held the memories, dreaded having her around.

The clock chimed three. Finally, thankfully, he felt the blessed relief of sleep overtaking him. He would sleep, drugged from the brandy. For a few hours at least, he would not remember.

Chapter Thirty-Six

Alexander did not appear for breakfast the next morning. When Joey asked a servant about him, she was told that Alexander rarely rose before ten. He did not join her for lunch either, and Joey occupied herself by roaming round the large apartment, looking at Alexander's books, paintings and belongings. She was in the library, examining the contents of an antique vitrine, when he appeared. He paused at the door, surprised to see her in the library. He was wearing an elegant smoking jacket; his face was pale and drawn.

'Ah, Joëlle, I'm sorry you were left alone all day. Not very gracious of me,' he said softly. 'I was feeling a bit under the weather.' He came into the room and gave her a charming smile. 'But what about you? Did you sleep well?'

'Yes. It's a lovely room,' she said. She looked at the glass case. 'I was admiring your collection. What are they?'

'Fabergé eggs. Each one unique, created for the czars. They're priceless,' he said, with a flat smile. He went to a French commode that held a selection of bottles on a silver tray. 'Would you like an aperitif before dinner?' he asked.

She shook her head and watched as he poured himself a small amount of clear liquid into a cut crystal glass.

'So,' he said, turning to her, 'did you call home?'

She nodded. Alexander looked at her thoughtfully. 'Is something wrong? Bad news?'

Joey shook her head.

'I thought perhaps that Jonathan . . .' Alexander paused. 'Well, frankly, I thought that he might not be too happy about your staying on here with me.'

'He was just a little surprised, that's all.' Joey glanced up at Alexander. He looked terrible, as if he hadn't slept at all, and she was beginning to wonder if she might not be imposing on him, and he was simply too polite to refuse her request to stay. He was not a young man, after all. And maybe she was expecting too much from him too fast.

Alexander set his drink down suddenly. 'I have an idea, a way to make up for my absence today,' he said. 'Tomorrow, you and I will go to the Bois de Boulogne.'

Joey looked up. 'A forest?'

Alexander laughed. 'Of course.' He picked up his crystal glass and held it out to Joey in a graceful salute. 'I'll show you everything in my beautiful city, Joëlle, everything.'

The early morning was grey and cold as their carriage drove slowly along the meandering paths of the Bois de Boulogne. The fog muffled the sound of the horses' hooves, and the bare trees advanced and retreated like ghosts. The bustle of Paris had receded; the whole rest of the world seemed far away. Joey had the sensation of being transported. She was suspended in some magic moment, out of place and time, as if the fairy-tale Paris of her childhood, the lost city that Jonathan had so vividly painted to her, had come alive.

The feeling stayed with her as the week went on. Alexander did not even bother to go into his office at the *Herald*; he devoted every moment to Joey. He took her to the Louvre to see the old-master paintings, then, at dusk, steered her to the Pont Neuf so she could see the luminous views as the day came to a close. In a bistro on Rue Jacob, he introduced her to death-black French coffee, *pelure d'oignon* wine, and abstract art by pointing out a Cubist design painted on the spiral staircase. Forgetting she did not read French, he took her to bookshops, buying her a copy of Colette's *Sido* and a translation of *Alice in Wonderland*. He took her to the *Herald* office and proudly gave her a tour. Joey was more interested in an exhibition of decor from the era of the Diaghilev ballet, designs by Bakst, Cocteau and Matisse that Alexander called 'symbols of *les beaux jours*, the days of civilized pleasures'.

One afternoon, he took her to Molyneux's couture salon, where he bought her a severely cut black velvet evening gown with pigskin belt and gloves. When Joey modelled it for him, he told her she was a beautiful woman.

On Christmas Eve, he presented her with a small, exquisitely wrapped gift. Inside was a green velvet box that held a crystal vial. She looked at it in curiosity. Jicky – an odd name for a perfume. Its scent was vaguely Oriental and more sophisticated than her usual perfume.

'I usually wear White Shoulders,' she told Alexander. 'Mr B. gives all his dancers perfume. He says it helps him keep track of us. I don't like mine . . .' She smiled. 'But I like this.'

'I'm glad,' Alexander said with a smile.

She wore the perfume and the Molyneux gown to a gala at the opera in honour of visiting British monarchs. The water in the opera house's illuminated fountains was sprinkled with gold dust for the occasion, and Joey watched, awestruck, as King George VI and Queen Elizabeth were escorted up the marble staircase by liveried torchbearers. She sat next to Alexander in his box, uncaring that she did not understand the opera's Italian. She was dazzled by Puccini's music, by the glamour of the glittering crowd, and especially by Alexander.

One day, Joey asked Alexander what the old Folies-Bergère had been like. He showed her where the old theatre was, but it was closed. So that night, he took her instead to a revue at the Casino, telling her it was much the same as in Cendrine's day. The revue featured pretty girls in scanty costumes doing much the same posing routines Cendrine had endured. There were musicians, comics and a juggler; the tiny chanteuse Mistinguett sang a sad love song; and at the end of the evening, Maurice Chevalier brought down the house singing a German song in a voice mocking Adolf Hitler.

This last event was the only intrusion of reality into the dream Alexander had so skilfully fashioned for Joey. During the week, as she spent her mornings alone waiting for him, she had time to read the newspaper, something she normally never did. She read the stories in the *Herald* about the possibility of war in Europe. She read with curiosity about Hitler's occupation of the Sudentenland, about Fascists, about Roosevelt approving the sale of war planes to France. Finally, one night over dinner, she asked Alexander to explain what was going on.

'It's nothing,' he said.

'But will France go to war?' she persisted.

'Joëlle, it's not something of concern to you.'

'But what if—'

'I don't want to talk about it,' he said brusquely.

Joey sat back, stunned by Alexander's tone of voice. 'I didn't mean to upset you,' she said. 'I was just reading about how a war would—'

'No,' Alexander said sharply. 'It won't happen again. It can't happen again.'

He rose abruptly and went into the library, shutting the door, leaving Joey sitting alone at the table, too shocked to move. By now, after three weeks, she had come to realize that Alexander was given to moodiness, but that didn't make it any easier to accept the shifts into darkness when they came. Although he did everything he could to impress and please her, he still held her at a distance, deflecting her attempts to get closer. He could be extremely charming, yet she could sense, beneath it, a sadness in him. She believed she understood now the reason why. He had never got over Cendrine's death. Alexander Profitt, living his solitary life in his exquisite Parisian apartment, surrounded by his paintings, books and rare objects, was the loneliest person she had ever met.

Her thoughts went suddenly to home, to Jonathan and Marion, and she could feel the warmth of the slightly worn old house on Oxford Street and the farm in Dryden. How lucky she was to have a family who loved her! She thought, too, of David. But Alexander – her eyes went to the closed library door – had no one; except for the *Herald*, he had nothing he cared about. That was why he was often melancholy and why he drank so much.

Her eyes fell on his empty wine glass. For several days now, a shadowy thought had been lingering in the back of her mind, a thought she had not wanted to face. Now it was pushing its way forward. Alexander Profitt, her father, was an alcoholic. She knew now that all those mornings when he was absent, he was sick from drinking. She stared at the wine glass, and her eyes filled with tears of compassion.

She rose and walked slowly to the library door. She paused, listening, before knocking softly. There was no answer, no sound at all. She tried the knob, but the door was locked. She stayed there for several minutes, listening, but could hear nothing within. Then she turned and went upstairs to her room.

It was after midnight when she heard the crash. She was just about to drift off to sleep, but the sound jerked her awake. She sat, her ears pricked to every sound in the quiet apartment. The crash had come from somewhere downstairs. She slipped on a robe and crept down the staircase.

The library door was open and a light was on. For a moment Joey saw no one. Then she saw Alexander, sprawled on the floor. The vitrine lay on its side, its glass shattered; the four Fabergé eggs lay amid the glass. Alexander groaned, and Joey rushed to his side. He was wearing the same clothes he had worn at dinner, and he reeked of alcohol. Joey put her arms under his, trying to lift him up to a sitting position.

'Go away,' he muttered, without seeing her.

'Let me help.'

'Leave me be, Brookes! Go away, damn you!'

His arm flailed out and hit Joey on the arm. She flinched and drew back. She watched, shocked, as Alexander struggled to sit up. He began to crawl away from her, across the shards of glass, which crunched beneath his hands and knees. Finally, he pulled himself up to sit against the wall. His eyes were unfocused, unseeing. When he brought up one hand to wipe his face, it was bleeding. He let it drop to his lap and closed his eyes.

Joey went to his side. She hesitated, her heart pounding, before taking his hand to pick the glass out of the cut. He opened his eyes and turned to look at her as if trying to figure out who she was.

'Joëlle?'

She didn't know what to do. Her eyes went quickly to the door. Should she go wake the servants? Find Brookes? She had to get Alexander to bed at least. She had to help him, but she didn't want to leave his side. She looked frantically at the door again. Why hadn't anyone come? Someone must have heard.

She looked back at Alexander's pale face, and tried to fit her shoulder under his arm. 'Let me help you,' she said.

Alexander shook his head. 'No . . . no. Go away.'

'Please,' she said. 'Let me help.'

'I don't need help.' He jerked away, leaning back against the wall.

She stared at him – at his ashen face, bloated with drink, and his stained, blood-spattered shirt. The man before her was her father. She felt her eyes brim with tears.

'You need help,' she said.

He glared at her.

'Please let me help you,' she whispered.

His eyes, for the first time, seemed to focus clearly on her. Suddenly he laughed, a loud, metallic laugh that made her draw back. The laugh echoed through the room, growing sharper and more angry, until it tapered off into a half-sobbing cry.

She reached for his hand and he pulled it roughly away. 'Go away!' he shouted. 'I don't want your help! I don't want your pity! Leave me alone!'

'I can't!' she shouted back, crying now. 'You're my father!'

'I'm not!' he cried. 'I'm not your father! It's a lie! A lie! I'm not your goddamn father, and I don't want your pity!'

His black eyes, deadened by the drink, glowered at her stricken face. Slowly, he pushed himself up to his feet. Joey sat frozen, too horrified to move. He found his balance and looked down at her, wavering.

'Go home,' he said tonelessly. 'Go home to Jonathan. I'm not your father. He's your father.'

He staggered out of the room, leaving Joey sitting on the floor amid the glass.

Chapter Thirty-Seven

Jonathan stood at the gate, searching the crowd of passengers disembarking the *Queen Elizabeth*. He spotted Joey and waved, calling her name. She heard him and came towards him. He drew her into his arms, holding her tight.

'God, it's so good to have you home!' he said. He pulled back to look at her, then hugged her again. Joey returned the embrace, shutting her eyes.

'Well! Let's get your bags and get going,' Jonathan said. 'We've got a long drive ahead, and your mother's anxious to see you.'

Joey was quiet during the time it took Jonathan to get through the Manhattan traffic. He glanced at her out of the corner of his eye, believing she was just tired from the long trip. He thought she would be eager to talk about Alexander and Paris, but she just sat silent, staring out of the window.

'So,' he said finally, gently. 'How did it go?'

'It was all right,' she said.

He waited but she said nothing more. 'Did you like Paris?' he probed.

'It was everything you said it would be.'

He hesitated, his eyes trained on the road. 'And Alexander?'

She said nothing. After a moment, Jonathan glanced

over at her and was surprised to see tears falling down her face.

He quickly manoeuvred the car through the traffic, then slowed until he could pull onto the shoulder. He switched off the ignition and turned to Joey.

'Joey, what is it?' he asked.

She was crying openly now, her hands covering her face. 'He told me to go away,' she said. 'He said he wasn't really my father. He said it was all a lie. He said you were really my father!'

Jonathan stared at her in shock, then pulled her into his arms. 'That bastard,' he muttered.

'Why did he say that?' Joey said, looking at him beseechingly.

'I don't know.'

'But what about the birth certificate?' Joey asked. 'His name is on it. That makes it legal, doesn't it?'

Jonathan did not answer. His mind was racing back to Iseltwald, and he was quickly calculating again the months between the last time he had seen Cendrine and Joey's birth.

'Doesn't it?' Joey asked again.

Jonathan took a deep breath. His heart was hammering. 'Joey,' he began softly. 'Alexander is . . . I don't think he meant to hurt you. He always—'

'Is he my father?' Joey demanded.

'Yes,' Jonathan said quietly.

Joey looked hard at him, then slumped back into the seat. She had stopped crying and was just staring vacantly out through the windshield.

Jonathan started the car and pulled back onto the highway.

Marion had prepared a special welcome-home dinner for Joey, decorating the house with balloons and streamers. But Joey was subdued throughout the evening. She

442

talked willingly about her experiences dancing in Paris, but avoided Marion's careful questions about Alexander. Marion looked at Jonathan across the table, and he could read the concern and perplexity in her eyes. He had not been able to bring himself to tell her about his conversation with Joey in the car, or about the questions about Cendrine and Joey's birth that were pounding in his head. He knew he had to tell Marion, but first, somehow, he had to face Joey.

It was only a little after nine when Joey announced that she was tired and asked to be excused. Marion and Jonathan watched her as she rose solemnly, kissed them each good night and left to go upstairs.

After a few minutes, Jonathan rose. 'I need to talk to her,' he said to Marion.

Upstairs, he paused outside Joey's door, and knocked. 'Joey? Can I come in?'

'Sure.'

She was sitting cross-legged on her bed, wearing an old chenille robe, darning the tip of a pointe shoe. Elton was curled up on the end of the bed. Jonathan nudged the old dog aside to make room to sit down. Joey glanced at him, then returned to her darning. Jonathan's eyes went up to the portrait of Cendrine and then back to Joey.

'You know,' he said softly, 'when you came walking across the pier this morning, I almost didn't recognize you. You looked different somehow. Grown-up. Very adult.' He paused. 'I want to have a talk with you, Joey, an adult talk.'

The darning needle paused in air for a moment, but Joey didn't look up. 'I already know that Cendrine was Alexander's mistress, if that's what you want to tell me,' she said.

'Did Alexander tell you that?'

'No, I just guessed it, from the way he talked. He said he took care of her.'

Jonathan said nothing. His eyes were riveted to her hands holding the shoe and needle. 'Joey,' he said, still not looking at her. 'There's something I need to tell you. Something I should have told you before now.'

'About Alexander?'

'No, about me . . . and Cendrine.'

She looked up at him. Slowly he raised his head to meet her eyes. 'I went to see Cendrine in Iseltwald,' he said, 'in 1917, about eight months before you were born.'

Joey didn't move, but he could see her mind working.

'I don't know if . . .' His voice faltered. 'I don't know if Alexander is your father. I don't know for *for certain*.'

'But my birth certificate,' Joey said softly. 'It says—'

'You didn't have one,' Jonathan went on quickly. 'After I found you in La Turbie, I tried contacting someone in Iseltwald, but there was no record of your birth. So I had a birth certificate made out for you in Nice. I had to have it to get you back into the States. I put Alexander's name on it because I just assumed—' He paused, shaking his head. 'But I could have been wrong.' He looked at her. 'I'm sorry, Joey, but I don't know the truth. I don't know if Alexander is your father or I am.'

Joey sat there, holding the pointe shoe, staring at Jonathan.

'But you could be,' she whispered. 'It's possible.'

Joey looked stunned. 'That's got to be why Alexander said what he did,' she said. 'He isn't my father and he knew it. You are.' Her eyes filled with tears. She set the shoe aside and put her arms around Jonathan, laying her head on his shoulder.

Jonathan's hand went up to cradle her head, and he kissed her soft hair. A faint smell came to him, a scent that sent him careering back in time. For a moment he couldn't place it, and then he knew. It was the perfume that Cendrine had worn the last time he saw her. He closed his eyes.

'God, I missed you!' David kissed Joey and shifted his weight to her side, pulling her into the crook of his arm. 'I missed you, I missed you, I missed you,' he whispered.

Laying her head on his chest, she could hear his heart still beating fast from their lovemaking. She listened until it slowed to its usual rhythm, until David's breathing deepened as he drifted into a light sleep. She lay still, watching the dusky light play against the curtains. The sound of a taxi horn rose up from below, and outside in the corridor, a cart clattered by, bearing luggage or someone's room-service dinner. The room grew chilly. Joey pulled the blanket over her bare shoulder, snuggled closer to David and closed her eyes.

But after a few minutes, she opened them, unable to sleep. Carefully, she extracted herself from David's arms and got out of bed. She went quietly to the window.

Far below, a line of red tail lights blinked on and off down snow-clogged Fifth Avenue, futile little SOS signals from the unfortunates caught in the Friday-night Manhattan exodus. Joey gazed at the red lights. It felt strange being back in New York. She had been happy to see David; she had missed him a great deal while she had been in Paris. But after a week, she still felt oddly out of place at Sumner and Katherine's, even in the city itself which she had come to love.

She leaned against the window frame. Perhaps it was an after-effect of Paris. Perhaps she was just feeling wrung out after finding out about Alexander and her father – having been taken to such heights by Alexander and then wrenched down so low. And she would never really know for sure that Jonathan was her real father.

'Does it matter?' David had asked her after she had told him everything that had happened. 'If you love him,

445

does it really matter?'

'No, but I just wish I knew,' she answered.

'Sometimes it's better not to know,' David said. 'I wish I didn't.'

Joey's eyes went from the window to David, sleeping soundly. He had never really known his own father, yet he was still so bitter about him. She had always felt sorry for him because of it; she had never really understood his wound. Now a part of her did. Growing up, she had always taken her place in her family for granted. Because she could never know Cendrine, she had looked to Jonathan for her identity. Knowing he was her father had made her feel connected to something. But now there was only uncertainty, and she felt as if an essential link had been broken. For the first time in her life, she felt alone.

Her eyes went back to the window and she shivered. Maybe that was why she had felt funny at home in Ithaca, too, as if a part of her didn't even belong there any more. She looked down at the street. But if not there and not here, then where did she belong? And to whom?

'Joëlle?'

David came up behind her, wrapped in a blanket. 'Are you all right?'

'Yes.'

He sighed and wrapped his arms over her shoulders, pulling her back against his chest. 'You're upset about having to come to a hotel, aren't you?'

'I don't mind, David.'

'Well, I do.' He kissed her neck. His lips and breath were warm on her cold skin and she closed her eyes, leaning back against him.

'I had a lot of time to think while you were gone,' he said.

'About what?'

'I think we should get married.'

She turned slowly to face him. His face was serious, his eyes unusually dark. 'I love you,' he said softly. 'I can't stand being away from you. I need you in my life, Joëlle.'

She felt her heart beating faster. 'Your mother,' she said, 'she doesn't—'

'She'll have to accept it,' David interrupted. 'We'll tell her tonight. I don't want to wait any more.'

He opened the blanket and drew her into it, against his warm body. He wrapped the blanket around their bodies. Joey held him tight.

'We fit, we fit so well,' he whispered. 'Marry me, Joëlle. We belong together.'

'Yes, we do,' she said.

David unlocked the front door and pushed it open. Joey peered beyond him into the marble and wrought-iron entrance hall. David's hand was firm on her back. 'Come on,' he said. 'It'll be all right, I promise.'

Joey entered the hall and stopped, taking in the details of the vast apartment. Her eyes focused on the huge Henry VIII tapestry hanging over the fireplace. 'Give me your coat,' David said, and she let him slip it off. 'She's probably in the library,' he said. He squared his shoulders and took her hand. His smile was meant to fortify her, but it seemed forced.

At the library, David didn't hesitate, he pushed the double doors open with more force than was necessary. Then he drew up short. His mother was sitting before the fire, with Oliver Thayer at her side. Both looked up, startled. Lucy's smile at seeing David quickly faded when she saw Joey standing behind him.

David recovered quickly, choosing to ignore Oliver. 'Mother,' David said firmly, 'I want you to meet someone.' He took Joey's hand and guided her forward. 'This is Joëlle LeClerc.'

Lucy did not move, nor did her expression change. Several seconds ticked by and the silence grew awkward. Oliver, on the other hand, looked suddenly interested. He set his drink aside and rose slowly, extending his hand to Joey.

'I'm Oliver Thayer,' he said with a smile. 'David has forgotten his manners. Undoubtedly blinded by a young lady's charm.'

Lucy shot him a venomous look. Joey took Oliver's hand and shook it, but she looked back quickly at Lucy. The hardness in the woman's eyes made her want to turn and run, but she held her ground, braced by the closeness of David standing behind her.

'Mother,' David said, 'I – we have some news.' Joey looked at him. His voice sounded peculiar, with a sharp edge to it she had never heard before. She knew that David's relationship with his mother had been strained lately, but he never really spoke of it. She saw now, however, that she was the reason. She could see it clearly in Lucy's eyes.

David glanced at Oliver. 'If you don't mind, Oliver, I'd like a minute alone,' he said.

'Oliver's my friend,' Lucy said tersely. 'Whatever it is, David, you can say it in front of him.'

David's mouth drew into a line. 'We're going to be married, Mother,' he said.

Lucy's face went white. She rose slowly, her eyes riveted to David's. 'No, you're not,' she said evenly.

Joey felt David's hand tighten around hers. 'Joëlle and I are going to be married – tomorrow.' Joey looked at him in shock. 'There's nothing you can do about it, Mother,' David added. 'I only came back here tonight because I hoped you might . . . give us your blessing.' The last words came out flat.

'My blessing?' Lucy said, her voice rising. 'You don't want my blessing. All you want is to hurt me, David.'

'All I want to do is live my own life,' David said, his own voice rising in anger.

'I've never stopped you!' Lucy exclaimed. Her eyes filled with tears. 'I've never stopped you from anything!'

'Yes, you have!' David shouted. 'You've stopped me from doing everything I ever wanted to do!'

'I only want you to be happy!' Lucy cried.

'Then give us your blessing!' David implored.

Lucy looked at Joey, who was staring at them both in horror. 'No,' she said. 'Not to marry *her*.'

The last word had emerged with such disgust that at first, David was too stunned to say anything. 'Don't talk to her like that,' he said, his voice low and measured.

Suddenly Joey wrenched her hand free from David's, turned and ran from the room. 'Joëlle! Wait!' David yelled. He started after her.

'David!' Lucy shouted. 'If you go, I swear I won't let you back in this house! I swear I'll cut you off. You won't have a dime!'

'I don't want your goddamn money!' David yelled over his shoulder.

The front door slammed. Lucy stood there, shaking. The room was as silent as a tomb.

'You know, I believe he really doesn't,' Oliver said.

'Shut up, Oliver!' Lucy began to cry, huge convulsive sobs that sent her falling back into her chair. Oliver watched her for a moment, then pulled a handkerchief out of his pocket, and held it out to her.

'I only meant that money doesn't seem that important to him, at least at this point in his life,' Oliver said. 'Here, for God's sake.'

Lucy grabbed the handkerchief and mopped at her face.

'I can't pretend to understand him as you do, of course, Lucy dear,' Oliver said placidly, 'but it does seem to me that he has a different sort of . . . value system. It's touching, really. You can't hope to control him by cutting him out of the family will.'

'So what do you expect me to do, Oliver?' Lucy cried in irritation. 'Just sit back and let him ruin his life?'

'He's not a boy, Lucy. Maybe you should just accept this girl and—'

'No!' She grabbed Oliver's hand. 'You said he'd forget about her. Well, you were wrong, Oliver! She's trying to trap my David. God, she's probably already pregnant.' Her eyes focused on Oliver. 'You said you'd help, Oliver. You promised! I want you to help me get her out of his life.'

'Good Lord, Lucy, get a hold of yourself.'

Lucy gave Oliver's hand a hard jerk. 'You promised me, Oliver! You promised!'

He pulled his hand free, staring at her. 'All right, all right,' he said, leaning back away from her. He reached for his drink and drained it quickly. 'I'll do what I can,' he said flatly. He rose, looking down on Lucy. 'It's late. I should be going.'

Lucy didn't even look up at him. She was sitting, slightly slumped, her eyes staring vacantly at a far wall. Shaking his head, Oliver walked away, letting himself out of the apartment.

David caught up with Joey on the pavement outside the apartment building. He grabbed her, spinning her round to face him.

'Stop, stop!' he said. He crushed her to his chest, holding her. Gradually, she stopped crying. She raised her head to look up at him.

'I can't,' she said. 'I can't go through with it.'

'Yes, you can!' he said fiercely. '*We* can.'

'She hates me, David. I saw it. I heard it. She hates me. I don't want to be caught between the two of you like that!'

'Listen! Listen to me!' He held her face between his hands. 'It doesn't matter! It doesn't matter! I love you!'

Her eyes filled with tears. 'It does matter David! I can't let you cut yourself off from your mother!'

'Is it the money?' David asked. 'Do you think I care about that? Well, I don't Joëlle! I don't need it. We don't need it.'

'No, it's not that. It's . . . your mother is all you have, David. I know you don't get along right now, and I know I'm the reason.' David tried to silence her, but she shook her head. 'No, listen to me. You may say it doesn't matter now, but you love her, I know you do. And some day, you'll regret this. I can't let you cut yourself off from your family.'

'Are you saying you don't want to marry me?'

'No, no . . . I love you, David. I do want to marry you.'

'What then? What do you want, Joëlle?'

She sighed. 'I don't know. Time . . . a little time, I guess. This has all been so fast. You haven't even met my parents yet. I have my dancing. You said you want to start a new play. We can do all this and still get married. We have time, David.'

He took a deep breath, then another. He ran his hands through his hair. 'All right,' he said.

She shivered.

'Your coat,' David said suddenly. 'Where's your coat?'

'Up there,' she said.

'I'll go—'

'No,' she said quickly. 'Just take me home.'

Chapter Thirty-Eight

Oliver emerged from the building on Madison Avenue and stopped in the middle of the pavement. He pulled the paper from his coat pocket and unfolded it, holding it as if the startling words he had seen there just minutes ago might now, somehow, be erased by the bright glare of sunlight. But there it was, right there in black and white. A one-paragraph biography, easily obtained in a quick trip to the press office of the American Ballet. Oliver read it again, reliving the shock that had struck him just minutes ago upstairs.

Joëlle LeClerc was accepted on scholarship to the School of American Ballet when she was eighteen. She was apprenticed to the American Ballet for a brief period and taken into the corps de ballet. A year later, she danced in George Balanchine's *Orpheus and Eurydice*. Born in Switzerland, Miss LeClerc was raised in Ithaca, New York, where she trained with Gladys Schweitzer. Her real name is Joëlle Caras.

Caras. Oliver stared hard at the name, then at the name LeClerc. No, it was just too easy, it had to be a conicidence. The fact that the girl was born in Europe meant nothing. He had to be wrong. His imagination was running away with him.

He put the paper away, pulled his collar up and began to walk down Madison. He had gone to the ballet school on a whim, not really expecting to find anything he could use to appease Lucy. He was just looking for an excuse so he could tell her he had tried. For a while, he had stood at a door of a classroom, idly watching the dancers. Then he had gone to the press office and asked, casually enough, for information about Joëlle. The young clerk had been only too eager to hand over the biography to the eminent *New York Times* critic. When she saw the shock on Oliver's face after he read it, she asked if he needed to sit down a while. He had simply walked out, clutching the paper.

Now, walking on slowly, he was still stunned; his mind was a thousand miles away, decades in the past. He was in a different ballet studio, watching different dancers, many long gone, some dead. He was watching Cendrine the day she had auditioned for the opera company.

He stopped. Dead. She was dead, too. For all he knew, so was Jonathan.

He walked on, his mind back in the present again. But was their daughter alive? Was this girl Joëlle somehow their daughter? If it were true, it meant that David and Joëlle were half-brother and half-sister. If it were true, it was all the evidence needed to end their relationship. If it were true . . .

Oliver came to a corner and waited for the light to change. Across the street, he saw a phone booth. The light changed, and he went quickly to it. He dialled long-distance information.

'In Ithaca, New York, please,' he said. 'The number for a Jonathan Caras. I don't know the street.'

The operator gave him the number. Oliver replaced the receiver and leaned back against the booth's wall. Jonathan was alive. He hesitated, then dialled the number in Ithaca. After several rings, a woman answered.

'Is Mr Caras in, please?' Oliver asked.

'No, he's not. Who is this, please? This is Mrs Caras.'

'*Mrs* Caras. Oh . . . ah, my name is Mr Hale. I work in the press office of the American Ballet here in New York. Mrs Caras, we're updating our biographies on all the dancers – just a little thing we do every so often. Well, I need to get some information about Joëlle.'

'You should talk to her,' Marion said.

'Well, she's very busy, you see, rehearsing for a new role and all. Mr B. doesn't like us to bother the dancers. I thought you could just fill in the blanks for me. If you don't mind? Just a few questions.'

Marion paused. 'All right.'

'Well, we know Joëlle's father is named Jonathan Caras. But we don't have much information about her mother. I mean her *real* mother, of course. She was also a dancer, I understand?'

There was a long pause.

'Mrs Caras? Are you there?'

'Yes,' Marion said softly. 'Her mother was a dancer.'

'Do you by chance know her first name, Mrs Caras?'

'Cendrine . . . it was Cendrine LeClerc.'

Oliver gripped the telephone.

'If there's nothing else you need, Mr Hale,' Marion said, 'I'm very busy.'

'No, no – you've been very helpful. Thank you, Mrs Caras. A good day to you.'

Oliver hung up, his breath coming in short heaves. He felt suddenly light-headed, as if he were about to faint. For some moments, he couldn't move. Then, slowly, with some effort, he manoeuvred his bulky body out of the booth and started towards Park Avenue.

The taxi made its way up Park Avenue. David reached

across the seat for Joey's hand. 'You're nervous, aren't you?' he said.

'Yes.'

'She wouldn't have asked us both to come unless she's changed her mind,' David said.

'I hope you're right.'

He looked out of the taxi's window. 'She's not well,' he said. 'I never told you that, did I? I never really told you much about her, I guess.'

Joey glanced over at him. 'You never seemed to want to talk about her very much, or anyone in your family,' she said softly. 'Or yourself, really.' She paused. 'And you don't know much about me.' She paused. 'I was thinking about this a lot when I was away. we love each other, David, yet we don't really seem to know enough about each other.'

David looked earnestly at her. 'That's going to change. Everything's going to change now.' The taxi came to a stop. David looked up at the building. 'Let's go in,' he said.

The maid let them in, and David led Joey to the library. Lucy was standing at the fireplace, waiting for them. Oliver was off to the side, pouring himself a drink.

David did not bother to hide his annoyance at seeing Oliver. But before he could say anything, Lucy came forward and kissed his cheek. She stepped back to look at him and then at Joey. Her eyes locked on Joey with intense scrutiny.

'Sit down, please,' she said tonelessly and took a chair. Joey and David sat down warily on a sofa.

'Would you care for a drink, Miss LeClerc?' Lucy asked.

'No, thank you.'

'David?'

'Nothing for me, Mother.'

Oliver brought Lucy a martini. David saw the look that passed between Oliver and his mother before Oliver retreated to stand near the window, but he couldn't read it. He looked back at Lucy. Something peculiar was going on: she was too composed. He had seen the flattening effects of her sedatives at work before, but this was different.

'David,' Lucy said. 'There's something I need to tell you and Miss LeClerc. It concerns you both.' She paused, staring at Joey strangely. 'It seems . . .' Her gaze turned suddenly vacant, then confused. She looked to Oliver, unable to go on.

He stepped forward. 'Miss LeClerc – that's not your real surname, is it?' he asked politely.

David looked at Joey in surprise. Joey looked at David and back at Oliver. 'Not, it's not,' she said slowly. 'It's my mother's name. I use it because—'

'Your name is Caras,' Oliver said.

'Yes, that's right,' Joey said, now totally bewildered.

David's mouth dropped open. 'Caras?' he said to Joey. 'You never told me that. Caras is *my* name, too.'

Joey looked at him. 'But your name is Savage,' she said.

'No, my real father's name was Caras,' David said. 'Jonathan Caras.'

Joey's face at first looked only confused. Then, quickly, the colour drained from it. 'Oh, God,' she whispered. 'It's not possible.'

She stared at David. She felt light-headed and her stomach began to churn. David's face grew blurry as the room began to spin. 'That's my father,' she muttered. 'That's my father . . .'

David stared at her in alarm. 'Your father? Joëlle, what are you talking about?'

'Jonathan Caras is her father,' Oliver said.

David looked up at him.

'She's your sister, David,' Oliver said. 'Your half-sister.'

David glanced at Lucy, who looked back with unfocused eyes. 'You're crazy,' he said angrily to Oliver. 'Why would you say that?'

'It's the truth, David,' Oliver said.

David looked back at Joëlle, seeing the shock and disbelief on her face. 'Joëlle,' he said. 'You said your father was that man in France, you said—'

Joëlle started to cry.

A hand on his shoulder. 'We'll leave you alone,' Oliver said.

David heard a door close and it was quiet, except for Joëlle's crying. Oliver and Lucy were gone. Joëlle was standing at the window, her back to him. David felt physically weak. Slowly, he rose and went to her.

'Joëlle.' He touched her arm and she drew back, almost imperceptibly. Slowly, her tears subsided, but her expression, as she stared out of the window, was dazed. She stood very stiff, yet looked very fragile.

'Talk to me,' he said. 'Please.'

She didn't move.

'Joëlle,' he whispered, 'who is your father?'

She turned to face him. 'I don't know,' she said. 'I don't know . . . I don't know.'

He grabbed her by the shoulders. 'What do you mean, you don't know?'

'Alexander told me he wasn't my father . . . Jonathan told me he didn't know for sure if *he* was . . . I don't know, David, I don't know. No one knows for sure. There's no record of my birth anywhere. Oh, God, David, I don't know . . .'

'Then we—' He stopped himself.

Joëlle started to cry again.

His arms dropped from her shoulders and he took a step back from her. He stared at her face. Sister, he thought frantically, his *sister*, his own flesh and blood. *Flesh and blood*. An image flashed into his mind,

457

followed by a flood of sensations. The feel of her body against his, his lips against hers, of himself inside her. He looked into her eyes and saw her struggling with the same thoughts and sensations. He saw in her devastated face the same mix of revulsion and longing that he was now feeling. *Flesh and blood, flesh and blood* . . . And a single ugly word echoed in his head. *Incest . . . incest . . . incest.*

He wanted so badly to touch her. Nothing had changed between them – no, everything had changed. He felt tears sting his eyes. 'There's got to be way to find out the truth,' he said. 'There's got to be a—'

'There is no truth,' she said woodenly.

'Joëlle—'

'I . . . I've got to go.'

'Joëlle!' He reached for her.

She pulled away from him. 'I'm sorry, David,' she whispered, crying softly. 'I've got . . . to go.'

She ran by him. Hearing the door close, he remained rigid at the window, looking down. After a moment, he saw her emerge from the building and run quickly across the street; she was gone.

With a loud, guttural cry, he swung his arm blindly towards the window. His fist hit the lead glass. He swung again and again, sobbing. A sharp sound, like a shot, rang out and the heavy old glass cracked against his bloody fist. It was only then that he stopped.

'Jonathan?'

He turned away from the window back to the room. His eyes fell on Sumner and Katherine sitting on a sofa, and then went to Marion.

'You can't blame yourself,' Marion said softly. 'You had no way of knowing about this.'

'None of us did,' Sumner said. 'If I had known . . .' His voice trailed off, and he shook his head slowly. 'He's

458

a nice young man, Jonathan. When Joey introduced us to him, that was our only thought. A nice young man . . .'

Jonathan looked back out of the window at the dark street. 'I can't help thinking that it's my fault,' he murmured. 'She's hurt, and I can't help thinking it's my fault.'

Marion rose and went to Jonathan's side. 'It's no one's fault,' Marion said. 'It's just a terrible, sad, horrible coincidence.' She touched Jonathan's arm. 'Joey's strong. She'll survive this.'

'She's been through too much, Marion, too much.' He paused, turning his head away. 'I've done things wrong with her. I sent her to Alexander and he hurt her. I can't even tell her who her father is because I don't know for certain. And now this. I've hurt Joey . . . and David, I've hurt him, too. My son.' He shook his head. 'I wouldn't even recognize him in the street, for God's sakes.'

'This is not your fault,' Marion said firmly.

'It's my payment,' he said flatly, 'for things I did a long time ago.'

Sumner and Katherine exchanged glances. Marion looked back at them, then at Jonathan. 'I'm going to go up and check on Joey,' she said, and left the room. The study was quiet.

'Will you stay on with us for a while, Jonathan?' Sumner asked. 'You're welcome to, you know.'

Jonathan turned. 'You've both done enough already,' he said. 'I don't want to impose any more than I have. Besides, I think it might be good for Joey if I took her home for a while.'

Sumner nodded. The sound of the doorbell made him look towards the hall. A moment later, the maid came in.

'I'm sorry to interrupt, Mrs Briggs,' she said to Katherine. 'But there's someone to see Joëlle.'

'Not now, Jean,' Katherine said.

'It's her young man,' the maid said softly. 'Mr Savage.'

Katherine looked quickly at Jonathan. He seemed bewildered at first, then the name registered. 'Let him in,' Jonathan said, 'please.'

Katherine left and returned with a tall, slender young man at her side. David greeted Sumner with a polite but wary nod. He stood awkwardly holding his hat, looking distraught, as if he hadn't slept well. He gave Jonathan a quick but uninterested look, turned back to Katherine and cleared his throat, readying his small lie. 'Mrs Briggs, Joëlle and I had a little fight the other night, and I'd like to see her for a moment. Would you tell her I'm here?'

'David,' she said hesitantly, 'we know what happened.'

David looked first surprised, then deeply embarrassed.

'David,' Katherine said, 'there's someone here you should—' She couldn't go on and looked to Sumner for help.

Sumner came quickly to her side and took her arm. 'Let's leave them alone,' he said. They left, closing the door behind them, before David could say anything.

David looked back at Jonathan in confusion. Jonathan had not moved; he was staring intently at David's face.

David frowned at the stranger's blatant, questioning gaze. He glanced back at the door behind which Katherine and Sumner had disappeared, then ran his hand through his hair in agitation. 'What was that all about?' he said, more to himself than Jonathan. He looked again at Jonathan's rapt face, now feeling very uncomfortable. What the hell was the man staring at?

'What am I doing here?' David muttered, shaking his head, and turned to leave.

'Don't go,' Jonathan said quickly.

'What?'

'Don't go.'

David looked again at the strange man – at the man's eyes riveted on his own; at the man's mouth and nose; at the way he held his slender, tapered body, as if poised to move. There was something intimate, close, something hauntingly familiar in it all. He stared at each detail of the man's face and, suddenly, he saw himself. With a piercing cold stab, it came to him. 'It's you,' he said, his mouth slack with stupefaction.

Jonathan took a step forward. 'David . . .'

Hearing the strange man utter his name sent a jolt through him so powerful he almost reeled backward. He felt his entire body beginning to tighten, first his fists, then his arms, up into his chest until he felt he was choking. 'What are you doing here?' he said.

'I'm here to take Joëlle—'

'Take Joëlle?'

Jonathan hesitated, fearful at the overwrought tone in David's voice. Hurting, he was hurting so much, Jonathan realized suddenly, there was so much pain buried there behind those eyes. Lucy's eyes – oh, God! Lucy's face. But not just Lucy's. There was still something there of himself, there had to be.

'David?' he said softly.

'Go on, then,' David said suddenly. 'Take her. You've taken everything else from me. Now you've taken Joëlle.' He was trembling with rage. 'Go on, goddamn you!' he shouted. 'Take her!'

The outburst hit Jonathan like a slap in the face. He couldn't move. The door opened and Sumner appeared, followed by Katherine, brought by the shouting.

David stared at Jonathan. 'Goddamn you,' he muttered. 'Goddamn you!' He turned abruptly and ran past Katherine and Sumner.

The front door slammed. Jonathan stood frozen for a second, then hurried to the window, but the street was empty.

461

David walked for hours, oblivious to the cold and the lateness of the hour. He walked aimlessly, heading north but not knowing or caring where he was going. Finally, he hailed a cab.

By the time the cab let him off in front of the apartment on Park Avenue, it had started to snow. He stood outside the apartment, looking up at the lights, then he went in. In the silent apartment a clock chimed twice. Quietly, he made his way to his bedroom.

Once inside, he didn't bother to turn on the light. He pulled a suitcase out of the closet and went to the adjoining dressing room. He contemplated the neat rows of suits and polished shoes, the crisp white shirts still bound with their laundry bands – banker's clothes.

Returning to the bedroom, he pulled a case off the pillow, stuffed a handful of underwear, a sweater and a few other pieces of clothing inside. He paused, looking around. Nothing, there was nothing else he wanted. He left, closing the door.

He crept down the hall, pausing when he came to his mother's door. Carefully, he opened the door. He could see Lucy's sleeping form curled beneath the blanket. He closed the door.

He left the apartment, walking down Park to the corner. Turning his face up into the falling snow, he headed west.

Chapter Thirty-Nine

It was almost dusk, and a cool breeze, moist with spring, blew in through the open window near Jonathan's desk. The radio was playing a soothing Bach concerto. Jonathan set aside his paper and listened to it for a few moments.

It was growing chilly. He reached over and closed the window. Joey was coming up the walk with Elton, and he watched her until she disappeared into the house.

A year had passed since they had returned from New York. At first, Joey had been so withdrawn and quiet that he and Marion had taken her to see a psychiatrist at the university. But finally, they decided the only remedy was rest and time – time to forget David. Gradually, Joey had emerged from her depression. She had even begun taking an occasional ballet class at Gladys Schweitzer's studio. For months now, she had not mentioned New York or David. She was quieter, it seemed to Jonathan, but Marion had been right. Joey was bruised, but she would survive this. What was strange was that the further into the light she came, the more into his own darkness Jonathan retreated.

With a sigh, he resumed his reading, a report of the English-deparment tenure committee. He hated this part of his job, hated the petty politics. When he became department head, he had not really foreseen how the

463

administrative routine would wear down his soul. Teaching had been different, it had been a balm of sorts after he had left the newspaper business. Working with young people, showing them the power and beauty of the written word, trying to strike within them the same spark that had burned so bright in himself once. But when the department-head position became available, he had been talked into accepting it. And now he felt trapped, knowing he had chosen the wrong road, knowing he couldn't go back.

The revelation had come to him suddenly last winter. He had gone down to the *Ithaca Journal* office one afternoon to place a classified advertisement to sell his old Studebaker. He had never been in the *Journal* office before, and as he stood at the desk, giving the woman the information for the ad, a smell came sharply to him. It was ripe, like a mix of moss and oil, and it sent a stab of recognition through him. Only one thing in the world smelled like that; a newspaper fresh off the press. The smell triggered a yearning in him so intense that he left without completing his business.

He stared at the tenure-committee report, not seeing the words. His work, he knew, was only a symbol of something deeper. He had wanted to be a great writer, yet he was an academic bureaucrat. He had known great, passionate love, yet had let it slip away. He had a son, yet had lost him. And the mistakes of his past had come back to damage his daughter, for whom he had wanted only happiness. He had lived sixty-seven years, travelled the world, done things most men only dreamed of. Yet sometimes he felt ignorant and lost.

He heard sounds coming from downstairs. Marion setting the table for dinner. The Bach concerto gave way to the news. John Steinbeck had won the Pulitzer Prize for *The Grapes of Wrath*. German bombers had smashed Norwegian towns in a blitzkrieg, and the war in Europe

464

was spreading. Fifty thousand American volunteers were being trained as air pilots. The Maple Leaves had beaten the Rangers to win the Stanley Cup . . .

Jonathan switched off the radio and went downstairs.

'Dad?'

Jonathan looked up from his book at Joey. She was wearing a jacket and was holding his hat and coat.

'Come take a walk with me,' she said.

He set his book aside. 'All right,' he said.

They made their way through the neighbourhood streets and down the hill. They were almost by the playground before Joey spoke. 'I need you to do something for me, Dad,' she said.

'Anything. You know that.'

'I need you and Mom to stop worrying about me.'

Jonathan stopped and faced her. 'Joey . . .'

'I'm all right, Dad,' she said. 'Really. I'm all right.'

Her face, lit from above by the streetlight, was sombre and determined. She started towards the playground, and Jonathan followed. They sat down on the bleachers.

'Your mother and I—' he began. He paused. 'It was hard for us, Joey, seeing you hurt so badly.'

'It's not your fault,' she said.

'What?'

'It's not your fault, Dad. I know that you think it is, somehow, but it's not. It just . . . happened. And I'll get over it. I'll get over it.'

He scanned her profile. She's changed, he thought sadly. She's so much older now.

'There's something else I wanted to talk to you about,' she said. 'Something I've been thinking about for a while.' She paused. 'I think I've got to go away.'

He gaped at her. 'Go away? What do you mean?'

Her gaze remained fixed on the dark baseball diamond. 'I have to get back to my dancing, Dad.'

He felt his throat tighten. He didn't want her to go back to New York.

'I got a letter the other day,' she said. 'The company's been disbanded. The opera didn't renew Mr B.'s contract, so he's gone off to work on Broadway.' Her lips turned up in a rueful half-smile. 'The rest of us have to fend for ourselves, I guess.' The smile faded. 'It's just as well. I don't want to go back to New York.'

'Then where?' Jonathan asked, fearing the answer.

She still wouldn't look at him. 'I heard from a friend of mine in the company. She's got a corps job with the Sadler's Wells Ballet in London. She said I could get in there, so I wrote them a letter. They want me to come.'

Jonathan let out a deep sigh. 'Oh, Joey, Joey . . .'

'Dad, please. I need to get back to dancing. If I don't, I'll go crazy.'

'Not London, Joey. It's too far away and there's a war going on.'

'There's nowhere else. There are no good companies in this country, no place I can go to keep learning, to keep moving forward. And I want to get away, far away . . . for a while, at least.'

'I won't let you go, Joey.'

Her eyes met his steadily. 'I'm not asking your permission, Dad,' she said softly.

In the moonlight, he could see her eyes – Cendrine's eyes. He felt a crushing heaviness in his chest. It was worse than that first time he had seen her go off to New York, worse even than the day she had left for Paris. Joey, little Joey, gone for ever, a woman in her place. A woman now seeking her own life somewhere far beyond him.

'I think it would be good for you and Mom, too, if I went,' Joey said.

'What makes you say that?' Jonathan asked.

'Things haven't been right since I came home. I mean, this whole thing has been hard on all of us,' she said. 'I

466

just get the feeling that you two need to be alone for a while.' She hesitated. 'You don't seem very happy.'

'Your mother and I are fine, Joey, it's—'

'No, I mean you, Dad.'

He glanced at her in surprise, but said nothing. He looked out at the dark diamond. 'When do you think you might go?' he said quietly, to deflect the focus off himself.

'In a week or two.'

He couldn't bring himself to speak.

'I know you understand,' she said. 'I know you understand how important it is to go after whatever it is you want out of life, not to settle for less. You taught me that, Dad.'

'Yes, I did.'

She was quiet for a moment, then added softly, 'I tried to tell that to David.'

'David?' The name sent a small jolt through him. He looked at her and saw tears forming at the corners of her eyes.

'David wanted to write,' she said. 'But something kept stopping him.'

'Write,' Jonathan said, almost to himself. He felt his throat constrict. 'He wanted to write?'

Joey nodded. She saw the brightness in Jonathan's eyes before he could look away. 'Do you want to hear about him?' she asked.

'Yes,' Jonathan said. And he sat motionless on the bleachers in the moonlight listening to his daughter tell him about his son.

David stared at the Victorian house. He was standing across the street from it, out of the beam of the streetlight, shielded by the dark. He glanced at his watch; it was after nine. A light came on in an upstairs window and he watched intently as a figure moved across the drawn shade. Then, the light went out.

Was it Joëlle? Was that her room? He shifted from one foot to the other to ease his tired legs. He had been watching the house since seven that morning, but had not seen one sign of her. Just an older woman – her mother, he guessed – who came out once to sweep the leaves off the veranda. She had looked at him, then gone back inside.

He took a few steps into the light to get a better view into the living room. Two people inside, or was it three? He couldn't tell. Where was she?

He leaned against a tree and pulled a pack of Luckies from his jacket. He lit one, cupping his hands against the wind. His eyes returned to the house.

What am I doing here? he asked himself. What had possessed him back in Phoenix? One moment, he had been sitting at a desk in a hotel room, pencil in hand, staring at a blank sheet of paper. The next moment, he had bolted. It wasn't just that he had been unable to write that night. In the six months he had wended his way aimlessly across the country and the time he had lived in Phoenix, he had written nothing worth keeping. What had he been thinking as he sat silent in the cars and trucks of strangers, travelling east, through the long days and nights? What had he expected to find in Ithaca? What did he expect to gain?

The wind blew, loosing a rain of dead leaves down on him. He pulled up his collar, his eyes fixed on the house. Joëlle . . . God help me, Joëlle. I can't have you. And I can't stay away.

Marion stood at the window, holding the curtain aside, looking out at the street.

'What are you looking at?' Jonathan asked.

'There's a man out there,' Marion said. 'He's been there since this morning.'

Jonathan came to the window. 'I don't see anyone.'

'There, in front of the Belkins' house.'

Jonathan saw the figure standing in the shadows. 'I'll go run him off.'

'He's probably just looking for a handout, Jonathan. His clothes are shabby.'

Jonathan had already gone to the front door. He switched on the porch light, stepped outside and peered out into the dark. 'Hey, you there,' he called out. 'What do you want?'

David didn't move. He looked hard at Jonathan, then dropped his cigarette, grinding out the butt. Slowly he crossed the street. As he came up towards the house, shoulders hunched, his unshaven face took shape in the light. Jonathan stared at him in shock as David came to a stop at the foot of the steps.

'I came to see Joëlle,' he said.

It took Jonathan a moment to find his voice. 'She's not here,' he said.'

David's eyes narrowed in suspicion. 'I want to see her,' he said evenly.

'I told you, she's not here. She's in England.' Jonathan paused. 'It's the truth, I swear it is.'

Marion came out onto the porch, drawing up short when she recognized David.

David looked at her, back at Jonathan, then at nothing in particular, his face reflecting his confusion and indecision.

'Come in for a minute,' Marion said suddenly. 'You look exhausted.' David and Jonathan both looked at her. 'Please, David, come in and have some coffee at least.'

David came up the steps, passing Jonathan without a look. Marion led him into the living room, Jonathan following behind. David stood awkwardly in the middle of the room until Marion told him to sit down. Jonathan stood at a distance, his eyes taking in David's worn trousers and sweater and the soiled summer blazer.

He focused finally on David's wan face.

'I'll make some coffee,' Marion said quickly and left.

Neither man could think of anything to say. David perched on the edge of a chair, elbows on knees, staring at his clasped hands.

'You shouldn't have come,' Jonathan said.

'I know,' David said, without looking up.

'I'm glad you did.'

David looked up.

'It gives me a chance to talk, to try to—'

David cut him off. 'We don't have anything to say to each other.'

Jonathan came around to sit on the sofa opposite David. 'I called your mother a couple of months ago to find out how you were. The person who answered the phone told me you had left, and they didn't know where you were.'

'Mother? How is she?' David asked flatly.

'I don't know. She wouldn't talk to me.'

Marion came in with the coffee, and handed David a cup. He thanked her and took a drink, cradling it between his palms. Marion looked at Jonathan and went back into the kitchen. There was a long silence.

'David,' Jonathan said, 'I wish you'd give me a chance.'

'You had your chance twenty years ago,' he said evenly.

'Give me another,' Jonathan said quietly.

David set the cup down on a table, shaking his head. 'You have a lot of nerve, mister,' he said. 'You run out on a wife. You run out on a son.' He looked straight at Jonathan. 'You run out on *me*. I don't hear from you – not one damn word – for twenty years! And you expect me to forget about it?' He laughed softly, bitterly. 'God, you have a lot of nerve.'

Jonathan stared at him. 'I hurt you. I know that.'

'Why?' David said. 'The question's been eating at me for years, and I never thought I'd hear the answer. Well, that's all I want to hear from you now. *Why?*'

Jonathan looked at the floor. 'Because I didn't love your mother,' he said softly. 'I loved someone else.'

'Oh, for God's sake!'

Jonathan looked back at David. 'I don't expect you to understand. I didn't understand it myself at the time. It was something that went beyond me, David. This woman . . . I was obsessed with her. That's the only way I can explain it.' He paused. 'And when she died, when I lost her, nothing else mattered. I couldn't work, I couldn't think; even breathing was an effort. For a long time, I didn't care about anything at all.'

David was glowering at him.

Jonathan rose. 'Wait here,' he said.

He went into another room and returned with a small bundle of papers. He held it out to David.

'What's this?' David asked.

'Letters. All the letters I wrote to you after I left. Your mother sent them all back.'

David stared at the bundle but would not take it. Finally, Jonathan dropped his hand. David rose slowly. 'I have to go,' he said. He started towards the door and opened it.

'Wait,' Jonathan said.

Marion was with him now. They both came forward. 'At least tell us where you're going,' Marion said.

'Fort Dix in Alabama. I got a low number in the lottery.'

Jonathan stared at him, feeling a knot form in his throat.

David gave Jonathan a final look that said nothing, then pushed open the screen door. He went quickly down the steps and started down the walk.

'David!' Jonathan called out. David turned, and

Jonathan came down the steps.

'Take them,' Jonathan said, holding out the bundle of letters. 'Please.'

David looked at the letters, then back at Jonathan. He hesitated, then took them, stuffing them inside his jacket. He walked off into the dark.

Chapter Forty

Joey hurried through the dark London streets, shoulders hunched against the misty rain. It was only seven but, as usual, the performance had finished early to allow everyone to get home before the blackout. Just in case tonight was the night that the bombs began to fall.

Tonight she had lingered at the theatre, talking with some friends, and now she felt a tickle of fear creep up her back as she made her way to her neighbourhood. She walked near the kerb, afraid of someone jumping out from a doorway and grabbing her. The ink-black night seemed sinister tonight. No lights beckoning from windows, no headlights, not even a moon. But moonless nights were safer. It made the city less of a target for the Germans.

She walked on, thinking about how naïve she and the other dancers had been about the war. When she arrived in May, the Nazis had occupied Norway and Belgium. But the other dancers were blasé, calling it 'the phony war' because England had not been attacked. Joey believed them, and when Jonathan and Marion's letters began to take on an urgent tone, begging her to come home, she wrote back that she was safe.

The phony war was soon over and the horror spread quickly. Though fierce air battles raged over the Channel and the English countryside, not one Nazi bomb hit London at first. The company embarked on a short tour of military camps. It was gruelling, seven performances a week, often on dangerous makeshift stages. The soldiers, looking for something racier than *Les Sylphides*, would sometimes bang loudly on their seats. More often than not, Joey returned to her shoddy hotel room discouraged, with barely enough energy left to choke down her only meal of the day; cold meat, apple pie and hot tea.

When the company returned to London, life settled into a more satisfying routine. The schedule remained hard, and as good food became scarce, life outside the theatre turned drab. But inside, the company closed in on itself like a family. Most of the male dancers were called up to do national service, and mere boys from the school took their place, eager but inept. Girls often fainted during performances, weak from poor nutrition and overwork. Admirers turned up backstage bearing not flowers, but little gifts of precious sugar, chocolates or butter. New tights became rare, and old ones with runs were sent out for mending again and again. But every night, six days a week, the magic was recreated anew on the stage, and every seat was filled.

That was what sustained Joey. No matter how dreary things became, no matter how afraid she sometimes felt and how lonely she was for home, the dancing always kept her going.

It kept her also from thinking about David. When she read the letter from Jonathan telling her that David had come to the house, she had been stunned. The shock was doubled when she read that David had been drafted into the army. She tried not to think about him; it was the main reason she often lingered at the theatre. Too often, when she arrived back in her dark flat, David's memory was there waiting for her.

She reached Piccadilly tube station and quickened her pace. As usual, there was a rowdy, drunken crowd swarming around. Last night, men had whistled and made remarks, so now she detoured to the other side and, head lowered, hurried on.

She didn't see the man coming the other way and smacked hard into his chest. She cried out and reeled back, holding her head.

'Oh, geez, I'm sorry. Are you all right?'

She wavered. 'Yes, yes . . .' she murmured.

'Are you sure?'

She felt him grip her arm and looked up. A young man with unthreatening eyes and wearing a uniform, dark blue, almost black from the rain.

'You don't look so good,' he said. 'You're not going to faint, are you?'

'No, no, really. I'm fine. I'm sorry. I wasn't watching where I was going.'

'Hey, you're American,' he said, smiling. 'So am I.'

She looked again at his uniform, but it was that of the Royal Air Force.

'Where are you from?' he asked eagerly.

'New York,' she said cautiously. 'Ithaca.'

'No kidding! I'm from New Jersey. Teaneck. We're almost neighbours!'

It was raining harder. Her head hurt and she wanted to get home.

'Listen, this's my fault,' the young man said. 'Let me buy you a drink to apologize.'

'I don't think so,' Joey said.

'Aw, come on.'

Joey shook her head.

The young man smiled politely. 'Look, I know you're not interested in being picked up. I mean, if you were, you wouldn't have gone out of your way to avoid those guys over there. It's just, well, it's been a while since I heard someone speaking real English.' He smiled, a nice smile. 'Please? One drink, and then I'll make sure you get home safe.'

Joey hesitated, then smiled. 'All right,' she said. 'One cup of tea.'

When they were seated in a nearby café, Joey took stock of the young man sitting across from her. He was in his early twenties, blonde and stocky, with clear blue eyes and a broad, pleasant face. He was very talkative, and she listened quietly to him as he told her about his friends back home, how he had made all-state fullback in his senior year of high school, and how he had worked in his father's garage and then left to go to California, where he learned to fly first crop-dusting planes, then mail transports, taking lessons and working his way into commercial work.

'And now I'm here, flying for Her Majesty,' he said proudly. He tapped the patch on his upper sleeve. 'Eagle Squadron.'

'But you're an American,' she said stupidly.

'There's only twenty of us,' he said. 'When I was working in Oklahoma, I heard these guys were getting together to come here and volunteer. Man, I was the first in line. The Brits were glad to have us. Roosevelt doesn't like it much; we could lose our citizenship. But it won't happen. Too many other people think like me, that we should be here.'

Joey just gazed at him. He seemed, suddenly, very young. 'Have you been involved in any fighting?' she asked softly.

He shook his head. 'Not yet.' Then he grinned broadly. 'But it'll happen. The way things are going, everyone's gonna be in it.'

Joey looked away, thinking of David.

'So what are you doing here?' he asked suddenly.

'I'm a dancer,' she said.

'Wow. No kidding. What, like belly dancing?'

She smiled. 'Ballet.'

'No shit. Oops, geez, sorry!'

She laughed. 'That's okay.'

He launched into another story, this one about his fellow pilots; and she sipped her tea. She felt herself relaxing, amused by the man's self-absorbed chatter. Her mind began to drift, and she found herself trying to remember the last time she had even talked to a young man. For several months now, her world had been populated only by the pubescent boys in the company and the old men who ran it. Men of her own age were rare in London these days. And before that, she had been in seclusion in Ithaca. She glanced at the young flyer, who was absorbed in his tale. When was the last time she had felt the simple pleasure of a man's company? When was the last time she had really felt feminine, not the curiously asexual female creature she had become? When was. . .?

David. He was there again, suddenly, filling her head.

She stared across the table at the polished buttons of the flyer's uniform. David – he was wearing a uniform now, too. Where was he right this moment? Was he sitting across a table from someone? Was he thinking about her?

Why was she thinking of him? It was wrong. Wrong. Wrong! Why couldn't she stop? She stared at the shiny buttons until they grew blurry. Her cup clattered onto its saucer.

'Hey, are you—' the flyer said in alarm.

'I have to go,' she murmured, rising quickly. She grabbed her coat and dance bag and ran out of the door.

'They're leaving. Everyone's leaving.'

Alexander stood at the windows of the *Herald* office, staring down at the crowds in the Rue de l' Opéra.

'Of course they are,' Harry Parkyn answered without looking up from the proof he was correcting. 'So should you.'

Alexander's eyes did not leave the swarm of cars and people below. 'I can't,' he whispered. 'I can't.'

Harry looked at Alexander's back, then, shaking his head, returned to his work. A few minutes later, he brought the proof to Alexander at the window.

'Want to check it?' he asked.

Alexander took the proof of the *Herald* front page. His eyes ran listlessly over the headlines, focusing on the biggest, blackest one.

REYNAUD GOVERNMENT FLEES TO TOURS
AS NAZIS REDOUBLE DRIVE FOR PARIS

He handed it back to Harry. 'Are there enough men left even to print this?' he asked.

'Barely. But there are no trucks to deliver it.'

Alexander turned his gaze back to the window. The day had begun calmly enough, a beautiful June day. Then word had got out that the government of Paul Reynaud was abandoning the city in anticipation of the Germans' arrival. The Nazis were a mere fifteen miles away. The uneasy calm of the last few months was over. And now, for the first time, Alexander was thinking the unthinkable. The Germans were going to take Paris.

Late that night, he left the *Herald* building. He walked the streets, staring at the kerbside piles of household goods, waiting to be piled in cars, taxis, trucks, wheelbarrows, baby carriages, whatever vehicles of escape could be found. Despite the hour, the streets were filled with grim-faced people, all heading south. It was as if everyone knew the city was now lost.

Alexander turned down the Champs-Elysées, walking under a silent marquee of a cinema that advertised *You*

Can't Take It With You. Once home, he fell into a deep sleep, knowing that the next day he didn't need to get up early. There would be no reason to go back to the *Herald* office.

Four days later, on a sunny, clear day, the German army entered Paris. Alexander stood with Harry outside his apartment building, watching the weary but triumphant soldiers march by. He watched as the French people wept, many turning their backs on the scene. He watched, his own sense of shame choking him, as the horses clattered through the Arc de Triomphe, the shrine to France's unknown soldier.

'You can't stay here any longer,' Harry said. 'It's dangerous for you now.'

Alexander stared at the soldiers.

'Your editorials made you a target,' Harry said. 'You can't count on the Germans being tolerant. You must leave Paris now.'

Alexander's eyes glistened. 'All right,' he said.

The village of Peille was a poor place, an eyrie of old buildings clinging to the mountains above Nice, just ten miles from the Italian border. Alexander had chosen the place because it was so remote, austere and insignificant.

He took up residence in an old farmhouse just outside the village, bringing almost none of his possessions with him from Paris. Just some clothes, a few books, a cache of brandy and a shortwave radio. Each night, he sat numbly listening to the BBC broadcast. The French signed an armistice with Germany that disarmed and demobilized its army. The country was divided into two parts, with the north occupied by the Germans. He listened to Churchill's eloquent pleas to keep fighting against Hilter. 'If we fail, the whole world and all that we have known and cared for will sink into the abyss of a new dark age.'

All summer, he remained secluded. Occasionally, he ventured out, going down to Nice, but he saw too many things that turned his stomach; resigned apathetic faces or, once, French officers toasting the German victory with champagne at the railroad station. He limited his travel to weekly trips to La Turbie, where he would sit for hours at the Roman ruins, looking down at the Mediterranean.

At the farmhouse, he drowned himself in drink, eating whatever food the housekeeper from the village fixed for him. The old woman was the only person who ever saw him. Alexander had no urge to mix with the rest of the villagers, and they were equally wary of him. Living in their fierce outpost, after enduring centuries of would-be subjugators, the people of Peille were suspicious of all outsiders, be they Nazis or Parisians.

It was September before Alexander saw a human being other than the old woman. One afternoon, while sitting outside the old stone house in a semi-haze of drink, Alexander saw a man standing outside the iron gate. The man was looking intently at Alexander. Alexander walked down to the gate. The man was about fifty and was wearing a badly soiled suit.

'What do you want?' Alexander asked.

The man looked at him warily, as if trying to decide something. 'To be allowed to sleep in your barn,' he said. 'For just one night. Please.'

Alexander frowned, trying to place the man's oddly accented French. 'Where are you going?'

'Spain,' the man said. 'I lost everything when the Nazis came through Alsace.' He paused. 'I'm a Jew.'

With an unsteady hand, Alexander unlocked the gate. 'Come into the house,' he said.

After that, a slow but steady stream of refugees found its way to the farmhouse. Refugees from the north, half-starved and dead tired; Jews whose property had been confiscated; people branded 'enemies of the Reich', fleeing the persecution of the Gestapo for the safety of Spain. Alexander offered food and shelter to all those who appeared at his gate.

Word spread in Peille of his actions, and one night, a small group of men from the village appeared at his door. 'We're here to invite you to join our group,' one of them told him.

'Group? What group?' Alexander asked.

'Le Cercle.'

Le Cercle was a loose gathering of local men, opposed to the German occupation, who were trying to organize the haphazard network of escape routes into Spain and devise ways to disrupt the Nazis' presence. Alexander had no interest in joining, but he allowed the men to gather round his radio each night for the BBC broadcasts. He listened to their vociferous debates with a sad apathy. What he did for the refugees was simple kindness. What else could be done? What the men of Le Cercle did was just petty acts of violence born of defiance or despair. It was hopeless.

He looked at their ruddy, rapt faces as they listened to the radio: Honoré the grocer, César the butcher, and Fabron, the gentle priest who spent his time gathering herbs in the hills. What good could these ignorant men do? What could any of them do?

The voice of Charles de Gaulle filled the room. 'Whatever happens, the flame of French resistance must not go out, and it will not go out.'

Hopeless, Alexander thought, it's all hopeless.

One day, Fabron asked Alexander to accompany him on his usual walk up into the hills.

'You think we're all just old fools, don't you?' the priest said as they walked.

'Yes,' Alexander answered.

The priest bent to pick some thyme. 'At least we have

481

something to believe in. You have nothing. You are like a dead man.'

'Yes,' Alexander said.

The priest looked him in the eye. 'If you will do something now to help me,' he said, 'perhaps I can help you.'

There was something in the priest's eyes that touched Alexander, in a way he had not felt in a long time. 'What do you want?' he asked.

'Come with me,' the priest said. And he turned to go further up the hill.

It was three days before Alexander and Fabron returned. They had made their way to Italy, across the ten miles of treacherous mountain paths, with the help of upland shepherds. They had established contact with a band of Italian partisans who were fighting Fascism. So began Le Cercle's role in the *réseau*, the network, as a conduit passing on information about Italian troop movements to contacts in Monte Carlo. Alexander soon became a functioning member of Le Cercle. If it wasn't something to believe in, it was at least something to keep him alive.

Chapter Forty-One

The rain beat steadily against the window. Cendrine sat in her usual chair by the window, watching the cars and people on King Street below. Seen through the rain-streaked window, the cars and people were reduced to smudges of muted colour and blurs of motion, distorted and unreal.

She saw a patch of bright blue and knew it was Mrs Bristol's umbrella. It was four o'clock; that was when the old woman returned home from Mass. The routine had never varied, not once in the last ten years. Even after the war had begun, the woman still had not missed one day.

Fifteen minutes, half an hour passed. Cendrine waited for the sound of footsteps on the stairs and the turn of the key in the lock that always announced Roland coming home for dinner. But there was only the sound of the rain. She picked up the hem of the dress she had been sewing; after a few moments, she set it aside.

Why was she feeling so depressed today? Was it because the rain had been so relentless lately? She couldn't even remember the last time she had been out of the apartment. Roland used to take her out for dinner once in a while, but the rationing had curtailed that. Sometimes, on Friday nights, Roland would insist that she go with him to the pub. He would drink with his small group of friends, and she would sit quietly at his side, watching the crowd, sipping a pint of beer. But she hadn't even done that for weeks now.

Was it the war? Was that why she couldn't seem to concentrate on anything? Was that why she suddenly didn't seem to care about anything? Was that why Alexander had been in her thoughts lately? The day she had heard the news about Paris falling, she had cried. She had cried for Alexander, wondering if he were still alive, but mainly, she had cried for herself. She had lived in London for more than twenty years, yet it was only at that moment that she had been able to admit to herself how much she missed France.

She picked up the dress in her lap. She had to get some work done. The woman was coming by the next day for her final fitting, and there were two others waiting for their alterations to be finished. Slowly, mechanically, her fingers moved, pulling needle and thread through fabric.

What right did she have to be depressed? So many others had lost more than she had because of the war. She could see it in Mrs Bristol's face every time she returned from church after praying for her dead son. She could see it in the face of the young woman downstairs every time she came back from visiting her children who had been evacuated to the country for safety.

Her own life was comfortable enough. The sewing kept her busy and brought in a little money to supplement what Roland made in his painting business. She had started sewing six years ago just for something to do, but neighbours were soon asking her to make things for them, and eventually word spread further. Now she had a long list of clients, many wealthy women who all told their friends about the wonderful French seamstress in the East End who could fashion beautiful custom dresses like nothing one could find in shops. Cendrine knew the women pitied her. She could always see it in the face of a new customer as she first entered the flat, her eyes flicking over the wheelchair and then back, discreetly, to Cendrine's face. They pitied her, but she steeled herself against it. That was why the sewing had become important to her. It gave her a small feeling of pride and independence, something she had not had in a long time.

The rain grew heavier, beating so hard on the roof that Cendrine didn't hear the door open. Roland took off his raincoat and hat and came into the sitting room.

'Cendrine?'

She turned. 'Oh, I didn't hear you come in,' she said.

Roland glanced at the untouched sewing in her lap. 'Did you have a busy morning?' he asked.

'Not really.'

He went through the room into the kitchen, put the kettle on and returned to the sitting room. 'We're a little low on things,' he called out. 'There was no butter again today at the market, so I used up both our egg coupons.'

'I'm not really hungry,' Cendrine said distractedly, turning back to the window.

The clattering of pans filled the silence. In the alcove off the sitting room, Roland set the small round table, and returned to the kitchen to bring out the dinner of boiled eggs and sausage. He waited for Cendrine to move, but when she didn't, he went to her.

'You're going to eat,' he said gently. 'And not in that damn chair.' He held out his hand and helped her to her feet. She took her place at the table and he sat down opposite her. He unfolded his napkin, stuffed it in the collar of his shirt and began to eat.

After a moment, Cendrine picked up her fork and took a bite of the ersatz sausage, the only meat available since rationing began. She grimaced slightly.

'Breadcrumbs in battledress,' Roland said with a smile.

'You didn't have to come home today in all this rain,' she said. 'I could have managed.'

'I know what your idea of managing is,' Roland said. 'A cup of tea and a biscuit.' He went to the kitchen, returning to place a cup of tea at Cendrine's plate. She regarded the cup and saucer for a moment. It was a beautiful setting: Spode china, a delicate pattern of violets on cream white. It had been a gift from Roland the year they moved to London.

She was surprised to feel a sudden sting of tears and kept her eyes on the cup, unable to bring herself to look up at Roland. It wasn't often that she indulged in self-pity, but for the last few days, she had been unable to shake it off. A single sentence kept running through her head: It wasn't fair. It wasn't fair.

It wasn't fair to Roland, especially. He had sacrificed so much of his life for her. He had made huge sacrifices that had started the day he had brought her to London. He had got her into a hospital to cure her drug dependency; he had found the flat in the East End behind the docks. It was a dreary neighbourhood, but it was all they could afford and it was right on a bus line that led to the hospital where she went for therapy for her hip degeneration. Roland had worked long hours to afford the therapy that had helped her regain some mobility.

And he had made innumerable small sacrifices. In those terrible early years of her recovery, he had helped bath her and dress her as if she were a child, and had sat with her when she cried in pain and despair. Talking to her, holding her, teasing her, cajoling her, he had done whatever it took to stave off the depression. He had been there, always.

Cendrine often felt she was a burden. Roland had never had a woman in his life, and had given up any chance of having his own family, just so he could be there to care for her.

Now, things were better. She could walk with a cane and could manage the tasks of daily life on her own. Yet the small sacrifices went on. He still liked to come home each day to fix her dinner, after which he would return to work well into the evening.

She held onto the violet cup, flooded with sudden remorse. What right did she have to feel so sorry for herself? She glanced up at Roland. He was nearly sixty now, and he looked older. She sighed inwardly, thinking how dreadful she must look; she was only a year older. She had long ago given up her notions of vanity. She relied on an unvaried wardrobe of simple dark dresses that she made herself, and wore her long hair pulled back in a chignon. Long ago, she had banished all mirrors from the flat. It was one thing to look down and see her legs; she couldn't avoid that. But she had no desire to confront the loss of her beauty.

'So, what are you working on today?' Roland asked.

She knew his question was his usual ploy to jog her out of her lethargy. She managed a smile. 'Letting out Mrs Pimm's cocktail dress again,' she said. 'She's put on another five pounds. I wonder where she's getting the food.'

Roland smiled. 'More?' he asked, gesturing to her tea.

'No, save it. We're getting low.' She smiled wryly.

They were silent for some time, both listening to the rain. Roland noticed Cendrine discreetly rubbing her hip. 'It's bothering you today, isn't it?' he said. 'Is that why you're using the chair? The doctor said that you don't need it, that the more you walk, the better—'

'It's the rain,' Cendrine interrupted.

He was watching her face intently. 'You've been kind of low lately,' he said. 'Do you want to talk about it?'

She shook her head and busied herself with her cup. He shrugged, got up abruptly and went to his room.

Returning, he placed a small envelope on the table between them.'

'What's that?' Cendrine asked.

He pushed it towards her. 'It's for you,' he said. 'It's your birthday present, but I think you should have it now.'

She looked at the envelope, slowly picked it up and extracted two small pieces of cardboard. Her brows knit into a small frown, then her mouth fell open in stunned surprise.

'Tickets . . . for Covent Garden?' she asked.

'To the ballet. I don't know how good it is, but the box-office fellow said it's sold out every night.'

Cendrine stared at the tickets, shaking her head. 'Roland, I told you before, I can't . . .'

'Yes, you can.'

She looked up, tears in her eyes.

'I won't let you put me off this time, Cendrine,' Roland pressed.

'Roland . . .'

'No. I won't listen to any more of your excuses about why you can't go to the ballet. I hate seeing you sitting up here making dresses for those stupid women. I want you to make yourself a pretty dress. Because next Saturday, we're going to the ballet.'

She set the tickets down. 'It's been so long,' she whispered. 'I don't know if I could stand it.'

'Well, it's time you found out.' Roland got up, cleared the dishes and came back. 'I have to get back to work,' he said, pulling on his coat. He kissed her cheek. 'I'll be home early. Get started on your dress. And don't make it black, for God's sake. Make it . . . make it blue, light blue.'

The door closed and the room was quiet except for the rain. Cendrine sat motionless at the table, staring at the tickets for several minutes. Then she turned her chair towards a closet. She sorted through the bolts of fabric inside, and finally pulled out one that she had hoarded. She ran her fingers slowly across the precious silk; then she reached up and ran her fingers across her cheek and through her hair.

She set the silk aside and went out into the hall. 'Mrs Bristol! Mrs Bristol!' she called out, rapping on her neighbour's door.

Moments later; the woman appeared, startled. 'Cendrine, what is it, dear? Do you need something?'

Cendrine looked up at her. 'A mirror,' she said softly. 'May I borrow a mirror?'

On Saturday night, Cendrine walked into Covent Garden, leaning on her cane and Roland's arm. He guided her carefully through the crowd and down the aisle, then went back to the lobby to get two programmes. Cendrine sat by herself, watching the last of the crowd trickle in, her eyes focusing on the women's dresses. She adjusted the neckline of her own pale-blue dress, wondering if she had made it too low. That was the fashion now; she knew that from the issues of *Vogue* her customers brought to show her what styles they wanted.

Her hand went up to pat her hair, and she thought back to that moment when she had first looked at herself in Mrs Bristol's hand mirror. The shock had taken her breath away. She had half expected, half hoped, to see the woman she had left behind in Iseltwald. In her mind, she had frozen herself at that age. But the woman she saw in the mirror looked old. Her once luminous skin had become lined and her white-blonde hair had turned into a mixture of grey and ashen yellow. She had cried, seeing herself as she really was. And then she had stopped, determined to change what she saw. She went to the hairdresser and had her hair done, but could not find any make-up in any shop. Such small luxuries, things she had once taken for granted, were very rare in wartime. Finally, she had borrowed what she needed from the young mother downstairs, and Mrs Bristol lent her a pair of fake sapphire earrings.

As the new gown took shape on her dressmaker's dummy, her spirits lifted as they hadn't in years. When she appeared shyly from the bedroom, Roland looked at her in shock. She was dismayed to see tears form in his eyes.

'Oh, dear,' she had said, her face falling. 'This is foolish. I'm foolish, a foolish old woman! I look terrible.'

'No, no,' he whispered. 'You look beautiful.'

Roland's reaction had given her a measure of confidence and restored something of her femininity, which she had not felt stir inside her for years. But it had also brought long-buried memories. They came back to her now as she sat in the auditorium, sharp and unheeded; thoughts of Alexander and Jonathan.

She thought about how much pleasure Alexander had taken in watching her dress for an evening out, coming up to encircle her corseted waist with his large hands, pulling her towards him. She thought about how much Jonathan had loved to feel her long hair brushing his chest when they made love. She thought of them now with a sadly ironic perspective. Their love for her had been so rooted in the physicality of her beauty, which had also been the way she defined herself. Seeing herself reflected in the eyes of Alexander and Jonathan, she had felt beautiful. Being able to dance had made her feel beautiful. And then it had been taken away from her. That was, she realized suddenly, the real reason she had been tormented by the vague, insistent unhappiness. The war brought back to her so clearly that October night twenty-two years ago. That night when the boat blew apart, throwing her into the Channel waters, she had lost more than the use of her leg. She had lost more than just her beauty. She had lost more than her dancing. She had lost all sense of what she was.

The lights dimmed. Roland slipped into his seat, handing her a programme. The orchestra began the overture. Cendrine felt her heart begin to beat wildly. There was still the ballet itself to be confronted. How would she be able to bear it without mourning its death all over again?

The curtain rose to reveal a stage with a simple set that suggested a ballroom. The music was by Emmanuel Chabrier, sweet and wistful. Then came the dancers, and Cendrine lost all sense of time and place as she became swept up in the ballet's magic. She watched, amazed by the daring choreography – it was like nothing she had ever danced! She watched, in awe at the technical skills of the dancers – they were so much more advanced than in her day! She was seduced, finally, by the ballet's bittersweet mood. The dancers were portraying young men and women at a ball, over which seemed to hover a poignant sense of doom.

Her gaze went from dancer to dancer and she focused finally on one girl in the corps, a tall girl whose long black hair hung down her back, tied by a ribbon. She was costumed, like all the others, in a long full skirt of tulle studded with little stars. Although not the loveliest dancer on stage, and far from the most lyrical, she drew the eye with her sheer verve. She turned faster and more sharply than the others, jumped with more abandon. She was very young and vibrant with raw energy.

Tears fell down Cendrine's face as she watched the young girl. She couldn't stop herself from thinking of her own first moments on stage. Finally, it was over and the curtain came down. As the lights went up, Cendrine wiped her eyes, but not before Roland had noticed. He handed her a handkerchief and feigned inspecting his programme to give her a moment to compose herself.

'Pretty, wasn't it?' he said.

She nodded, dabbing at her eyes. Finally, with a sigh and a smile, she picked up her programme.

'But what do I know, right?' Roland went on. 'I've never even seen a ballet before. I went to a vaudeville house once in Baltimore but it was—'

He looked at Cendrine and froze. 'Cendrine, what is it?'

Her face had drained of colour, and she was trembling. She was clutching the programme, staring at it with wide eyes.

'Cendrine!'

Her lips were moving, but no words came out. She just sat there, staring at the programme. 'It's her . . . it's her,' she said finally, her voice strained.

'What? Cendrine, what is it?'

'It's her!' she repeated, looking at Roland, her eyes wild. 'It's her! It's Joëlle! Roland, look, it's Joëlle!'

Bewildered, he looked to the line of the cast list at which she was pointing. The name was there, in small type: Joëlle LeClerc. He looked quickly back at Cendrine. She was visibly agitated and taking shallow, quick breaths. He didn't know what to do. He had listened to her talk obsessively in the past about a baby she had lost, a baby she had named Joëlle, but he had never believed the child really existed. Even if she had, she was lost long ago, and he thought Cendrine had finally let go of the thought. He stared at Cendrine's ashen face. How could this dancer possibly be the same girl?

The lights began to dim for the next ballet. 'What do you want to do?' he asked Cendrine urgently.

'I don't know,' she answered, shaking her head in confusion. 'I don't know . . . I don't know. Oh, God, I don't know!' She began to cry. Someone nearby made a shushing sound to silence her.

'I have to get out of here!' Cendrine said suddenly. She pulled at Roland's arm. 'Take me home, Roland, take me home, please!'

He got up and quickly drew her up into his arms. The others around them began to protest and call for them to sit down. Roland ignored them, picked up her cane and helped her fight her way through the dark across people's feet and knees. By the time he got her to the lobby, she fainted.

Roland was sitting on the side of her bed when she woke up an hour later. There was a cool towel on her forehead.

'I called the doctor,' he said.

'I'm all right,' she whispered.

After a few moments, she closed her eyes. 'It's her, Roland. I know it. It's her.'

Roland removed the towel, immersed it in a bowl of water and returned it to her forehead. 'What are you going to do?' he asked.

She opened her eyes but was silent and would not look at him. 'What would I say to her, Roland? After all this time, what would I say? How would I tell her that. . .?' Her voice trailed off.

'You don't even know for sure it's her, Cendrine.'

'I know it's her. I know it.'

He picked up her hand. 'There's another performance on Monday,' he said.

Cendrine looked up at him.

'I'll go with you,' Roland said.

She reached up to take the towel off her forehead. 'No, I'll go alone,' she said.

It was nearly four by the time Cendrine made her way backstage at the opera house. Rehearsal was just finishing, and she crept silently through the gloom of the wings and found a place where she could watch

493

unnoticed. Her eyes picked out Joey immediately from among the others and did not leave her. Her hand went up nervously to adjust the collar of her dress. She had taken such care as she dressed today, wanting to look as nice as she could for this meeting. But now, as she watched, her heart began to beat wildly; she forgot about her appearance and what Joëlle would think of it. What if she were wrong and this wasn't Joëlle? There was no way to be sure after so many, many years. Seeing Joey's glossy black hair, she remembered the baby she had held in her arms so long ago, remembered stroking her soft black hair. She scrutinized the shape of Joey's face, trying to connect it to the child who lived in her memory. If only she could be sure!

The rehearsal ended and the dancers drifted off. Joey remained behind, lingering at the back of the stage, her expression troubled. The sounds of laughter and doors closing came from deep backstage and then it was quiet. Cendrine stood in the shadows watching as Joey went downstage and stood in the centre, head bowed as if deep in thought. She struck a pose and began to dance, moving across the stage as she hummed the rehearsal music. Cendrine watched, holding her breath.

Joey stopped abruptly. She sighed and stood staring at the stage, her hands on her hips. She returned to her original position and repeated a series of steps. Again, she stopped, shaking her head in frustration. She tried it two more times, each time stopping at the same place.

'Damn!' she said. 'Damn it, damn it, damn it!' At that instant, she saw Cendrine standing in the wings.

'Oh, sorry,' Joey said quickly. 'I thought I was alone.'

For a few seconds, Cendrine couldn't move. Then, slowly, she stepped out of the shadows. 'No, I'm sorry,' she said softly. 'I shouldn't have been watching you like this.'

Joey stared at the strange woman, her eyes taking in

her slight figure and regal posture, and her hair, so carefully pulled back in a classic dancer's chignon. It crossed her mind that the woman might have been a dancer once, but then she noticed the cane. She looked away quickly, embarrassed, but not before Cendrine saw.

'You're a fine dancer,' Cendrine said. 'I saw you last night in *Cotillon*.'

'You did?' Joey said, surprised. 'But I was in the corps.'

'Yes, but you stood out.'

Joey sighed heavily. 'Yeah, I know. That's why I'm still here right now – because I stand out. And you're not supposed to do that in the corps.'

Approaching the young woman before her, Cendrine could now see the resemblance to Alexander. Her heart began to beat frantically as a multitude of questions rushed to the front of her mind, questions she had buried for so many years. Where did you go, Joëlle? What happened to you after I left? Can you forgive me? Can you ever forgive me for leaving you? She felt tears burn in her eyes and fought them back.

'You're having trouble with your dancing?' she said quickly to cover up her emotions.

Joey nodded forlornly. 'Mr Ashton – he's the choreographer – he says I dance too much like an American. He says I'm too athletic, too unmusical.' She shook her head. 'Mr B. used to tell me the same thing about music,' she said, more to herself than Cendrine. 'He told me once that I could jump and turn well, but that I have no music inside me. I don't understand . . .'

Cendrine's head was spinning. What should she say? Should she just tell her who she was? After all these years, how could they possibly connect?

Discreetly, she wiped at her eyes. Joey was looking at her oddly, waiting.

'Maybe,' Cendrine said softly, 'maybe he just wants you to listen to the music when you dance.'

'I *do* listen to it.'

'But do you *hear* it? Do you let it get inside you and carry you along?'

Joey was looking at her intently now.

Cendrine took a step closer. 'When you danced last night,' she asked gently, 'were you dancing to the sounds of the violins or the sounds of the oboes?'

'I . . . I'm not sure,' Joey said.

'The shape of your dancing changes depending on what you hear in the music,' Cendrine said. Her eyes became momentarily distant. 'It would be carefree to the violins; more sensuous, if it was the oboes you heard.'

Joey gazed at the woman before her in fascination. 'You're a dancer,' she said softly.

'I was, once.'

'When?'

'I stopped more than twenty years ago.'

Joey stared at her intently. 'You're not English, are you?'

Cendrine faltered. 'I'm French.'

'My mother was French,' Joey said hesitantly. 'She . . .'

Tears sprang to Cendrine's eyes. 'I am your mother, Joëlle,' she whispered.

For a moment, Joey did not move. Then she wavered slightly, as if she had been struck in the chest. The colour drained from her face and her eyes were wide and glazed with disbelief.

'My mother's dead,' she said, glaring at Cendrine.

Cendrine took a step closer, extending her hand. 'Please, Joëlle—'

'No!' Joey cried out, backing away. 'No, no! My God, how could you do this? Do you think this is funny? Is this a joke? To say you're my—'

Cendrine was crying, moving towards Joey. 'Joëlle, please, let me—'

'No! She's dead!' Joey screamed. 'My mother's dead!'

She turned sharply, running into the velvet-draped panels at the side of the stage. Disoriented, she thrashed at them, caught in their heavy folds. Finally she freed herself and ran into the wings. Cendrine watched her disappear into the darkness.

Joey had just finished taking a bath when the knock came at the door of her flat. She sniffed, wiping her hand across her eyes. She didn't need to have yet another person asking what was wrong with her. Back in the dressing room, she had been forced to dodge questions from the curious dancers. Then she had run home.

Wrapping a towel around her head, she opened the door a crack to see a tall, strange man. 'Yes?' she asked, pulling her robe tighter.

Roland peered at her with intense curiosity. 'Are you Joëlle?'

'Yes. Who are you?'

He hesitated. After what Cendrine had told him, the last thing he wanted to do was scare the girl again. 'The woman who came to see you today,' he said. 'I'm her brother.'

Her eyes became guarded. 'What do you want?' she asked.

'Just to talk to you,' he said. He waited, enduring her scrutiny. 'Please. Just for a moment.'

She shrugged and opened the door wider to let him in. He stood, ill at ease, filling much of the small room. Joey moved away towards the window.

'She doesn't know I'm here,' Roland said. 'She told me what happened at Covent Garden. And she said she should never have gone to see you, that even if you . . .' He paused, his eyes searching her face. 'She said that

497

even if you were her daughter, she was wrong to thrust herself into your life with no warning.' He paused again, awkwardly. 'It must have been a horrible shock for you. I know it was for her when she saw your name on the programme.'

Joëlle was just staring at him, her hands clutching her robe closed.

Roland had no idea what to say or how to go on. He cleared his throat. 'Years ago,' he began, 'when my siser was very ill, she talked about a baby she had lost. I never really believed her. But the other night, when she saw your name, she was sure that you were her child.'

He looked to Joey. Her expression hadn't changed. He sighed, running his hand through his hair. 'I don't want to see her hurt, you see,' he said softly. 'You're about the right age, but I see now you can't be her's. You're American, aren't you?'

Joey nodded slowly.

'Cendrine's baby was born in Switzerland and—'

'Switzerland?' Joey said.

'—after the war, there was no trace of her.'

'I was born in Switzerland,' Joey said. 'A place called Iseltwald.'

Roland froze. Joey's eyes were wide with incredulity.

'My God!' he whispered. 'It *is* you.'

Joey dropped slowly onto the bed, stunned. 'I thought it was a joke,' she murmured. 'I thought someone was just playing a mean joke on me. Everyone's always doing that in the company. I didn't believe her. I thought it was a joke.' She shook her head slowly, gazing vacantly at the floor. 'But then, I started to think. And there was something about her . . .'

She looked at Roland. 'The painting,' she said. 'She looks like my painting.'

'Will you come to see her?' Roland asked.

Joey looked up at him beseechingly, her face clouded

with confusion and mistrust. 'I don't know. It's—'

'Come with me, please. You have to see her. Please, Joëlle.'

There was something about the way he said her name. He was a stranger, yet he said her name as if he had always known her. Joey rose, pulling the towel slowly off her head. 'I'll go get dressed,' she said softly.

Cendrine was sitting staring out of the window when they came in. The room was nearly dark. Roland closed the door quietly. Joey stood, unable to move, trying not to look at the wheelchair.

'Cendrine?' Roland said softly.

When she didn't answer, Roland brought Joey around to face Cendrine. He turned on a lamp. Cendrine looked up, blinking. She stared at Joey, stunned, unable to speak and unable to look away.

Neither could Joey. She lowered herself slowly into a chair across from Cendrine, not taking her eyes off Cendrine's face. She had a strangely detached feeling, as if she were watching herself from above. The room was quiet. Neither Joey nor Cendrine noticed when Roland crept away, closing the kitchen door behind him. They just gazed at each other, taking in every detail of each other's face.

'I'm sorry,' Cendrine whispered finally. 'I had no right—'

'No, no,' Joey said. 'Don't say that.'

They were both silent again. Cendrine's eyes glistened in the lamplight.

Cendrine began to cry. 'So many years . . . so many years I thought you were . . .' She searched Joey's face in disbelief. 'How did you . . . when?' She faltered. It was a moment before she could speak again. 'I left you with Madame. How did you get to America?'

'My father took me there,' Joey said softly.

Cendrine's mouth dropped open. 'Alexander? He went to the United States?'

Joey froze. 'No, Jonathan.'

'Jonathan?' Cendrine drew back, stunned.

'He found me in France and took me to New York.' She paused, alarmed at the look on Cendrine's face, and took a deep breath to steady herself. 'But you said Alexander,' she said. 'Alexander really is my father?'

Cendrine nodded, confused.

Joey shut her eyes. She had to stay in control somehow. Alexander was her father, Alexander was her father. And David . . . David . . . David was not her brother.

'Is he still alive?' Cendrine asked softly. 'Is Alexander still alive? Do you know?'

Joey could only nod. Cendrine closed her eyes.

'But Jonathan raised you?' Cendrine whispered.

'Yes,' Joey said. She waited, feeling a heaviness grow in her chest, as if the revelations of the past weeks were suddenly crushing her. The control was slipping.

She searched Cendrine's face, looking for every similarity she could find to the portrait that hung over her bed. The painting had been her only link to the woman who had given birth to her, and it had been easy to idealize the beautiful woman in the portrait because she didn't really exist. Over the years, Cendrine had taken on a definite personality as shaped by Joey's imagination. But this woman sitting before her, claiming she was her mother, this woman was flesh and blood, and she was an unknown, somehow unreal.

Mother! The word raced through Joey's mind. How was she going to be able to let go of the perfect Cendrine who had lived in her mind and replace her with this . . . stranger?

The distant look in Cendrine's eyes was gone and she was smiling, a small smile touched with sadness and pride. 'You're a dancer,' she said softly.

'Yes,' Joey said, her eyes locked on Cendrine.

'And there *is* music in you,' Cendrine whispered. 'Don't let anyone tell you there isn't.' She reached up slowly and touched Joey's cheek.

The gesture surprised Joey so much that at first it didn't register. Then, suddenly, everything did – the warmth and softness of Cendrine's hand, the smell of her, the closeness of her. A sob came retching up from somewhere inside Joey. She was crying, and she couldn't stop. Cendrine pulled her daughter into her arms and held her, rocking her gently back and forth.

Joey stayed with Cendrine that night. They didn't sleep. They filled the hours with words and touches, trying to condense more than twenty years and their overflowing emotions into hours. Joey told Cendrine about growing up in Ithaca, about Marion and the farm. Cendrine told Joey about what her life had been like in La Turbie and Paris. Joey told her about her trip to see Alexander in Paris, but could not bring herself to mention Alexander's drinking. Cendrine answered all Joey's questions about Jonathan and Alexander. She saw the question in Joey's eyes and answered it before it could be asked.

'I loved them both,' she said.

When it was dawn, Cendrine drew back the blackout curtains and faced Joey. 'Do you hate me?' she asked, her eyes brimming. 'Do you hate me for leaving you?'

Overcome, Joey could only shake her head.

Cendrine shut her eyes in relief. She opened them, searching Joey's face again, as if memorizing each feature.

'I wish you could come home with me,' Joey said suddenly.

Cendrine just looked at her, sadly.

'I wish Alexander could see you,' Joey said.

501

'No,' Cendrine said quietly but firmly. 'It's enough that I know he's alive. I don't want to see him. And I don't want him to see me.'

'But—'

'I don't want Alexander to know about me,' Cendrine said. 'Or Jonathan either.'

Joey looked at her, puzzled. 'But I have to tell Dad—'

'No, Joëlle, no.' Cendrine gripped Joey's hand. 'Joëlle, listen to me, please. I don't want either of them to know about me.'

Joey was bewildered by the sudden resolute tone in Cendrine's voice. 'I don't understand. You said you loved—'

'I want Alexander to remember me as I was,' Cendrine said. 'Jonathan, too.'

Joëlle shook her head.

'Promise me, Joëlle,' Cendrine implored. 'Promise me you won't tell either of them about me.'

Joey started to cry. 'I can't,' she said. 'I can't pretend I never saw you. I can't pretend you don't exist, not now.'

'I'm not asking you to do that,' Cendrine said softly. 'We do exist . . . for each other.' She reached over and stroked Joey's hair. 'Promise me . . . please?'

Joey nodded weakly. Cendrine gathered Joey into her arms. The girl laid her head in her mother's lap, her arms encircling her waist.

Chapter Forty-Two

A droning noise, faint and distant.

'Now what in the world can that be?' the woman behind the counter said, glancing towards the shop window.

Cendrine shrugged. 'Do you have any sugar today, Mrs Goode?' she said with a smile. 'My daughter's coming for dinner tonight, and I'd like to make her a cake.'

'You might as well ask for gold,' the shopkeeper said, shaking her head ruefully.

The droning noise grew louder, and the shop windows began to rattle. The women looked at each other; without a word, both went to the door and stepped outside. People were standing in the streets, staring upward, hands shielding their eyes, against the afternoon sun.

Cendrine looked up. Planes – hundreds of them, filling the afternoon sky. She watched, transfixed by the sight. So many planes! But whose?

Then, without warning, the bombs began to fall. There was a deafening explosion so close it cracked the shop's glass. The shopkeeper screamed and darted inside, but Cendrine didn't move.

Another explosion, even closer, and the window of the butcher's shop across the street shattered, sending a spray of glass out over the paving stones. Another, and another. Suddenly, people were screaming and running wildly. There was smoke, black smoke, billowing up behind a nearby row of houses, coming from somewhere near the docks.

Cendrine stood frozen. She couldn't think. She could only hear the screaming, see the people running and smell the smoke. There was an ear-splitting explosion, and she screamed, holding her hands over her ears. Home, she had to get home.

She dropped the basket and began to half walk, half run, as fast as her limp would allow, down King Street. People pushed by her, their faces distorted with fear. The droning was right overhead now, a deafening roar. The sky was dark, the sun blocked out by smoke and planes. Another explosion. Shrapnel danced off the paving stones, and the suction from the blast pulled at her, threatening to suck her into it. She tried to scream but couldn't. She couldn't even pull in a breath now, as the thick air burned into her lungs like acid. The explosions kept coming, and the whole street was moving, rising and falling.

She reached the church a block from her building and stared at it in horror. The roof and front of it had been blown away, and its heavy stones were scattered in the street. Thick smoke billowed up from inside the sanctuary, and the shops next door were gone. She cried out in relief when she saw her building: it was still standing.

Suddenly, there was a flash of light, and she was knocked off her feet by a blast of hot air. She lay there for a moment, stunned, then slowly got to her feet. Wavering, bleeding from a cut on her forehead, she made her way into the building. She collapsed on the stairs, wiping her face.

The docks . . . the planes had been heading for the docks, she realized suddenly. Roland! Where was he?

Another explosion sent a spray of stones and glass into the doorway. She covered her head with her arms. The hallway filled up with black smoke. She gagged, her eyes watering. The smells, the darkness . . .

Suddenly, she was back in the tiny cabin on the boat that night in the Channel. She could feel the room tilting, she could hear the people screaming and running outside in the corridor, leaving her there alone to die. It was happening all over again. She was going to die . . . Her stomach heaved and she felt herself losing consciousness. No, no, she thought wildly, I can't let it happen! I'll never wake up again . . .

Slowly, she began to crawl up the stairs, making her way back into the flat. The droning and explosions kept coming. She crawled, groping her way in the darkness, feeling her way along the walls to the bedroom. She crept into the closet, drawing back into the furthest corner, and closed her eyes.

After an hour, the bombing stopped and all was quiet. But Cendrine didn't move. She looked at the crack beneath the door but saw no light. Her heart was beating frantically and her hip hurt, but she wouldn't move. The terror might start again, any moment. Finally, she heard someone calling her name.

There was a flood of dim light as someone opened the closet. In a moment, Roland's arms were holding her tightly.

'Oh, God, you're alive!' he whispered. 'When I couldn't find you, I thought . . .'

She saw the blood and dirt on his face, and reached up to touch his cheek. He helped her out of the closet. Cendrine got to her feet unsteadily, her eyes sweeping the room. It was still daylight, but the smoke and dust made it look like dusk. Pictures and shelves had been shaken off the walls. It was the same in the sitting room and in the kichen, where the floor was littered with broken dishes and glass. She looked anxiously at Roland.

'Is it over?' she asked weakly.

'I don't know,' he said. 'They were aiming for the docks. Everything's on fire. My shop is gone.'

A sudden noise drew their attention to the open front door. Joey stood there, breathing heavily, her eyes wide and panic-stricken. She saw Cendrine and came running, throwing her arms around her.

'I thought you were dead,' she said, crying. 'I thought you were dead.'

'I'm all right,' Cendrine said softly, holding onto her. She looked at Roland's grim face. 'Everything's all right now.'

At eight that night, it started again. The three of them huddled under a table in the dark sitting room. At one point, the window shattered, opening up a hellish view. They could see the searchlights raking the glowing red sky trying to pinpoint the German planes. They could hear the explosions of the bombs and the echoing blasts as the docks and warehouses erupted, with barrels of rum exploding and drums of paint flaring up in flaming white streaks. They could smell the stench of melting rubber, and hear the drone of the planes as they kept coming, wave after wave after wave.

Everything was on fire, burning out of control because the Thames was so low after the dry summer that the fireboats couldn't get their water pumps to work. Barrage balloons were hoisted, lifting a surreal forest of cables around the docks in an effort to force the bombers to fly higher, making their aim less deadly. In the neighbourhoods around the docks, whole streets disappeared, whole familes were crushed by falling homes.

When morning came, 2,000 people were dead. Roland

led Cendrine and Joey down to King Street, and they stood paralysed by the horrific scene. Some buildings were completely destroyed, and the remains of others thrust jaggedly upward like stange rock formations. Fires still burned, the black smoke blotting out the sun. Dazed survivors wandered the streets, looking for missing family members or possessions amid the collapsed homes. The hiss of a gas pipe mixed with the sound of weeping.

Joey looked up at the building in which she had just spent the night and shuddered. It was pocked with holes and shattered windows. 'We can't stay here,' she said.

Roland looked at her, but Cendrine was staring numbly at the surrounding rubble.

'She can't take another night like last night,' Joey said quietly to Roland.

Roland said nothing, but he understood. The previous night, he and Joey had taken turns holding and comforting Cendrine as she screamed. Cendrine seemed all right now, but while the bombs had fallen, she had slipped into a private world of terror.

'You'll come stay with me,' Joey said suddenly.

Roland glanced at the empty windows. 'All right,' he said.

Every night came the melancholy wail of the air-raid sirens. Every night the bombs fell, driving many people underground into the tube stations, tunnels and shelters, anywhere that might provide a safe niche. And every morning, people emerged to find that landmarks had vanished, buses had been swallowed up by craters, and that someone they knew had disappeared.

Two weeks, a month, two months passed. Still the bombing Blitz continued, without interruption, every night. Roland and Cendrine stayed with Joey in her small flat. It was cramped and uncomfortable, but they felt safe enough there and no one complained. At least they had a place to stay. At least they were alive, together.

During the day, the city seemed at times almost normal. The railway lines into London had been hit but people still went to work. Shops and business remained open, announced by a Union Jack flag stuck defiantly in the rubble or a wry sign, BUSINESS AS USUAL, MORE OR LESS. Everything closed early so people could get home before dark, but otherwise Londoners went on with their lives with a grim determination.

That was what Joey told Jonathan whenever he called. His first frantic call had come the day after the bombing had started, and he demanded that she return home. Joey tried to reassure him she was safe, but was sworn not to tell him the real reason she had to stay – for Cendrine's sake. Marion pleaded tearfully for her to come home. But guilty though Joey felt about causing them so much worry, she remained firm. She couldn't leave as long as Cendrine needed her.

After a while, the ballet resumed its performances, and Joey was glad to be dancing again. She knew Roland felt the same about his job as a warden in a shelter. After an exhausting, nerve-wracking night of bombing, it was a relief, when day came, to return to the normality of work. But Joey worried abut Cendrine, who had no such diversion. She remained in the flat by herself for most of the day, working on her sewing, emerging only to do the shopping. Finally, Joey was able to coax Cendrine to come with her to the theatre. The company was preparing a production of *Giselle*, and Joey was dancing a secondary but important role as Myrtha. Each day, Cendrine would sit quietly watching the rehearsals, and whenever Joey had a free moment, they would share a lunch and talk, often about Joey's dancing. Sitting in the cool darkness of the theatre, Joey saw a reviving serenity come over Cendrine. She would laugh, and she seemed so much younger. Joey grew to love those precious interludes, and she felt the bond between herself and Cendrine growing stronger each day.

'I think,' Cendrine told her one day at rehearsal, 'that you are too soft in the way you dance Myrtha.'

'Too soft?' Joey said, taken aback. 'But everyone's always telling me I need to be softer!'

Cendrine smiled gently. 'Yes, maybe, but Myrtha is not sweet like Giselle. I've always thought she should be danced as if she has a touch of evil in her.'

'Evil?' Joey said thoughtfully. Then she refocused on Cendrine. 'You should be teaching,' she said suddenly.

Cendrine's smile grew wistful.

'No, I'm serious,' Joey went on, excited. 'You know so much. I could talk to Mr Ashton or Madame de Valois about it. Maybe you could teach here.'

'Maybe,' Cendrine said softly.

The next day, Joey approached the choreographer about Cendrine. He seemed vaguely interested, but told her that there was no money at the moment to hire another teacher. He said that maybe after the war was over, some time in the future . . .

Joey thought about his words as she walked home early one evening in October. The future . . . who knew what that meant any more? Especially for Cendrine. Although she appeared normal during the day, at night, when the bombs began to fall, she became a different person. Cendrine tried to reassure her daughter that she was fine, but Joey could see that she wasn't. She knew that with every bomb that fell, Cendrine was reliving her own night of horror in the Channel.

It had become something of a grim routine now. Each night, as soon as the bombing started, Joey would take her mother into the bedroom. They would sit, huddled together on the bed, Joey holding Cendrine's hand, watching her break into a cold sweat, watching her screw her eyes shut, watching her jump with each explosion. Every night, Cendrine withdrew just a little further into her own world. And every morning, the crack in her fragile facade of calm was just a little more pronounced.

Joey walked on, her shoes crunching over the glass littering the streets. How long before she breaks? she thought sadly. How long before I lose her all over again?

She trudged up the stairs to the flat and unlocked the door. Roland was not home yet, and the place was quiet and dark. She saw the closed bedroom door that signalled Cendrine was taking a nap. She needed the sleep; she rarely slept at night. Joey quietly slipped off her shoes, turned on a lamp and closed the blackout curtains. She started for the kitchen to make some tea.

A knock at the door made her turn. With a weary sigh, she went to the door and opened it. Her mouth dropped open.

'Dad!'

Jonathan stared at Joey for a second, then drew her into his arms, crushing her to his chest. 'Oh, thank God, thank God,' he muttered. 'Thank God, you're all right!'

Joey pulled back, still in shock. 'Dad, what are you doing here?'

'I had to come to find out you were all right,' Jonathan said, searching her face. Tears came to his eyes and he embraced her again. 'I had to see for myself. Thank God, thank God . . .'

'But I told you I was—'

'We've been worried sick, Joey. God, if you only knew! We've been worried sick.' He embraced her again.

She was suddenly aware of the feel of Jonathan's arms, and an intense rush of love and homesickness flooded through her. She drew back to look at his face. It was so worn with worry that tears sprang to her eyes.

510

'But how . . . how did you get here?' she asked in amazement.

'Military transport. It wasn't easy, but luckily, I knew someone in the State Department.' His words tumbled over each other. 'Joey, your mother can't even listen to the radio or read a newspaper any more without getting upset.'

'Dad—'

'I can't believe this city. God, it must have been hell for you. But it doesn't matter now. You'll come back with me and—'

'Wait, there's something I—'

'There's a flight in two days, so—'

'Dad, listen, I have to tell—'

'Joëlle?'

Joey froze at the sound of the voice coming from the bedroom. 'Joëlle,' Cendrine called out. 'Who's there? Is Roland home already?'

Cendrine appeared at the bedroom door.

For a moment, no one moved. Joey saw the recognition register first in Cendrine's face, then she heard a sharp intake of breath and looked at Jonathan. His face went pale, his eyes wide and bright. He wavered, his hand groping for support. Joey grabbed it.

'Cendrine,' he said. It came out in a whisper, almost a question.

Cendrine's eyes filled with tears. 'Jonathan,' she said softly. She took a step towards him but stopped.

He went quickly to her, wrapping her in his arms. He held her gently, closing his eyes. Her arms went up to encircle his neck, and she buried her face in his shoulder. They remained locked in each other's arms, saying nothing.

Joey watched them, transfixed. She had tried so many times to see them together in her mind, and she had always failed somehow. Now, seeing them in each other's arms sent a flood of emotions through her: wonder, joy and a flash of confusion as Marion briefly entered her thoughts. She observed them, watching their intimacy, feeling intrusive but unable to look away. She heard weeping, but couldn't tell which of them was crying. Finally, overcome, she went quietly to the door, closing it behind her, leaving them alone.

'I thought you would find me ugly.'

'You're as beautiful as I remember.'

'I'm old,' Cendrine said, smiling slightly.

'No,' Jonathan said softly.

They were silent for a moment, sitting side by side on the sofa. Jonathan held her hand, pressed between his own. Half an hour had gone by. The shock had passed, but the aura of wonder and amazement lingered for each of them, joined now by the joy of rediscovery.

'Don't blame Joëlle,' Cendrine said. 'I made her promise not to tell you.'

Jonathan shook his head sadly. 'You should have called me. You should have—'

'No,' Cendrine interrupted. 'It was better this way.'

'How can you know that?' he asked. 'How can you know that for sure?'

They were silent, each searching the other's face. Finally, Cendrine withdrew her hand from between Jonathan's. She reached up and touched the tips of her fingers to his brow. Jonathan drew in a breath. Her fingers trembled as they moved from his brow down over his cheek and to his lips. Her eyes, filled with tears, held his.

For one moment, everything stood still. For one moment, it was 1913 again. For one moment, Jonathan was back in Paris. Then, slowly, she withdrew her hand.

She rose and took a few steps away, turning her back to him.

'You raised Joëlle well, Jonathan,' she said.

Jonathan stared at her back. He was afraid to ask the next question, but he knew he had to.

'Is she my daughter, Cendrine?' he asked.

She turned to face him. 'No,' she said softly.

Jonathan shut his eyes. After a few seconds, he asked, 'Does she know?'

Cendrine nodded.

'Good,' Jonathan whispered, his eyes vacant. 'It's good . . . for her and David.' He looked up at Cendrine. 'Did she tell you about David.'

'She told me everything,' Cendrine said proudly.

They were silent again.

'I can only imagine,' Jonathan whispered, 'what this must mean to Joey – finding you again.'

Cendrine's eyes filled with tears. 'And you?' she asked. 'What does it mean to you, Jonathan?'

He didn't answer. He rose slowly and went to her, taking her gently in his arms. Then he kissed her.

They had warned him about the bombs. But when it began that night, Jonathan was unprepared for the ungodly noise, the all-encompassing darkness, the feeling of helpless terror that came over him. Joey tried to warn him, too, about Cendrine, but when Cendrine let out the first scream, he drew back in stunned shock. He recovered instantly and started across the room for her, but Roland held him back. Jonathan watched as Joey led Cendrine into the bedroom, closing the door behind them. He spent the rest of the night sitting with Roland, in impotent horror, listening to Cendrine's screams and rambling speech. He heard only one coherent sentence. She was pleading, over and over, that she wanted to go home.

Joey emerged just after dawn. 'She's asleep,' she said wearily. She looked at Jonathan's stricken face. 'I'm sorry, Dad. It was especially bad last night.'

513

'It's getting worse,' Roland said.

'She's fine during the day,' Joey said quickly. 'You don't see her as much as I do. She's fine during the day.'

'It's getting worse, you know it is,' Roland repeated tersely, and he turned quickly away.

Joey sighed and looked at Jonathan. 'I'll make some coffee,' she said, and went into the kitchen.

Jonathan sank into a chair. 'She should be under a doctor's care,' he said.

Roland turned to face him. 'No,' he said. 'No doctors. I told you last night what happened to her on the boat, and about that place on that island. I told you what he did to her.'

'She should at least be given some sedatives,' Jonathan said, shaking his head.

'No!' Roland said. 'No drugs!'

'For God's sake, she needs some care!' Jonathan said. 'She shouldn't even be here. She should be in a hospital!'

'Who are you to tell me how to take care of my sister?' Roland said. 'Who are you to tell me anything?'

'I'm only thinking of what's—'

'I know what's best for Cendrine!' Roland said, angrily. 'I'm the one who's taken care of her for the last twenty years, goddamn it! I know what's best for her!'

Joey came into the room, holding a tray, her eyes going quickly from Roland to Jonathan. She set down the tray. 'Roland,' she said softly, going to him.

He ignored her. 'And I know what's best for her now,' he went on quickly. 'I'm going to take her home!'

'Home?' Joey said. 'You can't. King Street's completely bombed out.'

'La Turbie,' Roland said. 'I'm taking her home to La Turbie!'

Joey looked at him in stunned silence. Jonathan rose. 'You can't do that,' he said. 'You can't get to France right now.'

514

'I'll find a way,' Roland said abruptly.

'There is no way!' Jonathan said, his voice rising.

'I'll find one!'

'You're insane,' Jonathan said, shaking his head.

'I have to do it!' Roland shouted.

'You'll get her killed!' Jonathan shouted back.

'She'll die if she stays here!'

'Stop it!' Joey screamed.

The room went silent. They all looked to the bedroom, but there was no sound from behind the door.

'Stop it,' Joey said softly, her eyes welling.

Jonathan went to Joey and held her. Roland turned to the window and the street below. 'I have to get her away from this place,' he said quietly. 'If she stays here much longer, she'll lose her mind.'

'The bombing won't go on for ever,' Jonathan said.

Roland turned to face him. 'How do you know?' he said bitterly. 'It's been going on every night for two months. How do you know when it's going to stop?' His face was like stone. 'I'm taking her home.'

Joey looked at Roland beseechingly.

'You know I have to, Joëlle,' he said, his eyes softening somewhat. 'You've heard her, you've seen her. You know it's the right thing to do.'

Joëlle nodded.

'You're crazy,' Jonathan murmured. 'You'll both be killed.'

Roland said nothing.

Joey disentangled herself from Jonathan's arms. 'I'm going with you,' she said to Roland.

'What?' Jonathan grabbed her arm. 'No, you're not! You're coming home with me. Tomorrow.'

Joey jerked free. 'She needs me, Dad! I have to go. She needs me.'

'Forget it, Joey! I forbid you to do this!'

Joey backed away slightly. 'She's my mother,' she

said. 'I'm going with her.'

Her voice was soft but firm. Jonathan stared at her, at her unwavering blue-grey eyes. He knew suddenly, clearly, that there was nothing he could say or do to stop her. His shoulders slumped slightly and he turned away so she couldn't see his face. It was a moment before he felt composed enough to turn around again.

'All right,' he said flatly. 'We'll find a way.'

Chapter Forty-Three

It took nearly a week for Jonathan to find a pilot willing to fly them to Lisbon. It took several more days for the bank transfer to go through from the States so Jonathan could pay the man his exorbitant price. They rented a car and drove southwest through the countryside of Devon, stopping finally at an airstrip outside Plymouth. They boarded a small and very old commercial transport plane. The plane took off in the gloom of early morning, staying over land. But finally, the land gave way to blue-grey ocean, and as Jonathan watched the craggy peninsula of Land's End slip further behind, he closed his eyes. All week he had tried to talk Joey out of going, but had failed. The only concession he had got was her promise to return home with him as soon as Cendrine was safe in France. Jonathan stared at the expanse of ocean and then up at the empty sky. There was no going back now. Any moment, they could be blown to bits, but there was no going back.

The plane swung a wide arc west over water before heading south towards Portugal. Joey had told Cendrine beforehand of Roland's plan. She had accepted it without protest and had remained calm, but clung to Joey throughout the flight.

They arrived in Lisbon exhausted, and stayed one night in a hotel while Jonathan searched for a car and driver. Everywhere they went, he encountered people who told him what they were trying to do was suicide. But Jonathan quickly found that American dollars inevitably produced someone willing to risk his own neck. Once they reached the border village of Barca de Alva, another driver was hired, who transported them through the treacherous mountain roads of northern Spain. Three weeks after they had left London, they reached the French border. Under the cover of night, and with the aid of a French partisan, they slipped into France. It took them five more days to make it to Nice.

Jonathan installed everyone in a small auberge outside the city, and returned to Nice to find an estate agent. He was surprised at how normal the city seemed, but still felt uneasy. As an American, he drew stares of curiosity, but no one questioned him; still, he wondered how safe he and Joey would be once the United States threw off its cloak of neutrality. His uneasiness grew into anxiety when he spotted two German soldiers sitting in a café. In that moment, he felt more afraid than he had during the whole strange journey from London.

He found an agency, and within an hour he had made a deal to rent a small villa in the hill village of Eze. There was no place to rent in La Turbie itself, but Eze was only ten miles away. He paid for it without even seeing the place, wondering what he was getting into, but he was too exhausted to care.

The next morning they set off for the villa. Everyone was quiet, physically and mentally drained. They drove up from Nice, along the cliff-hugging middle corniche, enjoying the spectacular sight of the Mediterranean glittering in the sun far below nearly all the way. Jonathan watched Cendrine in his rear-view mirror, as she sat with Joey in the back. She was quiet but her eyes were avid, taking in every detail of the scenery. They drove higher and higher up into the hills, past vineyards flecked with workers. The sky turned hazy and white, and the air grew heavy with wild fragrances. They passed through Eze, an ancient village on a rocky outcrop. It was twilight when they pulled up in front of the villa.

Cendrine got out of the car first to look at the darkened villa. It wasn't really a villa, it was an old oil mill with a plain house, restored but run down, surrounded by umbrella pines and fig trees, and almost hidden by a riot of rambling bougainvillea vines. Cendrine reached for the purple flowers and picked a branch, turning it over in her hands, examining it carefully, as if she had never seen such a flower before.

Jonathan, Joey and Roland stood watching her. The only sound was the chirp of crickets.

Cendrine's eyes went back to the house. 'This will do fine,' she said softly.

Jonathan was sitting on the stone terrace. He held a pad of paper in one hand and a pen in the other, but his eyes were trained on the surrounding hills. Off in the distance to the west, he could see the sun hovering over the old grey buildings of Eze. Down below, on the winding road that led to the village, he could see a truck, its bed filled with baskets of grapes, on its way to the wine cooperative. The putt-putt of its engine reached him mutedly, mixing with the dwindling twitter of the birds that had taken roost in the fig trees for the night. From inside the house came the sound of Cendrine and Joey, talking and laughing softly.

He was filled with a strange, pervading calm. It was strange because it had come on him unexpectedly as soon as they had arived in Eze, and it arose from more than a simple feeling of safety after the dangerous trip. It came from some place deep inside him. He had fought it, distrusting it. Where was it coming from? And why now when he had never felt it before at any time in his life?

He knew he should be feeling something else, anything but this incredible sense of peace.

Somewhere else, a war was raging. somewhere else was a real world. Somewhere else was his life, awaiting his return. He closed his eyes and, for a moment, somewhere else vanished. There was only this perfect place, this perfect moment, the strange calm, and he desperately wanted just to give in to it.

A hand on his shoulder. He opened his eyes to see Joey standing there. 'Can I get you anything, Dad?' she asked. 'Your jacket? It's getting kind of chilly.'

He shook his head, covering her hand with his. 'No, I'm fine,' he said.

Joey went back inside. Jonathan looked down at the pad in his lap. The letter to Marion was finished. He folded it and put it in its envelope. He wondered if it would reach her. He had called her from London to tell her of the plan to go to France. He told her about Cendrine, but there had been no time to say much more. During the three weeks they had been in Eze, he had written several letters and had gone each day to the village post office to try to place a transatlantic call, but it never went through. He turned the envelope over and slowly addressed it. Oxford Street, Ithaca, New York, United States. It all seemed so far away.

He heard a sound and looked up. Cendrine was standing in the door of the house, wearing a simple dark dress and an apron. Her pale hair was piled haphazardly on her head, wisps of it framing her face. Standing there, caught in the slanting, burnished sunlight, she looked suddenly young, and Jonathan felt a catch in his throat, thinking of the first time he had seen her, standing in the door of the café more than forty years ago.

She came towards him, taking off the apron, and saw the envelope in his hand. 'Do you think any of them have got through?' she asked.

'I don't know,' he said.

Her eyes held his for a moment, then she looked away, out over the hills. 'It will be a nice sunset,' she said.

He stared up at her profile. Her face was lightly sunburned, her nose freckled. Roland had been right; since leaving London, Cendrine had undergone a slow transformation. In the three weeks they had been in Eze, the night episodes had disappeared and her nervous fragility had been replaced by serenity. Every morning, she and Joey went for a walk, which helped restore her vitality and agility. Joey had been right, too: Cendrine had needed her. It had been the girl's love that had brought Cendrine back.

'Jonathan?' She looked down at him. 'Will you do something for me?'

'Anything.'

'Take me to La Turbie.'

He looked up at her in surprise. It was the first time in three weeks she had mentioned the place. 'Now?' he asked.

'Yes,' she said. 'Please.'

Joey came out onto the terrace in time to see the old Citroën disappear down the hill. Frowning, she went back inside, just as Roland came in from outside.

'Roland, did they tell you where they were going?' she asked.

'Cendrine just said they'd be back soon,' he said. 'I'm going into Eze. Do you need anything?'

Joey shook her head. Roland left and she was soon absorbed in her task of clearing the dinner table. She heard the scrape of shoes against stone and turned.

For a second, she didn't recognize the man standing at the door leading in from the terrace. He was tall and ruddy-faced with a short beard, wearing an old tweed coat and a cap like those the local men wore. But then it struck her, and she almost dropped the plate she was holding.

'Alexander,' she said.

He took off his cap and came into the kitchen, his eyes discreetly looking, searching, before returning to Joey.

'I got your letter,' he said.

'But I sent it weeks ago,' she said, still shocked at seeing him. 'I sent it to the newspaper. How. . .?'

'I left Paris last summer. I've been living in a village not far from here. The letter was forwarded to me; I just got it today.'

Joey could remember Alexander lying, drunk and bleeding, on the gleaming parquet floor amid the broken glass. Now he looked different, and it was more than his simple clothing. His face was tanned from the sun and rendered less severe by the beard, and he had put on some needed weight. The Alexander she had known in Paris, who had beguiled her with his brittle elegance, was gone. Words flashed through her mind, the words he had spat out at her in his drunken rage that night. She focused on his eyes, trying to gauge whether he still felt the same towards her. She had written the letter to him without telling either Jonathan or Cendrine. She hadn't expected an answer, but it was somehow important to her that he should know the truth. No matter how he felt about her, it was important that he knew she really was his daughter. She had told him, too, about Cendrine, believing that he had a right to know she was alive. Now, as she looked into his anxious eyes, her heart sank. She knew that it was Cendrine he had come to see, not her.

'Joëlle,' he said.

'She's not here,' Joey said softly. 'She and Jonathan went for a drive.'

'Joëlle, I want—'

'You can wait here if you want,' Joey interrupted. 'I

522

don't think they'll be gone long.'

Alexander came towards her, pulling the letter out of his coat. 'Why did you write to me?' he asked.

She avoided his eyes, her hands flitting nervously over the dishes. 'I thought you should know. She didn't want me to tell you, but I know how much you loved her.' She stopped and looked up at him. 'And how much she loved you.'

Alexander just stared at her, clutching the letter.

'I just thought you should know,' she repeated.

He started to say something but stopped. There was something in her tone of voice, and a wariness in her eyes, that cut him off. He turned and headed for the terrace.

'Aren't you going to wait?' Joey asked, surprised.

He looked back at her. 'I can't. I'm going to go find them.'

'But I don't know where they went,' Joey said.

'I think I do,' Alexander said softly. And he was gone.

Chapter Forty-Four

Cendrine said nothing during the short drive to La Turbie, but Jonathan didn't mind. During the last three weeks, they had had plenty of time to talk. They had told each other about their lives, and they had shared memories of the past. They talked most often about Joey. It all felt so natural, so strangely normal, as if they had been separated only a month instead of more than twenty-five years. It was only when Cendrine talked about her life with Alexander that Jonathan felt uneasy. But he didn't know why.

Jonathan parked the car and they got out. He scanned the dusty square, ringed with sagging buildings and stunted plane trees. It looked exactly as he remembered it. He glanced at Cendrine, whose eyes sought the café. It was the only thing that had changed. It had been repainted and a new sign hung over the door: Café d'Antoine.

Cendrine noticed Jonathan watching her, and she smiled slightly. Taking his hand, she led him away from the square. They made their way through the labyrinth of dark, narrow streets and emerged into a clearing. Jonathan paused, looking up at the Roman ruins. Then, without a word, he followed Cendrine into the courtyard. The crumbling old monument was even more decayed, the massive stones scattered across the overgrown grass, the carved columns cracked and veined with moss. The mistral rushed through the cypress trees, and a bird sang plaintively somewhere nearby.

Jonathan looked at Cendrine. She was standing about twenty feet away, examining a pile of large stones, clutching the sides of her coat against the wind. He knew she was looking for the one on which they had lain together, but there was no way to pick it out among the rubble. Finally, she turned to him, smiled, and walked towards the terrace.

He followed. The stone bench was still there, and so was the breathtaking view of the Mediterranean and the village of Beaulieu-sur-Mer far below. They sat down on the bench, silent for a long time, each staring out at the sea.

Then Cendrine turned to look at Jonathan. 'What are you thinking about?' she asked softly.

'That bird,' he said. 'Do you hear it?'

She nodded. 'It's a song thrush.'

He smiled slightly. ' "That's the wise thrush; he sings each song twice over, lest you should think he never could recapture the first fine careless rapture." '

'Did you write that?' she asked, smiling.

'No, no! A man named Robert Browning did.'

They were quiet again, watching the setting sun.

'I used to come here often when I was a girl,' Cendrine said finally. 'It looks the same, but different somehow.'

'Maybe because you're different now.'

'Perhaps.' She looked back out over the sea. 'I used to come here to hide. I used to sit here and dream about growing wings, jumping off this cliff and flying away.' She paused. 'Now I am here again and I feel . . .'

He looked at her. 'Happy?'

'Peaceful,' she said softly.

He stared at her profile, at the still fine line of her throat. 'I loved you,' he said.

She looked at him, then took his hand. 'And I loved you,' she whispered, her eyes brimming.

'It was real, so real,' he said.

'It still is,' she said.

'And it's ours.'

'For ever.'

He raised her hand to his lips, kissing her fingertips. He gazed into her eyes for a moment, then kissed her on the mouth. When he pulled back, her eyes were closed.

'I have to go,' he said softly.

'I know.'

'We have to leave tomorrow morning. The plane—'

'I know,' she said quickly.

She was crying. He looked away, out over the sea. The sun was almost gone, and the sea was lavender in the fast-waning light. After a moment he rose, still holding her hand.

'One more minute,' she said. Her eyes swept out over the sea and down at the lights just coming to life in Beaulieu. Then she, too, rose. Arm in arm, they started back across the grass.

Jonathan saw a man coming slowly towards them. He was a tall man, bearded and dressed like a local. But there was something strange about the man, about his walk: it wasn't the walk of a villager. It was familiar somehow. Jonathan stopped abruptly, his arm slipping from Cendrine's. She was staring at the man, too, and suddenly she uttered a small cry. With a quick glance at Jonathan, she started to run towards the man.

Jonathan watched as Alexander folded Cendrine in his arms. He watched as the old man's hand came to cradle her head, and her arms wrapped round his neck. Jonathan watched, his throat constricting, as the two figures swayed together, locked in each other's arms. He stood there watching them, unable to move.

'Jonathan!' Alexander was calling his name.

'Jonathan!' Alexander's arm was outstretched.

They were standing, looking at him, their arms round each other's waists. Jonathan hesitated, but went to them. Alexander's tanned face was aged, his hair was white, but it was still the same Alexander. Except for his eyes: they were different now, no longer like glittering black stones, no longer so knowing and ironic. They had become subdued.

As for Cendrine, her face was infused with a light that hadn't been there a moment ago. Jonathan stared at her, at her hand resting possessively on Alexander's chest. He took a hard look at both of them. Alexander loved her, and she loved him. He had always known that, even though it was only at this moment that he realized how right it was. He felt a knot form in his chest, but he knew now that he could leave. He knew that, though a part of him would always stay with her, he could leave and know she would be happy.

'Jonathan?'

He reached out and took Alexander's outstretched hand. His eyes locked with Alexander's, and neither man moved. Then Jonathan drew back his hand and looked at Cendrine.

'I'll wait in the car,' he said, and left them alone.

Alexander watched Jonathan disappear into the shadows, and then continued to look at the dark ruins. He felt Cendrine's hand on his arm.

'He's all right,' she said.

Alexander looked down at her. His eyes swept over her face, then he brought up both hands, cupping her face. 'I can't see you,' he said softly. 'It's so dark, I can't see you, and I have to see you.'

His fingers moved over her face, over her brow, her eyelids, down over her cheeks to her lips. They trembled as they frantically traced each feature. 'I can't see you,' he repeated, urgent now, 'I can't see you . . .'

'I'm here, I'm here.' She covered his hands with her own, stopping them, calming them. She turned his hand over to kiss his palm. 'I'm here, Alexander, I'm here . . .'

He let out a sob.

'How did I live without you?' she said, crying now.

'I couldn't live . . . I didn't . . .' He too began to cry.

She pulled him down to her, kissing his lips. '*Je t'aime*, Alexander, *je t'aime* . . .'

He buried his face in her neck, holding her tight.

The sun was high in the morning sky when Jonathan emerged from the mill house. The chilly mistral was still blowing hard, stirring the fig trees and creating little whirlwinds of dust in the courtyard. A suitcase in each hand, he went to the old Citroën and put the luggage in the boot. He leaned against the fender, waiting, not wanting to go inside, afraid the dam holding back his emotions would finally give way.

He had not slept. None of them had. Alexander's presence in the house last night had created a strange and unexpected tension. There was too much to say, but no one really knew how to begin. And now there was no time left to say anything but goodbye. He and Joey had to get to Marseille to make the flight home.

Jonathan turned up the collar of his coat against the wind. He had spent most of the night sitting on the terrace. He had done it to leave Joey enough room to deal with Alexander and Cendrine together, and to give Alexander and Cendrine time; but he had done it, too, because he couldn't face Alexander. Seeing him again had unleashed feelings Jonathan was unprepared to deal with. Old wounds had been reopened, and the recent one – Alexander's cruel treatment of Joey – was still raw. A part of him wanted just to forget all of it, but something held him back.

He turned towards the mill house. Was it jealousy? After all this time, was it just simple jealousy? Jealousy because Cendrine loved Alexander? Jealousy because Alexander was really Joey's father?

Joey and Cendrine came out of the house, arm in arm. As they drew closer, Jonathan could see that they had been crying. Roland followed, bringing Joey's suitcase. And then came Alexander, trailing behind.

Roland handed Jonathan the suitcase. 'There's something I've been meaning to say these past few weeks,' he said. 'I want to thank you.'

'For what?' Jonathan asked.

'For what you did, helping us get here. We couldn't have done it without you.' He hesitated. 'When we were younger, back in Paris . . . I didn't think much of you then. I thought you were bad for Cendrine. I was wrong.' He paused, embarrassed. 'I wish we had known each other better.'

Jonathan nodded.

Roland held out his hand; Jonathan took it and they shook. 'Take care,' Roland said, and stepped aside.

Jonathan stashed the suitcase in the boot. When he turned round, he saw Cendrine holding Joey, who was crying again. The sight pulled at him, but he held himself in check.

He watched as Cendrine very gently pushed away from Joey. Alexander, who had been standing slightly apart, went over to them. Jonathan watched as Alexander stood looking down at Joey. Then Alexander opened his arms and Joey stepped into his embrace. Jonathan watched them, wondering what they had said to each other during the night, but knowing that somehow, the connection that Joey had so desperately wanted finally was there.

Jonathan's eyes travelled over the three of them – Joey, Cendrine and Alexander. Cendrine, small and pale; Alexander, tall and tanned; and Joey standing between them. The image locked in his mind like a snapshot.

He walked round to lean against the other side of the car. He heard the door open and close: Joey had got into the front seat. After a moment, he felt a hand on his arm and turned. Alexander stood before him.

'We didn't talk,' Alexander said.

'No,' Jonathan said.

'We may never see each other again.'

'I know.'

Alexander held out his hand and, after a fractional pause, Jonathan took it.

'Goodbye, my brother,' Alexander said softly.

Jonathan hesitated, then, with a sudden move, pulled Alexander to him. They embraced, holding each other tightly.

When they pulled back, Cendrine was there. They both turned to look at her. Her eyes were bright with tears, but she was smiling. The look on her face pierced Jonathan's heart. She reached up and touched his cheek.

'We had—' he whispered.

Her fingers touched his lips, silencing him.

'We have,' she said, 'a daughter.'

He nodded slowly, and reached for her hand. He looked at Alexander. 'Take care of her,' Jonathan said.

Alexander's eyes glistened with tears. He took Cendrine's hand from Jonathan.

Jonathan turned away quickly, got in the car and started the engine. Joey was slumped in the seat. He put the car in gear and it moved slowly out of the dusty courtyard.

Just as the car started down the hill, Jonathan looked up in the rear-view mirror. He watched as the man and the woman standing before the house grew smaller, blurred by his tears.

Chapter Forty-Five

Jonathan stood at the window, looking down on Madison Avenue. He was tired, very tired, and he was glad now that Marion had talked him into staying over in New York before heading back to Ithaca. He needed the time to recover, just to get used to being back from London . . . and Eze. One had been chaos, the other peaceful, but each had been intense and transforming in its own way. But he was back now.

'Jonathan?'

Marion came up behind him. 'That was Katherine on the phone,' she said. 'She and Sumner invited us to come for dinner tonight, if you feel up to it.'

'Mari, I . . .'

She smiled slightly. 'I told them maybe tomorrow night.'

He nodded thankfully and looked back out of the window.

'Did Joey say where she was going?' Marion asked.

'She said she was going for a walk,' he said without turning around. 'She's probably gone over to the ballet school.'

He felt Marion's hands come up under his arms and across his chest. She pressed against his back, laying her head on his shoulder. 'I'm so glad you're home,' she whispered.

Jonathan hesitated, then turned to face her. 'Mari,' he said, 'we need to talk.'

Her solemn brown eyes gazed up at him, and it struck him anew how much worry and pain he had caused her during the time he had been in Europe. He had seen it in her face immediately when she came running across the tarmac to the plane. She had grasped Joey to her chest, crying, and then reached for him. The three of them had stood there, clutching each other. She had said nothing, not asking a single question about what had happened, not one question about Cendrine.

'Mari—'

'Don't,' she said quickly.

'But what—'

'Don't,' she repeated. 'I don't want to know. You're back, that's all that matters.' Tears came to her eyes. 'Please, Jonathan, don't tell me that you still love her, don't tell me because—'

'Mari, stop, stop,' he said gently.

'—I know you do, I always have, but I don't want to hear it now. It was bad enough when she was dead, but she's alive now and—'

He shook her slightly. 'Mari, stop, listen to me, please.'

She waited, silent.

'I loved Cendrine,' he said slowly. 'Once, long ago in a different place, in a different time of my life that was very intense. I think a part of her will always be with me, just as a part of Ethan will always be with you.'

'It's not the same,' she said. 'I never loved Ethan.'

'Yes,' Jonathan said, 'but when Ethan died, you didn't forget him, did you? We can't separate ourselves from our histories, we can't forget things we did or people we knew or loved. They're the very things that make us who we are now.'

He pulled her close. '*Now*, Mari,' he said softly.

'That's all that matters: *now*. And I love you now, I know that with all my heart, I love you *now*. That's what I found in Europe.'

She didn't move for a moment, then she threw her arms around his chest. They held each other for a long time. Finally, Marion pulled back to look at Jonathan.

'But something has changed,' she said. 'Something is wrong.'

'Yes,' he said softly. 'That's what I want to talk to you about.'

She was waiting for him to go on, but it was suddenly hard. He took a few steps away from her, towards the window, to look down again at the street.

'I had a lot of time to think while I was gone,' he said slowly. 'A lot of time.' He turned to face her. 'I know you like our life as it is. You love that house, your friends and your clubs. I know you love everything about the university, the whole life that comes with it. But I don't.'

'Then what do you want?' she asked softly.

'I want to quit. I want to go back to newspaper work.'

'Here?' she asked anxiously.

He shook his head, confused. 'No, no, not here. In Ithaca.' He hesitated. 'The *Journal*'s for sale. I want to buy it.'

'Jonathan—'

'I know, I know,' he said quickly. 'It sounds crazy. But we could do it, Mari, because of the stock, the *Herald* stock that Alexander gave me. I could sell it all, or maybe talk to Alexander. I'm sure he'd buy it back.' He came to her, grasping her by the arms. 'It would be hard at first,' he went on, more rapidly now. 'But if we're careful about money, and work hard, then after a couple of years—' He stopped abruptly, 'Mari, what's wrong? Why are you smiling? Why are you crying?'

'You're home,' she said softly.

Joey stared up at the windows of the apartment on the top floor of the building. She shivered, pulling the scarf tighter. The doorman, who had been watching her, came out to the pavement.

'Are you looking for a certain address, miss?' he asked.

'No,' she said. 'This is the right building.' She drew in a deep breath. 'I'm here to see Mrs Pendrick.'

The doorman nodded and started towards the lobby. 'Come with me, I'll ring her apartment.' He held the phone. 'Your name, miss?'

Joey hesitated. Her eyes swept up and down Park Avenue and she had the urge to run.

'Name, miss?'

'LeClerc,' she said quickly. 'Joëlle LeClerc.'

Joey waited while the doorman dialled, said a few words, then hung up the phone. He came back to her, frowning. 'She said she doesn't know you.' Joey was about to walk away when the phone rang. The doorman picked it up, muttered something and hung up.

'Now she wants you to come up,' he said with a shrug.

Joey took the lift up to the penthouse. Outside the apartment's door, she paused, unwrapping her scarf and taking off her hat. She knocked and a maid let her in, telling her that Lucy was waiting for her in the library.

The apartment was dark, and the click-click of Joey's shoes on marble echoed through the rooms. At the library door, she paused. Lucy was sitting in a chair by the fireplace. Despite the wintry day, there was no blaze in the grate. In fact, the entire apartment was very cold.

'Come in,' Lucy said, so low Joey could barely hear her.

Joey entered the room.

'Sit down,' Lucy said.

Joey took the chair across from Lucy. No lamps had been turned on in the room, and the dim grey afternoon light coming through the tall windows cast a deep half-shadow over Lucy's face. It was an unforgiving light that made Lucy look older than Joey remembered.

'Why are you here?' Lucy asked finally.

'To see David,' Joey said.

Lucy's eyes did not blink. 'He's not here.'

'I know, but I thought you might know where he is.'

Her gaze turned vacant. 'I don't know where he is.'

Joey's eyes dropped to her hands, clasped in her lap. Then, drawing in a deep breath, she rose.

Lucy stared up at her dispassionately.

'Mrs Pendrick,' Joey said softly. 'I really have to talk to David. Please tell me where he is.'

'Why should I?'

The question caught Joey off guard. 'Because I love him,' she said.

'A sin,' Lucy muttered, 'a dirty sin.'

Joey shook her head. 'No,' she said quickly, 'it's not. You were wrong. David's not my half-brother. Jonathan is not my real father.'

Lucy stared at her. 'How do you know that?' she demanded.

'Cendrine told me.' Joey saw the shock register on Lucy's face. 'She's alive. And she told me herself that Jonathan is not my real father.'

It was at that moment that Lucy's face changed. Her mouth sagged, her whole body seemed to shrink. The last imperious layer fell away, leaving a small grey figure in the chair. Her eyes were trained on Joey but looked far past her, vacant and lost.

Joey stood over her, feeling only pity for the woman she had feared so much.

'I lost him,' Lucy muttered. 'I lost them both.'

Joey felt her throat constrict, thinking about David.

How would she ever find him now? Her eyes went towards the window. It was getting dark; she had to get back to the hotel. And she wanted suddenly to get away from Lucy. She turned and started towards the door.

'Fort Bragg.'

Joey turned at the sound of Lucy's voice.

Lucy was staring out of the window, tears streaming down her face. 'One card,' she whispered, 'that's all I got from him. He's stationed at Fort Bragg . . .'

Joey let out a small cry of joy and went quickly to the door.

'Wait,' Lucy called out.

Joey turned.

'Use my phone,' Lucy said.

Jonathan entered beneath a delicate latticework archway and sat down in a pew in the back. The vast sanctuary of Grace Church was silent and empty and cool currents of moist air carried a lingering scent of flowers. An organist was practising a Bach hymn, and the reverberations caused the pew to tremble slightly.

A man was clearing the altar of floral wreaths. What event had taken place that day in the church, Jonathan wondered as he watched the man. A wedding, a baptism, a funeral Mass? What kind of people had gathered, what kind of human rite of passage had been marked?

He closed his eyes, feeling a deep calm fill his body. He breathed deeply, fully, letting the calm seep into his muscles and bones. It was the same calm that always visited him when he was in a church, but now even more pervasive, more abiding.

His mind wandered, conjuring up dreamlike images from his past of himself in different churches. At ten, sitting between his mother and Marion in a cool green light. Much later, sitting in this same church, envying

Sumner's marriage. Standing in the tiny church in Iseltwald, with snow swirling through the broken roof, settling on Cendrine's face. And sitting before the altar of Sainte-Chapelle heaped with her white funeral flowers. A life, his life, each moment fully lived, but remembered now only in fragments.

The organist stopped, the last note bouncing, echoing against stone and finally dying. Jonathan opened his eyes, looked up and saw a man standing there.

It was David.

Jonathan rose slowly. His eyes took in the severe cut of the green uniform, the shining brass buttons and the fresh army-regulation brush cut. He focused on David's sombre face. Stripped of its frame of chestnut hair, it looked much more sharply angled. In fact, it looked almost exactly like Jonathan's at that age.

David shifted his hat to his other hand. 'I'm not late, am I?' he asked.

'No,' Jonathan answered.

The young man's mouth drew into a line, and he seemed to want to say something. But he didn't. And Jonathan could think of nothing to say to ease the awkwardness. The silence lengthened.

'David, I—' Jonathan began.

David withdrew something from behind his hat. 'I read the letters,' he said.

Jonathan registered the bundle of letters in David's hand. But before he could say anything, Marion came rushing down the aisle.

'Thank God, you're here!' she whispered. 'Hurry, we haven't got much time.'

David exchanged a glance with Jonathan before Marion ushered them both back down the aisle, through a side door and into an adjoining room. It was a small chapel, with a red marble floor and polished mahogany pews. At the altar, Joey stood waiting with the pastor.

Marion threaded her arm through Jonathan's and they sat down in the front pew. David went to the altar and took Joey's hand.

The pastor began to speak, but Jonathan heard none of his words. His eyes were trained on Joey and David, and his mind was filled with a kaleidoscope of shifting images and thoughts.

The momentous events of the past few days had happened so fast. Joey had called David, and he had arrived in New York the previous day on a two-day pass so they could be married. David was about to be shipped out to Europe. There hadn't even been enough time to buy a ring. Jonathan gazed affectionately at Joey and David. So fast . . .

Jonathan felt a catch in his throat. Looking quickly up at the vaulted ceiling, he noticed a carved moulding that rimmed the room with painted lettering. His lips whispered the words as he read.

Now abideth faith, hope, love, these three. But the greatest of these is love . . .

Cendrine was there suddenly beside him. And Alexander. There would be time, he promised himself, time to go back and see both of them again.

Love is of God and everyone that loveth is born of God and knoweth God . . .

His eyes found Lucy sitting in a pew by herself. There would be time, he promised himself, to heal.

For God is love. Love never faileth . . .

He glanced at Marion. Her eyes were locked on Joey, filled with tears. The wonderful feeling of peace that had been born in Eze was with him still, now even more powerful. He took Marion's hand.

The ceremony was over. The pastor pronounced David and Joey man and wife. Joey was dry-eyed and smiling; David stood tall and straight, his eyes brimming. Jonathan, Marion and Lucy rose as the young couple

538

came slowly down the little aisle.

Jonathan hung back, watching as Lucy went to David. They were silent, standing awkwardly apart. Finally, David embraced her. Jonathan watched as Marion, crying, hugged Joey tightly, then David. Then Joey was there in front of him. She was smiling, her face shining with love. He clasped her to him, burying his face in her shoulder. 'Be happy,' he whispered brusquely through his tears.

'I love you, Dad,' she whispered back.

She pulled away, and then David was before him. Their eyes locked, David extended his hand and Jonathan took it. 'Take care of her,' Jonathan said hoarsely.

'I will,' David said.

After a long moment, David pulled his hand away, looking down. Joey came forward, wearing her coat now. She wove her arm through David's. 'We have to go,' she whispered urgently.

They went to the back door of the chapel. The door opened to let in a gust of cold wind and a swirl of snow. David and Joey stepped ouside, David pausing to put on his hat and turn up the collar of his uniform. As he did, he looked back at Jonathan, standing in the doorway.

'Take care of yourself,' Jonathan said softly.

David hesitated, his eyes glistening. 'I will, Dad.'

David took Joey's hand and they started down the street. Jonathan watched them disappear into the black and white swirl of snow.

There would be time, he thought. He looked up at the snow, caught in the streetlights, up at the diamonds as far as he could see.

□	Foreign Parts	Sarah Harrison	£4.99
□	The Forests of the Night	Sarah Harrison	£4.99
□	The Flowers of the Field	Sarah Harrison	£4.99
□	A Flower That's Free	Sarah Harrison	£4.99
□	An Imperfect Lady	Sarah Harrison	£4.99
□	Song of the Wind	Madge Swindells	£5.99
□	Corsican Woman	Madge Swindells	£5.99
□	Shadows on the Snow	Madge Swindells	£5.99
□	Summer Harvest	Madge Swindells	£5.99

Warner Books now offers an exciting range of quality titles by both established and new authors which can be ordered from the following address:

Little, Brown and Company (UK) Limited
P.O. Box 11,
Falmouth,
Cornwall TR10 9EN

Alternatively you may fax your order to the above address.
Fax No. 0326 376423.

Payments can be made as follows: cheque, postal order (payable to Little, Brown and Company) or by credit cards, Visa/Access. Do not send cash or currency. UK customers and B.F.P.O. please allow £1.00 for postage and packing for the first book, plus 50p for the second book, plus 30p for each additional book up to a maximum charge of £3.00 (7 books plus).

Overseas customers including Ireland please allow £2.00 for the first book plus £1.00 for the second book, plus 50p for each additional book.

NAME (Block Letters) ....

....

ADDRESS ....

....

....

□ I enclose my remittance for _____

□ I wish to pay by Access/Visa Card

Number ☐☐☐☐☐☐☐☐☐☐☐☐☐☐☐☐

Card Expiry Date ☐☐☐☐